Saving KC

Saving KC

Grinnell Desjarlais

Third Printing, January 2025

ISBN: 978-1-59849-380-1

Library of Congress Control Number: 2024924276

BISAC Codes:
FIC014090 FICTION / Historical / 20th Century / Post-World War II
FIC000000 FICTION / General
FIC137000 FICTION / Native American

Printed in South Korea

Editor: Danielle Harvey
Cover Illustrator: Sarah Harris
Design: Soundview Design

www.savingkcthestory.com
www.grinnelldesjarlais.com
www.buzzdesjarlais.com

This is a work of fiction. Unless otherwise indicated, all the names, characters, businesses, places, events and incidents in this book are either the product of the author's imagination or used in a fictitious manner. Any resemblance to actual persons, living or dead, or actual events is purely coincidental.

Classic Day Publishing
206-860-4900
info@classicdaypub.com
www.classicdaypub.com

For an angel who was once on earth

and is now in heaven…

Chapter 1

Rescue

June 1971

Sun shined through the thick jungle, with its rays setting in a small shadowy clearing. Birds chirped, but it sounded more like screeching. Villagers moved around slowly. Sudden explosions littered the surface, and there were more to follow. Havoc wreaked, with bodies flying and people yelling and screaming in a foreign language while small automatic weapons fired, followed by more explosions. American troops in quick motions swept into the village, shooting and capturing inhabitants. Radio communications crackled back and forth.

"Street gang, street gang, confirm. I-Shackle, I-Shackle H.I. Fire mission, over."

The radio crackled a response, "Authenticate, I-Shackle, over."

A young lieutenant responded with a string of numbers and letters.

"Street gang, street gang, you have ten mikes, fire mission, out."

"Everybody out. Arty is coming in. Get moving, fast! Di đi mau," yelled the young lieutenant.

A sweaty soldier with no uniform shirt, only a flak jacket and an olive-drab towel around his neck, lowered his sawed-off shotgun barrel and cautiously lifted the bamboo hatch covering the ground.

He slowly peered over the edge of the opening, and his eyes widened. "Fuck me!" he exclaimed. "Sarge, over here, quick!" he yelled.

Two other GIs gathered and looked down, also wide-eyed.

The shallow cage revealed an emaciated, disgustingly filthy man. He was nearly naked, streaked and smeared with his own excrement. He was clothed in dirty rags, and his patchy blonde hair was thin and revealed bare splotches of scalp with a deep wound, blood oozing and covering his face. He slowly raised his hands against the light, and his blinking, deep-blue, azure eyes looked more dead than alive. He made only low moaning guttural noises.

A burly man in a sweat-drenched fatigue uniform joined the others. He looked down, and with slow realization became as wide-eyed as the others. He started yelling, "Jesus jumped-up Christ! Get him outta there and be careful!"

Three men gently lifted him out of the buried bamboo cage. As they pulled him to freedom, it was like picking up a small child. They saw the open sores all over his body and the deep lash wounds crisscrossing his back and oozing pus. Maggots were hanging from the open wounds, a putrefied mess that sent one of the men reeling and gagging.

The man was hoisted onto a makeshift litter and moved to a landing zone some distance away. He was loaded into the Huey chopper, along with other soldiers, and started to ascend as two other choppers quickly moved in.

Chapter 2

Dead or Alive?

Kelly Allen Chase drifted into consciousness, noticing how pain-free he was, like floating on a cloud. Maybe he had finally gotten his wish and been killed. If there was a God, why didn't he take him sooner? He drifted away again, hearing that angelic voice singing from somewhere… He was floating—floating and lost in that beautiful wood-smokey voice… Out again.

He was seeing bright light, along with voices—people speaking in low tones. As his mind started to clear, he heard a man's low, resonant voice. "Lieutenant Chase, you've finally decided to join us, welcome."

Two nurses were also there, pulling and tugging on bandages wrapping various areas of his body, bandages from head to foot. They spoke to each other in some unfamiliar language. He was eventually able to put the pieces and words together, realizing they were speaking in English…American English! He slowly became aware of tubes, wires, and other devices plugged into his body in various ways. He was dreaming—sure of it!

The man continued, "I'm Doctor Franklin, and you are in the Veterans Hospital in San Francisco. You have been here for about a week." Kelly was having trouble sorting the words out. "With a little diversion to a hospital ship in the Philippines." Doctor Franklin was a medium-built man with salt-and-pepper hair, who to Kelly looked like a soap opera doctor…or was it just the drugs? The man went on, "You have some very acute injuries that look like you've sustained over an extended period. I'm not sure what your circumstances were or how you got this way, but I can only say that you will be here for a bit longer while we help you heal. You have a severe case of malnutrition and some gross muscle loss that we will be helping you with. It also appears that you have had several bones broken and are still healing from those, mainly your fingers. The wounds on your back need watching, among others that we haven't been able to fully evaluate as of yet, and you have malaria. We now have that under control."

Kelly's head was spinning, barely able to keep pace with the doctor's assessment, as it appeared English was now his second language.

Dr. Franklin continued, "I know this is a lot to take in, and you are on some high-dosage pain-relief medications. I will cover this again with you tomorrow when you've had more time to rest. Are we about done here, nurse?"

She shot an unsmiling look at the doctor and returned her gaze to Kelly. He could see a great sadness in her eyes as she regarded him with a weak smile, adjusted his bed covering slightly, and moved away. He was thinking, still hoping, that he would pass from this place and go hear that angel sing again, and just be done with this hurt. Rita, Rita… He was out again.

Over the next couple of days, Kelly endured endless rounds of dressing changes, x-rays, IVs, and drugs, during which he was barely conscious. He realized he was very hungry. When did he last eat? How long had he been here? Where was he again? Maybe he was just dreaming again. Eventually he realized they must have been feeding him intravenously.

During captivity, his diet had been restricted to only a cup of rice a day or less and sometimes snake meat, each serving sometimes with some maggots as additional protein. At first, he would not touch the grim sustenance, but eventually after several days, it didn't matter to him; he ate anything with wolfish intent. His captors always kept him on the verge of starvation, so he was always weak. Sometimes he was given water, but most times, he was left to collect rainwater. Toward the end of his captivity, his gums were always bleeding. He feared he would start to lose his teeth. Sometimes his Viet Cong captors would feed him more the day before a night movement, where he was used as a pack mule for ammunition and other provisions. They moved all night long, and at dawn he would collapse and be caged again. He recalled the never-ending rain during the monsoon seasons and the unending misery and cold it dealt. This scene played out over and over during his ordeal. The only time things were different was after the three escape attempts. Beatings, bamboo lashings to his back, legs, and bottoms of his feet, along with wrist cuffing, would play out during the subsequent day or two. He received no rations during these treatments.

The effects of pain medications were ebbing away, and he could feel that old familiar throbbing coming back. His back was burning like fire from the last cane beating only days before his rescue. This was prompted by his final escape attempt. It was particularly brutal, as a heavy sharp-edged cane was used, and he lost count at twenty strikes and passed out. When he regained consciousness, his brutal captors set about splaying out his fingers and smashing them with a rifle butt. He had endured so much, and at the time he thought, thankfully, they were finally going to kill him. He would be so grateful when it came to pass. There was that final blow to his head that finally put him out. When he next came to, he saw strange men looking down at him and yelling, and he could hear a radio crackling somewhere and a man yelling orders at the rest. He recalled being lifted out of his cage and being transported. *Angels have finally come for me*, he'd rejoiced.

Kelly's fingers and back were starting to ache, along with the left side of his head. *So much*, he thought, *for trips to the beach*. Then there was Rita. If this wasn't a dream, he had to find her. But how would he dial the phone?

He didn't know how much time he had spent on mind-altering

pain drugs, but eventually he was able to make noises that somewhat resembled speech. "Rita. Help me call Rita," he rasped.

Nurse Winter, a middle-aged matronly woman, said, "Shhh, now. There will be time for that later."

"Now, please, now!" he begged, his voice nearly becoming a screech as he sprayed out droplets of blood onto her white uniform.

She told him he was not allowed to speak with anyone until he spoke with a reintegration officer, who was going to be at the hospital in the morning.

During the night, a small nurse awakened him to check his vitals. "What day is it? What year is it?" Kelly whispered to her.

She gave him a quizzical look and shrugged her shoulders. "July twenty-third, 1971, why?"

Kelly did not respond. Three years. Could it be possible?

The next morning, a lieutenant colonel swept into Kelly's small room, carrying a briefcase, and introduced himself. He was indeed a soldier's soldier, with handsome, ruddy good looks, which Kelly deduced played to his favor whenever it would work to his benefit. His US Army Class A uniform was to a tee and was something Kelly had not come close to seeing in years. Kelly was in awe for a bit as the colonel commenced to get right to business. Kelly was instantly suspicious and turned his head away.

"Lieutenant Chase, I am your reintegration officer, Lieutenant Colonel Flagg, and I will be guiding you back into the American way of life we have all so proudly defended and sacrificed for. I will be your liaison for all services Uncle Sam and the US Army can provide for you. You will be reassessed by the US Army and informed as to your continued fitness for duty. I will be a part of that assessment."

Kelly was having trouble understanding his rapid-fire delivery. Suddenly, he became aware of a headache and just wished for Flagg to go away.

Flagg continued, "You have been MIA for three years. According to any records we have, you disappeared from your unit with the 101st Airborne somewhere near the Laotian boarder during a nighttime fire fight. It was noted that some efforts were made to locate you afterward, but they came up with nothing. Units had to redeploy and were moved out of the area the next day. Does any of this sound familiar?" Kelly said nothing, frowning. Flagg continued, "Look, Lieutenant Chase, I'm trying to help you here."

Kelly croaked out, "When can I make a phone call?"

"Look," Flagg said, "we know you've experienced a lot during your ordeal, but we need to cover some ground here before you can move on, so you can make that phone call. Will you help me help you?"

"Dammit," Kelly croaked. "Somebody messed up. Me and two other grunts were cut off during this operation. We never should have been out there with only squad force. I guess it really doesn't matter now, but three of us were cut off." Kelly continued in his small raspy voice, "VC set upon us before we could move. They beat the shit out of us, ripped our clothes off, put ropes around our necks and dragged us off." Kelly had to stop and catch his breath; this was the most he had spoken in some time. "It was raining like fuck, and it was the most miserable feeling in the world. We were scared shitless."

Flagg pushed, "Did you in any way during your time missing collaborate or assist or aide the enemy?"

Kelly just stared at him. He could feel his headache really coming on now, and his back was really starting to hurt again. He was hoping for some medication to help.

Flagg finally broke the silence. "Look, it's my job to ask the question, and it has to be a matter of record. Please help us move on with this and get on the record with a denial. That's all I'm looking for."

Chase cooled off a little, trying to figure out if Flagg was trying to trap him somehow. *Oh, what the hell*, he thought. *What's he going to do? Throw me in jail? Given where I've been, it would be a vacation.* "Okay," he said, his voice cracking, "you have my official denial, a strong denial."

"What happened to the other two men?" Flagg inquired.

"They were executed the next morning—shot in the head, both of them," Kelly rasped. As he tried to clench his fists, he realized his fingers were starting to hurt. In his barely audible voice, Kelly pushed on. "Bastards broke all of my fingers again after my last escape attempt. Can't remember how many times they did that. Anytime they got mad at me, really." Flagg nodded, and a great sadness crept over his handsome features. "I really didn't know why I survived after Jonesy and Clemmons were executed and left behind. They discovered I was an officer, so maybe they figured I had some trade-in value or that I had some great secret. I did have some information on immediate troop movements, so I knew I had to hold out as long as possible. I eventually spilled my guts a few hours later. It happened after an intense session where I was hogtied with my arms held up around my back, twisted up to my shoulder blades and hung that way from a bamboo pen." He had to stop, breathe, and collect himself. "Can I get some water please?" Flagg held the container with a straw to his lips as he took small sips to clear his throat. "My shoulders were slowly dislocated. I pissed myself, and then I spilled. By that time, I hoped that anything I had shared was of no value to them." Kelly continued to rasp, sometimes in a near squeal. "I was allowed to heal, sort of. I was used every day as an ammo humping slave. I did try to escape three times but was captured. The day before my rescue was the last attempt, and I paid for it dearly." Kelly raised both of his thin arms, with IV lines dangling, his fingers bandaged or splinted.

Flagg hung his head and looked at the floor, remaining silent. "I will have someone help you with any phone calls you need to make, but they will need to stay with you to monitor conversations. Please do not discuss where you've been. I'm allowing this one time. So please don't get too upset with me, as I have orders and procedures to follow." Kelly nodded. "I think we'll leave it there today. I'll come back tomorrow and let you know the plan for you moving forward. Things are going to be okay, Lieutenant. I am here to help you, really. I will leave some information for you to go through after I leave." He dug into his briefcase and pulled out a brown envelope with red string closures. He set it on the hospital table, closed his case, turned on his heel, and left the room.

Nurse Winter came in shortly afterward. "Lieutenant Chase, don't be too hard on Flagg. He carries a lot on his shoulders. You're not the first who has had to answer those questions. Thing is, Flagg hears all the stories, too, and it takes a toll. I can tell you that from my own experiences."

Kelly only nodded.

Later that evening, a young MP, whom Kelly had discovered had been outside his door the whole time, brought a phone to his bedside and plugged it in.

"Sir," the MP said, "you will need to dial nine first, then the number to get past the switchboard."

It was a number Kelly would not forget for a hundred years. Instead of handing Kelly the phone, the MP dialed the number for him after dumbly realizing that Kelly could not work the dialer. Kelly weakly held the phone to his ear and listened to the first rings, his breath coming in short, wheezy gasps. He was finding it difficult to contain himself. He thought he might pass out before he could do this. Then, suddenly, a mechanical voice came on and announced that the number had been disconnected.

"No!" He croaked out, "You dialed the wrong number!"

The young MP sheepishly redialed, but the result was the same. Kelly calmed himself, working to recall the second number to try. He instructed the MP, who dutifully dialed again, and stepped back in case things did not work out again. The phone was ringing at the home of Rita's parents.

• • •

Nurse Winter, making her last check before her shift change, asked Kelly about his family and where he was from. He only told her Southern California and left it at that. She didn't pry and let the subject drop. Kelly started thinking back again, as he had hundreds of times during the last few years he had spent in captivity. Thinking about his family, relatives, friends. His dad, Aloysius Chase, was in Montana somewhere, probably still on the Blackfeet Reservation near Glacier Park. His dad, an old, full-blooded Blackfeet Indian, was used to living alone and did not want to be bothered by anyone since his wife Deena, Kelly's mother, had died just before Kelly was drafted into the US Army in the spring of 1968. They lived on the rolling foothills between the Blackfeet Reservation and the town of Cut Bank, Montana, where Kelly had attended school. Kelly guessed his younger brother, Frank, whom he had not heard from in years, was probably drunk somewhere. He had distant relatives throughout most of Montana. He hadn't spent any time with them in the years before he left home for Southern California in the summer of 1964. Truth was he really didn't have relatives available, and certainly not in California.

His father was, at one time, a bronco buster, womanizer, and rodeo rider who, between wild drinking sprees, managed to teach at the nearby Blackfeet Reservation. On one of his summer trips to Butte, where he worked in the copper mines, he came across his mother. Deena was a natural blonde, azure-eyed beauty. Kelly often thought about how he would have never put them together; they were so different. She, however, had a positive influence on Aloysius Chase, and he started to settle down. Kelly was born in September of 1947, and his brother about a year after. Kelly loved his mother, for she was smart, loving, and kind. Deena took an incredible amount of abuse from the Indians around; Kelly didn't know how she managed to survive it. Reservation Indians could be mean and intolerant to outsiders. Eventually they found she was an honest and genuine person and had finally warmed up to her. Once she was accepted, the Indians would defend and protect her from any outsider.

During the summer months, him and his brother, Frank, were Dad's ace cowhands, and they worked long days on the small ranch. His father was six-foot-three and built with a typical large, powerful Indian upper body with no rear end. A body type, some said, that was genetically built to ride horses. Aloysius kept his dark hair very short, always in a trimmed, crew-style cut. He was always quiet, but sometimes he could be rough, physical, and loud. His words were few, but when he spoke, the two brothers knew to listen. One piece of the old Indian's advice always stuck with Kelly after he had taken a particularly nasty fall from his horse Winger. He was trying unsuccessfully to cut out a young bull from the herd. The bull charged Winger, who scrambled to get out of the bull's destructive path. Kelly, being overconfident, was caught off guard and was dumped face first onto the hard ground. As the bull trotted off to parts unknown and Kelly lay curled on the ground trying to collect himself, the old Indian rode up to him, looked down, grinned, and said, "If you ever get hurt in life, remember it's your own fuckin' fault," and rode off.

Damn, how many times had that run through his mind during his ordeal? Kelly and his brother were never treated any differently by him, both always with his rough, no-nonsense demeanor. He was a tough, rugged man, and if nothing else, the boys always respected and—at times—feared his immense physical power. Kelly remembered the time the three were in the old Ford truck, trying to drive the muddy road to the back pastures, when the truck bogged down. Wheels spinning, it was clear they were stuck. Aloysius told them to stay put, that he would be right back. The boys felt the entire rear of the truck being lifted, moved sideways, and set back down. Their dad climbed back in, and they resumed the trip. Kelly remembered the look of amazement on Frank's face. Both looked out the back window of the cab to reassure themselves that the four hay bales were still there. It always struck Kelly how often his dad's mind was always elsewhere going over something, perhaps some memory. Kelly discovered later that he was taken from his tribe and home as a child to be educated by one of the missionary schools commissioned by the US Government to "get rid of the Indian to save the child." Those schools, Kelly learned, were brutal, harsh, and creative corporal punishment was encouraged, destructive, and ever present—sometimes ending in death. His dad had survived, but his dad's brother had not.

Kelly's mother was sweet, highly intelligent, and seemed to know everything about the world, but like Kelly's father, hid most of her past. He later discovered that she was a concert pianist and had learned her craft from some especially important people on the East Coast (Philadelphia maybe). She hooked up with a drunken rodeo rider in Butte, Montana, and remained a mystery until Kelly eventually wheedled the truth from her.

Frank never seemed to fit in anywhere. He wasn't a good student, only because he never wanted to be, and he always went out of his way to be in some shit-storm somewhere. Since they were not all white nor all Indian, they caught flak from both the whites and the reservation Indians. Their mother had coached Kelly through this and attempted the same with Frank. But Frank would have none of it. He was always in a brawl with one side or the other. Sometimes they were both in the same fight: black eyes, bloody noses, and bruises. This he recalled with a smile. Sometimes they would win, sometimes not. Frank never shied away from these battles, going out of his way to push back hard. Looking back, Kelly admired him for it.

They were brothers, but their looks were oddly different. Frank took after their father, with very dark skin, black hair, and amazing blue eyes. Kelly, on the other hand, had light-brown skin with streaky blond hair and his mother's striking azure eyes. This later helped him blend in on California beaches. Both Frank and Kelly stood about six-foot-two and had similar broad shoulders, narrow hips, and long legs. Both were raw-boned and lean. By the time they were nearing the end of their high school years, Frank started drinking and things started to go downhill for him. Kelly had memories of his dad when he was drinking, before his mother was finally able to exert her influence and get him to stop. He was never just a *little* drunk. After a couple of drinks, he was out of control and mean. Even back then, Kelly thought Frank was headed down the same trail. After their mother passed, their father started drinking again. He was isolated back on the reservation, becoming morose, sullen, and cruel. Kelly didn't have much to do with him after his mother had gone, but he still missed him and wanted the sober version of him back: a husband and a dad. He was sure his father had no idea what had eventually become of him, being drafted then missing in action.

Deena introduced Kelly to music and the piano at an early age. They played and laughed during the long Montana winters. Frank never took to music, and during the winter months was more of a caged animal pacing and whining about the weather. They would occasionally go hunting with the old Indian, which turned out to be more of a duel with survival in keeping up with the old man. Most of the time they were successful in bringing in a nice venison haul that would keep him and Frank busy and provide good meat for the winter. They had both become expert shots with the old .30-30 and knew how to skin and dress a buck.

Kelly's ranch life was ultimately something he always dreamed about in captivity. Those days were his most precious memories—next to Rita. His family was now dead: split, fractured, and scattered. Did he somehow cause all of that? He would have to consider this.

He adjusted himself in his hospital bed as best he could. He was placed on his side, allowing his back wounds a chance to heal. He waited for the night nurse to return with his next dose of pain medication. He continued to think about his family in Montana. What were his dad and brother doing? Were they still alive? How would he get the answers to these questions?

Chapter 3

California

Kelly had always yearned to go to California, as he had seen pictures of the sunny beaches and had read stories about a culture of carefree living. He just knew that was where he would live someday. In the summer of 1964, between his junior and senior year of high school, he got his chance. Kelly had been saving money from wrangling on the large Wheeler ranch, so he had a good nest egg going—it was his "California money." Two high school friends, brothers Marty and Joe Ames, were sons of a rich rancher who had struck oil on his place some miles down from the Chase ranch. The two brothers had the money and freedom during the summers to tour and visit faraway places. To Kelly, far away was a trip to Great Falls. He was always pestering the brothers with his big plans to head to California. On the last day of junior year, they announced to him that they had a trip planned to Huntington Beach, California, and they were flying for God's sake! Kelly was so envious he thought he would bust. Then the real surprise—they invited him along, and they were paying for the trip! Kelly was beside himself with excitement and couldn't wait to tell his mother. At first, she was skeptical, but she couldn't stand to see him crushed if she tried to stop him. Both his dad and Frank could not see what was so exciting about any of this and walked off. On the morning they headed for Great Falls to fly to paradise, Kelly's mother pushed a handful of twenty-dollar bills in his hand, and said, "I know this means a lot to you, and I want you to have this. Just be careful. I know how reckless you can be sometimes. Have fun!"

They landed in Los Angeles, the brothers rented a newer model car, and they headed to the weeklong rented condo. Kelly had never been away from the plains of Montana and was experiencing sensory overload. His first-ever airplane flight, the end-of-June warmth, sweet smells, tall palm trees, and general excitement were overwhelming. There was music floating in the air everywhere they went. “Walk Like a Man” was their background music. And the girls…ouch! The brothers had a beachside rental unit, which was pure heaven for Kelly. The nights were gorgeous and warm with fragrant scents wafting. Combined with the ocean-scented breezes, it was truly paradise. The brothers were seasoned travelers and had the wardrobe thing down. Kelly, on the other hand, showed up in worn Levi jeans, a faded denim shirt, and beat-up cowboy boots, so he was quite a sight. They went shopping and he bought his first pair of swimming trunks and accompanying beachwear. After nearly a week of beach bumming and seeing the sites, Kelly felt he had started to fit in. He had soaked in the sun and darkened up more than he ever had. Life was good… then the bombshell.

Her name was Rita Siva. They first met at an evening get-together on the beach. Both looking in opposite directions, they ran into each other spilling drinks on one another. They made their awkward apologies at the same time. She had waist-long, straight, raven-black hair. Her complexion was light-brown and flawless, and she was dressed in white hip-hugger jeans and a white pullover top with a loose collar. She accented her olive complexion with a fine silver necklace with small turquoise stones, a set of small silver hoop earrings, and an exceptionally fine turquoise inlaid silver bracelet. Her beauty startled Kelly. Then there was Kelly, outfitted as a slovenly beachcomber.

She immediately smiled, extended her hand, and announced, “Hi, I am Rita, Rita Siva.”

Kelly slowly took her hand and looked into the most radiant dark-brown eyes he had ever seen. Her touch sent a jolt through him, so warm and smooth. “Kelly…Chase,” he stuttered nervously.

She let out a small laugh, sounding like music. "Well, nice running into you, Kelly Chase."

"Likewise," Kelly responded, trying to be California nonchalant. He asked her if he could refill her drink.

"Yes, please, 7UP for me. Thank you."

Kelly hustled over to the bar and returned with two drinks. They took a seat on a nearby large chunk of driftwood. Both Ames brothers were stealing glances at them from their groups as Kelly and Rita talked. The brothers were not trying to be obvious but were. She was fascinated to learn Kelly was visiting for a week and was from Cut Bank, Montana.

"I have never met anyone from Montana," she said. "Please tell me about it, especially the Cut Bank part. What is that? Is your family there?"

Kelly tried to keep his story somewhat of a mystery. He knew that some people did not like Indians so much. He explained, best he could, where he was from, what it was like, and how it looked. He gave brief descriptions of the hard, cold winters. She appeared genuinely interested and started asking again about his family—the detective in her putting him on the spot.

With a curious look, she said, "You know, you kind of look Indian."

Shit! he thought. He knew he couldn't start their budding friendship with a lie. He blurted out his story—the brief version. He explained that he was half this and half that. His dad was a Blackfeet Indian and a small cattle rancher, and his mother was white with blond hair. He emphasized how hard she worked to take care of the three of them. Kelly explained that he also had a brother.

Her eyes grew even wider. "You're kidding. I'm Indian too! Morongo! Gosh, what are the chances?" Getting more excited, she continued, "I've read about the plains Indians and how they were experts with horses and amazing, courageous warriors." He could feel his face getting hot with embarrassment, hoping it was not showing through his newly acquired tan under the dim night light. "My reservation is east of here about ninety miles. We are not prolific warriors like your tribe. We are Mission Indians, a small tribe. We are awfully close and have large extended families." She lit up brighter—as if that were possible. "You should come visit before you leave. My mother and grandmother would especially love to meet you. They are such big fans of plains Indians."

The hotness again. She went on to talk about her father, who was tribal chair, and how her mother held the power behind everything, much like Kelly's. The Ames boys were now edging away from other guests and moving Rita and Kelly's way, each showing a curious, unbelieving look. As they joined them, Kelly introduced them to Rita and they each politely shook her hand. Kelly could have sworn a small bow was executed by both, much like one would do with royalty. Rita was gracious and greeted both brothers with a wonderful, winning smile. All four fell into easy conversations about Montana, California, and families. All four were seventeen years old and found that to be quite coincidental. Rita said she was attending her final year of high school at Banning High just outside the reservation. She was hoping for a scholarship to Cal State Long Beach. She wanted to study marine biology; she had a passion for ocean research.

"I know it sounds kind of weird," she said, "but I want to save the whales, you know? Do something really positive in the world."

The brothers were enthusiastic about this, but it was obvious to Kelly they were just fawning over her, but who could blame them. As for Kelly, he was caught flat-footed for a response. He wasn't sure what marine biology was all about. Kelly timidly went along with an affirmative nod and a smile, thinking a question would be the best route to show he at least knew something.

"How long do you have to go to school for that?" Kelly asked, trying to feign a real interest.

"Oh, God, at least six years, if I get an advanced degree, and about eight if I go for a doctorate. It's a long commitment, but I'm up for it." She turned to Kelly, giving him her undivided attention. "What about you, Kelly Chase? What are your goals? Are you going to college? Maybe in Montana?"

He was, again, at a loss, starting to feel like the proverbial deer in the headlights. Marty quickly looked away, but Joe could not hide his smirk. Kelly wasn't the only one stumped on this one.

"I really don't know. I haven't made up my mind. I'm thinking of a couple things. I'm just not sure yet," Kelly said with little conviction.

Joe piped up, "I'm gonna be taking over the ranch, so that will be a full-time job." Marty was nodding in agreement.

Rita said, "You know, I bet that lifestyle would be exciting and romantic. I'm envious you guys have that to look forward to." She shrugged. "Me, I've got all of this uncertainty about everything."

Kelly started to feel a real sense of uneasiness and maybe loss. He felt inadequate compared to the other three, especially Rita. Kelly's mother had tried to have the work-or-college conversation with him, but he was quick to dismiss her concerns. The truth was he had never really dwelled on it. He was busy dreaming about California. He hadn't considered the reality of making a decent living, much less an education. Kelly guessed he would be a ranch hand with his father or on the Wheeler ranch. Now, suddenly, the red lights were starting to flash—time to panic. He could feel the thought of a life with Rita slipping away.

Rita was busy giving Kelly an intent look, like the jury was out. It was like she had made up her mind and instantly changed the subject. "What do you guys like for music, and what do you listen to in Montana?"

Marty said, "Oh yeah, Marty Robbins, Jimmy Dean, Leroy… Ah, what's his name, Joe?"

"It's kinda tough," Joe said. "We only get one radio station, and it's country music."

Kelly said, "When I stay awake late enough, I get a station out of Great Falls. Like The Beatles, Jan and Dean, especially their song "Dead Man's Curve," and The Dave Clark Five. I love that stuff."

She seemed to come alive again. They continued to visit, never feeling the need to move around to other groups. Time had slipped into the late hours before they knew it. Two other girls suddenly approached the group. "Rita, where have you been? We've been waiting for you by the tent."

"You never showed," the other girl said and looked over at the boys. "Now we know why! Guess we can't blame you. We were busy anyway." They both broke out into giggles.

Rita introduced Nancy and Gina. They were both unbelievably cute. Each had blond hair cut short and were all smiles. Kelly liked them instantly. Rita said, "I'm so sorry, guys. I ran into Kelly Chase here. One thing led to another, and I lost track of time."

"It's okay, Rita," Gina said. "But we better get going. It's a long way to Morongo. Let's not make your mother mad"—she paused—"you know how hot she can get. We don't want to chance it." The three girls laughed.

As they were walking the girls to the parking lot, Rita, walking beside Kelly, linked her arm with his and said, "Kelly Chase, are you going to come and see us before you leave? I wasn't kidding when I invited you earlier. Nancy and Gina are staying overnight, so they'll be there too."

Kelly didn't hesitate. "Sure, we have two days left and tomorrow is Sunday. I will talk the boys into it." *Somehow*, Kelly vowed inwardly.

"Good," she said. I will give you directions and my phone number in case something happens. You'll call me, okay?"

On the way back to the bungalow, Marty and Joe agreed that a road trip was in order. "Thank you, Gina and Nancy," Kelly muttered to himself.

Normally Kelly slept like a rock, but his mind wouldn't rest that night. Kelly's thoughts of Rita filled his senses, remembering the way she looked, talked, and the fragrance of her hair as she stood close to him before they departed. Not since Thelma Joy in seventh grade had he felt this funny. Something was going on, and he was powerless to stop it. His thoughts turned to what he was going to do with his future. He was a budding failure. As he finally drifted off, he thought of his father and what he was doing just then.

The next morning, they ate breakfast at a small café next to their complex. By nine o'clock they were on the road with Joe at the wheel. Their conversation was all about the girls, obviously. They also talked about what the future would hold for each of them. Joe explained that he might go to Montana State University in Bozeman and study business so he could have a better chance of success when running and managing the ranch. Marty was all about becoming a country music star and touring the world. As for Kelly, he vowed to achieve better grades in his last year of high school, not committing to much beyond that. They eventually turned north from Highway 10 onto a narrow, paved road. They hadn't gone far before they saw the Southwest villa-style house on the left. It was incredibly attractive, surrounded by trees with a small circular driveway. Set at the base of the nearby desert mountains, it reminded Kelly of Montana. No sooner had they come to a stop the three girls came strolling out to the car waving happily. Rita was wearing denim jeans and a striking red blouse, a dramatic contrast to her beautiful look. Following them was an older, taller, sophisticated-looking woman. Hints of gray streaked her long black hair, and she wore a mid-calf length turquoise dress. Behind her was a smaller woman who was almost totally gray and had a dark, open friendly face. They both had genuine smiles and stood behind the girls. Under the entry portico stood a tall, dark man with an unreadable expression. He had dark eyes, distinct salt-and-pepper hair, and had an aristocratic air about him. He was dressed in light-colored slacks and an off-white, short sleeve, button-down shirt. He remained where he was.

Rita called out, "Kelly Chase!" She had taken to calling him by his full name. "Joe, Marty, so glad you came!" She continued to introduce everyone as she slowly placed her hand on Kelly's shoulder. "This is my dad Nance, my mother Victoria, and my grandma Weena. Gosh, we weren't sure you were coming. Gina was starting to get bummed out."

Gina, who was standing next to her, gave her a small hip check. All three girls laughed.

Joe and Marty were getting reacquainted with Gina and Nancy, and they were starting to move closer together, really starting to warm up to one another and exchanging compliments. Nance approached the group with his hands buried in his pockets and broke into a slow, soft smile. He held an outstretched hand to Marty, who was closest to him. Then Joe. He approached Kelly directly and took his hand with a firm gentleman's handshake. Nance Siva lifted his gaze to Kelly's eyes and gave him an intent look, still sporting a warm smile on his face. "So nice to meet you, Kelly. We're so glad you could make it. If you hadn't, I'm sure these three would have run away from home. They haven't slept a wink since they came home last night. Welcome to our home."

The three girls were turning three shades of red.

The boys laughed, enjoying the girls' embarrassing moment. Victoria joined her husband and gestured for them to follow them into the house. Joe, Marty, and the girls followed Nance. Victoria fell into stride beside Kelly and Rita. Grandma Weena trailed close behind. Rita latched onto Kelly's arm as they walked. The main room was homey but grand, with off-white stucco walls, high-beamed ceilings, and bone-white tile floors. A two-story high flagstone fireplace extended up through the mezzanine above. Kelly was starting to get that old "not in Kansas anymore" feeling again, as he was starting to gawk.

Victoria snapped him out of his reverie and asked, "You were born on the Blackfeet reservation then?"

"Yes, ma'am," Kelly quickly responded.

"Please, call me Victoria." She quickly glanced at her daughter, as if she were secretly communicating something, but he couldn't figure out what. Victoria continued, "You know, my mother Weena has a couple of lifelong friends up there somewhere. What were their names, Mom?" She turned slightly. "Where did she go? She's like a ghost, that one, up and appears and disappears."

Mother and daughter both laughed, and Kelly felt a brief stereo effect, as they sounded eerily similar. It was easy to see where Rita's beauty came from.

Victoria said, "We'll catch her later. It is so good to have you boys visit us."

As they approached the far side of the great room, it opened into a courtyard that was almost completely shaded with trees from the midday sun, providing a cooling effect on his skin. In the center of the large courtyard was an elegant fountain gurgling quietly. It was surrounded by round tables with chairs placed closely together, each with a small desert centerpiece bouquet.

Nance stopped and turned to them and gave a grand sweeping, welcoming gesture with his left hand and slightly bowed. "Welcome, friends."

Kelly was now thinking that they must have been expected, and preparations had been made just for the three visitors. Kelly was grateful that they had decided to come.

Joe and Marty, along with Gina and Nancy, were seating themselves at the same table. Rita, Kelly, Victoria, and Nance sat at an adjoining larger table. Weena joined them at the same table, and in that age-old Indian brogue English, which was common on most reservations, she announced that she was sorry but had to check on lunch. She looked at Kelly, and with a directness asked him, "Do you know anyone on your reservation with the last name Bruneau, maybe Ed or Anna?" As an afterthought, she added, "Probably passed on by now." She went on, "He was a big, tough Indian—I think mostly Cree. He held himself like a boxer who would take on all comers: Indian, white, anybody. By God, he would always beat the shit out of them!"

"Mom!" was Victoria's stern admonition.

Everyone laughed. It was an interesting question because Kelly did know of them. "Yes," Kelly said. "Old Ed was the tribal sheriff for many years, and Anna was quite well known as a whiskey cooker.

"Yes! Yes!" Weena practically squealed, partially standing from her chair. "I met Anna years ago when I went to a big stick game on the Blackfeet Reservation. We both fell in together and had so much fun. I stayed with them for a couple of days before my ride came back through and I had to leave."

Kelly said, "I believe Ed was related to my father, but I'm not really sure how, great uncle or something. I never did pay much attention to talk about my father's Indian relatives."

Victoria, Rita, and Nance were taking in this conversation, and by now, all three were staring in surprise. Nance was the first to speak. "Well, I guess it is true that Indian country is a small one."

"Boy, who would have thought," remarked Rita, with a new sense of wonder as she stared at Kelly.

Victoria was looking at her mother, and Kelly thought this kind of excitement must have been rare. The kids from the other table were now wondering what was going on. They had been wrapped up in their own lively chatter, at first not taking note of the conversations next to them. It was apparent now that Kelly was now at the center of some excitement. Now everyone was talking at once and Kelly wasn't sure his newfound notoriety was a good or bad thing, being held in higher regard than he ever deserved.

Weena sprang to her feet and said, "Lunch, I forgot, I'll get things ready," and then she flew from the courtyard.

Victoria leaned over to her husband and said something in a low tone, and Nance said, "Yes, of course."

Victoria stood and said, "I will go help mother with lunch," as she departed.

Rita had been sitting quietly, taking in the conversations around the tables and seemed pensive. Kelly noticed Rita deep in thought, like she was making some kind of decision.

Her father suddenly spoke up. "Rita, why don't you show Kelly around the house, give him the grand tour. I will show the other fellows around in a bit. They seem to be enjoying themselves too much right now to be disturbed."

The four at the other table were deep into discussing school, music, the beach, Montana, and California.

As Rita and Kelly stood and moved away from the table, she slipped her hand into his as they walked. "You know, you have the roughest hands I've ever felt. So hard and full of callouses. How did they get that way?" Kelly was immediately embarrassed and made a reflexive effort to pull away. "No, no, Kelly, it's a compliment. Please, don't freak out." She moved to grasp one hand in both of hers. "It just shows you're used to hard work, which I think is a long-lost quality. What kind of work do you do?"

Kelly was a little unsure of what to say, how to explain it in a way she would understand yet not make himself out to be too much of a rube. "Well," he started, "I work with horses, you know, riding a lot, sometimes all-day roping, herding cattle, horses too. We…me, and my younger brother, Frank, usually start early on Dad's small ranch, making sure all stock is accounted for, going after strays, and making sure all are corralled and fed. If we get caught up at Dad's ranch, we head over to a larger ranch owned by another man and do the same thing for him, usually till sundown. Only difference is we get paid for that."

With a quizzical look on her face, she tipped her head to the side. "So you're a cowboy?"

"Ahh…yes. I guess you could say that," he responded.

They were quiet, standing in a long hallway where a large

collection of pictures and wall portraits were mounted. "I guess that's why your hands are the way they are?" Rita asked.

"Pretty much," he said. "Mostly lariat—rope burns and such."

"You don't wear gloves?"

"No! My dad doesn't allow it," Kelly blurted, and instantly regretted it, adding, "but we have to when it gets colder."

Again, she gave the head-tipped quizzical look, her long raven hair bunching on her left shoulder. *So cute*, he thought.

"You know, Kelly," she said, "you are the most interesting person I have ever met. Joe and Marty are not far off, but you are quite different." He felt the blush coming. "And that part of you that is so humble, that you get so easily embarrassed, trust me, that is a rare quality. It's what first drew me to you." She was looking into his eyes intently as she talked. He could sense right then that he was probably in some real trouble. She broke away and waved her hands, gesturing to both sides of the hallway. "And these are all my relatives and family friends. Some really good folks, others not so much." She let out a small laugh and pointed out a couple of the more notorious toughs and briefly shared a history lesson on each.

"Wow, you have quite the history lesson here. It's pretty incredible," he said.

"Yes, our history is interwoven into Southern California history, for better or worse," she remarked.

They continued to walk through the large, beautiful home as she held his hand. Kelly felt like he was connected to a lightning bolt. They returned to the table, and on the way passed the foursome, along with Nance leading the group on a tour. The girls, Nancy and Gina, were along to keep the boys company, as they were keen not to let them out of their sight. Rita was waving at them across the large room as they passed. As they returned to the courtyard, a beautiful buffet was being set up by Weena, Victoria, and two helpers. Kelly was amazed at how wonderful it looked. The smell of different foods drifted through the air, and his stomach suddenly clinched, reminding him that it had been some time since breakfast.

Rita said, "I'll be right back," and moved to help her family with the remainder of the setup.

Kelly was left to wander the courtyard, carefully taking note of the many flowers, cacti, and local plant life staged and cared for so lovingly. Soon the others had returned, Nance went to Victoria and asked if things were ready. She nodded, smiling while wiping her hands on a small towel.

Victoria announced, "Everything is ready. Start on that end," she gestured to the left side, "and fill up."

The two brothers politely followed the two girls in line as they dished up and returned to their table. Rita and Kelly followed, along with Nance, Victoria, and Weena. The two helpers were invited by Weena to dish up as well, and they moved to a far corner table, chatting in some language Kelly didn't recognize. They ate and talked while drinking large, iced teas, followed by homemade apple pie for dessert. Kelly was stuffed and could barely move. All were chatting with one another when Nance looked at Kelly and made a quick motion with his head to the left. This had not escaped Rita, who was talking to Gina. She kept her eyes on Kelly, looking concerned. Nance rose and moved into the house with Kelly following. They walked through to a large den area off the main room. The room was trimmed in heavy dark wood with banks of shelves laden with books that all appeared to be the same. Nance walked over to the far bank of windows, extracted a small cigar from one of his breast pockets, along with a matchstick, and struck it on the nearby stone fireplace. He lit his cigar and blew out a small cloud of smoke.

He remained there, looking out the window for a brief time then turned to Kelly and said, "How old are you now, Kelly? Seventeen, eighteen?"

"Seventeen, sir," he responded, shuffling from foot to foot.

"Ah, point is you and your friends are all so young, as are Rita and the girls, all seventeen, going into their last year of high school. All of you have bright futures and unlimited potential. You know, when the kids came home last night, Rita could not stop talking about you. I wasn't kidding earlier when I said she hasn't slept." He chuckled, then puffed his cigar. "Those three were up all night comparing notes. Victoria and I are concerned, not only for Rita, but also for Gina and Nancy. We have been family friends since they were born, so our families are close. So you must understand when we heard of boys they met from Montana, we were concerned they were being taken advantage of. We are incredibly happy that you boys decided to join us today, and we have certainly had a good time learning more about you, Joe, and Marty. Joe has told me that his and Marty's parents are somewhat well off, with oil wells and a large ranch. It seems they have their futures mapped out. Our concern is with you, Kelly, and what your plans might be. You can understand our concern with Rita, as she is quite taken with you. Again, please excuse us for being so forward as to include ourselves in your personal business."

Kelly was reeling, not knowing what to say. It felt as if he were caught doing something he shouldn't have. "I…I…am not sure what to say, sir," Kelly stuttered.

"Easy, son, just be as honest as you can. Maybe there's a way we can help."

Kelly thought about this last offer and decided that if he was going to be a part of something other than reservation life, he had better trust this man and his family. They had displayed and shown so much kindness, kindness he had never experienced from people he hardly knew—even those he did.

Kelly responded, "It's true that I have not given my future much thought, and it's true that all I am is a reservation cowboy. All I ever wanted to do was come to California and have some fun. The brothers were kind enough to bring me along, and I am grateful. It has been a great, fun experience." He took a deep breath. "It is also true that I didn't see Rita coming. It was the last thing on my mind, yet here I am. My mother has tried to discuss education and work with me, but I didn't want her and Dad to be troubled about my future, so I wouldn't talk about it. We don't have any money other than the little ranch, and I know it's not worth much. And then there's my brother to think about. I have no idea what he's planning, yet I have to consider him. Truth is I wasn't thinking about anything but making it to California someday."

Kelly hung his head, as if waiting for some sort of rebuke. None came. There was a brief silence between them, but Nance finally broke it after a brief puff on his cigar. He said, "You know, Kelly, there might be an option for you to consider. After you graduate from school, if you find a way to move to California and establish residency, you could enroll in a university ROTC program. That might be your ticket to a paid education. Reserve Officer Training Corp, have you ever heard of it?"

"There were a couple of soldiers last year that came in and talked about it. I just never really took it seriously."

"That plan would give you a lot of what you want and some options you haven't considered. It may be worth exploring. Granted, it won't be easy, but most good things we all want come with a price, and this is no different. You have our number, and you can call me anytime. I will help you where I can if that's okay with you."

"That would be great, sir!" Kelly hoped his excitement wasn't showing too much.

They left the den and returned to the group. As they entered the courtyard, Kelly first saw Victoria find Nance's gaze, and Kelly noticed something wordless passed between them. Kelly saw her give a small nod and a smile.

Rita quickly came up to Kelly. "Where did you two disappear to?"

"Oh, just some man-talk," Kelly said, puffing out his chest.

She looked at him, then to her father, who had moved over

and was talking to Victoria and Joc. "Hmm, should have suspected there would be that." She huffed but gave him a smile.

Marty had somehow come up with a guitar and was entertaining all with a rendition of "Silver Wings" by Merle Haggard & The Strangers. It struck Kelly that he was rather good. Everyone was lost in the performance.

"Come on, walk with me," Rita said.

She grasped his hand and they moved out to the back of the house beyond a small hallway out a rear door to a small garden that was secluded and private. She stopped and turned to him. She tip-toed and kissed him softly on the lips and held it briefly. Kelly was in shock. He was sure his knees would start knocking. His heart was still churning from the encounter with Rita's father at Villa Morongo. He wanted so much to put his arms around her and bring her close, but he wasn't sure what to do, remaining frozen in place. She kept looking up at him, directly into his eyes, and let out a small laugh.

"Relax, Kelly Chase, God! You're such a wild Indian!" she exclaimed. "Here," she said as she grabbed both his wrists and pulled them around the small of her back and moved directly up against him.

Kelly had a sharp intake of breath as she again covered his mouth with her soft lips. This time biology took over and he returned her deep kiss as she melted in his arms. As they parted, she turned her head and placed it on his chest.

"Kelly," she said, "you have to promise me that you will come back to me. Please promise you will." She looked up at him again with a pleading look in her eyes, those deep, dark, warm pools.

"Rita, I don't know what it's gonna take, but I will. I don't even want to go home, but I know I can't stay in California, not yet anyway. When your father and I talked, he gave me some things to think about."

"Oh, I'll bet he did," she said.

Kelly dropped his hands down to gently hold hers. “Really, he was helpful, but I have so much to think about right now. I need some time, and I need to talk some things through with my parents, but I am coming back.” He tried to lighten up the mood and be optimistic. “Hey, maybe Labor Day weekend.”

His mind was racing. Where in the world was he going to get the money to pull this off? There weren’t enough strays in Montana to make that work. Kelly was inwardly starting to despair.

Rita gave him a small peck on the cheek. “Come on,” she said, “we’d better get back.”

They rejoined the group, and everyone, including the help, were all taking part in an energetic singalong to Marty’s rendition of Jerry Lee Lewis. He had moved to a grand piano at the side of the courtyard and was banging away with a “Boogie Woogie Country Man” tune.

Gosh, he’s good, Kelly thought. He had never heard him play. Maybe he was right about that country music bit. Rita turned to Kelly and gave the biggest smile, starting to clap her hands in time to the driving beat. Everybody was enthralled. Joe and the two girls were swinging and dancing together. Nance and Victoria were doing the same and having a great time. It was rocking. Even Weena was clapping and dancing with the help. They were bouncing off the walls, losing themselves in the energy of the music.

Once the song was over, everyone was yelling and clapping wildly. Marty made a sweeping grand bow and raised both hands together over his head and did the “I’m the Champion” thing.

Victoria came up beside Kelly and Rita. “Where did you two sneak off to? You almost missed the best part,” she said with a wry smile, winking at Rita.

“Oh, Mom, please.”

Victoria quickly changed the subject and looked at Kelly directly. “Well, Kelly, do you play?”

Oh, on the spot again. “Ah, a little, ma’am.”

"Great! Folks, the shows not over yet. Is it piano you play, Kelly?"

He nodded, a little embarrassed. Marty and Joe gave him an encouraging look and jumped in with, "Yeah, Kelly, show us what you've got!"

Kelly moved slowly to the polished grand piano, adjusted himself, and looked up at Rita standing to the side of the instrument. She had a hopeful look on her beautiful face. He was on. Kelly knew he had to make this work. His mother was a skilled pianist, and during the long Montana winters, she loved teaching him all she had learned over the years. She had surprisingly announced to him last January that he had a gift and there was nothing more for her to do. "The rest is up to you, Kelly," she'd said.

He started playing "Moonlight Sonata Opus 27." The grand was tuned to perfection, and he loved the instrument immediately. As he moved into the piece, everything became quiet. The sound was rich and resonant in the courtyard as he continued. In the corner of his eye, he caught Rita agape, eyes wide. As he continued stroking the keys with the gentle touch that his mother had taught him, it seemed that everyone behind him was holding their breath. This piece always reminded him of his mother, the beauty and softness with which she played. She possessed a patience, during which she taught him her perfect form. She insisted that a great piano player must have a heartfelt emotional connection to the music played in order to be great. He started into the closing moves. When he finished, the small group was completely silent. As he slowly turned, Nance had his arms around Victoria's waist and they both had tears in their eyes. All others suddenly broke into a wild applause complete with shrill whistles. Kelly looked at Rita, hoping for her approval, and she had one hand over her mouth while she used the back of the other to wipe tears away. Victoria and Nance both came to him and hugged him.

Nance said, "Absolutely stunning. I have never heard that piece played with so much emotion and beauty."

"Kelly, you are truly gifted," said Victoria, patting her eyes with a tissue. "Beautifully done, bravo."

He could feel that old hotness coming back.

The day had turned to early evening, and everyone had started moving to the front driveway. Rita had her arm in his as Weena came alongside him and nudged him with her elbow. "Well, Liberace, when are you coming back to see us?" she quipped.

Rita interjected, "Gram, he's going to call me as soon as he gets back to Montana and talks to his parents." Rita gave him a wide smile and a wink.

"Yes, ma'am, I sure am," Kelly quickly agreed.

Nance leaned in around Rita and touched his shoulder. "May I have a moment?" Rita released him as he and Nance moved to one side. In a low voice, he said, "Seriously, Kelly, you have a great talent for piano. I think it will take you places. I also want you to consider what we talked about earlier. I think ROTC would be a great fit for you. When you get back home, why don't you have your parents call us? Victoria and I would be thrilled to help any way we can. I have contacts at Cal State Long Beach."

As the boys drove away, Kelly was quiet, sitting in the back seat while the two brothers were talking excitedly about Gina and Nancy. Kelly was lost in thoughts of Rita. He had been catapulted into another dimension over the last two days and was still trying to make sense of it all. He had met and fallen in love with the most beautiful girl in the world, met her family, played a virtuoso performance, and been offered a chance to go to school and live in California. Yes, he was in trouble, just as he had first suspected. He knew he had just experienced the shortest, hardest fall in the history of mankind—probably. His mind was racing. How was he going to explain all of this to his mom and dad? Would they even believe him? How would he explain his feelings for Rita? He knew he could not lose her. He would move the stars in heaven to keep her.

Chapter 4

Back Home

The three boys landed in Great Falls the next evening, arriving at Kelly's house around midnight. They stood outside the car, lit by the small porch light. All three agreed they had had the greatest time of their lives and knew they had to do it again. They talked about going back for Labor Day weekend.

Kelly unloaded his bags from the trunk, hugged both his friends, and said, "I could have never done this without you guys. Thank you so much. I will never forget it."

"We need to thank you, Kelly," Marty admitted. "We would have never met Nancy and Gina if not for you. We are already dying to go back and see them."

"Hey, buddy," Joe said. "We gotta get going, it's late. See you later, man."

They both jumped in the car, turned around, and headed for the main road. Kelly stood and watched them leave until the taillights disappeared. He turned and went into the house. He felt as if he had been gone forever.

As he entered, his mother greeted him with a big smile, a huge hug, and a small kiss on the cheek. He didn't expect anyone to be up at this late hour.

"Kelly, honey, so happy to see you!" his mom exclaimed.

"You didn't have to stay up," Kelly said. "You should be in bed, Mom." He laid his bags aside.

She locked an arm in his and escorted him into the small dining table in the kitchen. She said, "I stayed up to hear about your trip. Come sit down and tell us about it."

There sat the old Indian with his hands cupped around a mug of coffee. "About time you made it home. Your mother was getting worried," he stated flatly, but with a small smile. That was big emotion for him. "Good to have you home, boy." He surprisingly got to his feet and gave Kelly a quick hug.

Kelly sat at the table across from his dad as his mother sat down next to him. He told them about his experiences in the past week. The feelings, sights, sounds, smells, the people. He found himself getting excited all over again, and it was clear his mom and dad were listening, as they continued to exchange glances and a couple of smiles. He was careful not to discuss Rita or the Siva family, saving that discussion for a later time. Something seemed off, he suddenly realized as he slowed his running monologue to a stop.

"Is everything ok here?" he said. "Where's Frank? Is he okay?"

They were both looking at him as his mother explained, "Frank has disappeared."

His dad jumped in, "We heard he was running with that bad reservation bunch doing drugs and drinking. I don't know what's happened to that boy's thinking." He squeezed his mug. "Maybe I did something wrong, I don't know." He moved both of his hands to the top of his head, brushing at his short hair, then interlocked his fingers at the back of his neck, leaning back into his chair.

"Now, Aloysius, we talked about this," Deena said. "You've done nothing wrong. You have been good to the boys and have taught them how to be good men—how to work hard, hunt, and provide for a family. We love you, and we will work together to bring Frank home."

Kelly knew before he left for California that Frank was a ticking bomb waiting to go off. It had finally happened. Now Kelly was fearful that everything in his life was in jeopardy. If Frank could not be reached or reasoned with, Kelly feared he would be stuck on the ranch for the rest of his life. He did not want his dad to shoulder the work all alone. But he was torn because he didn't want that future for Frank either. Kelly knew what he must do. He had to go find Frank and try to convince him to straighten up and help run the ranch. Hopefully, after another year, Frank would have a plan for his own future. "Thanks for waiting up for me, but I think we need to get some sleep. I know I'm bushed," Kelly said.

Aloysius rose from his seat slowly. "We have some catching up to do, son. I have fallen behind with both of you gone."

Kelly gave his father a nod, hugged his mom, grabbed his bags, and went to his bedroom.

• • •

It felt great being back on his horse Winger the next morning. The squeaks and creaks of the saddle, and the smells of the leather and Winger were comforts to his senses. As much as the noise and activity in California excited him, the peace and quiet of his home was welcomed. He didn't remember it being so quiet. So quiet he felt a soft tightness in his head, with only the occasional meadowlark and buzzing grasshopper to interrupt. It was great to be home.

At breakfast, his parents asked continuous questions about California. He was happy to answer and talk about his favorite subject. Kelly did catch his mother looking at him with some curiosity a couple of times, especially when she asked if he met any interesting people. To which he would answer, "A few."

He and the old Indian had rounded up over a dozen strays, counted and recounted the cattle, and noted brands and other new marks or scars after they had located broken fences. They had to ride onto the adjacent Wells ranch to follow another herd that had broken through the fence. They returned the strays back to the Chase ranch. They temporarily fixed the fence and moved the cattle further onto prime grazing land. They came up to what they called "the oasis," a large underground well-fed pond surrounded by cottonwood trees. This was his and Frank's favorite spot to hang out, swim, bullshit, and just escape and enjoy the warm Montana summer sun. Kelly felt a pang of sadness for his brother as he and his dad sat down with the lunches that his mother had packed for them. The old Indian let out a heavy sigh, took off his old, sweaty brown Stetson, and leaned his head back on the tree with his eyes closed.

Kelly removed his hat and opened the lunch bag. He handed his dad a sandwich, unwrapped his own, and took a large bite followed by a long pull from his canvas water bag. He lounged against the tree next to his father, taking in the rolling grassy fields before him.

His dad asked, "What do you think is wrong with Frank?"

Kelly chewed thoughtfully and said, "I think he's scared of what's going to happen to him." He swallowed before continuing. "He has always been restless and unable to focus on anything for long. I think my trip to California set him off, maybe scared him. He sees me moving away and doesn't know what to think of it yet."

The old Indian was silent for a moment, likely struck by such a coherent answer to something that clearly puzzled him. "Where'd you learn all this anyway?" his father asked, looking at him quizzically. The old Indian started to eat his sandwich and returned his gaze back over the prairie and sighed. Kelly thought it best for his dad to answer his own question. "Damned if I know what to say to him. I sometimes cannot figure out how you young guys see the world. Even being out here on the ranch, I don't feel right. There are still too many people around. And there is no one for miles. Folks my age, Indians, had it rough. We were sent to government schools, and they gave us the white man's religion. It killed my brothers and sisters and ruined my family. I…*we* wanted something different for you and Frank. I feel so powerless to help him." The old man hung his head. "The only thing that keeps me here is your mother. She keeps me going, and I will always love her and be wherever she wants me to be."

"Dad, I'm going to find Frank this afternoon and try to get to the bottom of things, if he's sober enough to talk." It was then that Kelly thought he owed it to his dad to outline his plans. "You and Mom have given me and Frank a good life here, but I am making plans to leave next year."

The old Indian looked at him sadly as he plucked a long grass strand and stuck it in between his teeth, using it for a toothpick. "I know, so does your mother. We are losing both of you too fast, yet we need to let you go."

Kelly shared every detail of the California trip he could remember, including Rita and her family. His dad listened with interest and finally commented, "All this happened in one week? Damn. Well, you'll be here until next spring, right?"

Kelly looked at him, nodded, and smiled.

"Well," his dad continued, "if you can find Frank, tell him we need him to come home."

"Sure, Dad. I will do my best to talk some sense into him."

"You know he is going to mess around on that reservation and get himself killed. It's a very dangerous place. That's the reason we don't live out there."

They roused themselves and gathered up the grazing horses. They mounted up, riding in silence while inspecting the fence line, each deep in their own thoughts. It was a typical Montana conversation.

Later that afternoon, as his father was putting up the horses, Kelly wandered into the house and found the courage to talk to his mother. "Hi, Mom," he said as he entered the kitchen, interrupting her putting a meatloaf in the oven.

She turned to him after closing the oven door. Wiping her hands on her apron, she asked, "Well, who is she?"

Kelly stopped in his tracks. "How… Ah, who?"

"Save it," she said, holding up her hand. "It was written all over your face when you came home last night. Moms can see these things, you know?"

He approached her. "Can we sit down for a minute?"

They moved over to the kitchen table and sat down, and his mother crossed her legs beneath the long dress she always wore. She crossed her arms, too, and looked at him expectantly. He related the earlier conversation that he had had with his father.

His mother smiled at him, looking deeply into his eyes, and said, "I am so happy you did that for him. I usually wind up having to give him the daily or weekly report on you boys because neither of you take the time to have a man-to-man conversation with him." She chuckled. "Sometimes he feels so left out. It serves to harden his feelings when that happens to him. How did he take the news of your plans to leave?"

Perhaps Kelly should have given his parents more credit. "I could tell he was sad about the whole thing," he said. "He is afraid of not having any help on the ranch, and he is worried about Frank being lost to him. With me making plans to leave, it just makes it tougher for him." Kelly was inwardly grateful that he had shared his plans with his dad already. "There's something else. I have a phone number for Mr. Siva, you know, Rita's father. He can help me get into the ROTC program at Cal State Long Beach. You probably need to call him and talk it over. Can you help with that, Mom?"

She put her hands on the table and interlaced her long fingers. "Wow, Kelly! Now you are starting to scare me. Please let me give this some thought, and we will talk tomorrow, okay?" She seemed excited, but there was still tension in her brow. "Are you going to look for Frank this evening? If you do, be especially careful. The bunch he has been seen with are real outlaws and it can be dangerous. Do you want me to call the tribal police to meet you?"

"No, Mom. Please, let me try to figure this out, okay?" Kelly paused for a moment. "Mom, can you tell me a little about how you and Dad came to be? You know, how you met and came here? I know you've talked about it in passing, but I have never been able to put all the pieces together enough for it to make sense."

His mother smiled, and color flushed her face. "Can we talk about that later too?" He was not going to budge, and she could see that. She sighed heavily. "I suppose you deserve to know, so I will do my best. Your dad and I first met in Butte in the old Copper King Saloon. I had come to Butte as part of an entertainment troupe that was originally created back East in St. Louis. It was a good opportunity for a young woman to make some money. It was the last leg of our tour before we needed to make our way back to Philadelphia, where I am from. Unfortunately, the manager of the show left us all high and dry in Butte—after he stole all the money we had earned as a group up till that time. Seems he ran off with one of the other singers in the troupe. To make matters worse, he had secured an advance on the three shows to be performed at the Copper King Saloon. The owner of the saloon was furious and wanted the remainder of the group to stay and perform the shows. Everyone except me had a means to get out of town. The saloon owner, Bart Steel, had his security men escort me to my room and watch over me. His plan was to make me play the piano and sing until he had what he considered proper restitution. His brother was the Silverbow county sheriff. I was trapped and knew Steel was never going to let me go. I was sure he had other plans for me other than just singing."

Kelly cringed, waiting for the happy ending.

"I had family in Philadelphia that had some means, but we were at odds because of my career choices, so I was cut off from any sort of help." She paused, stood, and got a pitcher of ice water from the fridge and returned with two glasses. She poured water into each glass and set one in front of Kelly. She sat down and continued.

"Enter, your father. I had just finished singing a song and was going up to my room. I'd noticed a growing crowd at a corner poker table. There were loud cheers and guffaws followed by moments of complete silence. I worked my way through the small crowd of men, and that's where I first saw him. A young Indian wearing dirty work clothes, a red bandana around his neck, and a dirty black cowboy hat. He had a pile of cash in front of him and was holding his poker hand before him. He was the perfect picture of a flinty-eyed, stone-faced riverboat gambler. I found out later that he was working in the copper mines, saving up for a piece of Montana grazing land he wanted. I was immediately taken with him."

She stopped to place her hand on her chest, as if to still her heart. She continued, "Across from him was Bart Steel. Bart had been losing big, and I could tell he was about to lose his religion."

"Wait, what does that mean?" Kelly asked.

"Oh, that is an old Southern saying, a loose expression meaning to blow up, come apart, or lose it," his mother explained. "Anyway, it was the moment of truth, and there was more money than I ever thought could possibly exist, just piles and piles. Your dad had just finished matching the latest large bet offered by Bart. The moment of truth had arrived. Bart turned over three kings, and your dad offered up a full house, three aces and two deuces. The place went wild. Bart was completely stunned. I was fearful for myself as I watched this play out. He would come after me later for sure. At that moment, your dad looked up at me, held my eyes briefly, and started stuffing packs of cash into every pocket he had. 'Gentlemen, I am out,' he told the group. When he started to get up to leave, Bart whined that he needed a chance to get some money back. It was funny. Your dad looked up at me again and sat down." In her best imitation of his dad's voice, she mimicked, "Well, Steel, I'll tell you what, one last bet. My money left on the table here against what you have in front of you—plus the blonde over there."

"He pointed at me with his chin, you know… how Indians always do." His mother laughed as she reminisced. "Well, they drew for high card and your dad won!" she exclaimed with delight.

Kelly could not contain the grin across his face.

His mother continued, "Your dad had come away with enough to buy this ranch and a woman to cook for him." She paused. "Well, it wasn't that simple," she said as she waved her hand in front of her face. "But we did eventually fall in love and got married. He is still my hero…" she trailed off. "Well, Kelly, go find that damn brother of yours." She slapped her knees and stood. "Be back here for dinner." She wagged her finger in his face with a smile.

Kelly eased the old Ford truck into the outskirts of Browning, the main town and home of the Blackfeet nation. It was a dusty, rough place. Some houses were barely standing, and it was hard to tell if anyone was living in them. Quiet blanketed the town. Abandoned cars littered each yard. There were a couple of old dogs wandering down the center of the old dirt road, barking while looking back and eyeing him with suspicion. He pulled into the yard of the last house on the dusty lane. It was no different than the others. Much of the asbestos-filled siding had fallen off, exposing tar paper and shiplap beneath. There were three worn-out, rusted, old cars resting on the rims beside the little dirt driveway. He caught a glimpse of curtain movement in the dirty window facing the front of the house.

He stepped out of the truck and kept a wary eye on the two rez dogs. He knew that the inhabitants of this house were acquaintances of Frank. Frank had met them on one of his party binges and had bragged them up to Kelly. He entered the small storm porch covered with stacks of boots, shoes, coats, and jackets on both sides, leaving a small path between the piles. He reached the back door and knocked. He could hear muffled voices growing louder and turning into some sort of argument. Suddenly, the door flew open and before him stood a skinny little Indian man. He had sunken cheeks and a face riddled with acne. The man's eyes were bleary, red, and unfocused—he was obviously intoxicated.

In his heavy Indian brogue, he said, "You lookin' for your brother?"

"Yep," Kelly said, unsure how this man knew who he was.

A younger woman entered the kitchen area. "He's in the back

bedroom. If he belongs to you, please get him out of here. I'm sick of him… Damn drunk!" she barked.

The house was dark and smelled of food turned bad, body odor, and some other things he could not identify. The small kitchen table was littered with beer and whiskey bottles, along with assorted drug paraphernalia. Above the table was an "End of the Trail" paint-by-number picture, and beside it was a plastic Budweiser beer representation of "Custer's Last Stand." Both pictures were probably in every house on the reservation. He followed the young woman to the bedroom, passing by a living room with two small children lined up on a dark sofa, one picking his nose. They stared at him absently. She swung the bedroom door open and stepped back, making a motion with both hands that silently said, "He's all yours!"

There, lying face down on a twin mattress with his arms extended along his body, still wearing his boots, was Frank.

"How long's he been here?" he asked.

"Oh, him and shithead there," she said, pointing with her chin to the skinny Indian, "have been smoking dope and drinking around here for two or three days."

Kelly guessed "Skinny" must have been her live-in man.

Kelly struggled with Frank's heavy, limp body but was finally able to drag him into the front seat of the old Ford and push the door shut securely behind his brother. Frank was out like a light. On the way to the ranch, Kelly's mind drifted to Rita. He needed to talk to his mother about the expense of a phone call to California. Maybe, if she decided to talk to Mr. Siva, he would have his chance to talk to her. But what would he say? Would his mother and father both be eavesdropping? And what about Mr. Siva on the other end? Would he be listening? How was any of this going to work?

Kelly looked over at his brother, who was beginning to stir, then raised his left arm to wipe the drool from his mouth. Frank cast an angry red eye in his direction, then appeared to successfully appraise the scene. He drew himself up against the passenger door and moaned aloud. Kelly noted what a smelly, pitiful sight he was as he pushed the old Ford to gain some speed so he could get this chore over with.

The sun had just set when he pulled in through the ranch gate and angled the truck toward the house. As he drove up, he could see his mother and father standing on the raised porch waiting for him. As he came to a stop, they both ran up to Frank's side of the truck and peered inside. They got Frank into his bedroom, removed his boots, and settled him onto the bed. He was snoring before they were out of the room.

The old Indian turned and looked at Kelly and smiled. "Thank you, boy, for bringing him home. God-awful mess he is," he said, shaking his head. Aloysius put his arm around his wife's waist, and they both moved toward the kitchen as she rested her head on his shoulder.

• • •

Everyone was up early the next morning, including Frank, who had managed to get showered and dressed in clean clothes. Breakfast was quiet, with no one willing to comment on the recent misadventures of Brother Frank.

Aloysius finally spoke. "Frank and I will be fixing fences today. Kelly, I understand you and your mother have some calls to make this morning."

Kelly nodded, and his mother responded, "Yes, about nine. It should be interesting. We will tell you all about it at lunch."

With his father keeping Frank busy, Kelly could focus on calling Rita. There were many dynamics to consider, but he thought it best to go for it and see what happened. Once his father and brother headed out for the fences, Kelly rushed to the phone with his mother in tow. Though he'd just eaten, his stomach growled.

The phone was answered by an unfamiliar voice, which momentarily threw him. He quickly gathered his wits and asked for Rita. He was asked to wait.

Shortly after, someone picked up. "Hello," the sweet voice sang.

"Rita, it's me! Er…K-kelly," he stuttered. "Kelly Chase!"

"I thought you would never call," she teased.

He felt his breathing quicken and his throat tighten as she continued to tell him how much she missed him and asked when he was coming back. Kelly had to consciously rouse himself, as he was lost in her voice.

"Kelly? Are you still there?"

"Yes, yes," he said, coming back to reality.

They shared a polite conversation until his mother came in and asked, "Is he there?"

Kelly quickly asked Rita if her father was there and that his mother wanted to talk to him.

"Can I talk to her?" Rita asked.

"Sure," he said, then reluctantly handed the phone to his mother.

"Rita?" she greeted.

An hour flew by as they handed the phone back and forth as the conversation went on between the four. Mr. Siva had eventually joined in. A plan had been proposed by Nance Siva and his mother had warmed up to it. Kelly was getting more excited by the minute for his prospects. Victoria Siva had soon introduced herself to Deena, and they seemed to enjoy each other's company as the conversation eventually wound down, and Rita and Kelly were left alone to say their goodbyes and spent time just listening to each other's breathing. Softly in the background, Victoria reminded Rita that it was time to hang up. They finally said goodbye for the tenth time and hung up.

Kelly and his mother had sketched out a plan by the time noon had come around. He and his mother were going to California after his spring graduation. Deena would travel with him to help him get settled. They had a standing invitation to visit the Siva family, which was also part of the plan. Deena would clear everything with the old Indian, so he was included. Deena kept promising Kelly she and Aloysius would take care of any money issues and not to worry, but he was still concerned for them. He loved them both deeply and didn't want to see them hurt.

Around 12:30, Kelly heard Frank and his dad stomping on the back porch. His dad led the way into the kitchen and walked through to the dining room without saying anything. Frank moved directly to the far side of the kitchen table quietly. He slouched insolently in the chair with a grim look on his face. He was pale and did not look well. A plate of sandwiches and a pitcher of iced tea had been placed at the center of the table.

Deena asked, "How did you fellas do this morning?" as she filled each plastic tumbler with tea.

Aloysius had returned and sat at the end of the table, looked at Deena, and gave a wide smile. "Really good, huh, son?" He looked at Frank, who looked up and gave a small smile, which Kelly took as an encouraging sign. "Well, my bride," Aloysius announced, "what news do you have?"

Deena related the details of the morning and generally laid out the plan of action for Kelly's future. Kelly was sure to correct her on a couple of points, as he was focused on his dad and brother, monitoring each and looking for any reaction. Frank sat impassively while his father was interested and nodding as the plan unfolded.

"Does this mean you'll have to join the Army?" his dad asked.

"It doesn't sound like it," his mother said. "He would have some reserve duty time to fulfill, but that's it. If he takes the required courses for ROTC, his education is pretty much paid for."

"Well," Aloysius said, smiling, "that seems like it solves a lot of problems. What is this Mr. Siva like?"

"Aloysius, they, Nance and Victoria Siva, are wonderful people," Deena said. "I really had fun talking to them. It seems they are already quite taken with your son here." She motioned to Kelly with a tip of her head. "Victoria's mother knows some people up here too. Remember the Bruneau family? She knows one of the elders that lives up here."

"What are you gonna do for money down there?" Frank interjected. "Ride broncs, break horses, and herd cows?" He slowly chewed the edges of a sandwich. He continued, "Do they even have cows in California?"

"Mr. Siva is going to help and get in touch with some people he knows," Deena replied.

Without saying anything, Frank rose from his chair, left his half-eaten sandwich, and went out the back door.

Kelly got up and looked at his parents. His dad was slowly shaking his head, and his mother shrugged her shoulders, sighed, got up, and started clearing the table. Kelly followed Frank out the back door. He had already found an old metal chair to lounge on and had crossed his legs and placed his dirty cowboy boots upon a short log just off the wood pile.

"Hey, big brother, thanks for the ride home," Frank said. "You didn't have to do it, though. Everything was under control."

Kelly looked directly at him and said, "Sure it was. You could've had a bear crawl up your ass and you wouldn't have known it."

Frank chuckled and smart-assed back with, "He only pissed in my mouth near as I could tell." He drew the back of his hand across his mouth with a bitter frown.

Kelly came around and leaned up against the short log fence ringing the back yard. "What's up, Frank? How'd you and Dad do this morning?"

Frank smiled to himself and said, "You know the old Indian. He was his usual quiet self, never saying much."

"That's because he doesn't know what to say to you. We both know he had it rough growing up, something we've never had to deal with thanks to him. Frank, he would do anything for us. If there is anything you ever need, he would go through hell to make it happen for you."

"Yes, I know, they both would." He fixed his eyes on the ground. "Kelly, I don't know what to do." He looked up briefly at the back door, as if readying himself to share a secret. "When you left," he paused, "I just got scared. I suddenly realized that you were going to disappear from my life, and it hit me that my brother was going to leave next year. What am I going to do? I don't have any interests, no desire to become anything other than a cowboy. That's not much of a life to look forward to, but it's all I've got." Frank looked away, embarrassed by the revelation.

"Frankie, you have two years to go, and that's a lot of time to get yourself centered and find what you like—what you're good at." Kelly scratched his chin, thinking about his brother's skills. "Hey, you are good with math and numbers. You would probably make a good businessman. Here's an idea. You know there are oil wells around here, so maybe you could look at that. See if there is any oil on this land, strike it rich."

"Boy, like the old Indian would stand still for that. He would have a fit," Frank said.

"You won't know until you ask him. Like I said, he would do anything for you. Just try, Frankie," Kelly begged. "I don't want to have to come back home and find you messed up like I just did." Kelly shook his head, the image of his brother on that mattress clear in his head. "You really scared the hell out of them. I hope you realize that. They were really worried about you. The old Indian was really hurting yesterday when we were herding strays. Promise me, Frank, that you won't do that again. You need to know that I will come back and visit every chance I get. I'm not leaving forever."

Frank got up, strode over to his brother, and hugged him hard. When he stepped away, Kelly could see his eyes had moistened up. Frank said, "I'll do my best, Brother, I promise."

Chapter 5

Return to California

Spring 1964

Kelly attended his last year of high school with a newfound goal and dedication. He now knew what he wanted. Rita was a big part of his plans. He did not miss a single day, even as the old Indian was haranguing him to help feed the stock in the winter. He would get up early on those days and get the feeding done before he and Frank caught a car ride to school with the Ames brothers. Kelly's grades had improved dramatically, including Algebra. His mother provided nonstop tutelage as he worked hard to improve. All A's and one B in Algebra were his reward. By the end of the year, his B became an A, and he had done all he could to aid in his own success.

Frank, on the other hand, had continued to drift both emotionally and scholastically as Kelly's ever-looming departure hung over him. Frank was naturally gifted in mathematics and critical thinking. Whenever he applied himself, schoolwork came easy, and his grades were consistently perfect. Frank, however, had other distractions: drinking and ever-increasing drug use. His grades suffered the entire year. Their mother had fretted constantly over his missing days, incomplete homework, and his uncaring attitude. Kelly tried his best to support his brother, but he knew how stubborn Frank could be. Ultimately, all anyone could do was just clean up any destruction in his wake and hope he would come back to earth at some point. The old Indian watched with interest, never judging or speaking ill of Frank's shortcomings. He spoke highly of his errant son when he could.

After Kelly's graduation, arrangements were made for a trip to visit the Siva family. Deena and Kelly had set aside any extra money they had earned throughout the year for the trip. Victoria had called his mother on several occasions throughout the year, and they talked at length. They discussed how they would, together, get Kelly enrolled at UC Long Beach and into the ROTC program. They had become fast friends. Nance Siva had made flight arrangements to the San Bernardino Airport, and they were scheduled to land June 13th on a Saturday. Nance had also arranged for a car to have them picked up. The Sivas also made plans for them to stay in the property guest house for the week, allowing them enough time to get all the logistics and school registrations started for the upcoming school year. A small apartment would be rented in nearby Long Beach so that Kelly could start establishing California residency, allowing for cheaper tuition.

As they drove east on Highway 10 toward the Morongo Reservation, Deena was watching the desert landscape slide by from the back window. She seemed uneasy, like she was wondering if she was going to lose her two sons forever. She looked over at Kelly. He was perched on the edge of the car seat in anticipation of seeing Rita again. It had been nearly a year since Kelly had last been here. Deena was likely worried that the relationship ultimately would not work out and that her son would be crushed. Rita had mailed photos of herself and the family. It was clear that she was beautiful, so a mother could easily see why Kelly had been so taken.

Their car soon turned off the main highway onto a narrow-paved road and drove into the circular driveway then stopped at the front of the Spanish-style villa.

Deena remarked to Kelly, "What a beautiful home. I've always wanted to live in a place like this."

The driver exited the car and opened the door for Deena and Kelly. As they stepped out, Victoria Siva quickly approached, followed close behind by her daughter, Rita. Rita quickly ran to the other side of the car and jumped into Kelly's arms, smothering him with kisses.

"Rita!" her mother warned. "Decorum, decorum, show some respect, please." Victoria gave Deena a friendly hug. "So nice to finally meet you, Mrs. Chase. Welcome, please come inside. We have some refreshments for you after your long journey."

Deena said, "Thank you so much, Mrs. Siva. Now, can we agree to start using our first names?"

They both laughed. Deena glanced at her son and Rita Siva; the pictures had not come close to capturing Rita's beauty. She held out both of her hands to greet Rita. Rita deftly slid between Deena's hands and gave her a gentle hug.

"So glad to meet you, Mrs. Chase," Rita said politely. "Sorry for the behavior. It's just that I missed Kelly so much."

"It is so nice to finally meet you, Rita." Deena scanned Rita up and down. "You are truly beautiful. Kelly is very fortunate to have found you."

"Oh, believe me, I found him," she chirped excitedly, gazing up at Kelly.

They continued into the house, with Victoria leading the way. A tall, handsome Indian man stepped into the foyer from a nearby hallway. Victoria slid in beside him and placed an arm around his waist. "This is my husband, Nance. You've talked to him on the phone."

They were both very well dressed, Victoria in a sleeveless, off-white below-the-knee dress—simple but elegant. He in black slacks with a semi-formal white shirt with the sleeves rolled up. Victoria's long black hair was kept in one loose thick braid held by a wrapped leather strip, accented by gray streaks that gave her a regal bearing. Nance's short salt-and-pepper hair served his distinguished look. When seen together, it was easy to see Rita in both.

Kelly looked to his mother, watching her evaluate the Siva's, and he hoped that she saw what he did. Life was so much simpler and easy in this place, and his mother was so used to the hard, sometimes harsh life in Montana, so any other way of life must have seemed casual and easy.

The group eventually made their way out to the shaded courtyard where Kelly had played piano nearly a year before.

Weena, Rita's grandmother, quickly moved into the room and gave Kelly a generous hug. "Well hello, Liberace," she greeted as she pulled away and turned to Deena. "You must be very proud of your son. He is good." She pointed to Kelly and winked at his mother.

Nance took the opportunity to comment, "Yes, he left a lasting impression on everyone with his piano skills. Did he tell you?" he asked Deena. His mother had a quizzical look on her face as a response. "Of course, he didn't. I suspect too modest by half," Nance said as he winked at Kelly.

Gosh, Kelly thought. Being around this family always caused his face to flash hot.

Kelly had never seen his mother enjoy herself so much. Becoming acquainted with the Siva family was the best thing that had happened to her in quite some time. Later, as they made their way to the neighboring bungalow, she shared with him, "These people are fantastic and so much fun. I wasn't sure how this whole idea about school in California was going to work out. It looks like, with the Sivas' help, this may be a very good thing for you." She nodded, unable to hold back a smile. "And Rita is just an absolute gem," she said.

The following week was packed with activities. Rita was the escort and Victoria acted as the chauffeur. Applications and paperwork for all educational needs were completed. When the enrollment forms were submitted for the ROTC program, Nance helped behind the scenes, and everything went smoothly. The Sivas were also helpful in placing a deposit on a small rental unit in Long Beach, just off the UC Long Beach campus. It was hard to tell who was more excited: Kelly or Rita. Everything was in place for the start of school in September.

On their last night as guests of the Siva clan, Deena played the piano for everyone after dinner. She was so skillful at her playing that she didn't leave a dry eye. Kelly too was moved, as he had never heard his mother play on a quality instrument. Kelly and Rita were able to spend time in the small garden where they had first kissed. They exchanged promises and talked about future plans. Rita surprised Kelly by telling him that her father had secured a part-time job for him at a small manufacturing plant near the school that her father had part ownership. Kelly couldn't believe everything was coming together. What were the chances that he would meet the most beautiful girl in the world and would be living in California? Rita sat appraising him as he quietly thought of his good fortune.

She leaned over and whispered in his ear, "I love you, Kelly Chase." They exchanged long, lingering kisses, but Rita broke off suddenly. "We have to stop," she said, breathing heavily. "Or I won't be able to stop."

"I love you so much, Rita. I don't know if I can stay away till September, but I have to save my money—"

Rita placed a forefinger on his lips. "You just come back to me when school starts. I will be waiting for you."

The next morning, after all the hugs and goodbyes were said, Kelly and Deena were taken to the airport. Early that evening, they were picked up by the old Indian. Aloysius gently placed their bags in the back of the truck and kissed Deena, then shook Kelly's hand and asked him with a gentle smile, "You riding front or back?"

"I'll ride in front, Dad," Kelly said with confidence.

Aloysius helped Deena carefully up onto the seat and returned around to the driver's seat as Kelly climbed in beside his mother. His mother talked nearly the entire way on the return trip home. Kelly would fill in between his mother's running descriptions of California and the most wonderful family she had ever met. Aloysius only smiled at her with his eyes gleaming. His wife hadn't been this happy in years. Kelly could see he was grateful that she was able to make the journey despite his doubts about the whole California adventure.

Kelly knew he needed to ask about Frank, but when he did, his dad issued a short response: “Good.”

Kelly wasn’t sure how to interpret this but decided to let it drop. Now he was concerned about Frank. The old Indian tipped his head forward as he drove down the road and peered around Deena at Kelly. “No, really, he’s okay. He misses you two but won’t admit it. He’ll be happy to see you both.”

That summer was one of Kelly’s happiest. The three men worked hard most of the day and genuinely enjoyed one another’s company. Kelly and Frank would spend two days of the week working on the Wheeler ranch cowboying and earning extra money. The other days were spent in the hot Montana sun swimming in the large pond beneath the big cottonwoods. They swam, ate, napped, and listened to stories the old Indian told. Deena joined them at least once a week for overnight stays at the pond. They cooked over an open fire, enjoyed the wide-open starlit skies above, and openly talked about Kelly’s upcoming departure. Kelly and Frank had never felt closer to one another or to their mother and father than during that last summer they spent together. Frank still had misgivings about what he would do after school the next year. He was afraid he would not be able to leave home. Unlike Kelly, Frank feared being a failure, and Kelly saw that.

Kelly spent lots of time with the Ames brothers after their return from California. They had some classes together in the last year and had grown even closer. The brothers had been discouraged from any long-distance relationships by their parents. Any plans to keep things going by returning to either girl was not supported. Marty had the most difficulty with the imposed restriction and at one point threatened to leave home early and return to Gina. Kelly wasn’t convinced that Marty had totally ruled out the idea. Joe had continued with plans to become a businessman rancher and succeed his father. Marty was still unsure of what he was doing. He was much like Frank in his thinking. Marty was still determined to become a country music entertainer and had started playing small gigs at area schools with his small band and had gained some success and notoriety. Kelly admired his determination, and he thought it took courage to go against the grain—especially one imposed by his family.

Summer eventually bled into early September, and it was time for Kelly to leave for California. Deena had been slowly shipping Kelly's possessions to the Siva residence so Kelly could eventually move them to his Long Beach apartment. Aloysius and Deena purchased a vehicle from a local man that had a car rebuilding and selling business. He had been around for years, and everyone knew his reputation. Aloysius acquired a yellow 1955 Ford station wagon with a three-speed manual transmission. Kelly realized that it was indeed the ugliest car he had ever laid eyes on, a reservation ride if ever. The old Ford did hum, he had to admit.

Kelly arrived two days later at his small apartment in Long Beach. It was strange being alone for the first time in his life. Though there was a lot of planning in getting here, he was unprepared for the quiet and the absence of his family. Luckily, exhaustion would offer some peace and reflection could wait. He was dog-tired and fell face-first in bed and slept until the next morning.

The next day he organized his belongings and left for the Sivas, stopping along the way for a breakfast sandwich and coffee. Kelly retrieved all his possessions from the Sivas and was served lunch and spent some alone time with Rita. She was so excited to see him that she completely forgot to eat. It was a Sunday afternoon, and they were to start classes next Tuesday. Rita's excitement was starting to become contagious, and his excitement only grew.

"Well, Kelly," Nance said, interrupting the lunch they'd hardly touched, "you are on your way. Your mother should be congratulated for pulling this all together. Make sure you tell her to come stay with us whenever she comes down to visit. Tell her to bring your father too so I can have someone to talk to." He started to leave, but then turned and said, "Kelly, make sure you call me if you need anything or have any problems with school."

"Yes, sir," Kelly said.

A couple of minutes later, Victoria came into the dining room and sat down across from the two. "I want to remind you two to always be respectful of one another and to remember that you will have an entire lifetime to spend together if you want it. Don't ruin it by rushing into things." She looked at each of them and stressed, "If you know what I mean."

Kelly couldn't recall a time when he had come to this house when he hadn't felt his face redden.

"Mother!" Rita chastised as she cupped her face in her hands.

"I just wanted you two to hear it directly from me, so don't disappoint me." Victoria walked around the table and stood behind them, kissed each on the cheek, and gave their shoulders a gentle squeeze, drawing them both toward her.

Rita was still pursuing a degree in marine biology. Kelly was less clear about his goals. He loved music and wanted to pursue it as a major but thought it might be perceived as wimpy. He decided on military studies as a major with a music minor. This would complement his ROTC studies and was something in which he had an interest. He would pursue both but knew his favorite was going to be music—he loved it.

They saw each other throughout the week and would study together in the large campus library or outside on the grounds when the weather was nice. Rita's family made the decision for her to stay with nearby relatives. On Saturdays, when not at the villa, she would spend time with Kelly at his small apartment. Remembering Victoria's warning, they were both hesitant about going too far and exercised restraint until one Saturday night when neither could stand it any longer. The experience for Kelly was something he had imagined many times, but the real thing was mind-blowing. He was afraid his heart would literally explode. This had been the first experience for them both, and Rita was particularly fearful. Her fears were soon overcome with an intense emotional outburst, and she wept with pure joy for the man she loved. They limited their intimate contact to once every two weeks, but even that became too much to bear at times. They had to redouble their efforts to their studies and purposely stay apart so there would be some sort of normal existence. Kelly always saw Rita as the exotic beauty with long raven hair complementing her olive coloring, high cheekbones, and coal-black eyes. She always saw him as the tall, long-haired warrior with his remarkably rugged handsome features. Those striking azure blue eyes set him far apart from any other man. They attracted attention wherever they went, together or apart.

Gina and Nancy were also attending the same school. They both spent a lot of time with Rita. Gina had made a habit of cornering Kelly and asking about Marty Ames. "What is the latest news on Marty?" she would always ask. Kelly found himself trying to avoid her, as he did not want to see her hurt look each time he had to tell her he didn't have any news.

Kelly took an Economics 101 class his freshman year. It was the first time he met Bradley Jenkins. He was the one who always sat front and center in class and always had the answers. This, of course, always elicited eye rolls from fellow students. One afternoon, during an intense exchange between Bradley and the professor over some arcane financial formula, it suddenly occurred to Kelly that the guy was really smart and had a backbone too. The professor finally found a professorial back door out of the argument, but the episode had won Kelly over. He decided he had to get to know Bradley Jenkins a little better. Bradley spent a lot of time alone and was about six feet tall and had a gawky gait to his stride. He sometimes wore his black framed glasses that added to his geeky persona. Kelly had purposefully sat across from him at the same table at one of the school's remote canteens. They were both silent at first.

Kelly ventured first with, "I enjoyed your little chat with Professor Barnes."

Bradley chuffed with a quiet chuckle. "Thanks," he said, "I did get a little excited—usually not like me. Brad Jenkins." He offered his hand over the table. Kelly took his hand and introduced himself. Bradley withdrew after the handshake and said, "Whoa! A working man, huh? Don't recall seeing that around here before," he said with an open smile.

"A remnant of my cowboy days. Sorry, still a little rough," Kelly explained.

"Well, you certainly have piqued my interest now."

Kelly went on to explain his brief history and Montana.

Brad exclaimed, "Well, you are a rare bird for Long Beach! You do have a bit of a beach-bunny look, though."

Kelly knew he was going to like this guy. Bradley Jenkins was originally from New Haven, Connecticut, and as he explained it, his father just got tired of cold weather and decided to move to California with the defense industry as an electrical engineer. Bradley had been in California since he was thirteen. He was a self-admitted geek and bookworm who had an affinity for numbers. He had a full-ride scholastic scholarship and was headed for some sort of greatness in the field of finance. Kelly was impressed. He in turn cautiously shared his educational credits with Bradley, risking harsh judgment.

Bradley's response was unforgettable. "Yes, but you are going with that beautiful dark-haired fox."

Kelly's mouth fell open. This guy might have looked like a geek, but man was he with it.

Kelly and Brad's friendship grew quickly. They were two men who were the exact opposites in most every way, yet those differences fit them together with very few personality gaps. Kelly was still rather gullible with some Montana-hick innocence, which played well off Bradley Jenkins and his wry, stinging wit and ever-present commentary about…well, everything. Things went well until Bradley found himself in Rita's presence. He was instantly transmogrified into a stuttering, babbling idiot that Kelly would awkwardly need to bail out. Rita was genuinely flattered and amused by Bradley's stage fright. She quickly warmed up to Bradley, and he eventually loosened up. He was soon able to elicit loud shouts of laughter from her normally reserved nature.

During his second year, Kelly had taken an Art class and met Henry Barney, a Navaho Indian. Henry was an organically grown artist and painter. Kelly considered him a professional, even at Henry's young age. Henry was the typical quiet loner with the stoic Indian persona. Kelly was able to see through Henry's implacable countenance, which, with Indians, was more intended to keep people at bay more than anything. Most Indians, with their quiet nature, did not suffer fools well and would normally opt to just skip the exercise. This worked well on someone who didn't know any better and would be halfway intimidated by the deep stares and unblinking response to questions. But having firsthand experience with Indians who presented themselves in this way, Kelly aped Henry's facial expressions until the Navaho broke into a chuckle.

"Okay, Indian, where you from?" Henry asked with a small smile.

The ice was broken. Kelly discovered again, as with most Indians, the art of deadpan comedy while delivering a deep observation of the obvious. Some of the other students said, "Is he kidding or what? I can never tell." Kelly, as a witness to many of these exchanges, could not contain himself and would have to turn and leave before he lost total control. Kelly loved Henry's quiet nature. They would be in comfortable silence with one other as they quietly observed others. Their conversations were economical, but when they did talk, things usually took a humorous turn and ended with gales of laughter. The real surprise was how Bradley, or "Jenks," as

Kelly and Rita had taken to calling him, had first interacted with Henry. It was akin to a mind-reading magic act, as they had started by finishing each other's sentences. It was eerie.

"Don't you find that unusual?" Rita asked Kelly. "In a sweet way," she added.

Here was this wholly urbane white guy having these disjointed, stilted conversations with this shorter Indian man—almost like a foreign language. Rita loved Henry. He had a stage presence that was unwavering. He was a true friend and the best person to confess your fears and transgressions. He would sit silently and finally offer his sage advice. The four amigos thusly joined and were to remain friends for life. Along the way, Nancy and Gina would join the group for many of their get-togethers.

The gang spent a lot of time together: studying, hanging out in the park, spending weekends together, going to the movies. It was the end of their third school year, and it was time to celebrate. The six of them loaded into Kelly's old Ford wagon, by this time christened the "Rolls Canardly" (rolls down one hill and Canardly make it up the next) and took a Saturday afternoon trip to the villa. They were a loud and rowdy group that turned into the Siva driveway. With the radio turned up all the way, they all laughed and talked at the same time. Nance Siva was leaning against one of the archway pillars with his arms crossed as he watched them speed around the circular driveway and stop at the front door—laughing, giggling, and being young. As they jostled each other on the way into the house, they ignored Nance, who said nothing, turned, and followed the gang into the house.

"Whoa, you kids, where do you think you're going?" Victoria asked, with her hand held up like an intersection cop.

"Out to the courtyard to mingle," Rita said. "What do you have to eat, Mom?"

Victoria stepped aside and allowed the group to pass. Nance came alongside Victoria and said, "Lively group today."

Victoria had a small lunch table set up for the group. Everyone was in a celebratory mood, for all had achieved great things during the year and life was good.

Kelly had called his mother earlier in the week to tell her how well the year had gone. Deena asked if he was going to come home for a visit during the summer. Kelly complained that he didn't have the money and was afraid the old Ford might not make it. They talked about Aloysius and Brother Frank. The old Indian was still working the ranch with two hired day hands. He didn't want to get behind again, as Frank would disappear for extended periods of time. Frank was in and out of school, trying to get enough participation just to graduate, which was apparently all he wanted.

"Mom, I'm going to ask Rita to marry me," Kelly finally blurted out.

He heard his mother's sharp intake of breath at the news. "Kelly, when are you going to do this?"

"Probably this coming Saturday," he answered. "We are—the bunch of us—going out to the villa to have a little end-of-the-year get-together, and that's when I'll ask her."

His mother was quiet for a moment, then said, "Do her parents know?"

"I sneaked out to their house last week and had a talk with Nance and Victoria. They were expecting it, and they're both happy with the decision, and especially grateful that I had taken the time to ask them for permission."

Deena was quiet again. Kelly thought she would have been instantly happy about the announcement, but he hadn't been home as much as he should have, so his mother may have felt as though another piece of her life was being taken away from her. "When are you thinking of getting married?" she finally said.

"I don't know, probably not until the end of next school year."

"Okay," she responded. "I will let your father know. You call me and let me know how it all turns out. I need a full report, okay?" Before Deena hung up the phone, Kelly could hear her softly crying.

Everyone was gathered around the large piano as Kelly played a medley of the Beach Boys favorites. He was leading the group as best he could. The help was busily setting up the plates and dishes, with favorite beverages in an iced tub. Once the tables had been set up with place settings, everyone moved to sit down. Bradley and Henry were involved in some deep discussion. Gina, Nancy, and Rita were chatting among themselves about some professor that had made an impression on them. Everyone was casually dressed, and Rita was again radiant with her white hip-huggers, white sandals, yellow blouse, and white hair band containing her long, flowing raven hair. Kelly couldn't take his eyes off her, as usual. She suddenly looked up and saw him looking at her. She gave him one of those puppy-dog, head-tipped looks with a slight narrowing of her eyes: her trademark look. Kelly sat down next to Henry and unconsciously reached in his jacket pocket to reassure himself that the small box was still there.

Henry elbowed him in the ribs and whispered, "You're on. Don't screw it up."

Jenks looked around Henry and surreptitiously gave Kelly a thumbs up. After everyone was comfortably seated, Victoria entered the courtyard. She was talking as she walked.

"Everyone, we have a surprise guest joining us today." She turned and made a grand gesture with the sweep of her hand. "Mrs. Deena Chase," she announced proudly. Nance followed with a wide smile. He had Deena's hand placed in the nook of his arm as he escorted her into the courtyard. Kelly was shocked and shakily got to his feet. It had been over a year since he had last seen her.

He ran to his mother and enveloped her in a hug as she kissed him gently on the cheek and said, "My boy, I've missed you so much." She hugged him even tighter.

"How, when…" Kelly trailed off.

His mom looked up at him and smiled. "We'll talk about that later. Do what you came to do." She squeezed his arm.

Kelly, dazed, dragged himself back to the task at hand. Everything had gotten quiet as Kelly approached Rita, who by this time had a thoroughly confused look on her face. Gina was leaning over to whisper into Nancy's ear, who immediately brought her hands to her mouth. Kelly hesitantly went to one knee and deftly withdrew the small box from his jacket pocket and opened it.

Rita, without waiting for the proposal, was already bouncing up and down. "Yes, yes!" she squealed. "I thought you'd never ask!" Her face had turned bright-red, and tears were already flowing.

Victoria rushed to her side, along with her two friends. Nance came to Kelly, shook his hand, and gave him a bear hug. "When's the big day?" he asked.

Kelly could only shrug at this question. Nance laughed and gave him a small slap on the back.

Jenks came up and said, "You are the first—"

"One to fall," finished Henry.

His friends both hugged him. Once things calmed down, Rita turned to Deena, went to her, and hugged her deeply. Standing back she said, "I will always take care of him."

"He's so lucky to have you, honey. I know you will," Deena said, lightly stroking Rita's cheek.

Kelly came up and hugged them both at the same time. He still could not believe his mother was there. "How did you get here?" he asked.

"Funny thing, right after you called, Victoria called me and invited me down. She said not to worry about the costs. She said once you were rich and famous you could pay her back." She chuckled, blinking back tears. "Victoria said she did not want me to miss this. This family is so sweet," his mother said as she looked around the courtyard.

Looking at his mother, he noticed for the first time that her eyes had a tired, drawn appearance, that some of the luster and brightness had disappeared from her.

Kelly introduced Jenks and Henry to his mom, as well as Gina and Nancy. Kelly caught up with Victoria, who was on her way to the kitchen. As they entered the kitchen, Victoria turned in surprise. "Oh, Kelly! Congratulations."

Kelly suddenly hugged her and said, "Thank you so much for bringing my mom down. You don't know how much it meant to her."

Victoria returned the hug. "I've got a pretty good idea," she said. "I was happy to do it. What's family for?"

Weena was preparing a dessert dish and had seen Kelly talking with her daughter. She walked over to him after wiping her hands on a small towel. "She's finally gonna make an honest man of you huh?" she quipped. She gave him a big grin and a quick hug.

Kelly enjoyed what was to be the single happiest event in his life for many years to come.

Chapter 6

Deena

For Kelly and Rita, their last year of school had begun. Kelly had done well with his studies and was certain he wanted to join the music industry in some way. He had taken many leadership courses, along with classes like business management. These would allow him to get an entry-level management position so he could learn the ropes. Rita was probably on track to post-graduate work. They might have needed to move closer to the San Diego area to be near the schools that offered quality degrees in marine work. Kelly was certainly willing to go anywhere for Rita. New classes had just gotten underway when the school's administration office sent a note to his first class. He was to call home in Montana immediately. Kelly quickly made his way to the admin offices, having no clue what kind of news was waiting for him there. He showed the desk person the note, and she escorted him to a small room with a phone on a small desk. He sat on the small chair provided as his heart started to race.

"Hello?" his father answered when Kelly called.

"Dad, what's going on?"

There was a long pause as he listened to his father's shallow breathing. "It's your mother, Kelly," his father choked out. Kelly held his breath. "She died last night at the hospital in Great Falls."

"Oh, please, God no. No..." he trailed off. Tears spilled from his eyes as he felt the room start to spin.

"Kelly! Kelly!" his father called. "Listen to me. Don't talk, just listen."

"What happened?" Kelly managed to say.

"She had what is called an aortic rupture," his father said, barely able to get the words out. "It was sudden, and by the time they got her to Great Falls, she was gone. The local hospital doctors could do nothing." He paused. "She's just gone."

Kelly could hear his father crying on the other end. Soon they were both lost in grief. "Dad, I will fly out as soon as I can catch a flight. I'll be right there. Bye, Dad," Kelly said before his father could try to change his mind.

They both hung up. He didn't remember walking across campus toward the class he thought Rita was attending. As he approached the building, a flood of students pushed toward him. He was buffeted about between the others, pinballing from person to person.

He heard Rita calling his name. "Kelly, Kelly!" She ran up to him, swung her book bag over her shoulder, and grabbed both of his arms. "What's wrong, honey?"

He was in obvious distress, with a stunned, tear-filled look. Kelly looked away absently as his mind wandered. She could see he was in shock. She yelled, "Somebody call the medics and campus police quick!"

She repeated the command until two students ran back into the building. Rita moved Kelly over to a nearby bench and sat him down. "What happened, Kelly?" she asked as she leaned in close to him.

He mumbled something low, and then louder, "My mom's dead. My mom's dead."

"Kelly, everything will be okay," Rita said, and her calmness surprised him. "I'm right here, and I won't leave your side. I will call Mom to come and get us, okay?"

Kelly nodded from a far-off place as he slumped to his side on the bench. Kelly could hear a siren wailing in the distance and then lost consciousness.

• • •

Kelly came to in a place surrounded by white. As he edged closer to becoming fully awake, he realized he was in a hospital—probably the emergency unit. The overhead curtain slid open, and a small dark-haired woman came to his side.

"Hi, I'm Doctor Leslie," she said. "I'm going to shine a light in each of your eyes, so please bear with me." She then checked him with her stethoscope. She stepped back and wrote on a clipboard attached to his gurney. "You experienced a shock episode and lost consciousness. I have prescribed some medication to calm you down. You should be okay. We are releasing you to your family. They are in the waiting room." She smiled gently, but Kelly didn't respond. "I will have you transported out to see them, and I will give them some instructions."

Rita, Victoria, Jenks, and Henry were waiting for him, all standing and advancing toward him as the doctor held up her hand. "Please, no excitement for him, just give him some time."

Everyone stopped in place, unsure of what to do. The doctor took Rita and Victoria aside, and Kelly could vaguely hear her issuing instructions to them. Both were nodding, then Rita asked some questions.

A nurse pushed him out the front entrance with all his friends following behind. The nurses must have assumed that he and Rita were married. Unfortunately, they had not set a date yet, but they were working on it. "Good luck, Mrs. Chase. I hope he gets better," the nurse said as she left.

As Kelly sat in the back seat of Victoria's car, he could hear his friends' voices discussing him. Jenks and Henry soon departed, and Victoria climbed into the driver's seat with Rita on the passenger side. "We're taking you out to the villa so you can rest for a couple of days. That is all we want you to do. We will make all of the arrangements for you to go to Montana. Don't worry about anything, just rest!" Victoria ordered.

Kelly said meekly, "Yes, ma'am."

For the next two days, it was all Kelly could do to get around and take care of his personal needs. Weena took care of Kelly, along with Rita. He finally ventured out into the main grand room and met with Nance and Victoria. Kelly sat opposite them on the deep leather couch, and his empty eyes found Nance.

Nance took a deep breath and started, "Son, you've taken a big hit and suffered a big loss. We realize you are still hurting, but you need to toughen up because you have some work to do. We have been in touch with your father, and he has made arrangements for your mother's funeral in Cut Bank. He needs you to be there tomorrow. He is having a difficult time holding it together and needs you to call him. Can you do that, Kelly?"

"Thank you," Kelly said, but his head started spinning with everything he had to take care of to make this happen. "I don't know if I have enough money to get there. I have some—"

"We have your flights taken care of, Kelly. Early in the morning, we will have a driver take you to the airport for your ten-a.m. flight home to your father. Let him know it's flight 3250. Do you have the number?" Nance said.

Kelly struggled to his feet, and they rose along with him. He made his way to the telephone and placed both hands on the table and supported himself, then took a deep breath. Nance and Victoria looked at one another, then quietly left the room.

Kelly dialed the number, and it rang five times. "Hello?" came his dad's voice.

"Dad, it's Kelly."

"You comin' home?" Dad was blunt as usual.

"Yes, I'll be there. I fly out tomorrow morning."

"Okay, I will pick you up."

Kelly hesitated before asking, "Is Frank there?"

"No," was his dad's quick response.

"I will see you tomorrow, then. Funeral is about two."

"Okay, Dad. See you—"

His dad hung up with a suddenness that surprised Kelly. He decided he would pull himself together to do this right, and he was determined to not be a burden to the Siva family. He turned and saw Nance with his arm around Victoria's waist, both with concerned looks. Kelly walked over to them, reached out, and gathered them both in his arms.

"Thank you so much," he said. "I will get ready and will be on that plane tomorrow."

"We will pray for you, Kelly," Victoria said. "Rita is out in the rear garden waiting for you. You should go see her."

He nodded, and as he left to find Rita, he let out the breath he was holding. This wasn't going to be easy, but he had to try.

Kelly found Rita, went to her, and kissed her gently. "I'm sorry for being a burden to everyone."

Rita moved her arms to encircle his neck, drew him close, and kissed him longer this time. She looked up at him. "You have the courage to go to Montana and take care of your family. We are all here for you if you need us." She pulled him down until their foreheads touched. "I love you, Kelly Chase. We'll get through this," she said, and gave him another small kiss on his lips.

"I love you, sweetheart," he said, pulling away. "Now, I've got some work to do."

• • •

During the flight to Montana, Kelly was thinking about the different scenarios that could play out during his trip. What was his dad up to? Would he be acting rationally? Would Kelly be able to hold it together enough to be of any help, or only make things worse? Where was his brother, and how could Kelly be of help? Where was she going to be buried? Who was paying for it? There were so many questions.

Kelly stepped off the airplane into a bitter, late September

Montana breeze that held an ominous portent for the upcoming winter. As he made his way into the main terminal, he saw his dad standing just outside the doors. He had his trademark black hat on, and Kelly noticed he had grown his hair to his shoulders, which was now streaked with gray.

"Been waitin' for you," was his dad's only comment.

He led the way through the terminal out to the parking lot, where Kelly loaded his two bags into the rear of the old Ford and jumped into the passenger seat. They rode in silence for some miles before Kelly spoke. "Where's Frank?"

Kelly looked at his dad, who looked straight ahead with the same expressionless face he'd held since meeting him at the airport. Aloysius shook his head silently and kept driving. Kelly was looking mindlessly out the passenger window at the barren pre-winter Montana landscape crawling by, when suddenly his father said, "There was nothing anyone could have done to save her. If we only knew she had this thing, we would have been able to fix her. She was having some trouble catching her breath sometimes and complaining of stomach and back pain. I kept telling her to slow down, but she never listened to me. She was out in her garden picking her last little harvest when she collapsed. I was walking back from the barn and saw her go down. I drove her to Cut Bank, but there was nothing to be done, so they put her in an ambulance and took her to Columbus in Great Falls. She was gone by the time we got there."

Kelly kept watching his father as a tear slipped down his cheek. Aloysius made no move to stop it and kept driving. "I don't know where Frank is. I had the sheriff looking for him. I think he's just scared and doesn't know what to do." He sighed, keeping his eyes on the road. "He may not be at the funeral." Kelly clenched his fists, but he held back until his father finished. "We had some savings, and I've used it to make all the arrangements. There is nothing left. I'm thinking of selling the place."

Kelly sat up in the truck seat. "No, Dad, you can't. That's our home!" He raised his voice, and it boomed inside the truck. "Please, Dad, don't," he begged.

His father was quiet for a minute. "Then you and your brother will need to live there and make it work."

"Where are you going?" Kelly asked, noticing his dad wasn't part of that equation.

"I'm moving back to the reservation," he stated flatly.

Kelly had to find Frank—that's all there was to it.

They arrived at the ranch, and Kelly unloaded the bags. He stopped outside the front door and looked around as the wind blew cold, dusty swirls at his feet. The place was still beautiful to him, although it had taken on a darker cast with faraway black winter clouds looming. Kelly took his bags into the house. Once inside, the house was so dark and quiet. Without his mother to provide the heartbeat that kept it alive, it too seemed dead. Kelly dropped his bags in his old bedroom and went to the bathroom to wash his face. When he walked back out into the small living room, his dad was on the phone.

"Well then you better get over here. We have some things to talk about." He hung up and looked to Kelly. "Frank," his father said quietly as he walked toward his bedroom. "I'm getting dressed."

A short time later, Kelly heard the front door open and close as Frank walked in. Kelly hurried to his brother and hugged him. "Where have you been, Frankie?" he said as he held him tightly. Kelly felt his brother's tears on his neck as they wept together.

"I just needed time to think," Frank said. "This has really brought things to a head for me." Frank stood back from Kelly and continued, "Don't worry about the ranch. I'll take care of things. I know Dad's leaving, but I will be here. Just get back to school when the funeral is over. Okay?" Frank chewed his lip, remaining strong as he shared his plan. "I've been in Great Falls going to junior college and looking for a job, but no luck. I just want to be home now and take care of things."

Kelly looked at his brother for a moment, unsure what to make of this. “Okay, but you’ll get ahold of me if something goes wrong?”

“Yep.”

“What’s up with Dad anyway?” Kelly asked, looking at the floor. “He’s so angry. Is it about Mom or what?”

Frank sighed, and a heaviness overtook them both. “He blames himself,” Frank said, “because he couldn’t save her. He somehow thinks he should have found a way to do that. He thinks he should have known what was wrong with her. He’s mad at the Creator for letting her die. He’s started drinking again, so that doesn’t help either.”

Aloysius came into the room, stopped, and looked at his two boys. “Frank, I’ll give you until the end of spring to make this ranch work.” The men locked eyes, and Kelly shuddered. “If you can’t do it by then, I’m selling it. If you want to buy it outright, I will consider it.”

“If you sign over the mineral rights to us, then in one year, we will buy it from you,” Frank proposed.

“Why, so you can drill for oil?” Aloysius smirked. “Frank, don’t be such a dreamer. So typical of you, always with your head up your ass looking for the easy way out.”

“Like you’ve been such a fucking success!” Frank yelled, but the real shot came next. “All you did was kill Mom.”

“You little bastard, I ought to knock the shit out of you right now!” He took a step toward Frank.

“Dad!” Kelly yelled, stepping in. “Stop it—both of you! This won’t solve anything.” All three men breathed hard as Kelly inserted himself between the two. “Come on, we have Mom’s funeral to go to. It’s time.”

Before the tension rose any further, they headed for the old truck. Aloysius climbed in the driver’s seat and Frank jumped in the bed and plopped himself down against the cab with his arms crossed.

"Are you going to be okay back here?" Kelly asked. "It's getting cold."

"I'm fine," harrumphed Frank.

Kelly climbed into the cab with his dad. They travelled in silence to Deena Chase's funeral.

The funeral was sparsely attended: a couple of old Blackfeet women, two couples from adjoining ranches, a Blackfeet council member, the Catholic priest, and a man in a blue suit who stood off by himself. The service was short as everyone stood in the cold, and the priest didn't know Deena, so he didn't have much to say. The priest, however, spoke highly of Deena, as if they had been old friends. He pointed out her qualities, all which Kelly could agree with. The two old women were nodding in agreement. Aloysius stood stoically silent with his new black hat in his hands. Kelly and Frank stood side by side, both fighting back tears as the service ended. The councilman H. Barnes came to each of the three men, shook their hands, and offered his condolences.

"If there is anything I or the Blackfeet nation can do to help, please let us know," he said as he put his hat on and slowly walked away.

The other members of the small gathering did the same and walked to their cars into the biting Montana wind. The lone remaining man introduced himself to the three. "My name is Stanley Jones, and I represent the National Harvest Insurance Company of Minneapolis, Minnesota. Please accept my sincere condolences." The men said nothing, but Kelly listened with interest. "You may or may not know this, but your mother had a life insurance policy with us. It was still in place at her death and is now payable to you three heirs. In the amount of," he dug into his internal suit breast pocket and pulled out a piece of paper, and read, "fifty thousand dollars."

The three looked at one another. "Really?" Frank said in amazement.

"I am happy to say yes," Mr. Jones said. "I came out personally since it was such a large amount."

Aloysius stood quietly with no reaction.

"If you three would like to follow me into town to the bank," Mr. Jones continued, "I have worked it out with the bank manager there to make good on a draft I have with me. Then you three can receive separate checks for the amounts due."

They were frozen for a moment as they each took in the news. Here they were trying to figure out how they were going to keep the ranch running on hope and Frank's timely determination, but this amount of money was life changing. Once they found their bearings, all three agreed and drove into town, Frank riding with the insurance man. Perhaps Mr. Jones was expecting more celebration, but when he handed them each their checks, he was met with silence and grateful nods. Grief weighed heavily on all of them.

After they arrived home that night, Aloysius told the boys to sit down with him in the kitchen. "I will make a deal with you boys," he said. "Give me half the money you got today, and we will call it good. I will sign a quitclaim deed and you can do whatever you want with the land after that. I will be out."

Kelly and Frank looked at one another, then back to Aloysius. "Why the change of heart?" Frank asked.

"Because your mother would have never wanted me to do that to you two. I will disappear from your lives and live on the reservation. Don't come looking for me. I don't want to be found. I need some time alone. If I need to see you, I will let you know."

Frank looked at Kelly again. "Well," he said.

"Sure, I'm all for it," opted Kelly.

"Good, it is done then," their father said. "We will conclude business tomorrow, and I will be gone by sundown. You guys can keep the truck; just give me a ride into East Glacier. If you sell the livestock, put my share aside, and I will get it later."

The discussion was based on money and logistics. Kelly wanted to ask his father why he wanted to disappear so badly, especially when his sons needed him. Perhaps they could have that conversation someday, but it clearly wasn't happening tonight.

The next morning, business was taken care of with the bank, an attorney, and the title company. Aloysius took all his money in cash and stuffed it in a leather satchel. The boys took their father to East Glacier as agreed. There was no fanfare.

"Bye, boys," Aloysius said as he exited the truck and walked away.

As Kelly watched his father walk away, he felt totally abandoned. As they drove back to the ranch, Kelly finally asked his brother where he was at when their mom had died. Frank gripped the steering wheel tighter and was quiet.

"Well?" Kelly insisted.

Frank glanced at him quickly. "What difference does it make?"

"Because I want to know," Kelly pushed.

"I was with some friends having a party," he finally admitted.

"So, once I jump on an airplane tomorrow, you're back to Great Falls to party?" Kelly shook his head, wishing he was surprised. "Then who's going to take care of the place, pay the hired help, feed and care for the livestock? Am I going to have to quit school to come home and run shit because my brother can't stop getting fucked up?"

"Fuck you, Kelly! Now you're starting to sound like Dad!" Frank yelled, briefly crossing the highway centerline.

"You have to admit that up until now you haven't been exactly reliable," Kelly calmly stated. "If I call the ranch next week and nobody answers or calls me back after I leave a message, what am I supposed to do then? Put yourself in my place, Frank."

Frank did not speak for the remainder of the trip home. Once they reached the front door, Kelly ran to the telephone and called Rita's apartment. Rita answered on the first ring, and Kelly told her everything was taken care of and that he would fly into San Bernardino the next day. She would make plans to meet his already scheduled flight. It was so good to hear her voice. He couldn't wait to get back to her and away from the mess of Montana.

Early the next morning, it was the Wednesday of the last week of September of 1968. It was already spitting snow on the trip to Great Falls. Kelly and Frank were just turning into the airport when Kelly asked, "What happened to my horse, Winger?"

"Had to put him down about a year ago," Frank said. "One of the hands was riding him and he stepped in a varmint hole and..." Frank trailed off.

Kelly looked at him and nodded as they pulled to the front of the terminal. "I'm getting married next spring. I want you to be there. I will not be coming back for a while, so if I call you and you're not here or you don't call me back, I can only assume the worst—that the ranch is lost—and that will be the end of it."

"I'm sorry if you feel I let you down, Kel. I will try harder—that's all I can promise. Love you, Brother." He offered a small hug across the truck seat, which Kelly reciprocated.

Kelly jumped out of the truck, gathered his things from the truck bed, and entered the terminal—without looking back.

On the flight back to California, Kelly felt uneasy. Once he was alone on the plane, the heartbreak over losing his mother started to settle in. He had been stripped from his moorings, exposed, disconnected, cut off, and was alone. The feeling of abandonment gnawed at his edges. How had he caused this? What was wrong with him? He could never measure up to be the son his father wanted. His father's love and affection were gone too. His brother, Frank, was emotionally bankrupt. He had lost his emotional anchor with them. Any history about him as a person on this earth was gone. He was empty.

• • •

Rita was waiting for him with a car and driver. He was especially quiet on the way to his apartment. Rita did her best to give him the space he needed. "It's Friday, do you want to join the gang at Shakey's for pizza?" she offered.

"No, I just need to be alone for a while," Kelly said flatly.

"Okay, I'm going to call you later and we'll talk."

He gathered his bags from the trunk and walked away once they reached the parking lot to his place.

Kelly's depression deepened as the holidays rolled around. He had started to isolate himself more, only leaving his apartment to go to work and visit briefly with Rita. Occasionally Jenks and Henry could coax him out for a quick beer, but he couldn't get away from the cloud that was his mother's death. His fractured family wore heavily on him. Rita always made a great effort to cheer him up, but it was a heavy pull for her too. Kelly knew she, Jenks, and Henry had many late-night discussions about how they could help their friend, but Kelly was slipping further and further away from them. Kelly's school counselor met with him to try to determine the problem, only to encounter a bitter, morose young man unwilling to help himself. His marks just prior to winter break contained several incompletes, and his other grades were well below satisfactory. His third notice regarding his tuition payments being withheld went unanswered. Kelly still had money from his mother's insurance policy, but he didn't feel the need to answer the demands made upon him.

Kelly spent most of the holiday break by himself. He did manage to go to Rita's house, where everyone was in great holiday spirit and had fun. Kelly just could not motivate himself to participate. Rita managed to finally pull him into their little outside garden, where she turned and lit into him.

"Goddamn you, Kelly. You have had your head up your ass since you came back from Montana. I am sick and tired of your insolent, selfish bullshit. Jenks, Henry, me, and my family, too, have bent over backwards and have accommodated your shitty behavior. I thought I had picked me a winner when I said yes to your marriage proposal." Kelly was coming out of his haze at the mention of his last hope: marrying Rita. "Now I am beginning to regret that decision, because right now the man standing before me is not the man who asked me to marry him. Now, whoever you are, do you want this goddamned ring back, or are you going to straighten up and get your shit together? You owe everybody that has had to deal with your crap a big apology, and you can start with my mom and dad, as you've hurt them the most. You in or out, Kelly?"

Kelly could see her face was furiously red under her smooth olive complexion. He rocked back on his heels as he dropped his head and placed his hands behind his back, right hand grasping the wrist of his left. The perfect picture of contrite humility. He had seen Rita's temper flare before, but only aimed elsewhere. Now it was twice the intensity he had ever seen before, but now it was aimed at him. He had not been this humiliated and chastened since his mother had treated him in a similar way some years before when he had behaved in a similar manner.

She took a step back, crossed her arms, and demanded, "Well?" She stared at him intently.

Kelly looked up, met her eyes, and finally said, "I'm sorry, honey. I don't have an excuse anymore. I love you and never want to lose you. I'll do anything to keep you, and you know that. I will do better, and I will apologize and make some changes."

Rita, still with a stern look, gave him a small nod, came to him, stood on her tiptoes, kissed him on the cheek, squeezed his arm, and left him alone.

Kelly, true to his word, made his apologies to everyone he had offended with his behavior. He retrieved money from his account and paid the Sivas some of the money back for their help with his airplane flights. Kelly recommitted to his schooling with Rita's encouragement. He also made several attempts to connect with his school counselor, but she remained oddly unavailable. Rita started making plans for a June wedding. She was an organizational whiz, and he was grateful for her help as he struggled to bring himself up to speed with course curriculum. They spent each evening together studying, making wedding and honeymoon plans. It was a warm and exciting time. At the third week of his recommitted efforts, Kelly received a message that his counselor was in and wanted to see him immediately. Kelly felt his stomach drop.

He sat waiting nervously outside her office, trying to imagine what the meeting would be about. Mrs. Reams escorted him into her office. "Please sit, Mr. Chase," she said as she motioned to a chair at her desk.

She quietly slipped to the other side and sat, her fingers interlaced over a manilla file, peering at him over her glasses. She opened the file and flipped through the contents before clearing her throat. "Mr. Chase, sadly, I must tell you that you are to be terminated from the ROTC program here at UCLB. This decision is based upon your refusal to cooperate on your own behalf despite repeated attempts by the ROTC program and this office, myself included. Your continual refusal to communicate with us has left us no choice. The decision to drop you from all programs and classes was ultimately reached. You also owe the school some uncollected balances that are due immediately. At this point, you are to collect any personal items you have here and asked not to return to the campus." Her delivery was cold and dry, leaving Kelly speechless.

Kelly found himself outside the administration offices feeling weak and shaken as his stomach clinched into a knot, causing a wave of nausea. What now? What did his future with Rita look like? An all-consuming dread enveloped him as he slowly made his way to Rita's apartment.

Later that afternoon, they sat at Rita's small table in her apartment and considered the implications of Kelly's expulsion. Kelly listened in as Rita called her father and asked if he knew if anything could be done. Apparently, Nance had learned through his contacts that Kelly was being terminated. He had exhausted all his efforts to try and save Kelly, but in the end, all his attempts were thwarted. When Rita hung up the phone, he couldn't think of a thing to say, and instead held Rita's hand and tried to stop himself from throwing up.

A week later, Kelly received his draft notice in the mail. This was something that Kelly and Rita thought was a remote possibility, but they didn't think it would happen so quickly. They slept fitfully and clutched each other desperately. During the following weeks, when Rita was not in class, she stayed glued to Kelly, never leaving his side and occasionally breaking down into uncontrollable crying fits. Reality was settling in for the both of them.

Kelly and Rita met with Jenks and Henry to give them the news. All sat quietly, not knowing what to say, not having a way to fix any of it. They had become aware in recent weeks of the deteriorating events occurring in Vietnam; it was now a full-blown war. Kelly had done his best to reach out to his brother, Frank, with no success. He could only leave a message, and no call was returned. He was inducted, sent to training at Fort Polk, Louisiana. Kelly was able to secure an officer commission in the US Army, thinking that this would limit any dangerous assignments, and was sent to Georgia for his officer candidate training. During his officer training, Kelly discovered that a newly minted Infantry second lieutenant's survival in Vietnam was measured in *days*. Kelly kept this horrifying news to himself.

His friends gathered, along with Nance and Victoria, to see him off on his final flight to Fort Lewis, Washington, where he would leave the country three days later. He hugged everyone, saving Rita for last.

She looked up at him with tears filling her eyes as she held his face in both of her hands. "God damn you, Kelly Chase. I don't care how you do it, but you come back to me. I won't be able to live without you."

Chapter 7

The Pact

August 1971

When Kelly called Rita's home, Victoria's familiar smooth voice answered, "Siva residence."

Barely above a whisper, he asked, "Is Rita there?"

A long silence followed before Victoria demanded, "Who is this?"

"Kelly Chase," he hissed, fearing he would lose his voice completely before he could finish. Another silence. "Please, Victoria, it's Kelly. Is Rita there?"

He heard fumbling, some muffled voices, and what sounded like her yelling. He could make out her calling for Nance. She came back with, "Kelly, is it this really you? What state were you born in?"

He croaked out, "Montana." Kelly could feel moisture in his eyes.

Suddenly, Nance came on the line, and Kelly could hear Victoria in the background say, "Nance, it's really him!"

Nance said, "Kelly, where are you?"

"San Francisco VA Medical Center," Kelly squeaked out.

Victoria was on the second line now and excitedly asked, "How? What? How long?"

"About two weeks, I guess. Where's Rita?" he asked again.

There was a long silence, until Nance said, "Kelly, Victoria, and I will be there tomorrow to see you. Can we talk to you about Rita then?"

Kelly had a deep sense of foreboding. "Is she okay?" he squealed.

"She's fine, Kelly. We just need to talk some things through. I promise you she's alive and healthy. What room are you in?"

He paused before his next loaded question. "Kelly, where have you been?"

Kelly heard Victoria on the second line sniffling and clearing her throat.

"Mr. Siva—Nance—I'm not supposed to talk about that with anybody. There is an MP monitoring my calls. I haven't done anything wrong. When you come tomorrow, you'll see."

"I understand," Nance replied. "I think I understand very well, son. You get some rest. We will be there as soon as we can tomorrow. What is your room number, son, and who is your coordinator at the VA?"

Kelly gave them the information, and Nance promised that they would be there in the morning. "Okay, Mr. Siva, I'll be here," Kelly said, and then they both said goodbye and hung up.

Kelly wasn't sure if he wanted more from them, but at least they were coming. Thoughts of Rita haunted him through the night. Her parents were holding something back, but he couldn't figure out what.

Early the next morning, Dr. Franklin entered his room with Nurse Winter and an aide. Dr. Franklin, after checking all his attached equipment and listening to Kelly's heartbeat and breathing with his always-cold stethoscope, started on what Kelly thought was a list of his injuries, although in a language he did not understand. The aide was scribbling furiously on her clipboard, trying to keep up with the doctor.

Nurse Winter had started tending to his IVs, bandages, splints, and stitches. "How's your pain this morning, lieutenant?" she asked.

"Not too bad, I think," he whispered.

Over the last couple of years, he had undergone unbearable, excruciating pain. Comparing what he'd been through to his pain today—how was he supposed to answer the question? The pain was not to the point of him passing out, so everything must have been okay.

Nurse Winter said, "Over we go now, Kelly. Roll onto your side so we can look at your back."

Once they adjusted his position, the doctor was silent as he checked Kelly's back wounds. Kelly was facing the closed door, which opened wide enough for him to see Colonel Flagg's head pop in and back out before he closed the door. He could feel the peel of bandages from his skin, followed by fingers probing and gently touching. The gentle touch of another human was something Kelly had not felt since Rita. He felt warm and oddly secure: safe. Maybe the drugs again? The doctor continued with his assessment. Eventually, they were finished with his treatment and were preparing to leave.

Dr. Franklin said, "Lieutenant Chase, pending Colonel Flagg's evaluation today, the plan is to have you transported closer to your home of record, which will likely be the VA medical center in LA this Friday, if Flagg approves. You seem to be coming along well considering the amount of damage and malaria. You, however, are still not ready for solid food, so we need to give it a couple more days before we try. Okay?"

Kelly only looked at Doctor Franklin, attempted a smile, and nodded. Nurse Winter remained behind to tidy up.

With the door open, the young MP poked his head in, looked around, retreated, and could be heard talking to Flagg. "He's ready now, sir."

Colonel Flagg entered the small room as Nurse Winter left and closed the door. He scooted a chair next to Kelly's bed and sat down. "How are you feeling, Lieutenant Chase?" he asked, sounding genuinely concerned.

Kelly raised his unrestrained arm at the elbow in greeting, nodded, and attempted a smile. The medications Nurse Winter had administered had started working.

Flagg continued, "I realize that you haven't been able to go over the contents of the brown envelope I left you last time I saw you.

That's okay, we'll go over that later. We have been looking for your next of kin and all we could come up with is a person that you listed as a friend, a Mr. Bradley Jenkins from the Long Beach area. I was able to speak to him. My reasons for talking to him were twofold. One, to see if he had any information on your relatives beyond what you had listed. All either of us had was an old telephone number and a PO box in some small town in Montana, neither of which panned out, so far. The US Army is still checking. The second thing is, we need something from you. You are required to have a next of kin on file who would be able to conduct business on your behalf if for some reason you become incapacitated or something unexpected occurs while you are being treated. Someone to assist in your estate affairs as well as help with medical decisions."

"The unexpected did happen—I came back," Kelly whispered.

Ignoring his remark, Flagg continued, "Lieutenant, we have a next of kin listed for everyone who is given services in the system. You, however, have a different set of circumstances. Do you think your friend Mr. Jenkins would be willing to sign some paperwork to fill that role? Temporarily, at least, until we can find someone else in your family. Would he have your permission to act in this capacity?"

"Sure," Kelly hissed. "No problem. If he is okay with it. Is he here?" Kelly asked, becoming excited.

"It does sound like he will be here this afternoon sometime. As you can imagine, he was quite surprised at your return. It sounds like you are awfully close friends."

"Yes, yes, we were," Kelly agreed, starting to get more excited about the prospect of meeting his old friend. Kelly felt a lump start to form in his throat. He swallowed hard to control any emotion.

"Okay, I will bring him up when he arrives, after we have him sign the paperwork. On another note, you are still in the US Army, subject to its rule and protocol. You will be assigned a temporary duty post, as your original unit has been deactivated. You will be attached to a military police unit based at the Presidio here in San Francisco. Your orders and further details will arrive by mid-week."

Flagg produced a document from his briefcase and began to flip through the pages, talking to Kelly as he did so. "At this time, I should add there was little to corroborate your version of events while you were missing. However, we have obtained final field reports from different sources in-country. The unit that found you has verified that you were in obvious distress and appeared to have been that way for some time. That, and your physical condition when you were examined later, indicates that your captors maintained you in subpar conditions and did not comply with international laws. You know, Geneva conventions and all that. All this to say that you have been absolved of any wrongdoing in the events surrounding your missing-in-action status and capture."

Flagg continued in his military style, "Furthermore, additional orders will be cut promoting you to the rank of captain in the US Army. In addition, you will receive full back pay for your time in-country as well as POW time, all tax-free plus any pay moving forward. Added up, you will have enough to start a new life. Chances are, too, that you will ultimately be retired from your rank and position as you will, in all likelihood be placed on full medical disability, given the extent of your injuries, and further treatment to help resolve any future consequences. Pending these events taking place, you will be reassigned, as mentioned before. This may take up to six months or longer." He finished placing the document back in his briefcase.

Kelly continued to take all this in and was hanging on every word.

"Services will be provided to support your continued rehabilitation. Anything you need, the US government will provide, Captain Chase," Flagg said, addressing him with his new formal rank. "I hope this eases your anxieties somewhat. You will be assigned a VA counselor-slash-coordinator in the Los Angeles area to make sure all your needs are met. The MP outside your door will be assigned to you personally as you transition. He will stay with you for as long as you need him. He is attached to the Presidio base, just as you will be, so this is not out of his ordinary duty assignment. Now, Captain, he is not with you to spy on you, he is with you to help you. The US Army is grateful for your service, and this is something they want to do for you."

Kelly struggled to adjust himself on his pillows, not having any luck. "Colonel Flagg, I'm sorry I was so rude at our earlier meeting," Kelly whispered.

Flagg visibly relaxed and said, "That's okay, it goes with the territory for me." Flagg placed a hand on Kelly's shoulder and gave a small squeeze. "You have been through a lot, and no one respects that more than me, so no apology needed." As he rose from his chair, he said, "There is someone here to see you. I'll come back this afternoon with Mr. Jenkins when he arrives." Colonel Flagg smiled and turned to leave.

Kelly steeled himself for his next visitor.

True to their word, Victoria Siva was in his doorway right after Flagg left. When he first saw her, he thought she must have driven all night—she looked drawn and tired. Kelly was on his side facing the door. They must have pulled some strings to get directly to his room. Victoria entered the room; she looked shaken, and the color was drained from her face. Then, to Kelly's surprise, Nance appeared behind her. Nance didn't look much better than Victoria.

She quietly said, "Kelly, my God, we thought you were dead. Where were you?"

Kelly could not take his eyes off her, this slightly older but equally beautiful version of Rita. He whispered, "I can only say that I was not in this country."

They both moved closer to his bed, and Kelly noticed Flagg had appeared briefly in the doorway and then backed out, gently closing the door as he left. Nance placed a hand on his shoulder and said, "It is so nice to have you back with us, son."

Nance's eyes were so sad that Kelly feared he might jump out of bed to try hugging them both. Victoria placed one hand on his bed rail and held out her other hand to caress his cheek, like she were touching him to make sure he was real. Her eyes had filled with tears, but her gentle touch was the most wonderful feeling in the world. His craving for human contact from someone who cared for him was beyond measure.

"You poor kid," Victoria said. "What the hell did they do to you?"

Kelly could not muster a reply, for he had no idea where to begin.

"Where's your family?" she pressed. "Have they called them?"

Nance started, "Vic—"

Kelly interrupted, "I have no idea where they are or how to find them. I just don't know." Kelly looked at both of his friends. "You know, you folks are my only real family. I don't think my brother or dad ever missed me," he rasped. "I mean, they didn't know I was missing, maybe didn't care."

"Don't you worry, Kelly, we're going to help with that," Nance said. "We will get with the reservation police in Browning to see what they know. Somebody knows something, and we will find out what we can do to get in touch with them." Nance, always the practical one with a plan.

Kelly looked at Victoria with pleading eyes. "Rita?" he almost squeaked.

They both looked at each other, then down at him.

"Kelly," Victoria said, waiting as long as she could, "Rita had lost all hope after two years, and since we weren't legally your family, we couldn't get any information."

"It almost killed her," Nance interjected. "She lost so much weight, and at one point had to be hospitalized. We were all devastated and had lost hope."

Then Victoria bluntly stated, "Kelly, she is married and has moved away. She has restarted her life."

Kelly showed no emotion, as he had already come to terms

with the outcome. After yesterday's conversation, he had guessed what had happened. During the night, he decided he was not going to whine about it. He was determined not to shed any tears. Although, his heart bled for her.

Victoria started to speak again, but Kelly stopped her, raising his thin IV-laden right arm with splinted fingers. "Please stop," again almost whispering. There was a heavy silence in the room. "Just leave her alone. She's been through enough."

He looked at each of them, but their gazes were fixed on the floor. He suddenly realized that his pain meds had worn off and a headache was starting to emerge. Kelly continued in his raspy whisper, "I don't want her to know. God knows I still love her, but I want her to be forever happy."

Another silence followed. Victoria stood looking at Kelly, stunned, her mouth open, unable to speak. Nance walked to the other side of Kelly's bed and moved to look out the window. "And you, Kelly, what's to become of you?" Nance asked, still looking out the window.

"We can't just leave you like this," Victoria said.

"I don't like it, but I can't put her through anymore. I have a lot of recovery to do, and I need some time to get through it. Truth is, if I hadn't been such a fool after my mother died, none of this would have happened. I know I am asking a lot of you, but will you help me with this?"

"Nance and I will always be here for you. All you need to do is call us…for anything," Victoria promised.

Nance turned back from the window. Kelly watched his reflection in the mirror on the far wall. Nance used the heels of his hands to wipe his eyes. Kelly couldn't hide the state he was in, and Nance saw a boy he loved with bloody wounds all over his exposed back. Some open wounds had been stitched, while others still oozed fresh liquid. They were too numerous to count. Nance raised his clenched fist to his mouth and bit into his knuckle. He looked away and came back to the other side of the bed and passed a handkerchief to his wife.

Kelly said, "If she ever finds out, you need to let me know. Okay?"

"Yes, we'll try to give you plenty of warning," Nance said. "Colonel Flagg told us that you will be coming south toward the end of the week. He was gracious enough to allow us your contact information as soon as he gets it. We are not family, but he knows you are an exception and is allowing it. We will come and see you then, all right?"

They said their goodbyes, each giving him an awkward hug. Kelly noticed how sad they were as they turned to leave, and said, "Victoria, Nance—I love you guys."

They both turned and looked at him one more time, and Victoria said, "We love you too, Kelly." Then they quietly left the room.

Knowing the Sivas still cared for him saved Kelly. Keeping his return from Rita wasn't going to be easy for them, but it was for the best. Here was Kelly—beaten, bruised, battered—watching the family that chose him walk out the door. Want was one thing, but need was another. Victoria and Nance would do their best to allow Rita to live a normal life, whatever that looked like, but it pained Kelly all the more that he would not be a part of it.

The door slid open, and Kelly heard voices coming from the hallway. The pain was settling in, and he wanted to ask for more meds, but he listened carefully, commanding his body to stay awake through the pain to hear their voices again.

"I can't believe we are going to do this. It just feels so wrong," Victoria said.

"I know," Nance said. "God damn it! The bastards beat him within an inch of his life," he hissed between small sobs. He took a moment to collect himself, and Kelly fought the urge to call out for them. "But he's right, at least for now. It will give him time to get his feet under him, and spare Rita the pain of losing him all over again. It's wrong for all the right reasons, and she will never need to know."

"I hope this didn't upset you too much," came Colonel Flagg's voice from the hall. "I know it's tough seeing someone you know in this condition. Hell, sometimes it's hard to believe it's the same person."

"Any luck locating his family, Colonel?" Nance asked.

"No, nothing for sure. The tribal authorities in ah…Browning? Is it?"

They were quiet for a moment, and Kelly assumed Nance confirmed the answer.

"Some remember the family," Colonel Flagg continued, "but they haven't seen anyone in two or three years. They think old man Chase is still alive and living somewhere up in a remote area near what is called…" Kelly heard crumpling papers. "Grinnell Glacier. Pretty rough country as I understand. We have discovered, too, that the tribal members are very private and are unwilling to give out much on fellow members. It really is hard to get information. Captain Chase's brother hasn't been seen for a couple of years, and what we have heard is that he has moved off the reservation. If anyone knows where he has relocated, they are not saying. As for Captain Chase's mother, Deena was well-respected among tribal members, and it is said they felt she had passed with dignity. No one we spoke to was sure where Kelly Chase was or what had happened to him. Most thought he was in California. That's pretty much it."

"As far as I know, Kelly didn't return to Montana after his mother died, so they most likely kept their distance," Nance assumed.

"You folks and Mr. Jenkins seem to be the closest he has for next of kin. Do you know Mr. Jenkins?" Colonel Flagg asked.

"Yes," Nance confirmed. "We met him two, maybe three times, some years back. He brought Rita to the house from Long Beach a couple of times."

"Very nice man," Victoria remarked.

"I certainly understand the circumstances that surround your relationship with Kelly, as you told me on the phone yesterday." He paused, and Kelly waited for more, but all he said was, "I'm sorry."

"It's fine, Colonel," Victoria said, and her gentle tone soothed Kelly, as he was sure it did Colonel Flagg as well. "You've been such a big help in all of this. Your job can't be a pleasant one. We thank you."

Colonel Flagg cleared his throat before saying, "Given the circumstances, I have asked Bradley Jenkins if he would act in Captain Chase's interest as his next of kin, at least for now. I will discuss it further with him when he gets here this afternoon, but I think he will help. Also, I will call you both when I have more details on his LA arrival—date, time, place—that sort of thing. So nice to meet you folks, and we thank you for coming to see Captain Chase."

Kelly heard some shuffling, but then the eventual footsteps of them walking away. He pictured Victoria and Nance holding hands, as they often did, but instead of their usual attractive confidence, he knew there would be sadness this time. He had always aimed to make them proud, not sad. So, he cried quietly—for them—not for himself.

Chapter 8

Return to Long Beach

Kelly could feel himself being moved, and as the aches returned, he slowly came around. Nurse Winter was performing her blood pressure and IV checks. She had gained possession of his right arm.

"Good, you're awake," she said. "I'll let them know."

She slipped out the door, leaving it ajar. The next moment, Colonel Flagg entered the room and announced, "Captain Chase, Mr. Jenkins is here to see you."

He ushered Jenks into the room, who stood frozen just inside the doorway. Kelly saw the blood drain from his face. That was the second time he had seen that reaction since his return. He could see that Jenks was struggling to collect himself, lest he upset Kelly in some way. Kelly thought he saw him take a small step back. Jenks wore his trademark outfit, the expected sport jacket and slacks. Kelly developed a lump in his throat again at the sight of his old friend.

"Kelly Chase! Is that really you?" Jenks cried out.

"Holy shit, Jenks, it's me!" Kelly responded hoarsely.

Colonel Flagg stepped back and gave Jenks room to come to Kelly and lean down to give him a hug. Kelly raised one tube-laden arm to accept him as best he could. Jenks embraced his shoulders, raising them up a little. Although it hurt, Kelly would not let on. He returned the hug as he felt hot tears dripping down upon his left cheek as his dear friend held him.

Jenks stood up and said, "Damn, Kelly, we thought we lost you, man. Where have you been? Were you a POW? How do you feel?" His emotion-filled questions slipped out rapidly.

Colonel Flagg stepped forward. “Excuse me, gents, but I need to make only one request. Please do not discuss where or what may have happened to Captain Chase. At least for now. It is just a precautionary measure. You are welcome to do so after leaving this facility. Having preached my bit, I will leave you two friends alone so you can catch up.” Flagg made his exit, gently closing the door.

Kelly looked back at Jenks and croaked out, “I think you have a pretty good idea what happened.”

Jenks nodded in jerky motions and was trying to catch his breath. “You’ve been gone over three years. I still can’t believe you survived,” he said. “I haven’t seen anything on the news or heard anything—not until Colonel Flagg called me. At first, I thought he was a crank caller or something. Then he swore me to secrecy and explained that you had been found in the jungle somewhere but wouldn’t say much beyond that. He told me two more times not to tell anybody. Then he gave me directions to get here. Kelly, I was never so happy to hear this. God damn it, we missed you, and Rita, shit, she had to go to the hospital during the first year of waiting after you disappeared, and we haven’t seen her since. She wrote me a note a couple of months later telling me that she was okay and that it was best if she didn’t come back, that I should just forget about both you and her. She had decided to move on,” Jenks explained. “Have you seen her? Called her?”

Kelly looked at him, expressionless, and with a small frown, slowly shook his head and said, “No, Jenks, it’s finished.”

Jenks braced both hands on the rack of Kelly’s bed and looked at the ceiling in silence, stifled a deep sob, waited a moment, and looked back at his friend. “Do you want to talk about it?” he asked.

“I can’t right now, Jenks, but I will later. I just have to think about it for a while.”

Jenks nodded, then reached over to the hospital tray and retrieved a handful of tissues, handed Kelly a couple, and used the others to wipe his eyes.

“How’s Henry doing?” Kelly asked, trying to divert the conversation away from Rita. “Your mom and dad?”

Jenks welcomed the shift and said, “Mom and Dad are doing well. Henry has been painting and selling art. He has gained a following and is starting to find some great success. I’m pretty proud of him.” Jenks chuckled to himself.

“And you, Jenks?” Kelly whispered.

Jenks sniffed once, swallowed. “I gained a post-graduate degree in business and work for a large brokerage house in LA. I still commute to Long Beach; I like it there too much to move,” he said, smiling as he explained.

Kelly sensed there was more that Jenks wanted to share, so he encouraged him by saying, “Jenks, I know this is hard for you too. What else do you want to tell me?”

Jenks described his conversation with Colonel Flagg, which held an ominous warning.

“I feel I must be honest with you, my friend, before signing the paperwork for you,” Jenks said. “Colonel Flagg had said, ‘Please realize, Mr. Jenkins, that you are going to see a man that may resemble only a little of the one you once knew. You must know, too, and I’m going to be blunt here, that when men come back home after having gone through similar experiences, their chances for successful reintegration are low. For many, it usually ends badly.’” Jenks paused and let Kelly absorb that before continuing. “I could see how deeply sad Colonel Flagg was. I realized then the gravity of the job Flagg was tasked with and how stressful it must be. I was shocked by his revelations, thought for only a second, and said, ‘Where’s your pen, Colonel?’”

After the two spent another hour catching up, the friends parted after agreeing that Jenks would try to meet his transport vehicle at the LA hospital. As Jenks left Kelly’s room, Kelly relished the pieces of the normal life Jenks seemed to live. War changed people, and Kelly was no exception. He was scared, as anyone would be, and his future was unclear—specifically who would be a part of that future.

• • •

Over the next three days, Doctor Franklin ordered Kelly's IVs be removed, leaving only a single means to inject pain and malaria medications. Nurse Winter and other aides assisted him into a wheelchair, moving him to a small garden area near the employee side-entrance to the hospital. This was Kelly's first trip outdoors since coming back to the world. The beauty and fragrances of the garden, with its wonderfully scented roses, brickellia, and primroses, were enough to send his senses into overdrive. These were simple things that he had not experienced in so very long. Scents so sweet Kelly was becoming heady as his nose revolted at the new experiences. He was wheeled to a nearby fountain, where the aide set the brake and told him she would be back in five minutes. Kelly furtively glanced around and there he was, his MP escort, never leaving his side. He still had not determined if this was a good thing. The large trees surrounding the garden were gently swaying in the mild coastal breeze. Kelly closed his eyes and drank in the sounds, smells, and feel of it all, finding a peace that he had not experienced in years.

On Friday morning, he was to be released and moved to LA. Doctor Franklin entered his room and asked what he would like for breakfast. Once off IV feeding, he was introduced to bland oatmeal, limp toast, and apple juice. He had managed to keep this down, along with soup and other food items they put in front of him.

"Eggs, eggs," he hoarsely responded. "Can you have them fried?"

Dr. Franklin shook his head and smiled. "You guys are all the same," he said. "Sure, Captain, I'll have it taken care of for you. This is your last day with us. I hope we were able to help you. I know you've had it rough, to say the least. Make no mistake, you still have a long recovery ahead of you. Your wounds are healing well enough, and we have removed some of your finger splints and placed them in bandages. Your stitches can be removed when you get to LA. The only real concern now is the malaria. We've managed to bring it under control with medications, which you will need to continue taking for a time, but realize that malaria can resurface years down the road. Just be careful! If you feel symptoms, get to a VA clinic right away. This is nothing to fool with—it can kill you. When you get to LA, they will X-ray those bullet wounds. Somebody did some meatball on you. Do you remember?"

Kelly recalled his first escape attempt. He'd worked his way out of his cage after a nearly all-night struggle. He'd crawled in the rain until the sun came up. He had finally found his feet and was immediately knocked down. His captor had been trailing him all along, waiting for the right moment to take it all away. He lay on his back as the pistol was leveled at him and fired twice—shot and left to die. An old village Momma-sun dragged him into a hut, and Kelly thought for sure she was going to kill him, and she almost did as she dug and dug until he went under from the pain. He spent days with a burning fever. She had saved his life, and he never saw the man who shot him again. Some days later, he was back in his cage.

Kelly was trying to listen to the doctor, but he was already visualizing those fried eggs.

Travelling south on Interstate 5 toward LA was a bewildering experience for Kelly. He had been down this road many times before, yet today it was so different than anything he could recall. He and his MP travelled in silence, as Kelly had insisted on the radio remaining off. It freaked him out for some reason. There was some small talk, but even that made Kelly uncomfortable. He wondered, *God, am I that fucked up?*

The other cars pushed past them at incredible speeds. His anxiety level quickly rose. The military sedan they were riding in had a spacious back seat, so they'd propped him up so his back injuries were relieved of pressure. Kelly slumped over on his right side so he wouldn't have to see the passing traffic, which helped. Eventually his thoughts went back to his family. Where was his brother, Frank? Why couldn't he be found? Where was his father? Were they still alive? Why had no one tried to find him? He was afraid he would never see them again. Then there was his love: Rita. He had to put her out of his mind, forget about her. Yes, it was over!

He started to think about what his life would look like from here on out. He certainly had made a mess of things so far. What would he do for work? Where would he live? He felt so lost, alone, incomplete. There were so many questions without answers. His head was starting to ache; he could tell it was going to be a painful afternoon. He started to recognize buildings and landmarks as they continued south on the 405, eventually turning off the freeway onto Wilshire, then made a few more turns that Kelly didn't recognize, and then they pulled up to a large multistory building. Had this always been here? Why didn't he remember this place—it was huge. They followed the circular drive and pulled into the front portico entrance. Two aides came out with a wheelchair.

"I guess we're VIPs," Kelly rasped.

The aides helped him into the wheelchair. His new MP, Jake, gave Kelly's name, rank, and other information as one aide checked boxes on a clipboard sheet. "Okay, we're ready," the man with the clipboard said.

They wheeled him to an elevator, punched some buttons, and were whisked up a few floors. Jake was still following close behind. Everyone was quiet during this part of the elevator ride. He was eventually rolled into a large ten-man ward. There were only four occupants in various stages of recovery. The Frisco VA was a constant beehive of activity compared to this place. Kelly was placed closest to the entry door. The bed next to him was empty. *It's so quiet—odd for a weekday afternoon*, Kelly thought.

Kelly was helped onto his bed and placed on his left side facing away from the door and the wall. A pretty young nurse came in and started giving directions, orders, and filling out a clipboard. She deftly hooked up an IV to his upper arm resting on his right side.

"Hi, Captain Chase," she said. "I'm Nurse Rosa, and I will be seeing to your needs this afternoon. I have just placed you on an IV to help continue to hydrate you. I will shortly administer a pain medication, as I'm sure you're starting to feel some discomfort after your trip." She paused, and a quizzical look crossed her delicate features. "As for the doctor… Who's on?" she asked an aide.

"Belmont," someone said.

"Good, Doctor Belmont will see you in a couple of hours. We'll give you some time to settle in. Are you hungry? Can I get you something?"

"An apple and an orange," he requested hoarsely.

"I can do the apple, not the orange. You're not ready for that yet. I will get you some other soft food too. Remember, eat slow, no gobbling, you'll make yourself sick."

Kelly only nodded. By the doorway, he spotted MP Jake. "Jake, where are you staying?"

"They have a room for me in a hotel nearby. Don't worry about me, Captain Chase. I will be here for a little while if you need me. I will tell you when I leave."

After Kelly ate his late lunch, savoring the sliced apple as if it were from the garden of Eden, the pain medications started working, and he felt himself drifting off. Prodding at his back welcomed him back to consciousness.

"Damn, they sure beat this kid up. We don't see many like this," came a voice beyond Kelly's blurry vision. "We need to take some X-rays tomorrow to see if there are any bullet fragments in his chest. There are some old, badly healed gunshot wounds present."

"It's a wonder he survived," said another voice, Nurse Rosa, Kelly guessed.

"Captain Chase," the man said, "I am Doctor Belmont. Welcome to the West Los Angeles VA Hospital. We are just doing some wound care back here. We will be done shortly and then you can get some more rest."

Kelly was out again.

The next morning, Kelly awoke to Jenks standing by his bedside. "Hey, Kel, good to see you again."

"Damn, these people are serious," Kelly croaked. He moved around, feeling somewhat agitated.

Nurse Rosa appeared in the doorway and said, "Captain, are you ready to get up and do some walking?"

"Yeah, as soon as I go to the john," Kelly said.

Jenks walked alongside him as he wheeled his IV pole. "I've been working with the VA and we have an apartment ready for you," Jenks said. He had apparently been taking his duties seriously. "It's in Long Beach near the campus, so you'll at least know the area. I don't know if you're ready for a car yet, though."

Kelly waved Jenks off. "That's the last thing I need right now. I've probably forgotten how to drive anyway."

They walked to the end of the long hallway in silence for a while, but Kelly could tell that Jenks was itching to ask him something.

"Kel," Jenks started, "you want to talk about Rita?"

"She's gone, Jenks. There's nothing to talk about. It's my own fault. She didn't do anything wrong. I've already told Nance and Victoria to never tell her that I've come back. She doesn't need to relive the shit she's already been through."

"Maybe she would *want* to know that you're okay," Jenks said.

"I don't see it doing any good right now—"

"Maybe it's because *you* can't face it," Jenks interrupted.

Kelly stopped, turned, and stared Jenks down. "We're not telling her, and that's final."

Later in the day, Kelly had MP Jake walk with him to the pay phones. Jake dialed Kelly's old Montana phone number, just to see what would happen. Sure enough, it was disconnected. The next day, Victoria came to see him. She brought him a box of candy and a get-well-soon balloon. Kelly was so happy to see her, for he always saw Rita in her, and she was a breath of fresh air that lit up the ward. Those who were awake gave appraising looks at the woman as she stood by Kelly's bed.

"Looks like Jenks has found you a home and is getting you started in therapy. Things are looking up," she said, trying to be cheerful.

They talked about happier times, and Kelly found himself feeling a lot better. Victoria could do that to him.

The US Army was slowly releasing its hold on Kelly. He was going to be mustered out with full disability with the rank of captain. A week before he was scheduled to be released from the hospital, a pastor came to the ward to visit the patients. He asked Kelly if there was anything he could do to help him. The kind, middle-aged pastor invited Kelly to Sunday service the next day at a nearby church in Downey. He talked with Kelly about the ability of the spirit of God to heal. No one knew more than Kelly how badly he needed healing and an outing.

Chapter 9

The Voice

August 1971

Kelly had agreed to take the pastor's offer. He managed to wrangle an outing pass and transportation was arranged, along with Jake to escort him. He was technically not finished with his reintegration process, so Jake would follow along. Kelly had no clothes of his own, but Nurse Rosa had managed to come up with a pair of old Navy dungarees, a button-up Navy deck shirt, and black shoes. He was so thin he floated in the makeshift garb. He was tall, so the jeans rode up above his ankles, exposing white socks. His first outing under the California summer sun felt glorious, as long-ago experienced aromas, noises, and public activity filtered in. But suddenly, an overwhelming sense of panic surrounded him. He needed to get away and hurriedly gimped to the waiting car. Jake opened the back door for him. Once inside, he closed his eyes, leaned back in the seat, and sighed. Jake slid into the front seat, put the car in motion, leaned over, and turned on the radio. Kelly instantly reached panic mode again and covered his ears.

"Please, please turn that off," Kelly pleaded.

"Sorry, sir, forgot."

They rode to the church in nearby Downey in silence.

MP Jake escorted Kelly to the main entry of the church and gave him a small salute. "I'll be right here, sir."

Kelly became aware of the small limp he still had from his knee injury. He was starting to think this was a big mistake, but then the pastor hurried toward him in his Sunday best, carrying a bible.

"Good morning, Captain Chase. Welcome," he said cheerfully. "I am so glad you could make it. Please, sit anywhere you want. We are about ready to get started. I will come visit you after the service to see if there is anything I can help you with."

Kelly rasped out a thank you and sat in the last pew, judging it to be far enough from prying eyes. His hair was mostly cut close to his scalp, exposing the scars, knots, and stitch marks. His thoughts moved to Rita, wondering where she was at that exact moment, wondering if she ever thought of him anymore. It didn't matter. He, Nance, and Victoria had closed that door forever.

The service started with the large church at about half capacity. A choir had started singing from somewhere on the other side of the church, immediately drawing his attention. The voices were low, sweet, and pleasingly harmonic. The priest picked up with a sermon about eyes of needles, camels, rich men, and man's inhumanity to man. Kelly's thoughts instantly shot back to his tormentors and the apparent enjoyment they took in his misery. After the service, he quickly exited the main church area as others started filtering out into the main entry foyer. He passed by an open doorway to a small, elegantly furnished room with a red shag carpet. An old piano stood as the center of attention facing away from the doorway.

Kelly slowly moved over to the worn Baldwin and cautiously pecked a couple of keys as he carefully perched himself on the bench. The volume of other church members' conversations grew as they gathered in the foyer outside the room. Kelly could hear some talking with the minister. He started to hit some old notes of a song that his mother had once taught him. He was drawn to it because it captured the very essence of his isolation and loneliness. As he started to press each key, it slowly started coming back to him. *As time goes by…* He moved through the beginning of the tune. *You must remember this kiss is just a kiss…*

He felt the need to keep playing even though his fingers started to hurt, each of them bent and misshapen. Two splints remained on two fingers of each hand. He tried to keep his playing soft so it would not disturb anyone. Suddenly, he heard a beautiful voice start singing the song behind him. Was he going crazy? She was directly behind him, and he made no effort to turn, just painfully kept playing. He had heard this voice somewhere before but could not recall where. The voice was beautiful. The tonal quality was low, smooth, almost unnaturally low, then would rise higher in pitch, creating a flawless connection with the lower notes as she continued. Her vibrato was perfectly controlled yet smooth except for the occasional small vocal fry at the end of some phrases. He was filled with an emotion he knew he would not be able to contain. A small crowd of church people had started to gather around them in the small room. He had not been able to conjure up any sort of emotion for years. He was…dead inside. Now, there was this! And worse yet, in front of people he did not know!

Then there was that voice that continued behind him—he was consumed. He could not choke it back, and tears welled in his eyes, almost brimming over, as he continued to play haltingly, painfully, as the woman continued to draw him along into the song.

He could feel sobs starting, but he kept playing. Tears fell onto the keys below him. He felt a soft hand on his shoulder as she gently squeezed assuredly, softly stroking his shoulder. She kept singing. *Oh, my God,* he thought, *she will feel how thin and boney I am!* She kept her hand on his shoulder as the song was ending, her soulful, beautiful voice continuing to move him to tears. The song came to an end, and he moved his hands to his lap and lowered his head. He felt her move her arms around his neck from behind, wrapping around him, again probably feeling how thin and frail he was. She smelled and felt so good. His senses were overwhelmed by the gentle human contact, he felt that he did not deserve. What was that perfume? Crazy thought.

She gave a small laugh and said, "Damn, the first real man I've met in a while," and gave him a small peck on the cheek.

He struggled to his feet, turning as she released him. He saw a beautiful young woman with what struck him as the most expressive brown eyes he had ever seen. She was short and very petite. She had long, straight dark-brown hair with bangs over her forehead. She wore a simple light-yellow sleeveless dress. He was entranced. He kept hearing her voice in his head as he gazed stupidly at her with his tear-streaked face. It then occurred to him the small audience they had gained was giving them an applause. Someone sternly insisted, "Kaitlin, we have to go now."

She turned and nodded to the small mustached man with dark shoulder-length hair. She returned her gaze to him, held his eyes deeply, then reached out her hand to grasp the back of his hand. "What is your name?" she asked.

"Kelly," he croaked out. "Kelly Chase." He looked at her, expecting a quick response, only to receive a deep stare with a small smile on her lips.

"Kaitlin," she said, then broke off. "I gotta go, sorry."

She rushed away with the man. She glanced back at him over her shoulder one last time as she reached the doorway then left, leaving him there, knees knocking, to weigh the surreal experience.

Chapter 10

Madness

1971–1974

Kelly was lost for almost three years. It was as if aliens had dropped him off from another galaxy and were not coming back to get him. Men on the moon, men with long, shaggy hair, having conversations he could not understand with words that had no meaning. It seemed America, as he had known it, had spun out of control. *Humanity gets an F,* he reasoned.

He rarely left his Long Beach apartment. Jenks often called to remind him of his VA rehab appointments, and then came, picked him up, escorted him to see his therapists, then stopped by the drug store on the way home to pick up his meds.

Kelly had developed a fear of public places, radios, and TV. He had trouble being out in public—it terrified him. He found himself yearning for the protection of the bamboo cage in which he'd spent so many years. It was misery, but at least it was misery he knew. Out here…in this place…thoughts of that place were more comforting.

A year earlier, in his therapy sessions, the shrink had started edging toward the subject of caged confinement and how it made him feel. He felt weirdly peaceful talking about it, so much so that the doctor must have seen a very visible relaxed change in Kelly's countenance, something tranquil. The doctor quickly changed gears and started asking about public appearances, going to the mall, or to the park, or taking a trip somewhere. The effect on Kelly was instantly ruinous and scary. He felt his heart start to race, a headache starting in his temples. His eyes widened as he grew intensely agitated, then he stood up and started pacing back and forth. His doctor backed off and instead asked questions about Kelly's drinking. Kelly vigorously denied any problems and inched toward the door.

In this new world, Kelly had trouble processing the overwhelming amounts of information. He rarely turned on his rental TV that Jenks had arranged for him, and he seldom used his small radio, listening only occasionally to an old country station when he did. He preferred the quiet. He was alone, isolated within his painful existence and loneliness. These things had replaced the cage. He drank almost continuously in the days he did not have psychological or physical therapy appointments. Jenks always dropped off weekly supplies of food because he knew Kelly would not eat otherwise. He rarely did anyway.

Kelly only ventured out late at night when the streets were empty. He staggered from block to block, sometimes losing his way for long stretches of the night and early morning. He always managed to make it home before the sun came up. *Like a god damn vampire*, he thought.

He spent his days playing his old guitar, learning how to compensate for his injured fingers, and writing melodies and lyrics he suspected no one would ever hear. Then his thoughts would return to Rita, his dad, his mom, and Frank, starting the cycle all over again. He then set rules for drinking. Nothing before five in the afternoon, which then became four, and then three. Soon he gave up on the idea entirely. It soon became his constant state as he ping-ponged from lucidity to semi cognizance to insanely intoxicated. On his nightly wanderings, he would stop at the 7-Eleven or a small bar to buy his MD 20/20 wine and two-fifths of Jim Beam whiskey, a ritual he had developed. Always staying with the familiar. Somewhere along the way, he had started smoking cigarettes when taking his pain meds. He felt they comforted him in the anxious periods between his daily afternoon sprees. He never slept, fearful that the terrors would stalk him and jar him back awake, sweating and fitful.

One night, Kelly showed up at the local 7-Eleven. The new clerk eyed him suspiciously, as he had dirty, matted long hair, a month-long growth of beard, and had not bathed for days. As he was casting about looking for his wine fix, he stopped dead as he heard that wood-smokey woman's voice. He flashed back to the woman in church… Her? Where? He zeroed in on the small radio on the shelf behind the clerk. He gazed unfocused beyond the clerk to look at the small music box playing. His mind was still reeling from the last chug of JB minutes before entering the store, and it seemed like he was dreaming as he stared toward the clerk.

The clerk asked him, "Hey, man, what's your problem?" Not getting a response, he repeated the question. "What's wrong with you, man?" His eyes narrowed. "Hey, get your booze and get out of here, weirdo."

Kelly came back to reality, gathered his bottles of temporary relief, and set them on the counter. He struggled to pull out the cash from his front pocket, scattering the bills before the agitated man. Kelly said nothing as the man gathered up the wadded bills and haphazardly straightened and counted them. The man bagged the bottles and slid them over the counter, offering some change in return. Kelly ignored the offer, hugged his bags, and shuffled toward the door. He stopped and turned when he heard it again, "the voice," and briefly hesitated, then departed the store.

• • •

Late in July 1973, Kelly returned home early with his bottles ready to try the only thing he knew how to do. A thing he knew had stopped working. He suspected now that it was only a matter of time before it would kill him. He knew now that he was powerless to stop it. How many times had Jenks and the doctors warned him over and over, always harping? He had tried a couple of times and found it useless. Jenks and an AA guy named Fred would get him to agree to an AA meeting after a therapy session. They knew it was their only chance to catch him not drinking. He had quickly surmised that whatever this AA shit was, that he was beyond their ministrations. *Blab away*, he thought. *All this shit about a higher power and God. Fuck!*

He had seen what the Catholics had done to his father, hollowed him out like a Halloween pumpkin. He wasn't going to buy into that shit. But he strongly suspected that the alternative was grim.

He started with the Jim Beam and used the wine as a chaser and added pain medication in doses he dared. He started playing his guitar and singing. He did this for some time, interspersed with the sweet relief, chasing that elusive dead zone he hoped would come. He later collapsed onto the floor and passed out. In the early hours of morning, he came to, never actually waking up, just "coming to." He slowly crawled toward the small bathroom off his small studio apartment. He thought he had to take a piss, but he lost track of time and urinated in his jeans. He climbed the bathroom doorway, finally finding his feet. He found the light switch, and the dingy bathroom's low light came from the dim bulb dangling from the ceiling. He slowly gazed up, catching his hazy, unfocused image in the mirror. As his vision began to clear, he exploded! He swung his right fist up, and with all his might, punched himself square in the face. Bringing up the left fist, he punched again. Now both fists—punching, punching, punching.

As he punched, Kelly screamed, "You son of a bitch! You son of a bitch! I fucking hate you! You dirty cocksucker!"

Blood squirted from Kelly's face, splattering on the mirror before him. One last punch, square on his left eye, and his vision instantly clouded. He rocked backward against the wall, breaking the towel rack free; it clattered to the floor. His body slid to the floor.

Blood ran freely from his nose, mouth, and eyebrows, pooling on the bathroom floor. He refused to cry. He wasn't sure if he could. He soon collected himself as best he could and crawled to his small bed in the corner, crawled up, and again, passed out.

For the second time, later that morning, Kelly came to. He was face down on his bed. He tried to move but could not lift his head. He struggled to raise himself up and could feel the bed sheet tearing away from his face and his hair. He could not see. Had he gone blind? Where was he? Numbly, he extricated himself from his bed, slithered to the floor, and inched toward the bathroom for the second time, not recalling the first time. As he crawled into the small room, his hands were sticking to the bloody floor, sending a message to his brain that his hands were really hurting. He was starting to become fearful, trying to force himself awake. He knew this was a night terror. Nothing happened. He tried again. Nothing. He struggled, pulling himself up using the small vanity, still not seeing. He mechanically reached for both faucets, pulling them toward him and was rewarded with the sound of running tap water. He put his sore hands beneath the running water, collected the liquid, and flushed his face, quickly realizing that his face was a mask of pain.

"What the hell?" he said, and then it started coming back. The beating he had inflicted upon himself. "This wasn't a night terror. It was real!"

He flushed his eyes some more, then again, and again. His vision slowly starting to come back as he washed the dried blood that had welded his eyes shut. Things came into focus, again for the second time during his spree. Shocked, he stepped back. His face was a bloody mess, with both eyes nearly closed and thickly swollen. His lips were split and thick, his blond hair thickly matted with dried blood. His first thought was that he should kill himself somehow…finish the job. He was so tired of fighting and being this way. He had lost, and he knew it. He staggered back, hit the wall, and crumpled to the floor for the second time. Tears began to flow for the first time since he had met the woman at the church. He put both his hands to his face and did the only thing left to do.

He cried out, "Dear God, if you're there, please help me! Please help me! I can't do this anymore! Please save me or kill me, please!"

He dissolved into more tears. He laid his head on the floor and fell into a deep sleep.

Chapter 11

Wreckage of the Past

Jenks stopped by Kelly's apartment after work to check on him. He knocked on the door several times, then decided he needed to let himself in. It wasn't like Kelly to be gone this time of day. Jenks opened the door of the stifling hot apartment. The sickening smell of stale alcohol, cigarettes, and body odor was stomach turning. Another smell too. What was that? Blood? Jenks saw bare feet extending from the bathroom, not moving.

"Oh, my God, it's finally happened," he said.

He had feared this day, and knew it was fast approaching. He knew his old friend was not going to make it much longer. And here he was. Jenks saw blood-soaked bedding, along with a trail of dried blood going to the little bathroom. The light was on in the small room. Kelly was motionless on the floor, with his back to the wall. The bathroom walls and floor were spattered and caked with more dried blood. Jenks cautiously nudged Kelly's bare foot with his loafer—nothing—again, a little harder.

Kelly lay slumped over on his side with his right arm extended above his head along the base of the bathroom wall, his left arm resting back around his waist wedged between his body and the wall. His face was flush on the floor when Jenks gave him another, sharper, kick to his bare foot.

"Kelly!" Jenks probed. "Kelly," he said again, insisting on an answer.

"Yeah?" Kelly mumbled, looking like he was trying to open his eyes and lift his head, unsuccessfully.

"Thank God, you're alive!" Jenks shouted.

Jenks guessed if he didn't act fast that Kelly may not stay alive.

He ran to the phone and dialed for an ambulance. He ran back to Kelly and could see that his face was a mess. He tried to rouse him, but it did no good. Kelly was mumbling something about "Please God, please God."

The medical personnel arrived with a stretcher, medical kits, and other equipment. It was then when Jenks could see that his friend had been stuck to the floor in crusted, dried blood. *At least he's alive,* Jenks thought gratefully.

The next morning, Jenks and his friend Freddy, who at one time had his own drinking problem, were anxiously waiting for word about Kelly, who was still in the hospital ICU. Freddy had been diligent with Kelly, taking him to AA meetings and spending a lot of time talking with him, sometimes for hours. A doctor finally walked down the hall and asked them if a Mister Kelly Chase was theirs. They both nodded, looking sadly at him.

"Well, your friend is lucky to be alive," the doctor said. "Despite how damaged he looks, that is not the worst of his problems. He still has an abnormally high blood alcohol content that is extremely toxic. Looks like he's been that way for some time, judging by blood tests. His liver is borderline, and he is dehydrated, anemic, and malnourished." He looked at the two men. "Veteran?" he asked, and they both nodded again. "He has the most God-awful scars on his body. Even my battle-hardened nurses were in shock."

"He was a POW," Jenks offered.

The young emergency doctor was quiet for a moment, then said, "That explains the malaria indicator." He shook his head, and then his expression grew more serious. "He absolutely needs to stop drinking, right now!" the doctor stressed, stabbing his right index finger into the palm of his left hand. "He won't last much longer at the rate he's going."

"Yeah, we know," Freddy replied. "We're doing our best, but he's been pretty uncooperative."

"Well, maybe this will help convince him," the doctor said.

"Say," Jenks said, ignoring the fact that the doctor seriously thought it was that easy, "what happened to him anyway? How did he get so beat up? He was alone in his apartment."

"Judging by the evidence, he did it to himself," the doctor answered.

Jenks had never heard of such a thing. "How's that possible?" he said, turning to Freddy.

"I've seen it a couple of times," Freddy said. "It's the ultimate expression of self-hatred and self-loathing. Usually, people don't have much longer before they kill themselves when that starts happening."

The doctor nodded grimly, and said, "He wants to see you guys. You can go in if you want. Just keep the noise down, okay?" The young doctor quickly walked away, his white lab coat flowing behind him.

As the two men approached Kelly's bedside, he raised a hand in greeting, and they both could see he was trying to smile. His face was a mask of bruises, and stitches in his eyebrows, his upper lip looking like a small sausage.

"Man, you scared the shit out of me, Kelly," Jenks said. "I thought you bought the farm."

Kelly looked directly at him. "I did. I died," Kelly said, and smiled again. "I heard that beautiful angel's voice again, and I knew I had to come back to find her. That's what I was told to do—come back to save the angel," Kelly said dreamily, half-awake with the most serene expression on his face.

Jenks and Freddy looked at one another, and Freddy shrugged. "Must still be dieseling from his last drunk," Freddy guessed.

Kelly looked at Freddy. "Can you help me, Freddy? I'm done drinking now," he announced.

Jenks and Freddy again looked at each other in stunned silence. "Sure. I've just been waiting for you to give the word," Freddy said, sounding a little unsure.

Once they were back in the hallway, Jenks asked, "What the hell was that?"

Freddy gave Jenks a puzzled look. "Shit, Jenks, I think we just witnessed a profound spiritual awakening. I've read and heard about them, but I've never seen one like this. If your mind is open to the word 'miracle,' just accept it and move on."

"Yeah, right," Jenks said, somewhat unconvinced. Jenks looked up and saw a police officer coming their direction. "Uh oh..."

• • •

In the coming weeks, Kelly's progress was phenomenal. He attended a meeting once a day, sometimes twice. He started coming out of his self-imposed confinement. He attended VA therapy religiously and started lifting weights and running each morning. His physical growth was amazing, as he was building muscle for the first time in years. He started to gain his former good looks and naturally handsome features. There were still some remaining phobias to address. TV and radio still bothered him, so he had them removed from his apartment. He was getting much better around people, even strangers. Freddy's ever-present council was having a positive effect, as Kelly started acting out the language of recovery. Freddy would always remind him that "growing up in public is a bitch." Or, as he often said: "It's not for those who need it, but for those who want it." Freddy had hundreds of these little sayings, so many that Kelly had lost count and only focused on trying to remember them all…real clever folks, those AA people.

Freddy and the other recovering people in his life supported him at every turn. On bad days, when he would slip back into his morose, isolating moods, and days when he was almost manic with the excitement of the new freedom he was experiencing.

"Kelly," Freddy would say, "you are on an accelerated spiritual journey. Your creator knows exactly what you need, only when you need it and are ready for it. It works in perfect symmetry with the universe. Keep yourself in the center of the path. Remember, it's about being balanced every minute of the day, so stay in the here and now. If you have one foot in tomorrow and one foot in yesterday, you will be pissing all over today." Just too much to remember.

Jenks took Kelly to the beach on the weekends—usually Sundays were best. As they walked along the beach one afternoon, Jenks asked Kelly, "Do you remember when Freddy and I came to see you in the hospital after I found you in your apartment?"

Kelly jammed his hands into his pockets as they walked. "Well, I remember you guys being there, and I know we talked." Kelly paused and then continued, "I don't remember exactly what was said. I think I remember telling you I'd died, and there was something about an angel, or something like that. I do remember I had this feeling of complete peace, a floating feeling in the pit of my stomach, like I was sailing above the clouds. I don't think it was the booze, because it never made me feel *that* good. Something happened. I know it. I just can't remember what it was. I've been trying since that day, and it's driving me crazy. Why do you ask, Jenks?"

"Oh," Jenks said, "just trying to fit some pieces together, but I'm like you. None of it seems to make sense."

"When it does, please let me in on it, okay?" Kelly said, looking at his friend with a smile.

At the end of his first year, Kelly had progressed to moderate radio listening. His brief listening times were limited to country stations. Hard rock was still foreign to him. He had not yet gained an appreciation for some new types of music. He was still not convinced that a television held much value. Since he had not grown up with television, it was not something he missed. Where his family lived in Montana, they were limited to three stations of snowy viewing. He was content to play his guitar and write lyrics to his songs. He was now spending more time reading and was enjoying it. Kelly avoided most social outings and did not actively pursue relationships with women, mostly because they still made him nervous, and he still felt an unwavering loyalty to Rita. There were some AA women who pursued him, but he was able to escape and avoid them, not wanting the complications they might bring. Freddy had laid down the law on relationships with the opposite sex during the first year. It was simple: none!

"You can't even take care of yourself, so how are you going to take care of anybody else?" Freddy had explained.

One night, after his first year sober, Kelly, Freddy, and Jenks met at a local diner after a meeting that he and Freddy had attended. The subject of dating women came up. Kelly was silent as Jenks and Freddy exchanged views and recent experiences.

"What are your plans in that department?" Freddy asked in his cigarette-heavy voice.

"I have no plans," Kelly said softly.

"You must have—"

"No!" Kelly interrupted slapping the tabletop with both hands and then got up and walked out.

• • •

What the hell is eating him? Freddy wondered as he stroked his bristly chin after Kelly left the diner.

Jenks reached over and tapped the back of Freddy's hand, and said, "I've got something to tell you."

Jenks related the story of Kelly and Rita and how Kelly had to give her up, never telling her that he had returned from Vietnam. Freddy looked down at the coffee cup he was grasping with two hands, and said, "Damn, tough deal. Poor kid. It's good for me to know that. I will do my best to help him move on. Man, some guys come in here with some unbelievable stories, but I've never seen anyone with as much damage as Kelly."

• • •

There was a soft knock on Kelly's door. He put down his guitar and his composition book. When he opened the door, he was surprised to see Freddy standing with his head down and his hands in his pockets. "I came to apologize," Freddy said. "I didn't know, man. Jenks told me the story."

"It's okay, Freddy. I just have to deal with it," Kelly said as he turned to the small table and made a motion to the opposite chair. "I just had to let her go, and I did. Now I only need to find a way to accept it. Right now, it's still torture. Freddy," he made sure to hold his sponsor's gaze, "will I be this way forever?" As they sat down, Kelly's eyes were turning red. "Will I ever be whole? Because right now, I have a great big piece missing."

Freddy reached out for Kelly's hand. "I can't ever promise you that, Kelly. I can tell you that you will in time learn to live with it. I can tell you, too, that you will meet someone someday that you will cherish and love, and you will still love Rita, but in a better, more complete way. You will have those relationships with them for the rest of your life. You are into your second year of sobriety, and you've come a long way. You've had a spiritual experience that I cannot explain, and you are a two-legged miracle. Do you remember what you told me in the hospital?"

"Not really. Maybe something about an angel, I think."

"You told me, 'I'm done drinking now, Freddy. Can you help me?' And you had the most serene look on your face, like you had been in direct contact with the Creator. I've never seen anything like it. Kelly, you are truly blessed, and you are in a very human process that you cannot avoid or wish away. This experience will build you into the Creator's man-to-be. It's like I've always told you, hang on to your ass; you're in for a wild ride. Will you feel? Yes. Will you have pain? Yes. Will it ever get better? Yes."

Kelly let tears flow down his face without trying to stop them. He only nodded at Freddy's words.

Chapter 12

The Party

September 1974

As promised, Henry and Jenks stopped by Kelly's small apartment. They said they had been invited to a small party in a nearby town not far from UC Long Beach, where they had all attended school some years earlier. Kelly had just finished packing, as he had been planning a trip to Cut Bank. He wanted to try and find his family, or what was left of it, but the thought of the journey and what it might hold weighed heavily on his mind. He had been self-isolating again and thought it better to accept the invitation and get out for a bit. Being around too many people still bothered him, but it was something he knew he needed to do. Freddy had been all over him about isolating, and that guy was a god damn mind reader, so Kelly decided to accept when his friends offered. Jenks and Henry had not shared many details, so this was going to be a surprise.

When they arrived at a large, fairly ordinary two-story suburban residence that seemed to stretch halfway down the block, Kelly became nervous. He hoped there wasn't any shit going on at this party. He would have to leave if there was.

Greeting them at the door was a blond man about his own height and build. He had a wide grin on his face as he welcomed Henry and Jenks and offered his hand to Kelly. "Hi, I'm Roland Chapin. Any friend of these two old alumni are friends of mine. I understand you went to Long Beach too?"

Kelly answered as he shook Roland's hand, "Yes, attended in sixty-seven."

Roland had a firm grip and met his eyes directly, and Kelly immediately liked him. He followed his friends as they went further into the home, following Roland. "Welcome to our home," Roland said. "We're glad you could make it. Please feel free to try the buffet tables. There's also plenty to drink: beer, wine, or soda. I'll be right back." He bowed slightly as the doorbell rang, and he turned to greet more guests.

Kelly followed his friends into a larger family room at the rear of the home, just off a large kitchen area. Beatles music was softly playing in the background. There appeared to be about fifteen to twenty people having casual conversations, sipping drinks, and hovering around several standing tables. The home was much larger than it looked from the outside. The rooms to the rear were large, with evermore people talking and laughing. The large rear doors were opened to a lush backyard garden, where more people were mingling about. No one really seemed to notice they had entered. Everyone was dressed in varying degrees of California casual, and here he was ready to go to Montana—dressed in denim jeans, a snap-button shirt, and beat-up cowboy boots, his usual armor for any public outing. There was a sumptuous buffet layout with some sort of iced sculpted logo with a guitar in the center. It had some wording that had started to melt, which he didn't recognize. Pretty swank. Whoever these people were, they were apparently well off.

Kelly sidled up to Henry, and in a low voice asked, "Who are these people anyway?"

Henry was forever giving him the "where in the fuck have you been" look. In the grand scheme of things, Kelly was socially stunted and unaware of people, places, and things. However, he was getting better.

"Man," Henry said in a hushed voice, "these are the Chapins! You know, they make music? Remember we were talking about them last week?"

"Oh, yeah," Kelly said, not really remembering the conversation.

"See, look. That's Kaitlin over there."

Kelly looked over toward the backyard doorway, and there was a beautiful petite woman with long dark hair chatting and laughing with two other young women. She had a powder-blue blouse and white jeans with matching white open-toed string sandals. She looked vaguely familiar, so she was probably famous, and he had probably seen her picture before. He immediately made a note to himself that he must avoid her at all costs. He probably would not do well with people like that…too pretentious.

Kelly smiled at Henry, and said, "Great, let's eat!"

Henry shook his head and walked away. Jenks was chuckling behind him, and said with a smile, "Fucking Kelly, you can't be impressed by anybody. At least try to be a little user-friendly, okay?"

Kelly nodded and moved to the banquet table and started dishing food, somewhat unsure what it was. He reasoned it was best to choose potato salad. He couldn't help noticing that the other people nearby all seemed to look familiar as well. Now, getting a little worried, he started to wonder how and when he could make an escape. Kelly filled his plate and went to the nearest empty corner. He ate and slowly scouted his surroundings. He had to admit the food was amazing. His gaze settled again on that star singer, but he still could not place where he had seen her before. He was deep in his mental file cabinet when a man wearing a shiny polyester suit moved in beside him. He was complete with a wide tie and a colorful scarf hanging loosely around his chubby neck. He was holding what looked like a martini, complete with an olive.

The man muttered out of the side of his mouth, "Lions and tigers and bears, just look at 'em. Lots of 'em here tonight. I'm George Shipley." He extended his hand, which Kelly took. His hand was overly smooth, and his grip was of the dead, cold fish variety.

"Kelly Chase. Nice to meet you, Mr. Shipley," Kelly said, remembering Jenks's admonishment. "What do you do, sir?" Kelly asked.

"Kelly, may I call you Kelly?"

"Sure," Kelly responded, inwardly rolling his eyes.

George said, "I don't do much, mostly write occasionally—gossipy stuff. And you?"

"Not much," Kelly responded. "Looking for a job."

George stopped mid-sip and turned to look at him. "Man are you in the wrong crowd. Probably the only honest man in the room," he said, chuckling. "A refreshing departure from most present company. The only exception is little Kaitlin over there. Fascinating person she is, not a judgmental bone in her body." He pointed with his glass. "How she manages to survive is a true testament to her courage. I don't know where she gets it. Her mother is an overbearing menace that she always has to deal with." George seemed to slur the last few words, and it suddenly occurred to Kelly that old George was gassed, or well on his way. Kelly decided to disengage.

"Good talking, George," Kelly said. George gave him a small toast as he eased away, looking for another unattended corner to occupy. He set his empty plate on a service tray as he passed by.

Kelly turned to look for Henry or Jenks. He couldn't find them, but he could see that no one was occupying the doorway to the back garden. He took the opportunity to exit and do some more exploring. He saw some people gathered around a fountain area. There was a famous comedian he recognized standing in the center of a small group of guests telling a long joke. Kelly moved to the other end of the patio area to a small table with two empty chairs. There was an old guitar leaning against one of the chairs. He looked around for any potential owner. Not seeing anyone, he slowly picked it up, examined it, and sat down. He checked the tune on the old acoustic, and it was perfect.

His mother had taught him how to read music at a young age, and he mostly performed on the old Baldwin piano. They sometimes practiced on two older acoustic guitars that his brother, Frank, had bought with the full intention of becoming a rock star. That never developed, for he later abandoned the project—no surprise there. Kelly had become proficient on the acoustic thanks again to the long Montana winters and his mother's musical knowledge and talent. He had spent many recent days isolated in his small apartment in Long Beach playing, writing, and singing new songs in private, never thinking they would be played for anyone. He'd had to develop new methods to play, as his bent and misshapen fingers presented problems. He had managed to compensate, and in some weird way, he had developed a style that surpassed the original skill he had learned from his mother. Anyone who was good with a guitar could spot it immediately, but most people could not tell that his methods were unusual.

Kelly had come across an old vocal coach from UCLB who then talked his way into letting him help with his speech problems. Kelly agreed under the condition that he wouldn't need to leave his apartment. Kelly had developed this almost breathy quality to his voice, which Kelly thought was because of the screaming he had done while in captivity. The additional beatings and abuse had taken their toll on his voice as well, such as being strangled into unconsciousness. The coach in turn knew a speech pathologist on campus who was willing to help. Kelly learned later that the VA would pay for their services. As a result, his voice had been nursed back to health, and with some great coaching and therapy, he had developed a wide and strong vocal range. He had come into that raspy quality some vocalists had chased over the span of their careers and never achieved. In his continuous escape from life, he developed song and lyrical abilities that had become comforting. He did have a lot of life experiences to draw from. It had become his ultimate escape from the reality of pain, booze, loneliness, and Rita.

Just as Kelly finished tuning the guitar, Roland came up to him, and with a small smile said, "Are you gonna show us how it's done, Kelly? Can you play?"

It was then when Kelly gazed toward the open garden door to the house and saw her again; she was talking to one of her friends. She looked up at him and met his eyes directly, locking for a moment. It hit him like a ton of bricks. It was her! It was her! His mouth fell open, and he nodded absently to Roland. Kelly started to play, slowly strumming, working into the song. As he started to sing, his voice started low and soft and raised in pitch and power as the song progressed. He had written it almost two years ago. The song was of an unrequited love, emotional desolation, isolation, and remoteness. Raw feelings carelessly cast aside, and the emotional destruction to follow. He started to create slow power in his voice as the raspy quality started to come through. Looking squarely at her now, her eyes again met his, and he looked away and continued to sing his ballad. He could sense that she was moving closer to him, until she stood a short distance away with her hands to her chest. The small crowd had become hushed, and the only sound other than his voice and guitar was the slight gurgling of the fountains nearby. As he moved into the middle of the song, he glanced at her and saw her eyes becoming moist under overhead string lights. She put her hands to her mouth, and he looked away and continued singing with the pleading raspy quality that the song demanded, his voice complementing the lyrics. As he brought the song to an almost abrupt end, he lowered his head. It was unearthly quiet. As he slowly looked up, everyone was staring at him, some with open mouths. He wasn't sure if he had just screwed up or what.

Slowly, a small applause started, growing into whistles and shouts. Someone yelled, "What the hell was that? Wow!"

Kelly looked at Roland, who had a wide grin across his face as he said, "Damn, Kelly, you are one hell of an opening act!"

Kelly glanced *her* direction as she moved toward him. Her eyes narrowed and her head tipped to one side. Her two friends were trailing close behind her. Their eyes locked as he stood up and set the guitar on the table.

She looked up at him and said softly, "That's twice now you've broken my heart. Who are you again?"

She wrapped her arms around his waist and squeezed as she placed her head on his chest. It occurred to Kelly that it was the same familiar perfume scent that he had mentally filed away as he rested his cheek in her hair. It took him back to that day over two years ago at the church in Downey. He had constantly thought about her, but he had given up hope that he would ever see her again. Yet here she was.

She pulled away and looked up at him again, then turned to her two friends and introduced them as Brenda and Ramona. They were still looking at her curiously. Brenda whispered something to her, and he thought he could hear, "KC, we need to talk!" More of a hiss than anything.

She looked back at him and said, "Kelly Chase, wasn't it?" and extended her hand toward him in an introductory motion.

He nodded and said, "You remembered?"

"How could I forget?" she said.

Both of her friends were smiling awkwardly at him as they started pulling Kaitlin back toward the house, one with each arm pulling her backward, as she said, "I'll be right back. Please excuse me." Her friends led her into the house.

Roland had been standing nearby, observing. "Well, I don't know if I even want to know what's going on with her, but I do know that you and I should talk."

By this time, Henry and Jenks had come over, both with curious, concerned looks. Jenks said, "Now what have you gotten yourself into? Are you okay?"

Roland said, "Oh, he's doing fine. It's just my sister being weird again. By the way, where did you two meet? It's obvious that she knows you from somewhere. If I didn't know any better," he smiled, "I'd say you really don't have a clue who she is. Am I right?"

Kelly looked at his two friends, who were no help and both looking down with their hands in their pockets.

"Well, I guess she is some sort of singer," Kelly said. "Maybe I've heard a song on the radio somewhere."

He was telling the truth, and then sheepishly confessed to Roland that he had not made any connection. How could he tell him he was a loser with a very strange past? Kelly's social contacts were few, and he didn't even own a radio. They still scared him. It may have been the DJ's voices, but he wasn't sure. He was certain that Roland would find out about him soon enough.

Roland said, "Well, maybe that's why your artistry is so good. You haven't been negatively influenced."

Jenks piped up, "Hey, me and Henry knew you had some voice issues and were working on them, but damn, we had no idea there was such a dramatic change. Since you came back, we only knew you as hoarse and raspy."

"And crazy," Henry added.

"Now this," Jenks paused, "is amazing!"

Henry nodded in agreement.

Suddenly, Kaitlin walked up to the group, without her friends, and said, "Came back from where?" She had her hands in her pockets, and everyone, including Roland, regarded her but said nothing. "Why are you such a mystery, Mr. Chase?" she said, calling him by his surname. "And how did you find me?"

"Miss Chapin, m-ma'am," Henry stuttered, "we invited him. He had no idea where we were going. It was going to be a surprise."

She continued to press. "So you're telling me that this is just one big coincidence?" Roland said. "Kaitlin, I invited Henry and Jenks, and they asked if they could invite one friend and I said yes. I don't understand why you are so upset?"

"Roland, you know how hard it is to trust anybody in this business," she said. "You agreed to limit the guest list to only people I knew. You promised me and Mom." She sounded genuinely hurt and upset. Kelly guessed this was something her two friends had cooked up.

Getting defensive, Roland said, "Well, apparently, you know Mr. Chase from somewhere, so he doesn't appear to be a stranger."

Kaitlin looked at all of them, as they tried not to meet her gaze. "Mr. Chase, will you please come with me for a minute?" she asked.

Kelly nodded meekly and followed her inside the house to a bar area off the large kitchen. There were just two couples chatting nearby. She turned to confront him. Kelly thought this woman was obviously crazy, and he just wanted to leave.

"You need to understand the number of crazies that try to approach me every day with love letters, marriage proposals, and various other devious ploys, all bogus and creative. My friends have my best interests at heart because they know I can still be very naïve and fall for things I shouldn't." Between the anger, there was sadness too—maybe even fear. "I know we met a couple of years back, and now here you are again, and I'm expected to believe it's just a huge coincidence? As much as I dearly want to believe and trust you, please, again, I need to know who you are, where you're from, and where you've been before I can really believe you."

Kelly felt that old hotness returning, building its way up to his neck and into his head. He knew by now it was a combination of fear and self-loathing—fomented anger. When he got this way, it was Hulk-like. There was no going back. Something bad was going to happen. He rose to his full six-foot-two height and growled as he jerked open his snap-button shirt and pulled it down to his waist, causing the sleeves to hang at his wrists. Kaitlin stepped back into her friends Brenda and Ramona, as they had crept up behind her. They all three stepped back and stood agape, witnessing the multitude of scarred-over stab wounds, and bullet holes on his muscular chest, stomach, and arms. He quickly turned around so they could get the whole show. Old, puffy red whip wounds stood out in stark profile on his back. A woman somewhere let out a loud scream, a glass was dropped and shattered, and there were gasps of shock and surprise. The three young women put their hands to their mouths and then to their chests, almost in unison. Kaitlin's eyes were wide with horror.

As Kelly turned to look at them, with his azure eyes blazing at her, he yelled, "Okay, you want to know where I've been? Well, I've been working for you! If you want to know what your fucking tax dollars have bought you, take a *good* look!"

He shrugged his shirt back on and stormed out of the room, almost running to find the front door. The guests quickly parted for him as muffled screams had started anew. He found the front door and ran into the darkness.

• • •

Roland watched Kaitlin collapse into Brenda's and Ramona's outstretched arms. Roland, Henry, and Jenks had come running upon hearing the screams. They entered the kitchen in time to see Kelly's meltdown and exit. Everyone was shocked into silence, and there was scattered crying and sobs among those guests in the kitchen and adjoining rooms. Others were streaming into the kitchen to investigate. Kaitlin was wide-eyed and in shock, as were the other two women. Kaitlin kept repeating, "No! No! No!"

Her friends carried her over to a nearby sofa in the next room. She brought her hands to her face and sat, stunned.

"What's going on, Roland?" Jack Chapin asked calmly, holding his car keys loosely in his hand as his face carried deep concern as he looked around, sizing up everyone's excitement.

Before Roland could answer, Marie Chapin, carrying her purse, pushed her way past Jack to reach Roland. Marie, too, wore a look of concern. Their parents had gone to dinner with friends and had just come in from the garages.

Roland wasn't expecting them back so soon, and their timing couldn't have been worse. The situation was getting out of hand, and he was losing his grip.

"Roland!" Marie exclaimed. "What's happened? Kaitlin, are you okay? Roland, what's wrong with your sister?" she demanded.

Roland rushed to explain as Henry and Jenks stood back and watched. "Mother, it was just a misunderstanding." Roland reassured her, "Everything is okay, really."

"It doesn't look like it!" she shot back. "I kept telling your sister this was a bad idea, and now look what she's done to herself! Roland moved his parents aside and explained as best he could what had happened."

Marie shook her head, eying Kaitlin. "Girls, can you take Kaitlin upstairs?"

Kaitlin still had a stunned look in her eyes and was moving upstairs in a trance, with her two friends escorting her. Roland knew his mother would try to take control no matter what. "Jack!" she called to her husband. "Can you please help Roland until he calms down?"

"Mom, I'm okay. Just please let it be," Roland begged.

"Roland, see that Kaitlin's guests are helped out." Ever the hostess.

Roland turned to the two men and asked, "Boys, can you help me, please? I would appreciate it."

It wasn't as if any real help was needed, as everyone was already leaving. The guests made appreciative comments and asked about Kaitlin's wellbeing on the way out.

Ramona came down as the house started to clear. "She's in bed," she said, "and Brenda is staying with her. I must get back to my husband, but I'll be by tomorrow, Roland." She kissed Roland on the cheek and departed.

After everyone had gone, Roland said, "Let's go out back and sit for a bit." He motioned the boys toward the patio, ready for some peace.

The elder Chapins had disappeared somewhere into the home. Henry looked back at Jenks, nodded, and said, "Sure, we'll stay."

As they sat at one of the small tables, Roland said, "What just happened? Is Kaitlin in trouble with this guy?"

Henry responded, "I don't know. I think the bombs are in the air and haven't landed yet."

"When they do, man I do not want to be around," Jenks said.

Roland wanted more answers. "Jenks, Henry, what can you tell me about this guy? I need some answers. My mother is freaking out, and KC," he paused, "what the hell am I gonna do with her? I gotta tell her something." A sad expression crossed his handsome face.

"Roland, I have known Kelly longer than anyone, and I'm not going to step out on that ledge," Jenks said. "Kelly will literally kill me. It's his business, and I'm not going there. You guys will need to get that from him. I'm not touching it."

Henry nodded in agreement, and said, "Yeah, man. We just can't, sorry."

The boys thanked Roland and apologized for Kelly as they rose to leave. Roland implored, "If he is willing to talk to me about his music, please give him my personal number and have him call me."

Jenks and Henry agreed and left.

Chapter 13

Where Have You Been?

Early the next morning on Sunday, Jenks was preparing for work the next day when the phone rang. “Hello?” he answered. The other end of the line was quiet, so he said, “Hello, anyone there?”

A small voice on the other end said, “Mr. Jenkins?”

“Yes,” he replied, but another silence followed, and then a small sniffle.

“Mr. Jenkins, this is Kaitlin Chapin,” Kaitlin timidly announced.

Now that was a surprise. “Yes, yes, of course,” Jenks said. “Miss Chapin, how can I help you?” With a little more thought, he had already guessed the reason for the call.

“First,” she said, “I want to apologize to you and your friends for being so rude and offensive last night. It was all my fault. Please forgive me,” she begged. Something was going on behind this apology, and Jenks could hear the hurt in her voice.

“Miss Chapin, no need to apologize. I don’t think anyone is really to blame.” He paused, working up the courage to continue. “Excuse me for prying, but can I ask you a question?”

“Certainly, Mr. Jenkins, anything.”

“It appears you and Kelly have met before. Is that true?”

There was a pause before he heard her sniff again. “About three years ago, I was at our Methodist church facilitating a donation for a charity event. He was there, struggling to play an old tune on the piano. He was in terrible shape: fingers in splints, his head shaved and scarred, his face bruised, and he was so thin—my heart broke for him. We had a moment as he struggled with the piano, and I sang to the song he was trying to play. We had just finished when we finally introduced ourselves. Me with my first name only, him with his full. I never forgot his name. Odd thing is I don't think he knew who I was. I had to leave in a hurry. My assistant was going crazy. I assumed he was a homeless person the pastor was trying to help." Jenks ignored her harsh judgment, remembering how rough Kelly looked in those days compared to now. She had developed a reflective tone as she continued. "I have never forgotten him. He had me in tears before I got to the car."

"When exactly did this happen?" Jenks asked.

"In the summer of seventy-one. July, maybe August, I think."

"Then last night this man shows up out of the clear blue at your house, at a private party, and you managed to recognize him?"

There was a long pause on the other end. He could hear her breathing hitch as she swallowed and said, "It was his eyes, those azure-blue eyes that first caught my attention. Halfway through his beautiful song, it came to me that he might be the same man from that time long ago. Although his appearance had changed dramatically, I just somehow felt it was him. I noticed him when he first came in with you guys, and I didn't think much about it. I knew I had seen him somewhere before, but we meet so many people in this business." She stopped again, collecting herself. "By the time I reached him last night, he seemed to have recognized me too. It didn't…go well from there." Jenks held back a sigh. "My two friends Brenda and Ramona took me aside and convinced me that there was no way the whole reunion was anything close to real, and that I should confront him. You saw the result…" she trailed off.

Jenks started, "I'm so sorry for the way things ended—"

"Mr. Jenkins," she interrupted, "I know you told Roland that you wouldn't have anything to say about Mr. Chase," she paused, "but do you know where he is?"

Jenks paused for a moment, knowing that after an episode like that Kelly might be drunk somewhere. "No," he said, which was true.

He and Henry had searched for Kelly until late into the evening.

They checked his tidy apartment and saw his duffel bag was gone. Jenks hoped he had managed to make it out of town. There was a heavy silence between them before he continued, "I think he may have gone to Montana. That's where he's from."

"Is there any way to contact him?" she said, her voice quivering with palpable emotion.

Jenks felt himself giving way to her. Her sadness stirred deep sympathy. "No, not that I know of, Kaitlin," he said, risking the use of the familiar name.

"Will he come back?" she asked.

"I don't know." He heard a small choking sound and knew he was going to crack.

With a resigned, shaky sigh, she said, "Okay, we are leaving the week after next for an extended tour, probably for about four to six months. I was hoping to get some information so I'm not left wondering if there is any hope of—"

"Kaitlin," he interrupted, "where can we meet?"

It sounded like she could hardly contain her excitement. She gave him directions to a home in an adjoining Long Beach suburban area. He felt her building excitement and relief. He dressed in a newly cleaned and pressed button-down shirt, tan slacks, and a blue sport jacket. He should be somewhat prepared, just in case.

About an hour later, he pulled up to a non-descript home with a neat appearance and finely trimmed yard. There was a late model black Mercedes coupe parked in front with personalized California plates that gave away the owner, if you knew her.

He knocked on the door, and Ramona answered with a big smile. "Please come in, Mr. Jenkins."

"Please, it's Jenks," he said as he entered.

"You remember me, Ramona?"

"Sure, you and Brenda."

"Yes, she's here too, and that's all, I promise. And KC, of course.

We're sorry if this seems like a trap, but I can assure you we are all on the same side. Please join us."

Ignoring the word "trap," he walked into the small dining room where Kaitlin and Brenda were seated at a small table in a very neat, orderly room. The windows nearby were partially open, and the gauzy window coverings were moving with the breeze. Kaitlin quickly stood and looked up at him with a grateful look. She had on a simple white blouse with long sleeves and a slightly open collar, with faded blue jeans. Her long dark hair that cascaded down her shoulders was held in place by a small white headband. She was very neat and conservative, and he appreciated that.

"Thank you for coming, Mr. Jenkins. I can't tell you how much I appreciate it," Kaitlin said.

He nodded and smiled at her as he took her hand in a polite handshake. "I hope I can help in some way, Miss Chapin, and please call me Jenks," he said.

"Please, KC is fine."

He nodded to her.

"Can I get you something to drink?" Ramona asked.

"Water, please," he said, sitting with Kaitlin on his right and Brenda on his left at the table.

Ramona returned with the drink shortly, placed it before him, and sat down opposite him. All three, he sensed, had nearly stopped breathing. Ramona said, "We made a big mistake. We owe you, Henry, and Mr. Chase—er, Kelly—an apology. We stampeded into things last night, and we are truly sorry for causing so much trouble."

Jenks held up his hand. "Please, it's okay," he said softly. They both nodded. He had decided earlier he would not put Henry in jeopardy with Kelly. He would do this alone. He said, "Let me just get on with it," and they all three looked at him with anticipation. "Kelly is from a small town in Montana, Cut Bank, I think it's called. He came to California when he was about seventeen years old. He met a Morongo Indian girl, you know, from the Morongo Reservation over by Palm Desert?" They nodded, following along. "Her name was Rita, and she was absolutely striking and beautiful. She was a wonderful person and had a great personality, full of charm, smart. She was a marine biology major at UCLB, where they both went to school. Kelly was in the ROTC program and taking on a full load. He was using ROTC to pay for his tuition, and he had to pursue a military curriculum. He was also pursuing music as a second major. They were both in their last year and engaged to be married. I became friends with them during our first year at LB. Then, in our last year at school, Kelly's mother in Montana died suddenly. Kelly is half Indian—Blackfeet tribe. His dad is full blooded, and his mother was an attractive, blond, non-Indian woman. She had given up her other life and moved to the small Chase ranch near the reservation with her new husband, Aloysius. Kelly and his brother were born and raised there. They were brought up as ranch hands and cowboys by Kelly's father. They were expert horsemen and tough as nails. Kelly has always referred to his dad as 'the old Indian.'

"Anyway, when he returned to California after his mother's funeral, he was not the same person. He was shattered by her death. Apparently, he and his family had some sort of falling out, and things hadn't been resolved. After he returned, his family had not once contacted him. So essentially, he no longer had family. His commitment to his education took a stumble and his grades suffered. He couldn't pull himself out of his emotional downturn. Believe me, we tried everything. Rita finally had a hard talk with him. She managed to get through, and he seemed to have turned a corner. Unfortunately, he unwittingly exposed himself to the draft board and was drafted in 1967. He realized the seriousness of his situation and went for an officer commission and entered the US Army Infantry as a second lieutenant in late 1967. As soon as his training was completed, he was sent to Vietnam. He was sending us all letters for about six months, and then everything just stopped. We never heard from him again. I'd heard that a second lieutenant's survivability was measured in days. Of course, I had never shared this with Rita.

"Rita's family had some political pull, too, but could not get any information since they weren't related. So, no luck. Looking back, it's doubtful anyone in the Army had any idea either, just listed him MIA, missing in action, and moved on. Rita's family loved Kelly and thought the world of him. She was devastated when he left and was inconsolable when he stopped writing."

He paused and took a drink of water. The three women were rapt and tense. Kaitlin's eyes were starting to redden as she stared straight ahead, unfocused. He continued:

"In July of 1971, Kelly was found by a US Army infiltration unit when they overran an enemy jungle encampment near the Laotian border. Kelly was found lying in an underground bamboo cage." Jenks paused as his emotions started to rise, his eyes starting to sting. *Damn*, he thought, *this is tougher than I thought it would be*. Kaitlin reached out for his hand and gave it a gentle squeeze, as did Brenda. He took a deep breath, swallowed, took another drink, and continued.

"He was in miserable shape, nearly dead, with a raging case of malaria. He had been tortured, whipped, fingers broken, shot—you saw…" Kaitlin sat with her hands in her lap, head nodding in jerks, looking down. Jenks continued, "He was so emaciated there was nothing left but skin and bone. He was covered in filth and had some serious wounds. They extracted him and took him to a hospital ship in the Philippines, where he was stabilized. He was then sent to the VA hospital in San Francisco, where he was placed in a coma, giving him time to heal. He was out for a week or so and then revived."

He stopped again. The three girls had tears in their eyes and were quietly wiping them away. Ramona got up and brought back a box of Kleenex. Each of them thanked her and pulled one.

He continued, "He couldn't talk right away, but soon started calling for Rita. The US Army and the VA finally allowed him to call her, but her phone was disconnected. Rita waited for him for over two years. He was the love of her life. Eventually, she met another man, a lawyer from San Diego, married, and moved there. I understand she has a son. Kelly then called her parents, Victoria and Nance, who came to see him. I wasn't there, but when they saw Kelly, he made them promise to never tell Rita that he had been found and returned. He felt that he had hurt her enough."

Kaitlin leaped to her feet, hands to her mouth, and ran out the back door, unable to contain herself any longer. The other two girls sprang up and quickly followed her. *Her friends are so loyal and dedicated*, Jenks thought, *and here I am betraying mine*. Jenks had been made aware of Kelly's military details through Colonel Flagg.

Jenks was starstruck by Kaitlin, and he felt that he must try to warn her about what Kelly had been through. He knew that Kelly had enough going on with trying to maintain his tenuous recovery. She could only complicate his life, and if she was trying to *fix* him, this could only lead to bigger problems—for both Kelly and her. However, Jenks was now convinced that there was much more going on. Kaitlin had had such a physical, emotional reaction to Kelly's experiences that he was forced to rethink his original motivations in meeting and talking with her. He now realized that something deeper was present in Kaitlin and that some emotional hook had taken place between the two. Now he was afraid he may have gone too far in trying to warn her away from Kelly.

He went out the back door and saw Kaitlin in the grass—bent over at the waist with her hands on her knees, vomiting. Brenda and Ramona were doing their best to console her, each holding her long hair back. As he neared them, he was so taken with the scene of this beautiful, talented girl crying and puking her guts out at the same time. It suddenly hit him that the bombs had started going off, and there he was, where he had earlier vowed *not* to be.

After about fifteen minutes, everyone had regained a measure of composure. They were back at the table. Kaitlin managed a sheepish smile and a weak apology. "Sorry, Jenks, please go on."

He was impressed by her persistence. He started again. "Kaitlin, I need to warn you, Kelly can be an unpredictable person. He is sometimes very emotional, as you have seen. This can sometimes make him dangerous."

"But how can someone so dangerous have such beautiful, expressive talent and be so gentle?" Kaitlin asked.

"I know," Jenks replied. "I wish I had the answer. I'm just telling you what I know. Me and Henry have seen him get pretty rough with other men. He can be mean and brutal. He has this self-destructive side that he always wrestles with. He's not a typical social worker's project. His recovery since he returned has been long and painful. This morning, KC, you told me about the meeting you two had some years ago. Judging by the way you described him, it was probably only weeks after his return. He would have had no idea who you were. Since that first time with you, he started drinking heavily. He finally had an alcoholic breakdown, and he has been in AA for over a year now and is now doing well." *Thank God*, he thought.

"He's had a terrible time with isolation, even in recovery," Jenks explained. "He still doesn't watch much TV, and very seldom listens to the radio. Something about them can send him into a panic. Me and a few others have been working with him, trying to get him out into the world and get him plugged back into society."

"Why would he act that way?" Ramona asked.

"I don't know. I do know that men who have gone through similar experiences are usually unable to overcome them."

"Meaning?" Kaitlin said, coming to full alert, her posture becoming very erect at the table. She interlaced her fingers and stared directly at him.

Jenks only returned her gaze in silence. He finally pursed his lips and looked away. Kaitlin looked back down at the table.

"Me and Henry were invited over by Roland, and he gave us permission to bring one person along," Jenks said. "We told him that our tag-along guest was a UCLB alumni as well, so no one was concerned, and we thought it would be a great outing for Kelly. KC, Ramona, Brenda," he said, looking at each one. "Trust me, Kelly had no idea who the Chapins were—he was clueless. Today, though, that has all changed. He will find out who you are and may go out of his way to avoid you, especially if he thinks there is any pity involved."

Kaitlin placed her elbows on the table and crossed her arms, nodding her head slowly.

Jenks could see a decision had been made. He continued, "On the other hand, he is very keyed into the only thing that has helped save him so far…music. As you've heard, his music and lyrics can be very emotional, powerful, and wrenching, probably because of his experiences."

Kaitlin looked up at him, giving him a deep, intense stare. "Would you please help me contact him? Tell him that I must see him? Can you do that much for me?" she pleaded.

He rocked back in his chair, placed his hands flat on the table, and slowly drew them in, leaning forward and blowing out a heavy sigh with puffed cheeks. "You ladies do realize that I am going way out on a limb here, don't you? I'm risking any trust he ever had in me, and Kelly does not take trust lightly. If he tells you something or trusts you, it is unequivocal. Much like the relationship you three have. He is not a liar or a bullshitter. You can see what happens when he is confronted about trust."

Brenda and Ramona nodded silently, and Kaitlin slowly shook her head. "Well, girls, we sure screwed that up, didn't we?"

"That is between you and him. Like I said, my friendship is at risk with him now too," he warned again. "Just be careful, KC. He would never hurt you physically, but he is still an emotional train wreck at times."

All were quiet. Jenks stood to leave, and Kaitlin came around the table and gave him a hug, and then gently kissed him on the cheek. Pulling back, she said, "This couldn't have been easy for you. Thank you. Friends for life, Jenks?" She extended her hand and smiled. "You can call me anytime from anywhere," she said.

Jenks was taken aback by the offer, and more than a little flattered as he took her hand. Brenda and Ramona did the same and thanked him profusely. They agreed to stay in contact with one another until Kelly was located. Kaitlin handed him her phone number on a slip of paper as they said their goodbyes.

Jenks returned to his car. Once inside, he put his hands to his face and broke down, unable to contain the pressure any longer. He would die for both if it ever came to it. Fuck the bombs!

Chapter 14

Her Story

Ramona and Brenda watched Jenks walk to his car. Standing back from the living room window, Kaitlin was thinking about what Jenks had said. Ramona and Brenda both looked at each other, and at the same time said, "Did you see that?"

"What?" Kaitlin asked.

"He's crying out there," Brenda said. "Or it looks like it." She shrugged toward his car. Kaitlin rushed to look, but Jenks had started to leave, and it was hard to see through the glare of the car window.

In the last two days, she had met two men who had exposed her to more truths about the world than she would have ever discovered from her small circle of acquaintances, friends, and family. Her world, since her and her brother's early fame, had become so small and insulated that her existence no longer felt real. She had willingly become part of the unrealistic universe they had created for her. She knew that damage control was already in motion, and the events of the previous night would be finessed or outright snuffed out. Money could do that.

Instant fame and adulation were heady drugs, exhilarating and intoxicating. There was nothing that could prepare a person for the acceleration to full-blown overnight fame. Now she could feel herself cracking at her emotional seams. She thought she could see some differences in Roland as well. Their mother, managers, and record label were working full time to protect, counsel, direct, and schedule all their activities each day, year in and year out. The grind was becoming exhausting. The pressure to always look her best had started to exact a toll. Remarks made by callous music industry gossip types were rarely positive, always looking for some angle to exploit. Her hair, makeup, weight, craft, on and on.

"KC, what are you going to do?" Brenda said, interrupting her thoughts.

Kaitlin thought for a moment, looking at each of her friends with a small smile. "Man, you guys," she said, "I have been on such an emotional ride for the last two days, I am just spent. Hearing Kelly Chase's story, I…I just couldn't take it anymore. How can one person be hurt that much and still survive?"

"I need to go home and think about all of this," Ramona said. "KC, you really aren't considering searching for him, are you? You haven't fallen for him, have you? You know his story now, but that doesn't mean you know the man."

Kaitlin looked at her and could only shrug. "I don't know what I feel. I do know that I really hurt him, and I have to fix it somehow."

"There may be no way to fix it, KC. Maybe you should give it some time, think about it, and just move on," Brenda suggested.

"You have a short tour coming up soon and a longer one after that. You and Roland are going to be busy," Ramona reminded her.

"Look," Brenda said, "we are here for you. We will go to the mat for you, and we will help you find him if that's what you really want. We just worry about you, and you've started to lose so much weight lately. We are concerned that adding another stressor will really burn you out."

Kaitlin looked at her two friends with a loving frown and moved in to hug them both. "Thank you both so much for today. I love you guys," she said.

"Besides, how many boxes does he check on your Ideal Man List?" chided Brenda.

Kaitlin said, "I need to get going. Mother and Roland have the search party out by now."

As if on cue, the telephone rang. Ramona walked over to pick it up as Kaitlin furiously made slashing finger-to-throat motions. Ramona nodded her understanding. She answered the call and went on about having seen Kaitlin earlier but that she had left about thirty minutes ago. Kaitlin made a little prayer-and-bowing gesture to Ramona as she backed toward the front door, grabbing her purse and keys as she went.

Kaitlin was again deep in thought as she drove to her mom and dad's home, which also doubled as a rehearsal studio and band hangout. She thought about the first meeting between her and Kelly. She couldn't believe his physical transformation. Three years ago, when she first saw him at the church, he looked like a man who was barely salvageable. Last night, aside from all the scars, he was well muscled, and his blond hair was neat and trim. She didn't remember him being as tall as he was. His face had that chiseled Native look, and he looked like he had spent a lot of time outside. It was hard for her to judge height, as she was only five-foot-four. And those damned eyes! Now she was fearful that she had forever damaged her chances. It was true, as Brenda had mentioned, he didn't check any of her boxes on her "Ideal Man List." He probably didn't have a cent to his name, so there was the risk of him living off her wealth, just lying around playing the guitar all day long… *Wait, wait, dammit!* Kaitlin thought. *He's probably not like that at all,* she scolded herself. "Man!" she whispered to herself. "What a voice!"

Her thoughts continued as she pulled into the driveway of the Chapin home and personal studios. How was it possible for one person to have experienced so much in such a short amount of time? *How much personal pain can one person endure?* she wondered.

She was so curious about what made Kelly Chase tick. How was he able to function? Was he even going to live much longer? Where did those lyrics come from? How could he possibly sing with so much personal feeling without coming apart? How could a person walk away from a person they loved so much? Kaitlin felt the lump in her throat again. She swallowed hard as she got out of her car. Her questions about all these things and more kept stoking her to new heights of curiosity. She knew she had to meet him again…somehow. She entered the house and there was her mother, arms crossed.

Marie Chapin was a formidable personality. She had made it her business to manage her talented offspring over the music business hurdles, exerting her influence whenever she could. At first, she was up against sometimes powerful record companies that could exert their will capriciously. The companies were not unfamiliar with parents of her type, as many of the recording artists were minors. Despite Marie's behavior, she was only judged by the industry executives to fall somewhere on the middle of the scale, yet she could never be underestimated. Her two children, although they were now adults, were always seeking to maintain her approval. Her husband Jack was more laid back and more willing to let the kids be themselves and handle their own affairs. Jack's views, however, did not hold much sway with Marie. She came from an old-fashioned conservative background, and she remained a force for the siblings to reckon with. At first, she was able to handle the kids' affairs when they were unknown, but later, that all changed.

Marie was focused on Roland because she was certain any success would be because of his musical education and talents. The family support was all geared to his success. Kaitlin, who was about four years younger, loved her brother and would do anything for him. She was the tag-along at her brother's jam sessions with bandmates. She loved music and discovered that she loved playing the drums, despite always hearing from her school bandmates that "girls don't play drums." She became progressively better, surprising many during her last years of high school.

Kaitlin was eventually able to enlist Roland as her accomplice in the pursuit of her first drum kit purchased by her parents. Roland reasoned that his new band always needed a drummer. The other drummers that they had enlisted became unreliable and seldom showed up for rehearsals and performances. This left Roland to scramble to fill the drummer slot or cancel the weekend performances. Their parents purchased a starter drum kit. Kaitlin had mastered all time signatures and had developed an internal metronome that was deadly unerring. She studied and emulated the great jazz drummers through recent musical history and adopted bits and pieces of what she determined were the best qualities, then expanded and enhanced those. During a couple of sessions, the group was short a backup singer, so they asked a seventeen-year-old Kaitlin to step in, and she agreed.

Her performances were uneventful and fulfilled the needs of the band. She was able to perform backup vocals and still maintain her drum duties. Some months later, Roland's band, "The Roland Four," had connected with Burt, a person who had some connections to the music business. He invited Roland's group for a recording session at his garage studio, telling them he could help get their demo out to important record people he knew. Kaitlin was drafted again, as their backup singer had recently quit. Midway through the session, Kaitlin was to participate in an extended piece of background vocal. Her first attempt was somewhat uneven. Her brother and Burt both suggested that she drop down an octave, to find her vocal floor. She performed the second take. As she finished, all heads turned to her, mouths open. Roland calmly asked her to perform the piece again. She sang again, and the result was the same. However, this time the group started talking excitedly.

"Damn, Roland, you didn't tell me your sister had such a stunning voice," Burt said. "Where have you been hiding her?"

One member of the group commented, "Sounds deep, almost contralto. Amazing because you don't hear many of them."

Kaitlin couldn't understand what had just happened. It felt utterly natural, and it flowed freely from her. Roland and Burt were busy talking off by themselves, both nodding in agreement. They finished the session with a completed demo ready for Burt to do his work. As for seventeen-year-old Kaitlin, she was thoroughly embarrassed for being the center of so much attention.

"Hi, Mom," Kaitlin said when she reached the door, facing those crossed arms.

"Where have you been?" her mother asked. "We've been looking all over for you."

"Ramona's."

"Yes, Roland finally talked to Ramona," Marie said.

Kaitlin deftly sidestepped her mother and ran upstairs.

Marie called after her, "Remember we have dinner together tonight."

Kaitlin did not respond. She navigated directly to her own bathroom, fortunate to find relief. This was so damned difficult. Kaitlin suspected that trouble might be looming for her, as she was trying to recall if she had enough laxatives to outlast her mother's dinner tonight. It was sure to ignite another binge-and-purge cycle, with subsequent high and emotional numbness that would follow. Yes, trouble may have been on the horizon, but even with that, Kaitlin held out the notion that this was just a temporary condition that she would be able to overcome and gain full control of her life.

Lately, her reaction to eating anything was oddly repulsive. She had somehow slipped into the idea that her weight was out of control. Her weight had ebbed downward steadily, but whenever she looked in a mirror, she always saw herself as chubby, just as she had been as an early teen. She had begun to consume copious laxative dosages to ensure she would stave off the ugliness of any perceived gains. The machinations involved in maintaining this part of her life were exhausting: the constant purchasing, hiding enough laxatives to keep ahead of any gains, and planning the timing of it all. Then there was the constant bloating and lower stomach pain. It was all so tiring. Yet she knew it was the price of holding everything and everyone together.

Later that night she returned to her upscale, secure condominium and took care of immediate business. She had become an expert at making herself throw up. Using her fingers was an effective tool for expelling stomach contents. She carefully positioned herself before the toilet, kneeling as if getting ready to pray before the porcelain God. She carefully slid her fingers along the top of her tongue until she could feel a gag reflex growing. She applied more pressure and went a little deeper, triggering the full convulsive reflex. She then quickly removed her hand when she felt her stomach clench into a full contraction, feeling as if it were against her spine. She made a loud choking sound as the slimy, chunky substance flew past her throat and out her mouth. She was rewarded with the sound of splashing toilet water. She repeated the process until there was nothing remaining to expel, only a dry choking sound. Her attempts to hold her long hair back failed, long strands hanging into the unpleasant contents of the toilet. Her eyes were filled with hot tears that streamed down her face. A long string of nasal substance hung from her nose, the nasal passages stinging with stomach acid as she tried to sniff some of the grim substance back. She reached for a nearby towel and wiped her face. She struggled to get her footing but could not stand. A wave of dizziness overtook her, her vision dimmed, and she slid to the floor unconscious.

A short time later, Kaitlin came to. She lay still for a couple of minutes to collect her thoughts. This passing out was a new occurrence that she would have to consider when she emptied herself in the future. That is if she ever did it again. Each time she purged herself she swore inwardly that it would be the last time and she would never do it again. But there was always a next time, and each time she was unable to stifle the urge. What was happening to her?

She struggled to her knees, her arms leaning on the long, tiled bathroom vanity. She caught a reflection of herself peering just above the counter in the wall-length mirror. A light sheen of sweat covered her pale features. Kaitlin pulled herself up to her feet, with another wave of dizziness threatening to take hold. Her hair hung stiffly, in matted tangles. Since she looked like a mess, she cleaned herself up as best she could and wrapped a towel around her head. Her legs started to quiver in protest. She wobbled to her bedroom and managed to put on her pajamas, and then she collapsed face down on the bed and fell unconscious from sheer exhaustion. Her last thought was how good it was to be in control.

• • •

Kaitlin awoke sometime later thinking of Kelly Chase. She wondered what he was doing, where he was at that very minute—in Montana? Drinking somewhere? Had she driven him over the edge? She couldn't sleep, for thinking of him was maddening. She felt so alone, so in need of companionship. Rare tears started to come. The price of fame was lived in a gilded cage, which she had not bargained for. She thought back to the day when her and Roland had been offered a record contract from B&M records and had officially changed their name to "The Chapins." Barry Herb, one of the executives, happened to catch the garage demo being pushed by Burt. He'd obtained it through an obscure contact he had at a local radio station. Barry had taken it to Martin Gary, the other executive, and persuaded him to buy off on extending a contract offer to the Chapins. Roland and Kaitlin were stunned by the offer, as were their parents. Her mother immediately began fussing over Roland, praising his success as Kaitlin stood by dutifully waiting for a congratulatory hug from her mother. One that never came. No one would know that the recording contract was ultimately offered mainly on the strength and quality of Kaitlin's vocal ability. Her father had finally come to her and offered, "Congratulations, my sweet girl. I knew you kids had it in you!" They had laughed, cried, and celebrated until the early morning with fellow bandmates, friends, and relatives. Kaitlin was so happy.

She got up after about an hour, shuffled into her large walk-in closet, took her measuring tape off the shelf above her hanging wardrobe and begin to check the exact measurements between the hanging garments. "Has to be exactly one and one quarter inches," she said, repeating this over and over as she checked each one.

The hanging wardrobe was sorted and arranged by type, color, and size, everything hanging and presented just so. She took out her ironing board and iron and started at one end of the pantsuit wardrobe and again ironed the creases to exacting tolerances. Two hours later, she finally made it back to bed, completely exhausted again.

Kaitlin's alarm woke her at five-thirty a.m. She was tired and needed more sleep, but she had to get to a rehearsal session. They were getting ready for a series in Las Vegas, then a tour of the eastern states. They would be in and out until November. She decided to allow herself five more minutes to stay in her warm bed. She was experiencing an ever-present chill that she could not shake, but she was eventually able to force herself up, go to the kitchen, put on a pot of coffee, retreat to her dressing room, remove her pajamas, and step on her scale: 108 pounds.

"Dammit," she muttered. "It must have been mother's dinner last night."

She donned shorts and a sweatshirt and headed for her workout room. Her Pacemaster treadmill faced the bank of windows looking to the south, overlooking Century City from the twenty-second floor. It afforded a commanding view of her surroundings. The sun was just starting to peak over the hills to the east as she stepped on the machine and started to jog at a moderate speed. The same thoughts always crossed her mind. How soon would her mother make her first call? Then how soon after would her brother? She reflected on how much of a struggle it had been for her to move into her own place. She always felt guilty about leaving her parents and Roland alone. Why was she so conflicted? Kaitlin wanted so much to be free from her family entanglements, but she knew her most important function was to hold them all together. It was family before anything, including herself. She would die for them if she had to. She worshipped her brother, and hadn't he guided them to this wonderful success? She owed him everything and would never let him down…ever! Yet why did she have this hole, this yearning for freedom? Freedom from what? These thoughts pushed her to speed up her run to nearly unsustainable pace. She needed to be punished for her thoughts. She didn't deserve all she had. Her bad thoughts must be dealt with and exorcised. *Run harder, harder…*

Finally, an hour had passed, and she was exhausted as she struggled to get to her sumptuous bathroom. She sat on her soft bathroom chair, searching for her breath. As soon as she was able, she stepped onto the bathroom scale. One hundred seven and one-half pounds. She would have to do better. She sat on the toilet and emptied herself, straining with effort to make sure nothing remained. She stepped on the scale again, but the result was the same.

She made her way to the kitchen and poured a coffee, in her head counting down, five, four, three, two…the phone rang. It was her mother asking the usual questions. "What time did you get up? When will you be here? Roland is already here. I am worried about you Kaitlin. You need to eat more. Come and eat breakfast when you get here, okay?"

It was mind-numbing. She had to come up with a way to avoid her mother's pushy attitude towards eating. Kaitlin finally managed to get off the phone, sipping her coffee as she went back into the bathroom, stripped again, and stepped into her shower with a gleaming glass enclosure. She started scrubbing herself vigorously, as she had to make herself clean. She was a dirty person for thinking ill of her mother this morning. She must be made clean…cleaner.

Once she finished with her shower, she scrubbed the shower

glass, tile floor, and walls until they gleamed once again. Kaitlin stood before the full-length mirror, and it was obvious that she was getting fat. She had to redouble her efforts. After perusing her closet, she settled on a pair of denim jeans with sharp ironed creases and an oversized Long Beach T-shirt. Once dressed, she dried and styled her hair. She started applying her makeup as she quickly moved to the coffee pot to get another cup. She crawled under the bathroom sink and reached deep in the back for a large, sealed plastic container. She removed three packs of laxative capsules and placed them into an inner zippered pocket of her purse. Finally, she was ready to go. When she was home, the ritual was always the same. She left her condo at eight-fifteen, already calculating travel time to the home studio. If she timed it right, she would be able to go directly into the rehearsal session with Roland pushing for them to get started, giving her the opportunity to ignore her mother's insistence on breakfast.

The plan appeared to work, as her mother was nowhere in sight. The house that fronted as both their parents' home and headquarters for the Chapins' lucrative music industry business had been recently built with their parents' newfound wealth created by their children's success. Both siblings, along with their parents, agreed this was practical and offered a way for all four to stay in close contact. It was more convenient overall for Kaitlin and Roland. Just inside the non-descript home entrance was a darkly paneled foyer coupled with a second similar space. Numerous gold records and photos with prominent people from the entertainment and music industry covered the walls. Kaitlin rushed through the rooms to the adjoining rehearsal studio. The newly constructed studio took up a complete wing, which was considerable in size. Kaitlin and Roland each had a bedroom upstairs and came and went as they pleased. Marie and Jack occupied a master suite on the main floor that was kept private from the rest of the house. The suite contained a TV set, a refrigerator unit, and other personal necessities her mother had built in. Kaitlin thought her mother must have been wrapped up in a TV program, so her attention was elsewhere. *Great, I don't have to get past the guard*, she thought as she bounded down the hallway to meet up with the other members of the Chapins' band.

The studio provided a professional and comfortable setting in which to work. The equipment purchased for these purposes was the most current and modern. When recording a new album, they went to the B&M recording studio because it was acoustically sound and had a much wider array of tuning and mixing capabilities. Their home studio was a private, homey haven to create and plan the next foray into the live entertainment world.

Later that afternoon, the group was wrapping up the session with Roland beginning to tone down his directions and critiques of the other band members. Kaitlin was stowing her drum kit under their appropriate covers. For this session, she had stood in as drummer. She started thinking back to the old house where they practiced in the cramped little basement, remembering how she'd felt pure joy from playing her kit with absolute perfection as her brother beamed at her with approval. That was the moment she knew she had found her place in life.

Two years later, after their first hit album was recorded and the "Chapins" had started touring, Roland and their manager had made a request that sent her into an emotional tailspin. They had wanted her out from behind the drum set to front the group. She'd done her best to defend herself from the opinions the two were using to leverage her to the front of the band. Roland had eventually said, "It's best for me and the other band members that you do this. You would be helping everybody."

"Roland, please. I can't do this," she'd cried.

"At least give the ballad numbers a try and we'll see how it goes, okay?"

Kaitlin remembered being in tears as she'd reluctantly agreed. She was being stripped from her moorings, exposed, made to be something—someone—she knew she wasn't. She recalled the early rehearsals with the session drummer the manager had found. She would stop and offer her advice and critique the new drummer to be sure the timing and sound were just right. After gaining some confidence after their first live show, being the center of attention was both exhilarating and terrifying. *Just don't make a mistake*, she kept telling herself as she clutched the microphone close to her mouth. It was like she had gotten lost in time, and before she knew it, the set had been completed and the crowd was cheering, clapping, and whistling. She numbly took her place at the drums again and the band finished out the more upbeat numbers. It was a triumphant night for Kaitlin. But she wasn't sure she could ever warm up to this new role. She was still terrified that she would never be good enough, never perfect.

• • •

About two o'clock that afternoon, Lyn Phelps came rushing into the room clutching several large bags and took them to a long table at one end of the room. "Lunch!" she said. "Sorry I'm late. I got held up at the airport. Got here as quickly as I could."

Lyn had been the band's personal assistant and gopher for a little over two years. Lyn had been tasked, along with two other team members, as the advanced party to Las Vegas. Lyn came up to Kaitlin, gave her a warm hug, and whispered in her ear, "All right, what have you been up to? I've been getting reports." She winked at Kaitlin and started unpacking lunch for the band members.

Roland and the others had started converging on the lunch buffet. They were getting a little rowdy, so Lyn and Kaitlin moved toward the edge of the room.

"Are you okay? I've been worried about you," Lyn asked in her East Texas twang. Lyn was about Kaitlin's height, had short dark hair that curved around her face, and was a bundle of energy, which was one of the reasons Kaitlin liked her. Lyn continued, "I got the blow-by-blow from Brenda. She said I'd find out anyway. Is there anything I can do?"

"I don't know," Kaitlin said. "I don't think there's much anyone can do right now. He may be in Montana somewhere." Kaitlin looked at the floor, quickly getting lost in thought again.

"Damn, KC, Montana is a big place," Lyn said.

"A place called Bank Cut—no, Cut Bank," Kaitlin clarified.

"So you think this is the one, huh?" Lyn chided.

"Don't even go there, Lyn," Kaitlin said seriously.

"Hey, you guys better grab something," Roland said. "KC, there's a chicken salad here for you." He pointed with his fork.

"Sorry, Kaitlin," Lyn said. "I just thought you were somewhere else with this."

With her fingers hooked in her jean pockets, Kaitlin looked uncomfortable. "I'm sorry, Lyn. Look, this whole thing has consumed me for some reason."

"Well, I know someone who can refer us to his contact at a certain law enforcement agency. I can do some asking. Is that okay?"

Kaitlin lit up. "Oh, would you, please? I would be in your debt."

"Oh, you already are, woman," Lyn teased with a smile.

They both turned to the lunch table, and Kaitlin dished up only about half of her salad. She sat at her drum kit, rearranged her food, and slowly picked at it. *Is that the real reason?* She asked herself. She realized that she never would have considered going to this length for another person, except her family. *Is this how love starts?* Kaitlin wondered. She felt herself swoon.

"Kaitlin, are you okay?" Lyn asked as she moved beside her. "You look a little pale."

"Oh, no, I'm fine," Kaitlin said. She got up and made her way to the end of the room, depositing her plate on the table as she passed by. It was time to call Jenks.

• • •

For as long as Lyn had known Kaitlin, she could never recall her being so distracted. Kaitlin was the epitome of focus and drive when it came to her craft. Lyn knew Kaitlin possessed a determination to do whatever it took to be the best. She was usually the first to show up at rehearsal sessions and the last to leave. She and Roland were in constant competition for who could exhibit the longest staying power. As far as Lyn could tell, they were running a tie. Now, Lyn was seeing another side of Kaitlin. During this rehearsal, she had stood in for the session drummer who had personal business that day. After the session, Lyn heard a couple of bandmates discussing how Kaitlin had missed a couple of tempo changes, which were obvious to Roland as well. If Lyn didn't know better, she would think Kaitlin might be in love. She weighed the possible repercussions. If what she suspected was true, she might want to take her concerns to Roland and let him get to the bottom of it. After all, Lyn wanted what was best for the band. However, if Kaitlin ever found out that she was complicit in such a thing, she would fry her alive. She had seen the confrontational side of Kaitlin, and she was a force to be reckoned with. Most saw Kaitlin as a wilting flower. Upon casual observation, Kaitlin appeared that way. However, if she were pushed, cornered, or otherwise trifled with, her claws would come out. Lyn had seen her bulldoze fellow band members for not bringing their A game to the stage. She would raise her voice and become a commanding presence, never yelling or using profanity, though, as she rarely cursed. Anyone on the wrong end of Kaitlin's guns always got the message. Lyn made up her mind to look the other way and see how things played out. She decided to stay loyal to Kaitlin, especially since she was the closest she had to a sister.

Chapter 15

Connections and Reconnections

The rocking Greyhound bus shook Kelly awake. Kelly readjusted himself in his seat and looked around, feeling grateful that the seat next to him was unoccupied. His thoughts drifted back to the moments after the party. He'd been angry. "Pompous asses," he'd mumbled as he'd stomped down the sidewalk, aiming in the general direction of home. He had become aware that his anger had turned to hurt and disappointment. His regret started to build as he walked with a purpose, taking long strides. He knew that Jenks and Henry would be hot on his trail, so he decided to hitch.

He'd arrived at his apartment. His packed duffel was parked on his small neatly made rack, ready to go. He'd grabbed his keys, cash, and a checkbook, and swiftly departed. He made his way to the street and started looking for a taxi. His luck held and he caught a yellow. He knew he was steps ahead of Jenks and Henry. There would be explanations demanded and more questions that he did not have the answers to…yet.

He had traveled for well over a day when the bus finally hissed to a stop in Great Falls, Montana, on Sunday evening. He walked into the bus depot with his duffel only to discover his connection to Cut Bank was a one-hour wait. He walked for two blocks and found the Barrel Restaurant, which had an odd exterior barrel construct. He entered and moved over to a shiny, red, faux leather booth. He deposited his duffel on the seat, moved to the opposite side, and slid in. A small, cute, red-haired waitress came over with a plastic-enclosed menu and announced specials so rapidly he could not keep up. He ordered a burger and frics with a Coke, and she quickly departed with the menu. His thoughts went to his family and the talks at the kitchen table when he was seventeen and eighteen. They talked about the neighbors, horses, cows, and sometimes school. It seemed like a lifetime ago. A jukebox nearby was playing a country song he was unfamiliar with. The song ended with him still deep in family memories, and then the jukebox sent her voice to him. He froze, and the hair on the back of his neck and his arms stood on end. There it was! So beautiful, so emotive, hurting, and haunting. He scrambled out of the confines of the booth and ran to the jukebox, not knowing where to look for the song, the name, anything! He turned and looked for help. On a Sunday night, the place had few customers.

Kelly yelled, "Hey, waitress, hey! Where are you?"

She ran up to him, wide-eyed and concerned. "What's wrong? Are you okay?"

He had lost his breath and gasped as it came back. He looked at her, caught her name tag, calmed, and asked, "Jenny, who is that singing this song?"

She looked surprise, probably thinking he was crazy since this was far from an emergency. After collecting herself and stepping back, she said, "Where have you been?"

"Who?" he demanded.

"The Chapins. Kaitlin Chapin is the singer, and this song is called 'Next to you.'"

His jaw dropped as the name clicked: Kaitlin. The realization staggered him.

Jenny grabbed his arm. "Damn, cowboy, are you okay? Are you sick or something?"

"No, no, I'm fine," he answered absently as he walked back to the booth in a daze, sitting down with a new heaviness that came with this knowledge.

His mind started arranging the pieces of his memory together, anything having to do with Kaitlin. When he played the piano piece in the church in 1971, she came up behind him and sang to him, accompanying him with that beautiful voice. He recalled her name: Kaitlin. There was no way in hell he could forget a voice like hers. At the time he'd thought he had heard it somewhere in a dream. It could have been the effect of high-powered pain medications and someone's radio…maybe. He remembered those eyes, too, those big, brown, expressive sad eyes. He could see they had already experienced great sadness—the same sadness he'd felt during that first encounter. More Freddy AA wisdom came to him: "That goddamn radar alcoholics have, it's always running, pinging, looking for that same level of disfunction, and finding it!"

Jenny brought his order, and upon setting his dish and drink in place, she asked, "How you doin', cowboy? Gonna be okay?"

Kelly looked up at her, met her eyes, and smiled. "Gee, I'm sorry for being so rude. Thanks for helping me."

"No problem. We get a lot worse in here." She placed his receipt on the table, wheeled on her heel, and marched off. He suddenly realized how hungry he was. He ate his meal and tried to clear his mind the best he could.

After he had finished eating, he packed up his duffel, paid, and left. He glanced back and saw the waitress and the cook, spatula in his hand, looking at him and exchanging glances. Kelly overheard the waitress saying something to the cook, "Strange bird."

"Yeah," the cook responded.

"He acted like he'd never heard of Kaitlin Chapin, but the oddest part was that I got the sense that he knew her…"

As he continued his journey on the bus, Kelly thought back to the party, and even more was making sense. He realized he'd recognized her right before he sang. And afterwards, when she came up to him, he'd tensed when she stood close. The familiar scent of her perfume came to him in that moment, something he couldn't forget.

He realized now that she was indeed famous, finally making the connection. That was why she'd been so upset and confronted him, because she was scared. *What a catchy disease fear is*, he thought.

Kelly was the poster boy for fear turned to anger then to rage. His response to her, he realized, was full-blown and had exploded all over the house, a tornado that sucked everybody up in its wake. He was now aware of the damage he had caused, especially for Kaitlin. She hadn't deserved any of it. This being sober and growing up in public shit was overrated. He suspected his sponsor, Freddy, would suggest he apologize at the first opportunity. "Might as well eat the crow while it's fresh," Freddy would advise.

He would then be expected to make the proper amendments to his future behavior. Freddy once told him, "Dammit, Kelly, amends are not apologies. They are intended to amend your present behavior into something different, something good! Remember, it's all about the action, never just the thought! An alcoholic's apology is worth shit!"

Fuckin' Freddy is always right, Kelly thought as he dozed off, finally falling asleep.

Kelly awoke both times the bus stopped before reaching Cut Bank. It was late by the time he shuffled into the small bus depot. The lone attendant behind the counter greeted him with a nod and a soft, "Good evening, sir, have a pleasant journey?"

"Yes," Kelly answered, then asked if he could get change for a five-dollar bill in quarters.

"Yes, sir, let me help you with that."

Kelly walked over to the nearby phone booth, set his duffel nearby, and closed the door. He deposited a quarter and dialed Freddy's number.

"Hello?" came a gruff voice.

"Freddy, it's me."

"Damn, Kelly, where are you? I have Jenks up my ass over here. He's been calling me every hour. What the fuck did you do?"

Kelly explained the events of Saturday night and brought Freddy up to date, all the way up to him standing in the bus station in Cut Bank. Freddy listened patiently. That was what Kelly liked most about him. He just let him talk until he was finished, and then there was a silence between them. It was like Freddy was waiting for the bucket to empty out completely before he would speak.

"Shit, son," Freddy said. "How do you keep fitting ten pounds into a five-pound bag? Hell, I just talked to you Saturday morning and here it is, early Monday, and you are in Broken Neck Montana? If my life were even half as wild as yours, I wouldn't be sitting here talking to you. And who is this girl? What kind of party was this?"

"That's kind of a problem." Kelly hesitated. "I think she's famous."

Freddy cleared his throat after emitting a loud smoker's cough. "Just a minute, I've got to get out of bed, man."

Kelly could hear the phone being set down as the pay phone dinged, and the operator asked for a dollar and a half. He could hear Freddy striking a match and lighting a cigarette, taking his first drag. "Now, is this the one you yelled obscenities at?" Freddy asked.

"Yes," Kelly said meekly.

"Okay, what's her name?"

"Chapin, Kaitlin Chapin."

A long pause followed suit as Freddy stopped breathing. "Hold on, son." Freddy said. "You mean the singer Kaitlin Chapin?"

"Yes, I had no idea she was who she was. I just put it together today—yesterday, actually." Kelly unfolded the events that took place in the Great Falls restaurant.

"Shit, how do you *not* know who Kaitlin Chapin is?" Freddy muttered, "Have you been under a rock?" Freddy sighed. "Sorry, Kelly, forgot."

"There's more," Kelly said, ignoring the unintentional jab.

He told Freddy about his first meeting with Kaitlin Chapin some years earlier, and the feelings she had brought out of him, how he felt he somehow knew her before then. He heard Freddy take a long drag from his cigarette. “I don’t know what to say, Kelly,” Freddy said. “Who could make this shit up? What does this have to do with a trip to Montana?”

“I was planning the trip anyway because I wanted to find my family. It was late, and,” he paused, “I got scared, afraid I might drink, so I bought a bus ticket, and here I am.”

“Why didn’t you call me?”

“Well, it was late, and I didn’t want to bother you—”

“How many times have we talked about this Kelly?” Freddy interrupted. “When this kind of thing happens, you need to process it with someone…like me!”

“I just thought—”

“Bullshit! You know where your best thinking got you last time, a near trip to the nut house. I’m sensing a question here, so ask it!”

Kelly, thoroughly chastened, said, “How do I fix this, Freddy? I know I have to do something. I just don’t know what to do, how to do it, or anything…” Kelly trailed off. “It’s bothering the hell out of me.”

“Well, here’s one thing to consider,” Freddy said, calming down. “When I’m confused, I usually give the feeling time to settle. I don’t do anything, and instead, I just wait. Sometimes the best thing to do is nothing. Be careful not to charge in and make things worse. Remember, when one door closes”—*I know, I know*, Kelly thought, mouthing the words to himself—“another one opens, but it can be hell in the hallway. You find a place to get some sleep, and we’ll talk later in the morning.”

“What do I do about Jenks?” Kelly asked.

“Call him and tell him the truth. He’s deeply invested in you, and just like me, he loves you. Remember, you are special in the eyes of the Creator. Have you ever heard the saying”—*Here we go again*, Kelly thought—“big crosses for big hosses and little crosses for little hosses?” *Nope, never heard that one.* “Surely you must be blessed, Kelly. Your creator loves you enough to allow you to carry the biggest cross, yours and sometimes those of others. And the little hosses, they just aren't there yet, only able to carry the small problems of life. You are blessed. Now get some sleep." Click!

Kelly could feel the glow in his stomach, that inexplicable feeling after he had one of these talks with Freddy. What was that anyway? Maybe it was because he knew he was loved.

Kelly stumbled into a nearby motel, checked in, and slept until late the next morning.

• • •

Kelly found a phone booth outside the motel office. He entered the office, got change for more quarters, and called Jenks's work number. After being routed to his extension and two more rings, Jenks picked up. "Bradley Jenkins, may I help you?"

"It's me, Jenks," Kelly said.

"Kelly!" Jenks said, sounding surprised but relieved. "Where are you? I've been calling everyone I can think of looking for you."

"I'm in Montana. Did you talk to Freddy?"

"Oh, yeah, he told me to talk to you and hung up."

"Well, you know how he operates." Kelly chuckled.

Ignoring his comment, Jenks continued, "Hey, Kelly, we have a problem."

"Yeah, I know," Kelly said. "I owe you and Henry an apology, and I will limit my public interactions from here on out. Pretty bad, huh?"

"Oh, that's not the half of it. Kaitlin Chapin is scouring the countryside for you. Have you finally figured out who she is?" Jenks asked.

"I finally put all the pieces together on the bus ride. I figured out she is pretty well known."

"Shit, Kelly, she and her brother are world famous, and she is one of the wealthiest female entertainers on earth!"

Kelly was stunned by this new revelation. Now he knew for sure he was never going to see her to apologize and try and make things right. She was probably pissed off at him anyway. She was a highflyer and would soon have no regard for him. He needed to do what Freddy suggested and lay low for a while. Hopefully, she would just go away.

"She called me first thing Sunday morning and started pumping me for information. Man, she sounded close to tears, so I agreed to meet with her. Kelly, I couldn't resist. She was practically begging me for the low down on you. Those big brown eyes... Man, I caved."

"What does she want with me? What did you tell her?" Kelly asked.

"Ah, pretty much everything," Jenks admitted, leading to a brief silence. "Everything, didn't leave anything out."

"That must have scared the hell out of her," Kelly said. "What does she still want from me. Is she mad?"

"No, not at all," Jenks said. "I think it was the part about Rita that shook her up," Jenks said sheepishly.

Kelly didn't know that "everything" included Rita. "Jesus tits, Jenks, you told her about that too? What else?" Kelly asked, wanting to know if anything was off limits.

"Well, it must have scared her. She ran outside and threw up, and her friends were crying—"

"What? How many people were at this little shindig?"

"KC and her two friends who were at the party the night before."

"Oh, now it's KC! Boy, you two got awful chummy in a flash."

There was another silence between them as Kelly could feel Jenks cringing over the phone. "Jenks, it's okay man," Kelly said, letting Jenks off the hook a little. "You didn't do anything wrong. It's my fault for doing what I did. It's on me." There was an audible sigh from Jenks as the pay phone cried for more quarters. "After all of that, why is she still looking for me?"

"I don't know, but something is going on with her. It has to do with the first time you two met, you know…at the church."

"She told you about that?"

"Yeah, why didn't *you* ever tell me about meeting her?"

"Was I supposed to tell you about a strange woman who sang to me in church?"

"Oh, I guess you're right."

"Yeah, you and Freddy both give me too much credit," Kelly said, getting tired of people forgetting that he was in a literal hole in another country, so he wasn't up to speed on what had been going on in the rest of the world.

"You know, she's sorry about the things she said to you. I think she wants to find you and apologize," Jenks said, but Kelly felt that he was hiding something. "She is probably going to call me anytime soon wondering if I've heard from you. What am I going to tell her?"

"Well, Jenks, you're just going to have to tell your old friend KC whatever you want. You two, being old pals, can work it out."

"Come on, don't do this to me," Jenks begged.

"Tell her the truth if you want. I mean, what the hell is she going to do? Chase me down in Cut Bank, Montana? There's no way for her to get a hold of me, so just let her down as easy as you can. The last thing I need is some woman trying to push her pity on me. I don't care how fucking famous she is!"

With that, the phone chimed, and the call ended.

• • •

The Chapin group was kicking back after a late lunch and relaxing after the Monday afternoon rehearsal. Kaitlin was in the rear storage area by a phone and searching in her purse for Jenks's phone number, and once she found it, she dialed. She reached his office receptionist, asked for Mr. Jenkins, and was placed on a brief hold. Though she was just going to ask for an update, she felt that there was a lot on the line. With every minute that passed, she was risking losing Kelly further and further. She had to press on when she could, so she hoped Jenks would have something—anything—to tell her.

"Bradley Jenkins, can I help you?" Jenks answered.

"Jenks, it's Kaitlin Chapin. Have you heard anything?"

Jenks was starstruck the moment he heard her voice, being caught flat footed for an answer. He thought of his possible responses quickly and decided to tell her the truth. "K-Kaitlin," he stammered, "he called me this morning."

"And you were just getting ready to call me, right?" A silence. "Come on, Jenks, I'm just pulling your leg." She let out a small laugh. Poor Jenks. He was in a tight spot, so she sympathized with him.

"Well, I-I…"

"It's okay, Jenks. I appreciate the spot you're in. I know you're caught in the middle. Well, what'd he say?" she pushed.

"First off, he is in Montana, and he's okay. I think he's looking for his brother. I told him about our meeting and what was said."

"Was he angry?" she asked, remembering how important trust was to Kelly according to Jenks.

"Not as bad as I thought. He pretty much took the blame for what happened at your house. He's finally figured out who you are, and like I said before, he might think you're on a pity trip and won't want any part of it."

She was quiet for a moment. "He *is* mad at me then," she concluded.

"No, KC. I just think he's a little intimidated by you and doesn't know what to do."

"I know. It's a big problem I have with men."

"So I think he's more comfortable being by himself for now."

"There's no way I can contact him then?"

"Not unless you actually go to Montana and track him down. He didn't give me a way to reach him either."

"Will he ever talk to me again?"

"Oh, yeah, sure," Jenks lamely offered.

"Jenks, when you talk to him again, please tell him to call me and give him my number. Tell him to leave a message and I will call him back. Will you do that for me? We will be in Vegas starting next month, in October, and then I think we're touring the Midwest. Look, we will be back in early December, just so you know. Please call me if you hear anything. Promise?"

"I will. I promise."

• • •

Kelly dumped more quarters into the phone and dialed Freddy's number. The familiar gruff voice answered, "Hello?"

"It's me, Freddy…"

"Call around and find the closest AA meeting and get your ass there. If you can't find one, stop and ask a local deputy dog. He'll know. So what's with Jenks?" Kelly recounted the conversation with Jenks, and then waited for a response. "You're trying to find your family, right?"

"Yep, looking for my brother. I'm trying to find out what happened to him."

"Long overdue, I'd say," Freddy said.

"I'm going to catch a ride to the old ranch and see who lives there now, see what they know. I'll try to find one of my old friends to see what they know."

"What are you going to do about Superstar?" Freddy asked.

"Taking your advice and leaving her alone. I told Jenks not to lie to her about where I am. I don't think she's interested in coming to Montana, so I'm safe for now. I'll call him later to find out what's going on with her."

"Why in the hell is she so invested in you anyway?" Freddy asked.

"She's doing the pity thing, and I don't want anything to do with that," Kelly said dismissively.

"What if it's something else?"

"Like what?"

"Maybe she's attracted to you. You know, good girls love bad boys."

Kelly was taken aback by Freddy's suggestion. "I don't think I would ever be on her dance card," Kelly demurred. "She's a big star, beautiful, and she can have anybody."

After a brief silence, Freddy continued, "Now, you first met her in a church in seventy-one, right?"

"Yes, I told you all about that."

"It sounds like that really meant something to her. If that's the case, you need to handle her very carefully. She's probably pretty fragile, and you don't want to compound the damage you've already done," Freddy suggested. Kelly took this in and continued to listen to Freddy. "Don't lie or try to manipulate her. Easing your discomfort and guilt at her expense is not allowed. You get that? You two can work things out from there."

God, the old fart was right. *Where'd he learn all this shit anyway?* Kelly wondered.

"Does any of this make sense to you, goofball?" Freddy asked when Kelly didn't respond right away.

"Freddy…I'm scared," Kelly confessed.

"It's just like all of the other things you've worked through. It looks hard, scary, and impossible, yet you always get through it. Call me tomorrow." Click.

Kelly hoisted his duffel bag over his shoulder and walked into downtown Cut Bank. It was a typical small Montana town, with diagonal parking and old brick buildings. At almost noon on a Monday, it was busier than he ever recalled it being. After six years, many things must have changed. He walked to the old Pay 'N' Pak grocery; it was still there. This was comforting and cheered him up some. He went to the coolers at the end of the store, noting the old wooden floors had developed more squeaks. The sounds and smells took him back in time, as if he had never left. He selected two wrapped sandwiches from the deli and a bottle of Coke. As he made his way back to the front of the store, he realized he was passing through the flashy magazine aisle. Suddenly, there she was, on the front of a popular weekly star tell-all. The banner flashed "Kaitlin Chapin tells all." It was accompanied by her image with a beautiful smile.

This can't be happening, he thought as he picked up the magazine. He waited in line behind an older woman as she fished through her little coin purse for the proper change. She and the clerk were talking about the weather and the prediction for a hard winter. She shuffled off toward the door as the clerk started to ring up his items.

"She sure is beautiful, isn't she?"

"Huh?" Kelly said, looking up in confusion and glancing at the old woman, then back to the clerk who had picked up the magazine, ogling the cover as he heaved a sigh, placing it in the bag and handing it to him.

"Yeah, she sure is," Kelly acknowledged, looking directly at the clerk before heading out. The clerk trailed him with a curious look, shrugged his shoulders, and greeted the next customer.

Kelly walked to the small park across the street, found a wooden park bench, and eased himself down as he dropped his duffel beside him. The park bench with green, peeling paint felt good, having warmed in the bright September sun. The leaves on the trees had started to turn to the reds and yellows of early fall. There were only two couples strolling nearby as he surveyed his surroundings before unpacking his sandwiches and surreptitiously opening the magazine next to him on the bench. He flipped through to find the article. It described how wealthy she and her brother had become within the last three years, that they had both lived at home until recently. Kaitlin had purchased an expensive condo somewhere in the LA area. The writer went on to talk about the stresses of touring and Kaitlin not being able to establish any lasting relationships with potential suitors. She explained that she just didn't have the time because of their hectic touring and recording schedules. Also scattered within those dates were benefit shows in which they would donate all the proceeds to some charitable cause. Kelly was impressed by that. It went on to explain that she was regrettably unattached. Her final remarks were quoted as: "Someday I will marry that special man, have kids, and live a quiet life. It's just not possible right now." The magazine writer chided the readers, telling them that they too were still in the running. At the end of the article was another photo of Kaitlin playing the drums. *Now, that's weird*, Kelly thought. *Girls don't play drums.*

As he finished up, he collected his belongings and stood to find another phone booth. A pickup truck bearing a Glacier County Sheriff logo was easing toward the intersection as he started crossing the street. Recalling Freddy's suggestion, he held up his hand as he passed in front of the truck, met the driver's eyes, backed up, and approached the driver's side. The man inside had one beefy elbow partially extended from the window.

"Can I help you?" the sheriff said, eyeing Kelly.

"Sir, do you know where I might find an AA meeting in town?"

The big man held up one meaty index finger. "Hang on a minute." He reached for his radio. "HQ, can you…" The big man talked over the radio for a few seconds, then looked back at Kelly. "You're in luck, son. Right around the corner here above the moose lodge is a meeting starting at noon, so you're just in time."

"Thank you…deputy."

"Sheriff Potter, Blaine Potter, glad to help. You new in town?"

"Well, sort of. I used to live just south of town down toward Valier."

"Really?" the sheriff said, his interest piqued.

"The Chase place. My dad was Aloysius."

"Well, I'll be damned," Sheriff Potter said. "You must be that long-lost brother, Frank, is always taking about."

"Ye..yes," Kelly stammered.

"Your brother is sure you were killed in Vietnam. He still lives there. I'll be damned," he said in wonder.

Kelly's heart started to race. "He…he's still there?"

"Yes, sir. When are you going out there, son?" he asked.

"After I get out of the AA meeting. I was probably going to hitch a ride."

"Hell, I'll come by in about an hour to pick you up. I'd be more than happy to take you out there," the sheriff said excitedly. "Your brother is going to shit." He shook his head as his truck eased away.

Kelly climbed the stairs to the meeting. He entered a large room with tables running down the center end to end.

"Hello!" an older man shouted at the end of the table. He was wearing worn, striped coveralls with a small brimmed dark hat. "Welcome," he said with a big smile, "I'm Tracy."

An hour later, Kelly threw his duffel in the back of the sheriff's truck and clambered into the cab. "Gosh, if you don't mind me asking, where have you been?" the sheriff asked with appraising eyes.

"Let's just say I was kind of tied up for a while," Kelly responded.

The big man nodded and left the subject hanging. They drove in silence for a mile or two before the big sheriff said, "You know, there were two government types moseying around town some time back, maybe three years ago or so. They were looking for your brother or your father. Course, we out here are suspicious of those types, and we rarely help them. Think that might have something to do with you?"

"Yes," Kelly acknowledged. "Probably the US Army looking for my next of kin."

"I guess that makes sense. Word was they went on the reservation to find Frank after they left town. I wished them luck with that," Potter said. "The Blackfeet don't give nothing up," he said with a big grin.

"Yeah, I know," Kelly ruefully said.

"I remember your family. I think you went to school with my nephew, Tim Potter."

"Could have," Kelly replied absently. He gazed out the open truck window and saw the often dreamed about rolling countryside that was his home. Off in the west stood the outline of the great Rocky Mountains, another vison that he kept returning to while in captivity. How many times had he prayed that he would one day return home again to see these things? Now, here he was, feeling that old familiar lump forming in his throat. Kelly tipped his head back on the truck seat and closed his eyes, breathing in the smells and listening to the sounds as they drove down the old familiar two-lane road. The big sheriff soon announced the upcoming turn into the old Chase family ranch. As they turned into the main gate, Kelly could see that the place was in a general state of disrepair and hadn't been painted in years. The corral was dilapidated, and tall weeds had taken over. The old barn roof had partially collapsed. There was no sign of livestock, and Kelly assumed that the ranch's working days were over. The old house had a ghostly appearance and was barely recognizable. Kelly's feelings were in collision. His sadness from seeing his old home in such a broken state was immense, but at the same time, he felt this growing excitement at the possibility of seeing his brother for the first time in years.

The sheriff pulled his truck near the front of the old house next to a gleaming new Ford pickup truck still wearing the new dealer window stickers.

"Somebody must be doing well," Kelly muttered in a low voice.

He and the sheriff exited the truck. Potter strode up the steps and knocked on the door. They could both hear the footfalls of a small child pounding on the floor. The door was opened wide by a small Indian boy of about four. “Hi,” he announced, “I’m Danny. Are you here to arrest me?”

The big sheriff squatted down to address the small boy. “I’m Sheriff Potter, and it’s nice to meet you, Danny. There are no warrants out for your arrest today, so you’re free to go. We’re just here to visit your dad if he’s home today.”

At that moment, a small Indian woman appeared in the living room doorway. Kelly was lost in time for the moment, trying to remember the last time he was in this room. Everything had changed so much. The room was so dark and small now. It had not been cleaned in some time and was sorely in need.

“Hi, I’m Shelly. Can you wait for just a minute? I’ll get him for you. It’s been a bad day for him, and he’s in bed.”

Kelly heard voices at the end of the hall. “I don’t know, Frank, it’s the sheriff and some other guy.”

After a brief time, Kelly’s brother, Frank, appeared in the doorway wearing a bathrobe. He was horribly gaunt, had a yellowish cast to his skin color, his eyes were grossly bloodshot, and his hair stood in all directions. Frank stood frozen at the sight of his brother. His eyes widened as he shuffled to Kelly with his arms outstretched. Kelly walked into his brother’s arms and hugged him, feeling his thin frame beneath. He could feel Frank’s body shaking with each sob-filled breath his brother took.

“I’m here, Frankie, I’m here now,” Kelly said as he stroked the back of Frank’s head.

Frank said nothing, just hugged his brother tightly, quietly crying.

“Mom, what’s wrong with Daddy?” Danny asked, tugging at his mother’s sleeve.

“Nothing, honey. Everything’s okay.” Shelly kneeled and pulled her son to her.

“Kelly…Kelly,” Frank managed to finally say. “My God, I thought you were dead.” Frank stood back from their hug, holding on to Kelly's shoulders, looking directly into his eyes. "Where were you? What happened?"

Kelly wiped the tears from his eyes with the backs of his fingers, dropped his hands, and looked down at the floor. "They captured me, Frankie. They kept me for three years," Kelly confessed tearfully to his brother.

Sheriff Potter had been standing quietly back as he dangled his hat gingerly in his fingertips. This was a sight that nobody could forget.

Frank turned to Shelly. "Shel, this is my brother Kelly I've always talked about."

Shelly stood and politely shook Kelly's hand, wiping her tears away with her other hand.

Everyone thanked Sheriff Potter and shook his hand, including little Danny. As he walked to the door, the big man turned to Kelly with a sad look in his wet eyes, and said, "I know it's a little late, and no one was there for you when you were brought back, but welcome home. We're proud of you." He nodded once, placed his hat on his head, and turned to leave.

Frank and Kelly sat at the kitchen table until late that afternoon, talking about experiences they had each had during their nearly six years apart. Kelly answered each question his brother asked about his years missing, pulling no punches. There were long silences after some responses, with Frank shaking his head and looking down at the table. Shelly had prepared dinner, and they continued to talk while they ate. Frank wasn't eating much but seemed to be trying his best. They laughed and cried over old stories and experiences. In the early evening, Kelly excused himself. He knew he needed to call Jenks to report in.

Kelly went to the phone in the living room and dialed Jenks's home number.

"Hello, Kelly, is that you?" Jenks's said when he answered.

"I found Frank!" Kelly announced to his friend excitedly. "He still lives at the old house."

"That's good news. I was hoping you would find something. It's about time you had something really positive in your life. I was worried you wouldn't find anything. Why hasn't he tried to get a hold of you?"

"He thought I was dead. The Army reported me missing, and that's all he ever knew. The local sheriff told me the feds had come snooping around about three years ago when I was found. They were looking for Frank or my dad, but nobody told them anything."

"They should have checked property records."

"Yeah, well the Army isn't too bright about such things." Kelly paused, but then decided there was no way to put the next sentence delicately. "He's dying."

"What?"

"He has liver cancer, so he doesn't have long, maybe a month or so. I'm just happy that I got to see him."

"Is there any way I can help? Do you need me to come up there?"

"No, we're fine. I may ask you to come up later, though. Maybe you can come up and get me, haul me home?"

"Yeah, sure. You just let me know." Kelly was about to hang up, but then Jenks said, "Say, one more thing…"

"Yeah?"

"Miss Chapin wants me to give you her phone number. She asks that you call her and leave your number so she can call you back if she can't pick up. You should call her, Kelly. At least to get her to stop hassling the hell out of me."

"Okay, okay. Dammit, I thought we were done with this," Kelly complained.

He wrote down the phone number and gave Jenks the ranch number so he could reach him later. Kelly paused for a moment after hanging up. He decided he would call and leave a message if the recorder came on. If she answered, he would quickly hang up. He did a quick mental check to see if it still complied with

Freddy's demands about lying or manipulating. He decided the plan would meet approval and dialed the number. For some reason, he was scared shitless. The recorder picked up after the sixth ring. A mechanical voice repeated the number and asked the caller to leave a message.

"Look, I know you want to talk to me, so I am leaving you my number," Kelly said. "Sometime tomorrow morning should be fine. I'm at my brother's house, just in case someone else should pick up. Just ask for me. Okay? Bye."

Kelly returned to the kitchen to continue catching up with his brother. Frank sat looking at him red-eyed with a gentle smile on his face. "Kelly, I have to tell you something important. Please sit."

Kelly was thinking the worst as he slowly sat down. Shelly and Danny had gone outside for a walk. Kelly could see them through the window, holding hands and walking down the weeded backyard path in the dim evening light.

"Kelly, you are about to become a very wealthy man," Frank said. "By the end of the week, I would judge about one hundred fifty million all tolled." Frank was clutching a water glass, then took a small sip.

"What are you talking about?" Kelly asked warily.

"Remember when you told me that I should maybe think about a career in business?" Kelly nodded. "Well, I did take some junior college classes. Turns out it lit a fire. I started going before Mom died, and I liked it. After Mom died, Dad disappeared into the mountains, and I lost myself for a while there. I did a lot of drugs, which is why I wound up with this liver problem. I contracted hepatitis. Anyway, after I came back around, Dad was still gone. I got a loan using the ranch as collateral and started drilling for oil. Lo and behold, we struck our first well. Did you get my letters telling you I had a surprise for you when you got home?" Kelly shook his head; he had never received those letters. Frank went on, "I continued to drill and continued to strike. I bought more ranch land and continued to drill. We struck even more oil. The markets started paying good returns and I started investing in commercial property all over Montana, California, and other places. These properties have increased significantly in value over the last few years. We have invested in some little-known stocks, mostly energy, coal, utility companies, and something called technology. These investments for the most part have continued to pay handsomely."

Kelly was taking all this in, going down the rabbit hole. "Why are you still living here, Frank?"

"Because I have been ill for some time, and this is my home. I don't need to be anywhere else," he said, taking another sip of water. "I thought you were gone forever. I was making plans this week to give it all away to charities, in grants, trusts, and other worthwhile causes. Hell, Dad is up in the mountains and doesn't want anything to do with it. Anything that takes from Mother Earth he wants nothing to do with."

"When's the last time you saw him?"

"About a year ago. I tracked him down, went up on horseback, and finally found him living in an old makeshift lodge. You know folks on the reservation say he's an important medicine man, a shaman."

"No way!" Kelly exclaimed.

"Yep, has some sort of special powers some folks say."

"What do you think?" Kelly asked.

"I've thought about that many times. You know, last time I saw him, he told me that you were still alive and that you were going to come and see me before I died. I asked him how he knew I was dying, and he told me it was written on me, saying it would be a 'good thing.' Now with you showing up like this, along with everything else that's happened, I think there's something to it."

Kelly was reeling from all of Frank's revelations: the company, the money, his dad.

"You and I have a lot of work to do before it's too late," Frank said. "All of what I just told you is buried in layer after layer of corporate dead ends and blind alleys. No one knows who we are. We only come out when we need to, and that will be through attorneys, CPAs, and other representatives. Some of them don't even really know who we are."

"Why all of this secrecy and shit, Frank? Does this company even have a name?"

"REO Chase: Real Estate and Oil. It isn't advertised much, though, but you can change it if you want. Might be a touch expensive, though. I set it up this way because I didn't want anybody to know who we were. I just didn't want to be bothered by anybody. To people around here, I'm just Frank Chase, the poor rancher. I have never spent money extravagantly or even attempted to stand out in any way. Are we rich and powerful? Yes, you could say that, but it's just not something I really value. Granted, I have made some things happen for people that would have never happened otherwise. But these are people and places that really needed help and deserved it. I help only as much as needed, and they are expected to finish the job with their own resources. I only keep an eye on their progress from there on."

"God, you're a weird bastard, Frank," Kelly said, shaking his head.

"Fuck, I know." Frank smiled and toasted Kelly with his water glass and took a drink.

"What about your wife and son? How do they fit in?"

"Oh, Shelly is my caretaker, and Danny is her son. I'm not his father, and we're not married. I am careful not to have any legal entanglements or loose ends. No ex-wives or kids, nothing. That new truck out there is in Shelly's name, the only real extravagance we have. The oil wells on this land show ownership by others. I'm not shown as involved." They were both quiet for a moment.

"So, is this leading to something? I know you. What's up?" Kelly asked.

Frank looked directly at him, holding his attention. "I want you to promise on Mom's grave that you will continue as I have for the most part. Never use this money or power to harm anyone. Stay below the radar and just be a good human. Don't fuck anybody over and help where you can. You can grow the company as big as you want, but be careful. Just because you are big doesn't mean you can't go broke," he said with a red-eyed wink. "I get that it might take some getting used to, and I get that you'll want to spend money on yourself, and that's natural. There are tons of ways to do that without exposing yourself. You will find it hard to keep this all under your hat, but again, you'll get used to it. Will you promise me, Kel?"

"What if I ever get married?" Kelly asked.

"Get a prenup!" Frank said, followed by a hearty laugh that dissolved into a coughing fit.

• • •

The next morning, Kelly was sitting in a chair by the telephone reading the latest *Oil and Gas Journal* magazine, drinking a cup of coffee. Frank was still sleeping. Shelly and Danny had driven into town to stock up on groceries. The phone rang, and he was instantly on alert. He hoped it wasn't her, and then hoped it was. No! *Don't answer it. Let the machine pick it up.*

He had gone over this conversation a hundred times and what he would say to her. He steeled himself. "Hello," he greeted in a normal voice.

"Is this Kelly Chase?" He recognized her unforgettable voice and started his rehearsed lines. "Miss Chapin, I am so sorry for having caused you, your friends, and your family any embarrassment due to my actions. I probably shouldn't have been there anyway, and I am truly sorry—"

Suddenly, there was a loud tapping on the other end of the line, something a sharp fingernail would do.

"Hello?" she said. "I want to speak to the *real* Kelly Chase. You're not the man who was in my kitchen last Saturday night," she stated flatly.

Kelly instantly responded, "What's the matter with you, lady? Are you nuts?"

"Oh! There you are, Kelly Chase."

His antenna was up instantly, for Rita would always use his full name, even in casual settings, only between the two of them. He knew he had better shut up and listen.

She continued, "Most men in my world tend to be simpering, whining cowards, and you appear to be the exception." He said nothing. She said, "First, let me compliment you on the song you performed at the party. It was beautifully done, sung with such passion and rawness. I have never heard anything quite like it." Kelly suspected that his weird world was taking another turn. "Did you write that?" she asked.

"Yes, I did," he said quietly.

"Beautiful," she remarked again. "Do you remember when we first met?" she asked.

How could he ever forget the first soft touch of a female he had felt in years? It triggered tears he thought he did not have. Kelly cleared his throat. "Yes," he responded weakly.

"Do you remember what I told you?" she asked.

Kelly was quiet, his memory taking him back, playing that old familiar scene again. The lump was coming back. He could hardly get the words out as he said, "Something like, the first real man I've ever met?"

He was shaking inside now, and the old fear was creeping back in. He knew if she asked him another question, he would not be able to respond. There was a silence between them until she finally spoke. "You made me cry that day," she finally said. "What you were doing at the piano was so pure and expressive, you drew me right in. I have never forgotten that. I confess, I thought you were some down-on-his-luck homeless man the pastor was helping.

Kelly could not resist a chuckle. “Yeah,” he admitted, “not one of my better days.”

“Sure, it was!” she insisted. “You met me. What was even more charming was you had no idea who I was. Kelly Chase, I don’t know what you’re doing now, but if you want me to set you up with studio people I know, it might be a good direction for you.”

“Thanks, Miss Chapin, but I don’t think I would fit in very well.”

“Okay, maybe later, and stop calling me that. To you, I am KC. Okay?”

“Yes, ma’am—I mean—KC.”

She let out a small giggle. “Well, let me know if I can help you with that. This is not pity. You have talent, and you should benefit from it.” She took on a more serious tone. “You know Jenks thinks the world of you. He’s told me quite a bit about you, but please don’t be angry with him. I can be a bulldozer sometimes, and I kind of ran over him. It wasn’t fair. It was my fault. Please forgive me.”

“I thought that’s what might have happened,” Kelly said. “He’s my best friend, he saved my life, and I love him. I’m not angry with him over any of this. My affection for him is not conditional.” It was her turn to be quiet.

Kelly wasn’t usually this expressive, but KC pulled this out of him. He didn’t often share his affections so openly, but he couldn’t help but be anything but honest. Honesty was his way, and he hoped she’d understand.

“How long will you be in Montana, and when are you coming back?” she asked.

Kelly could sense something change in her tone. “Why do you ask?” he said, putting her on the spot. “I just think we should meet is all. Me, you, and Jenks maybe?”

“My brother is dying,” he abruptly announced. “Probably any day now.”

"Oh, no!" she exclaimed. "I am so sorry. What's wrong with him?"

"Liver cancer, I'm told." He didn't need to share this with her, but he wanted to. "We have some legal things to take care of, and I don't know how long it will take."

"Did your brother know you had come back? I mean, did he know you were alive?" She paused. "Is there anything I can do to help?"

Kelly could hear genuine concern in her voice. What the hell was going on with her anyway? Why would she care about him so much? Maybe she was crazy, he worried. "I need to take care of things, and it will take some time. I need to spend all the time I can with him. He had no idea I was back—or alive—and I thought he was gone too. It's a long story." He sighed, thinking of the weight of it all. "It doesn't look like I will be back for some time, a month at the longest."

She inhaled a long breath before saying, "We are starting a tour next month and won't return until just before Thanksgiving."

Why was she telling him this? He thought about what Freddy had said to him, that she might be interested in him. He refused to entertain this thought, as it was so farfetched. "I should be back in Long Beach by then," Kelly said. "This thing up here is just complicated, that's all."

"Well, you have my number, so feel free to call anytime. I'll always find time to return your call."

Kelly heard the disappointment in her voice and wasn't sure what to say. So, he offered, "I want to thank you for the kindness you showed me in the church that day. I was in real trouble, and it really helped. I will tell you about it when we meet up in November."

KC perked up and offered, "I will take you and Jenks out to dinner. Does that sound fair?"

"Yes, ma'am. Er, I mean KC."

She let out a small laugh and said, "Bye, Kelly Chase," and hung up.

• • •

Kaitlin felt lost after her talk with Kelly, but she couldn't put her finger on why. *Dammit, I probably handled that whole thing wrong*, she thought as she made her way out of the rear storage room, which was called the phone booth.

It was mid-morning on Wednesday when she joined the rest of the group in the main studio area, smiling at everyone as she sat down in the chair next to Lyn. They had started setting the agenda for the next tour outing, including dates, times, and venues. The group's manager, Jerry Mellis, was at the center organizing and putting the pieces together. The group would start in Las Vegas the first part of October, tour the Midwest after that, then return to California in mid-November. It would be a typical tour: perform, travel, perform, travel. The pace was grueling, and any sort of personal life was not possible. They had to give up everything and move at a frenetic pace to capitalize on fame while it was still there. Once the fruit ripened and fell from the tree, you were done. Kaitlin's isolation during these trips was crushing. She had given up so much of her young-adult freedom, and for what? Money? It always came down to that in the end. She loved meeting new fans and being in new places, and she loved to perform live, too, and she had to admit that she still loved the attention. Then there was her mother, brother, and record company. They were always pushing for more. The pressure was immense, and it was out of her control. She was the good daughter and would always go along with the program, never objecting, never complaining. She suspected that something was very wrong, but wasn't she able to control her life in some way? She cleared her head, dragged herself back into the meeting, and looked across the table at Roland, who mouthed the words "You okay?"

• • •

Just before noon, Frank shuffled out into the main living room to look for his brother. He gently opened Kelly's closed bedroom door, and Kelly was standing with his back turned and pulling items from his duffel. He was in a pair of sweatpants and a towel hung from his head. Frank gasped when he saw the patchwork of thick scars covering his brother's back and shoulders.

Kelly turned and smiled at Frank. "Quite a sight, huh?" he remarked, perhaps hoping to quell his brother's shock.

Frank said in a wispy voice, "I think Shelly has some lunch ready."

"I could use a bite," Kelly said as he turned back to his duffel bag and extracted a T-shirt.

Frank backed away, headed for the kitchen, and shook his head. *God*, he thought, *if I can help him live his life in happiness, please help me*.

• • •

The two men reconvened at the kitchen table, where Shelly had prepared soup and sandwiches. Kelly was hungry and immediately thanked Shelly.

"Where's little Danny?" Kelly asked.

"I dropped him off at our neighbor's place down the road. They have two kids about his age, and he could use a little play time today."

After Frank sipped some of his soup and then set his spoon down, he said, "We don't have much time, Kelly. I need to get right to business."

As if on cue, Shelly left the room. Kelly nodded as he motioned with one hand for his brother to continue.

"I made a call late yesterday," Frank said, "and I have some men showing up here shortly. They will chopper into Cut Bank, and I have a car there waiting for them. I don't want them landing out here—it will cause too much commotion. I have already made most of the arrangements to roll things over. They will bring a pile of paperwork for you to sign and me to witness. They are good men, and I trust them, for the most part," he emphasized. "We will get part of it done today and the rest tomorrow with a different group of folks. I keep them separate so one doesn't know of the other." Kelly was impressed with how his brother had thought everything through when setting up the businesses. "By the end of the week, it will all be finalized, and you will be in charge," Frank continued. "The other part we need to talk about is this, you will need one or two people with you whom you can trust with your life, preferably someone who is business savvy and knows a few things. Do you know anybody who would be willing to help you out?"

Kelly thought quickly and said, "Mr. Bradley Jenkins, you heard me talking to him yesterday on the phone. Jenks works for a large Wall Street firm and manages investment portfolios." Kelly worried that Frank would not agree with his second choice, but it was his to make. "As for the second person, Nance Siva is someone I trust. He is a Morongo Indian tribal chairman and the father of my girlfriend"—Kelly caught himself— "old girlfriend."

"Did you part with her on good terms?" Frank asked.

As the memory of her came flooding in, Kelly felt a deep pang in his stomach.

Frank's eyebrows shot up with an intense curiosity. "What's the story behind that? I'm thinking I need to hear it. Sorry for being so nosy, but I am guarding your best interests here."

Kelly leaned back in his chair and unpackaged the whole story behind Rita, Victoria, and Nance. Kelly continued with his alcoholic breakdown and recovery and how he would always need to go to AA meetings, remembering to mention Freddy and his relationship. He told Frank about KC, holding nothing back. He had rambled on for the better part of an hour.

When he was finished, Frank had his fingers interlaced on the table, had his lips pursed, and was looking down at the table. He remained silent for a moment, and then said, "You have had to give up so much, Kel. I want this thing to change your life." Then he reached over and clutched Kelly's wrist with both hands, and whispered, "*The* Kaitlin Chapin?" as he narrowed his eyes and smiled wide.

"Yes," Kelly said. "To be honest, she's been pestering me ever since I lost my cool at her house party."

Frank straightened in his chair and said, "Whoa, buddy, it sounds to me like it's a little more serious than you're letting on—or willing to admit." Kelly could feel his neck getting hot. "Well, I'll be going to fucking hell," Frank remarked with a big smile. "You need to be careful, big brother. This thing could blow up in your face, so be careful."

"I know," Kelly said.

• • •

Roland quickly moved around the table after the meeting, coming to Kaitlin's side and placing a hand on her back and guiding her away from the group. "What's wrong? Are you okay?" he asked, with furrowed brows and a concerned look. "You look like you've just seen a bad accident or something."

"Oh, Roland, you can't be serious. I'm fine," she said, giving him a reassuring look.

"Okay, but I'm not convinced," he said, locking eyes with hers. "This doesn't have anything to do with that troublemaker at the party the other night, does it?" he asked, tipping his head down, still staring directly at her.

"Now, Roland, you stop this right now," she said defensively, pulling herself away from him.

"Ah! I thought so!" Roland triumphantly exclaimed.

She escaped to a conversation that was ongoing between Lyn and Jerry Mellis. "Hi Kaitlin," Jerry said and nodded, and broke off with, "We'll talk about this later, Lyn." He smiled at Kaitlin and made his way to another group.

"How did things go?" Lyn asked.

"I'm not really sure, to be honest. I just can't seem to get a read on him. There is so much going on in his life," Kaitlin said.

"Kaitlin!" her mother called out as she made her way down the hallway. "Your father has come home for lunch, and I want you to come and join us. He hasn't seen you for a few days and wants to visit with you, so come on," she urged with a smile.

Kaitlin knew there would be no excuse to avoid this invitation. Besides, she had missed her father as well. She had become an expert at moving her food around her plate, cutting everything into ever smaller pieces and taking a bite occasionally. This tactic seemed to work. Most people would never notice. However, she was aware her mother was watching her every move. The three talked about her new condo, the rehearsals, and the upcoming tour to Las Vegas and where they would be staying. Her father was always so kind and gentle, never prying too much into her personal life and letting the small things pass. She loved him and thought the world of him. Her mother was inquisitive and wedged her way into every facet of her life, never holding back and offering her opinions on everything. Condos, men, cars, weight, food, sleeping, and on and on. Kaitlin felt utterly smothered by this sometimes.

When lunch ended, her mother said Kaitlin should stay the night. Kaitlin knew there was no point in fighting the battle, so, as usual, she acquiesced.

"Good," her mother said. "We can watch TV together tonight."

"What's on?" her dad asked, rubbing his hands together in anticipation.

Kaitlin was happy to see this pleased him so much, which made her feel better. She went upstairs to her private bathroom and purged.

• • •

In the late afternoon, after Frank and Kelly had finished their business and the other men had left, Frank went back to bed. Shelly followed with his medications. Kelly took the opportunity to take the new truck into town. As he pulled out of the ranch and onto the road, he realized he was a little unsure of his long unused driving skills. By the time he arrived in town, he had gained enough confidence to move with some assurance. His first stop was at the small record shop in downtown Cut Bank.

Chapter 16

Death and Business

The telephone rang.

"Hello?" came a man's voice.

"Nance?"

"Yes?"

Thank God he's in his work office, Kelly thought. "It's Kelly Chase."

"Well, how are you, son? It's sure good to hear from you."

"Nance, I have a situation, and I need your help. It's terribly important, and things have to move fast. I'm sorry to be so short."

"Sure, Kelly," Nance said, sounding a little uneasy but interested. "How can I help you?"

"If I asked you to hop on a private airplane out of San Bernardino and fly to Montana, would you do that for me?"

There was a long silence.

"Kelly, are you okay?" Nance finally asked. "This sounds serious."

"I'm fine, Nance, really," Kelly said.

"Okay." Nance sounded unsure. "Where would this airplane be taking me?"

"Your ultimate destination will be Cut Bank, Montana. You will touch down first in Long Beach to pick up Bradley Jenkins, then on to Montana. I will have you flown in by helicopter for the last leg of the trip. Are you okay with that?" Kelly asked. "I've found my brother and he—er—*we* have some financial things going on, and they are…weighty, let's say. You and Jenks are the only ones I knew I could call."

"Okay, son, how long will we be there?"

"I'll have you back the next day," Kelly promised.

"I'm really curious now, Kelly. What time do you want me there?"

Kelly shared all the trip details with Nance and finally hung up.

"Sounds like it went well," Frank observed.

• • •

The next morning, Monday, Nance Siva had his driver take him to the private ground-level departure area at San Bernardino. He was looking for a small Cessna-type aircraft but saw none. There was only the sleek Learjet 25C on the tarmac with stairs extending to the ground. A young man in a neat blue suit tapped on Nance's car window, which Nance rolled down.

"Mr. Siva?" the man said.

"Yes," Nance confirmed.

"I'm here to escort you aboard, sir." The man extended his hand toward the sleek new jet.

Nance was led aboard the jet, with his overnight bag and briefcase. He could smell the fresh leather scents emanating from the ten plush, beige seats interspersed with leather divans, and mahogany storage cadenzas with a small bar area.

"Anywhere you want, sir. My name is Paul, and I will be taking care of you on your flight today. Can I get you something for breakfast? Omelet, bacon, eggs, sausage, coffee? If there's anything you need, I will be more than happy to help."

Nance slid into the soft leather seat closest to him. He ordered coffee and scrambled eggs with bacon. He was still stunned by the whole experience. "Say, who owns this jet?" he asked Paul.

"Sir, it is owned by a private corporation. I can assure you this is not a lease or a rental."

What in the world is going on? Nance thought.

"You'll be happy to know that you and Mr. Jenkins will be the first passengers to enjoy her," Paul said proudly, and made his way to the small custom galley of the craft. The jet flight to Long Beach was silky-smooth and quiet.

Jenks timidly peeked around the entry bulkhead of the Lear, and upon seeing Nance Siva, broke into a smile. Paul stood aside as he welcomed the newest passenger aboard. Jenks approached Nance with his small bag in hand and deftly slipped into the seat across from the small table facing Nance.

"Mr. Siva, so good to see you again," Jenks said as he extended his hand.

"I wasn't quite expecting this, you?" Nance said. They shook hands in a warm greeting. "Do you know what's going on?"

"Not a clue. I thought you knew," Jenks said, and shrugged. "I got a call at home late yesterday asking me to be here. I thought I'd be boarding a Cessna, but this?" He looked around, obviously surprised.

"I guess we're in the same boat, my friend. Let's see where this adventure takes us," Nance said with a grin. "Order the eggs and bacon, it's delicious."

As they settled in on the flight, Jenks asked how Rita was doing. This subject always wore on Nance. He suspected that at some point there would be a reckoning, a price to be paid for the vow he and Victoria made with Kelly. He had a feeling that someday it would all blow up and they would risk losing the affection and love of their daughter.

Nance smiled and said, "She's doing great. The boy is growing like a weed, smart as a whip. Ben, her husband, is working his way up the corporate law ladder. Rita continues her research on her latest marine biology project. She loves her work. They have a good life." Despite sharing the news that his daughter was well and happy, Nance looked serious as he took a sip of his coffee.

• • •

Jenks had learned about the agreement between Kelly, Nance, and Victoria shortly after it was made, and he was tasked by Kelly to maintain the lid of secrecy. Now, after these last few days, Jenks had even more secrets to maintain. He wondered if he should share these with Nance. He had shared too much already this past week, so he decided to hold back this time. The thing with Kaitlin Chapin had really put him in a tight spot with both her and Kelly.

Nance was absently staring out the porthole window when he said, "I wonder what sort of trouble Kelly has gotten himself into. All this mystery is concerning, and this," he waved his arm around to indicate the jet, "is a lot to take in. Have you ever met his family?"

"I met his mother once, at your home, but never his brother or father. His mother was incredibly beautiful and charming."

"Yes, she was," Nance agreed.

Two and a half hours later, the jet landed at the airport in Great Falls, Montana. The two men were escorted off the plane and directly to a waiting Bell Jet Ranger helicopter. It immediately lifted off, and in about forty-five minutes, they were landing in a pasture outside an old ranch house that had seen better days. The men were deposited with their bags and the Jet Ranger was gone in an instant, leaving only a cloud of dust.

• • •

From behind the old house, Kelly and Frank stepped out from the back door and walked toward Nance and Jenks. Kelly and Frank met them halfway to the house.

"Nance, Jenks," Kelly said, "I sure appreciate you gentlemen coming on a moment's notice. I wouldn't have done it, but this is extremely important." Kelly continued with introductions.

Frank asked how the trip was, and Nance grinned and said, "I would have to say rather surreal and quite the adventure."

Franked laughed and said, "Please, come into my home and I'll get right to it. Again, thanks for trusting us, and I don't think you'll regret it."

Once they were all in the small dining room seated around the table, Frank began. "Gentlemen, I am dying…soon." He let that settle for a moment. "My brother, Kelly, whom I thought was dead, appeared on my doorstep Tuesday morning this past week, and you can't imagine my shock. It was emotional as hell for both of us."

Shelly came out of the small kitchen with a pitcher of iced tea, glasses, and sandwiches. "I will be out back if you need me," she said. "The little one is down at the Smith ranch." She quietly disappeared.

"Your wife?" Jenks asked. "No, she's my caretaker. I've never been married. I have terminal liver cancer, and I'm sad to say that my days are numbered." Frank took a deep breath. "Let me preface this. Once you've heard me out, you can choose to not be involved and we will both understand."

Jenks looked at Nance. "Okay, I think we understand," Jenks said slowly. "You guys aren't in some sort of trouble, are you?"

"It depends on what you call trouble." Frank smiled and suddenly went into a coughing fit. Everyone waited for him to recover. Frank wiped his mouth with a handkerchief and started again. "Your friend Kelly Chase here is now worth about one hundred fifty million—give or take." It was so quiet one could hear a pin drop.

With a jovial smile on his face, Nance said, "Come on, gentlemen. We didn't come to hear delusional stories."

"I wish it was just a story," Kelly said. "Please listen."

Nance and Jenks turned their attention back to Frank.

"Kelly, can you help me please?" Franked asked.

Kelly opened the sliding door by a nearby credenza and removed four four-inch-thick binders full of files and deposited them on the table before the two guests. For the next two hours, Frank explained everything the same way he had to Kelly. Nance and

Jenks were busily sharing the files back and forth, flipping through pages as Frank continued, sometimes stopping and pointing out a particular document and its significance. Nance and Jenks, at the conclusion of Frank's presentation, were both shaking their heads in disbelief.

"As we sit here today, Kelly's fortune continues to grow, and so does the responsibility," Frank explained. "This is where you two gentlemen come in. Kelly trusts you both, and he is going to need help managing all the details, projects, endowments, and charities related to this 'empire.'" Frank's yellow-eyed gaze settled on each man across the table, and all were silent again. "Before you answer, I have one qualifier that I demanded of Kelly before we came to an agreement. Kelly has promised me that he will never use his fortune and power to damage another person, place, or thing. He's assured me that there will be no lying, cheating, or stealing. I'll need those same assurances from you both." Frank let that settle. "Well, what do you say?" Before they had a chance to answer, Frank said, "Oh, by the way, you both will be handsomely compensated, but you may need to curtail some of your present employment commitments if you're going to be involved."

Nance looked at Kelly and said, "Son, you have had a lot taken from you and have suffered untold amounts before coming back to your family—back to us—*we* are your family. Speaking for both Victoria and I, we would be honored to become involved in this very worthy venture. Hell, I have a corporate law degree from Stanford that is collecting dust. I'm in."

"Will I miss my Tuesday-night bowling league?" Jenks asked, looking concerned. The others laughed as Jenks broke into a grin and gave two thumbs up to Kelly and Frank.

The group took a recess. Kelly followed Nance, who had walked into the back yard to enjoy the last of the warm Montana fall day.

"Nance, how is she doing?" Kelly asked with concern when they were alone.

Nance turned to him. "She's doing fine, son." Nance related the same details he had shared with Jenks earlier.

Kelly stared down at the ground, with his hands in his pockets. How could anyone understand how much he loved and missed her?

"Kelly, what you have done for her is one of the most unselfish acts another human could possibly do for another," Nance said, but Kelly kept looking down, and then he nodded his head and wiped a tear from his eye with the back of one finger. Nance pulled Kelly into a tight hug. "We all love you here and at Morongo, we will always be there for you."

• • •

Later that evening, Jenks and Kelly were walking around the old corral. Kelly asked, "Have you heard from Miss Chapin since we talked last?"

"Nope," Jenks replied. "Not a word. My understanding is they are preparing for a stint in Las Vegas, then travelling to the Midwest somewhere, then back home in late November sometime."

Kelly nodded as they continued to walk back toward the house. "What in the world is going on with her anyway?" Kelly asked.

"I don't know, maybe she's working on developing the talent she sees in you," Jenks suggested. He wasn't willing to reveal what his real suspicions were yet.

"Well, what you heard today probably removes any possibility of that happening. I am going to have my hands full for a while." Kelly was looking out across the rolling fields. "And I still need to figure out how I'm going to stay sane during all of this. This could drive a man to drink."

• • •

That night, after everyone had gone to bed, Kelly retreated to his own bedroom. He retrieved the records and small stereo system he had purchased, along with the new headphones. He had bought all the records that the Chapins had made, starting somewhere in 1970. There was that hauntingly beautiful voice. Every song was an adventure to him. So well put together and arranged by her brother Roland. Her vocals were flawless, impeccable. He had never heard anything—or anyone—like her. When had he first heard her voice? He couldn't be sure. Why had their lives come together? There was something about her rolling around in his mind. He just could not put his finger on it. Like a small sliver you couldn't see, yet you could feel it was there, somewhere.

The next morning, Shelly prepared a full breakfast for everyone. Danny was there, busy with his rubber army soldiers between noisily slurping from his cereal bowl and chatting away to himself. Kelly found the child's voice soothing. He hadn't been around small children for the entirety of his life. He found little Danny fascinating, both to watch and listen to. His pure innocence was a curiosity. He found himself wondering if he had been this way at one time.

Frank had not gotten up yet. Shelly sat at the table with the men and said, "He doesn't have much longer, and he's getting weaker by the day. The doctor will be in later today to let us know what to expect."

"We should stay at least until tomorrow," Nance proposed.

Kelly thought about it. "No, if something happens, then you'll feel obligated to stay longer, and that might keep you away from your other responsibilities."

Jenks said, "Hold on, I thought we were your closest advisors now. This thing that you've entrusted us with is a huge job, and you'll need our help. Besides that, I expect to give up my position at the brokerage. Frank suggested that I meet with the eastern group and get involved with their ongoing projects. I will fly out toward the end of the week. Nance and I have talked about it already, and we will hang out for a couple of days to keep Frank company and keep developing a strategy. We need to get as much information from Frank as we can for as long as he can share it."

"I only have a couple of months remaining as tribal chairman," Nance said. "After which I will retire from Indian politics. Lord knows it's been brutal. I am available right now and am excited to get started."

Doctor Jacobs was flown in from Great Falls to evaluate Frank that afternoon. In Frank's bedroom, he administered some medications, replenished the IVs, and fussed with the vitals monitor. Frank had not awakened that day, and there was already some general concern.

While fiddling with his stethoscope, Doctor Jacobs said, "He's resting with the help of the sedatives that Shelly was instructed to give him this morning, and the IV will continue to administer what he needs to stay as comfortable as possible. He may or may not regain consciousness again."

"I thought he had more time!" Kelly shouted. He had just gotten his brother back, and he was already losing him again.

"This type of sickness is unpredictable," Doctor Jacobs said. "Ultimately, it's a guessing game. I will stay here until…"

Kelly left the small, dark bedroom and went out the back door to get some air. Nance followed him out and said, "Kelly, with this new start, we can set this all up to allow you as much freedom as you want. I would encourage you to do the things you have always wanted to do, go places you've never been, enjoy life. I spent a little time with Frank yesterday, and he made me promise that we would make that happen for you. He told me he was so sorry that he wasn't going to have more time with you. He also told me to tell you to go find your father. Frank has left you a map so you can do that. Son, you have unlimited resources, so take advantage of it."

Kelly looked at Nance and said, "I'm scared of this whole thing. I'm afraid I will screw something up."

Nance let out a laugh and put his hand on Kelly's shoulder. "You couldn't screw this big machine up if you wanted to. Don't worry about it. That's why you have me and Jenks. We will protect you and all your interests, but you will need to make key decisions regarding money. We can't do that for you."

"I'm afraid it will turn me into a bad person," Kelly admitted.

"Kelly, I've witnessed firsthand the way you have handled yourself since Victoria, Rita, and I have known you, so I don't think that will happen. You are hardwired to do the right thing, and you'll know what it is each time you need to make a decision."

"She's going to find out, isn't she?"

Nance hesitated, looking out over the brown September fields. "Yes, she will eventually. She is smart and resourceful. With one loose thread, she'll figure it out. With all of this happening now, it may make it easier to hide, but it won't work forever."

"Then what do I do, Nance?"

"As we discussed before, you can only sit down and talk with her. She is certainly not going to leave what she has now." Nance paused again. "You will just have to let her go, and for you it may be best to find another person to devote your life to."

Kelly kicked at the dirt with his boot, nodding his head quietly. "Are you going to tell Victoria what has happened here?" Kelly asked.

"That's up to you. What do you want me to do?"

"Tell her everything. I want her to be involved. She is the closest thing I have to a mother." Kelly paused. "I better go check on my brother."

When Kelly turned to go back into the house, Nance was again left to ponder what the future would hold for Kelly.

• • •

Brother Frank died later that evening without regaining consciousness. Kelly was there to hold his hand as his heart stopped beating and the monitor beeped its final complaint. Although Kelly had already accepted Frank's death, it didn't help. He shook with tears as the doctor filled out the paperwork.

Looking at Kelly and shaking his head, Doctor Jacobs said, "A remarkable man. There are a lot of people who owe this man everything, and they didn't even know who he was."

With Shelly's help, Doctor Jacobs secured all the equipment into two large luggage containers. Jenks had made a phone call to Kelly's new concierge group. The Jet Ranger was dispatched, and once it landed, it scooped up the doctor and left the ranch just as the last rays of sun disappeared. Jenks got Sheriff Potter's phone number and notified him of Frank's death. The sheriff said he would have the local mortuary come right out to help.

Two days later, the three men, Shelly, and Sheriff Potter, along with a priest, gave Frank his last prayers, and then they silently lowered him into the ground. He was laid beside his mother, Deena. *She would have been so proud of him*, Kelly thought.

Shortly after the service, Nance and Jenks were carried away with another dispatched Ranger. They lifted off from the cemetery on the edge of Cut Bank. Sheriff Potter approached Kelly just as he had finished waving goodbye.

"Must be some pretty high-up folks, being able to travel around like that," he said, tipping his hat back on his head.

"Yes, they are, Sheriff. Yes, they are."

Chapter 17

Aloysius Chase

Kelly didn't get much sleep that night. As he lay in bed, he thought about all that had happened in the last three weeks. The party, the bus ride, the restaurant episode, Frank, Kaitlin Chapin, becoming a millionaire, and losing Frank again. He slipped on the headphones and put on a Chapin record. Her soothing voice came on, and tears filled his eyes as she eventually lulled him to sleep.

Early the next morning, Kelly awoke to breakfast prepared by Shelly. She and little Danny were sitting at the kitchen table. Danny was eating Cheerios and humming a tune. Kelly stepped out the back door, with his small AA book in hand, and walked some distance until he stopped to read the daily prayer. He continued walking, contemplating how it applied to him, and then he said a prayer of his own to his own personal Creator, asking for the power and strength to do the right thing on that day, to treat others well, and to not be an asshole.

After breakfast, Kelly talked with Shelly. He told her that it was his wish that she and Danny would always remain at the house. It would be their home as well as the Montana Headquarters of "REO Chase." He had decided to keep the name, for it was fitting and Frank's legacy. He would prepare to have a full remodel of the ranch house, keeping its original character intact along with expanding the square footage. It would look as it always had, until you went inside. The interior would be upscale and contemporary, with an abundance of overhead natural light and larger rooms. He wanted to bring the ranch back to its original purpose by adding a new corral, barn, and other amenities. Kelly made plans for a bunkhouse with a kitchen to house the crew that would maintain the ranch. He would stock it with horses and cattle again, thinking this would act as a good cover for anyone snooping.

Around mid-morning, Nance called with the latest information on all enterprises that were scattered around the country and other ongoing business projects. “I can’t tell you how much I continue to be impressed with what your brother has built. It’s amazing and so well organized. He has top-notch people wherever I look. They all knew who I was and who you are, and they are just wonderful,” Nance said. “We have been invited to every site the company owns, which we should start visiting next week. I discovered, too, that the company REO Chase owns a large commercial corporate jet. It will make overseas flights much quicker and more comfortable, and you can stay out of airports.”

Kelly’s head was reeling again. Nance finished his report with an update on the work that Jenks was doing in the investment arena. “He found a couple of things that needed some adjustments, so while he’s in New York, he will work on those fixes. Unfortunately, we need to make the name a little more visible. It will help things immensely. You know, names on buildings and such. I’m impressed with Jenks, too, being particularly great with people.”

“How’s Victoria?” Kelly asked.

“I haven’t told her anything yet,” Nance admitted. “I felt that you should be the one to deliver the news,” Nance said as he chuckled.

“Please tell her I love her, okay?”

“Sure thing, son. What are your immediate plans?”

“I’m going to find my dad.”

• • •

Kelly drove the Ford truck through the main gate entrance to the Ames’s ranch house. It was a large brick structure with grand arches and similar brick out buildings and garages. The spread was neatly trimmed with manicured grass surrounding the main house. Kelly leaped out of the high truck as he pulled his Carhartt jacket collar up. He could already feel the beginnings of the coming October chill. Before he could reach the front door, Joe Ames appeared in the doorway.

"Kelly!" he cried as he rushed out to greet him with open arms. "Old Sheriff Potter told us you had come home, but we were sure he was on drugs or something." Joe gave him a bear hug, grabbed his arm, and dragged him toward the house. "Where the hell have you been anyway? Somebody said you got killed in Vietnam or lost or something."

"Lost is a good word for it. Where's Marty at?" Kelly asked quickly, changing the subject.

"Oh, he's in Great Falls. He and another fella have a junky little recording studio that they've been trying to develop, but they're not having much luck I'm afraid. Come on in, let's catch up," Joe offered. "Did either of you boys happen to meet up with those girls from California again?"

Joe poured them each a cup of coffee and they both sat at the marble counter in the kitchen.

"No, not me," Joe said. "Dad kept me too busy. I think Marty was staying in touch with Gina for a while, but I don't think anything ever came of it. I could be wrong, though, so you'll need to ask him."

"What about Rita? I thought you two were getting married." Kelly looked at him and silently shook his head. "Too bad," Joe said with a shrug. "She was beautiful. You missed out."

"Yeah, I know. Wasn't in the cards, I guess." Kelly knew he had to follow up with Marty, as he had to close any possible loop back to Rita through her friends. "How's your dad?" Kelly asked.

Joe frowned and shook his head. He explained that their dad had been killed two years earlier when he was thrown from his horse and suffered a critical head injury. Kelly offered his condolences.

"Yeah," Joe said, clearing his throat. "Boy, that really threw us. I had to figure out this business thing overnight."

"How's the ranch and everything going?" Kelly asked.

"Well, truth be told, Dad spent a lot of money on some things he probably shouldn't have," Joe rolled his eyes, "and some people he shouldn't have. We're okay, but not as good as I would have hoped. Even with the oil money coming in, we're struggling." Joe looked away when he said, "We heard your brother died. I'm so sorry."

They both sat in silence for a moment before Joe said, "I see Frank still lived at the ranch, but it didn't look like he had much going on, though. Heard you boys had found oil on the property but that you didn't own the wells. I don't know how Frank survived."

"Yep, he was struggling," Kelly said. "Joe, I came to ask a favor. Can I use your horse trailer for about three days?"

"Sure, anything you want."

"And a horse with tack?"

"You want me to ride him for you too?" Joe chuckled. "Where are you going?"

"Up into Glacier."

"Let me call out to the barn and have somebody get that together for you. Your keys in the truck?"

• • •

Kelly drove through the little reservation town of Browning and into some even smaller towns until he was on a narrow road where the pavement eventually ended and became a rutted trail, which he travelled for about five miles, climbing higher into the heavy timber with the truck in four-wheel drive. He slowly navigated as to not injure the horse in the trailer. Kelly eventually reached a clearing where he was able to turn the truck and trailer around and secure it. He fed and bedded down the horse for the night and put together a fire with extra wood. He brought out his pre-cooked beef patties and warmed them up over the open fire. He set up his tent, and finally crawled into his sleeping bag with his .30-06 tucked next to him. His thoughts drifted to the girl with the beautiful voice as he sailed into sleep.

The next morning was cold, as the temperature had dropped considerably. Kelly cautiously picked his way up the mountainside, nudging the oatmeal-colored horse named Mush as he went along. He rode all day, taking several breaks to feed and water Mush and to check the hand-drawn map from Frank. Having not ridden a horse for so long, the feeling was glorious. It set him free and caused a wave of nostalgia as he recalled his earliest days of riding: his father's gentle coaching, the spills he took, riding full tilt through the hills, the feeling of a free soul. The only noises he heard were the breezes blowing through the treetops and the creaking of the woods. The smell of pine filled the air, and occasionally he would breathe in deeply to take in the scent. The temperature had gone up slightly, the wind still stinging his cheeks as gusts blew around him.

He had been trekking for some hours when he suddenly caught the scent of fire. He looked around, up, down, side to side. He saw no sign of smoke or where the smell could be coming from. He checked the breeze direction and moved into the wind, moving slowly and checking his surroundings. When he looked up again, a man appeared. Kelly moved closer. The man stood with a rifle cradled in his arms, wearing heavy buckskin worn to smoothness with a few fringes remaining along the sleeves. His father's skin was darker, more wrinkled and weathered than he remembered. His totally gray hair was in long, neat braids with leather twine encircling the ends. He wore leather leggings that extended close to his knees. He looked hard and tough. Aloysius Chase waited until his son came to a stop in front of him.

"Been waitin' for you," his father said as he turned and walked away.

Kelly followed his father into his camp, where a large, single lodge was standing. To the side there was a small sweat lodge covered in old tarps and blankets. To the other side were a pile of animal skins and a mound of antlers and skulls.

"Put your horse over there." Aloysius pointed to an oat bucket and water trough, so Kelly fed and watered Mush. "Come eat," he commanded, leading Kelly into the lodge. It was warm, with a smoldering fire in the center. Kelly removed his jacket and hat as his dad said, "Sit," and pointed to a hide that was carefully arranged.

It was clear to Kelly that his appearance was no surprise to the old Indian. Kelly did as he was told. Aloysius had his back to Kelly as he squatted down to retrieve something. He turned with a plate in hand and gave it to Kelly. Pemmican, roots, and wild berries. He followed up with a canvas canteen still cold from the water held within. Kelly realized he was hungry and ate with his fingers.

After some silence, Kelly said, "Dad, Frank is dead."

There was no reaction from Aloysius as he continued to look down at his plate and chew his pemmican. "I know," was all he said at first.

Again, the damned silence, Kelly thought.

"The last time we met I saw it in him. I have already grieved for my son," Aloysius finally said. "And you? Are you still dead too?" his father asked.

Kelly didn't know what to say. This man before him resembled his father, but his speech and actions were so different from the man he remembered. He moved easy, slow, deliberate, but with a confidence that struck Kelly as panther-like. He sat across from Kelly with that question in his eyes.

"I," Kelly started, "did die, but I came back."

His dad stared at his son and said, "Yes, you came back for the angel." Again, Kelly didn't know what to say. His father continued, "Sometimes we must trade what we hold dear. We look to trade them for something else of worth. These new things that we trade for sometimes look like they have no value, and sometimes we do not know what they are. In time we learn what they are and what they are worth. The Creator will lead us to these important things as he sees fit and when he sees fit. Smoke?"

Aloysius held up his pipe toward Kelly, who took the pipe, and Aloysius lit the bowl of tobacco. Kelly drew in the smoke, which was surprisingly smooth and tasted faintly of raspberries. He returned the pipe to his father. Kelly was thinking, *What the hell is he talking about? All in riddles.*

"Dad, what do you mean?" Kelly asked.

"I just told you, you'll know it when you know it."

Argh! Kelly thought, totally frustrated.

"Come, let's sweat!" Aloysius said.

Kelly hadn't been in a sweat lodge in years, the last time being when his dad constructed one years ago. They'd used it a couple of times, but it fell into disrepair. Aloysius stripped down to nothing and crawled into the small opening. Kelly did the same as the cold breeze burned his scarred skin. He crawled in behind his father.

Kelly entered the dimly lit lodge. He adjusted the mat on the floor and turned to sit cross-legged across from his dad. He saw the reflection of the hot rocks in his father's eyes. His dad was sadly appraising the scarred landscape of his son's body.

The heat was nearly unbearable for Kelly, and he felt as if his scars were on fire as he felt himself going numb, feeling nothing. He was sitting cross-legged with his head down, unable to move. He could hear his father's low chanting cadence as time was kept on a small hand drum. The smell of sweet grass came to his nose. Visions were passing through his mind like a large movie screen. Guns, strange languages, the cage, beatings, pain, Rita looking back at him and waving goodbye. There was the strange apparition of the female singer reaching out to him and weeping. Kelly began to feel a slow burning in his stomach that spread throughout his body and seemed to levitate him off the floor of the sweat lodge.

He suddenly became fully awake, sweat stinging his eyes. He felt like he'd just awakened from a long sleep. He crawled weakly from the lodge, found a water bag and drenched himself with the cool liquid, causing a large intake of breath. His father remained in the lodge for a minute before he came out and rinsed himself as well. Aloysius carefully arranged a bed for him in the large lodge. Kelly drank more water and realized that he was tired, more tired than ever before.

As his eyes grew heavy under the softly tanned hide covering him, he drifted away with her voice softly echoing in his head.

• • •

The next morning, Aloysius came into the lodge as his oldest son was coming awake. "Breakfast?" he called to Kelly.

Kelly was still groggy. He slept heavily but eventually found some energy. He realized that he hadn't felt this peaceful and relaxed since he was a small child. For the first time, he could not feel the healed wounds on his body. Being in the presence of his father added to his serenity and peace, feeling totally comfortable and protected. He made his way out of the furs covering him to a breakfast of fresh mixed berries, soft oats, and sweet roots he didn't recognize.

Afterward, his father led him to a mountain stream that rolled down from Grinnell Glacier. The old Indian handed him a large bar of handmade soap and took one for himself as he plunged onto a shallow backwash, yelling out loud as he landed in the near-freezing water. Kelly did the same, his voice sounding almost like his father's. They frolicked in the clear, icy water and enjoyed one another's company. Finally crawling to shore, completely spent, both men returned to the lodge to dry and dress in the warmth.

• • •

Kelly finished saddling up Mush and climbed up as his father gave him a small leather bag with a tied end. "Food for your trip down," he said.

Kelly stowed the bag, then looked down at his father for a moment, jumped off Mush, and engulfed his dad in a hug. "I love you, Dad."

Aloysius hugged his oldest son hard, and when he released him, he said, "When you think you have found this thing of great importance, bring it to me so we can talk about it, eat, smoke, and sweat. Okay? You will know what it is." Then he turned and walked away, disappearing into the woods.

As he made his way down the mountain, the old feelings of abandonment crept in. Thoughts of his mother, then Rita. When he reached the truck, he thought about what his dad had said about the angel, things of value; he was still confused.

Kelly secured Mush into the trailer and made his way down the mountainside. When he finally found the main road, he pulled over to check on Mush and then resumed his trip back to the Ames's ranch.

With his father and brother on his mind, the trip back was long. He was grateful for the time he was able to spend with them both, even though he had lost so much. The old Indian was coping in his own way, and he was at peace with it. His father had developed spiritually in a way that Kelly would probably never understand. Kelly had become oddly calm, serene, and, most importantly, pain-free. He was sure his mother was happy for how things had turned out for her husband and her son Frank. Once Kelly figured out what he wanted—and needed—maybe he could understand his father's questions. Time would tell.

• • •

"How much will you take for Mush?" Kelly asked Joe after pulling up to the Ames's ranch.

"You damned Indians, always trying to steal someone's horse," Joe said, shaking his head with a smile.

"I'm looking to buy some stock. I want to reactivate the ranch, so I'll buy whatever extra you have at a fair price, both beef and horse."

As they walked toward the house, Joe placed his hand on his old friend's shoulder. "I can help you with that. Come on inside, and we can make a deal."

The deal struck included a couple of herds of cattle and horses, Mush, and an old jackass named Burrass.

"What's with him?" Kelly asked.

"Fucking beast. You can't get within ten feet of him, or he'll kick the shit out of you."

"He must have been a real asshole in a past life," Kelly noted.

As long as he got Mush, Kelly was willing to take the bad with the good.

Upon returning home, Kelly called his assigned corporate assistant, whose job it was to do, get, and go anywhere Kelly wanted. Kelly thought he was based in San Francisco. "Mr. Cortez, can you please get me a ticket for a group called The Chapins? They're performing in Las Vegas on the twenty-second of October. Something private if you can." Mr. Cortez started asking all sorts of questions. "No, I do not want to meet them," Kelly clarified. "And I will need the name of a resource there to meet me at the hotel. Can you arrange that too?" Mr. Cortez assured Kelly he could do whatever he needed. Kelly thanked him and hung up.

Kelly had his company interview all the new positions he needed to run the ranch, including a general contractor who could do the specialty work requested on the ranch house and other structures. Everyone involved in the project signed non-disclosure agreements to keep the work on the ranch private. Work would begin the following week.

Kelly took some time in the afternoon to brave the worsening cold spell to ride Mush out to the old pond over the hills behind the house. As he rode over the top of the last two hills, Kelly could see several oil pumpjacks slaving away in the distance. Thankfully, none of them had been placed near the clear pond. He rode up to the pond, and when he dismounted Mush, he felt the wind blow gently against his back. Kelly took out his daily prayer book and began to pray, meditating as he looked out across the little pond, which had started to develop a thin icy sheen. He prayed for his remaining family, all his good friends in California and Montana, Rita, wherever she might be. He also prayed for her new family. After some consideration, he added a prayer for the somewhat bizarre Chapin girl, Kaitlin. As he stood thinking about her, he could hear her voice in his head again.

"Beautiful," he said to himself.

She was clearly a beautiful exotic creature. Her large, brown, haunting eyes that seemed to be crying for help. Dammit, though, didn't she have all those people and family around her? Wouldn't they know if something was wrong? Through the words to the songs she sang, her pain squeezed its way into your heart, then made it bleed. A chill crawled up his spine, not from the cold, but a different kind, the kind that made your hair stand up.

Chapter 18

Music

October 1974

Jenks arrived at his apartment on a Sunday evening after work, and the first thing he noticed was that his answering machine was blinking with messages. There was a call from Kaitlin Chapin.

"Jenks, I thought I had better give you a call to see if you had some time to call me back later tonight—it's Sunday. Call me around ten-thirty if you can. I should be home by then. You have my number."

Jenks thought about the last time they had talked on the phone, which seemed like ages ago but was less than a month. So much had happened since then. Kelly and his newfound wealth had completely upended Jenks's life. He had a difficult time explaining to his friends and family why he had quit his high-profile, highly compensated brokerage job for some job he could barely discuss. He could only tell them that his future was completely secure, and it was a job he loved. He was working for the best boss in the world, but one he could never talk about. All he shared was that he now worked for the "Chase Company." Jenks was fine with it. This job was more than fun. It was a non-stop thrill ride.

He wondered why Kaitlin would want to talk to him. If she wanted to talk to Kelly, she should just call him now that she had his number. Jenks made some phone calls and reviewed realtor flyers advertising some nice condos for sale. Moving was long overdue, for his current place was really dated. He heated up a TV dinner, made some more phone calls, and wrote out reports for his phone meeting tomorrow with Kelly and Nance. At ten-thirty, he dialed Kaitlin's number.

"Jenks, that you?" she asked after the first ring.

"Yes, it is, KC. How are you doing?"

"Good. Say, I've been worried about you. I tried to get a hold of you at work, but they said you didn't work there anymore. Are you okay? Do you need some help?"

"No, no, I'm fine. I just took another offer, one with better pay, benefits, and perks with a great employer. But thanks for asking. That is sweet of you to be so concerned about me. I don't get that often," he said with a small laugh. "Now, what do you really want, KC?"

"Jesus, you aren't a sucker for feminine wiles, are you?" She laughed, but then she turned serious. "Look, I haven't heard a thing from Kelly Chase, and I'm worried about him. It's just—"

"KC, you can call him. You have his phone number in Montana. He'll talk to you." He paused. "He likes you," Jenks offered.

"I…ah…I wasn't sure if he would want to talk to me or not. He didn't call, so I—"

"Call him. He'll talk to you. Okay?"

"Got it. He'll talk to me, but is he okay? Did his brother die?"

"Yes," Jenks said flatly. "I think he passed the day after you and Kelly last spoke. Kelly has a lot of family-business loose ends to tie up. It will take him some time."

"Would you be willing to join Kelly and me for dinner—if he agrees to it?" she asked.

"Where?"

"In LA, of course."

"Sure, I would love to. Set it up with Kelly. I'm all in," he said with real excitement.

• • •

The following Monday morning, after his Sunday prayers at the pond, Kelly's bedside phone rang at six. He had just gotten out of the shower and had finished getting dressed.

"Hello?" he said. "Nance, is that you?"

"This is Kaitlin Chapin—KC."

"Well hello, KC! You're up bright and early," he said. "Or have you not gone to bed yet?" he teased.

She responded indignantly, "I don't drink and do stuff like that, Kelly Chase!"

"No, I suppose you don't," he said with a smile.

"How can I help you, KC?" he asked genuinely.

"First, I wanted to offer my sympathies for the death of your brother, Frank."

"Thank you, KC. It was tough—still is."

"Yes, I understand that you had just reunited."

"It made it much harder, yes," Kelly agreed.

"Maybe this will help. I called to invite you to our last Vegas show on the night of the twenty-second. If you can get to an airport, I will send a plane for you and fly you down. All eats and stays will be on me, and the trip home, too, of course. There, that's my pitch. What do you say?" she finished.

He paused for a moment, wondering what the chances of such a coincidence were. He would gladly cancel his own plans to include hers. "I would be more than happy to take you up on your offer. When do you want me there?"

"Just like that?"

"Sure, why not? I've bought all your records and have listened to them all. In fact, you put me to sleep every night."

"Hey, did somebody kidnap the real Kelly Chase and replace him with a man with a personality?"

Suddenly, he became serious. "KC? Are you okay?"

"Why would you ask that, Kelly Chase?"

"I don't know, just call it a funny feeling, I guess." He quickly continued, "Look, I'm sorry. I apologize for asking. I don't know you well enough to be asking such a question."

"Kelly, I don't want you spending time worrying about me. I want you to come down and have a good time. I think you could use it. Heck, I will even throw in an official Kaitlin Chapin autographed picture." She laughed brightly.

He thought her laugh was the most musical he had ever heard… since Rita. "Thank you for thinking of me, KC. This means a lot, and I really appreciate the invite."

"One more thing," she said. "Remember, you still owe me and Jenks a dinner date in LA."

His mind was racing to recall their last phone conversation about her dinner offer.

"And," she continued, "did you know that Jenks has quit his job for another?"

"Really?" he said, deciding to play along. "Gosh, I'll have to call him to get caught up."

"You should. He thinks the world of you, you know?" She paused. "So we'll set up the date when we meet in Vegas—"

"Date? Miss Chapin, now I'm concerned," he said, mocking her.

"Oh, stop it, Kelly," she said, sounding embarrassed. "I will have our PA, Lyn, call you with all the details, okay?"

"Yes, ma'am."

• • •

As Kaitlin hung up the phone, she thought, *He could be thoroughly enjoyable and fun. Heck, I might have to put him on my list after all. Except for that question about me being okay—that was odd.*

She stepped on her treadmill and started running, ignoring the grinding feeling in her stomach. Well, he didn't have any money, but he didn't strike her as a gold digger either. She always remembered what he said about his unconditional love for his friend Jenks. She asked her friend Brenda what she thought it meant, but she didn't have an explanation. Then she called her pastor and asked him. She still remembered his answer: "Kaitlin, unconditional love is one of the purest loves, as it contains no motive, nor does it seek one."

Maybe it could still work, she thought.

• • •

Kelly hung up the phone, with Freddy's warning about seeking levels of dysfunction coming back to him, always sending out those pings looking for an echo. He didn't want to admit it, but he kept picking up those signals from KC. Why? She certainly wasn't a drunk or a wild-eyed drug addict—he was sure of that. There was something he just could not place. That unseen sliver.

Kelly made a call to Cortez, his PA, asking him to set up a flight for a future date to San Bernardino and to arrange a ride to the Morongo Villa. He had to meet with Nance and Jenks. He also needed to see Victoria, as he had not talked to her since he had come to Montana and his life had taken such an unusual turn. They used to have long talks on the phone, supporting him in his continued sobriety. Maybe it was a little strange, too, but he almost felt like he was talking to Rita.

He called Freddy.

"Hello," came the gravelly voice.

"Freddy, it's me."

"Damn, Kelly, I was just thinking about you this morning. I haven't heard from you in quite a while. Jenks has filled me in on most everything. In fact, just talked to him yesterday. Did you know he quit his job and went to work for somebody else?"

"Really?" Kelly said. "I guess I better call him and get caught up."

"What can I help you with, son?"

"Do you remember that talk we had about guys like me always

pinging signals out and sometimes getting pings back? And you told me to be careful because I was probably seeking a level of dysfunction."

"Yes, I remember. I have that talk with just about everybody I work with."

"Does that ever go away, Freddy? I mean…will I ever be normal?"

Freddy laughed out loud and broke into a dry, hacking cough. He covered the receiver, likely regaining his composure. He soon came back. "Does this have anything to do with that Chapin girl?" he asked. Kelly did not answer. "I'll take that as a yes. Next you're going to ask me if I think she's fucked up. I will tell you that I have no idea. But here's how this usually works, if you're wondering. As we progress in our sobriety and achieve some emotional maturity, how we view the world and the people in it changes. We are no longer drawn to the people we once were. They no longer hold an attraction to us. In fact, they repel us, and, at some point, we find it impossible to be around them." Kelly could hear Freddy strike a match and light a cigarette. He took his first long drag and then continued. "Now, your emotional antenna is always moving and changing as you grow physically, spiritually, and emotionally; it gains and loses stations as you go through life and continue to work your spiritual program. It will probably do that until you die—or if you drink again. It will all turn to static, and you may need to start over again. Does any of this make sense?"

"What if I feel funny around someone?" Kelly asked.

"Okay, knucklehead, what are you trying to say?"

"What if there is just something off about someone and I can't figure out what it is?"

"I mean, maybe it's not a bad thing."

"It's…just…something."

"Does she repel you? Can you not stand to be around her?"

"No, nothing like that."

"Welcome to the human race, Kelly. It sounds like you have the same problem the rest of us men have: how to figure out a woman."

With that, Freddy hung up.

Later that day, Kelly had Shelly drive him into Cut Bank. The first stop was the bank. He verified the account numbers that Jenks had mailed him. He now had a corporate account containing $250,000 for business expenses and a personal account containing $100,000. The bank president, Mr. Simmons, gave him a briefcase containing checks for both accounts, with a separate envelope holding two credit cards with unbelievably high limits. Kelly also requested a thousand dollars in cash just so he could actually feel what it would be like to carry a thousand dollars.

Mr. Simmons took him aside and said, "Mr. Chase, I've signed a non-disclosure agreement regarding you and your accounts. I can assure you that you have my complete discretion when it comes to your personal and business dealings."

Kelly, of course, had seen the bank statements and financials that described other bank accounts holding large amounts of cash moving in and out daily. Jenks and Nance were still teaching him how to understand these high financial reports and banking. The small bank accounts that Jenks had created in a small Montana town were a matter of convenience for Kelly. His head was again spinning with the reality of what was happening. It was too hard to comprehend.

"Thank you for your help, Mr. Simmons," Kelly said.

As Kelly walked out the door, he could feel the banker's eyes on him. He knew he didn't look like someone with such large amounts of cash and available resources. He looked more like a ranch hand who had just come in from a day of herding strays. Dressed in worn denims, worn cowboy boots, and with his shirt tail out, he was very hard to figure out.

The day had turned warm as the early October cold front had moved on. Kelly had Shelly drive him over to the only Ford dealership in town, where he took his briefcase, jumped down from the high Ford truck, and told Shelly not to expect him home for dinner.

He told her he was going to Great Falls and gave her a piece of paper with a business name and phone number on it. He also stayed in constant contact with his PA, Cortez. Nance or Jenks needed to have him available within an hour's notice if possible. He knew he needed to fix this somehow. He bought a used, one-year-old, four-wheel-drive highboy, black in color—a beautiful truck.

Kelly located the small recording studio owned by Marty Ames. He had done his homework and knew when Marty was most likely to be in. Kelly entered the front door and stood near the front counter. He could hear someone talking on the phone behind the partition curtain, speaking in an imploring tone.

"Come on, Mr. Bealer, if you just give me another week, I will have your money for you. I'm begging you, don't shut us off right now. We are so close to our big break." There was a pause. "Okay, okay, Thursday. You won't be sorry, sir. I'll see you then. Bye."

Marty Ames slowly came through the curtain and immediately saw Kelly. "Kelly Chase, as I live and breathe." He hurried around the short counter to give him a hug. "My brother told me you were back. Where in the hell were you? We heard you'd been killed. Man, this is a surprise. Kelly only shrugged. Come on back and sit down."

They moved back into the studio, and it was clear the little enterprise had serious intentions, given the equipment and console control equipment they had in place. Marty pulled two director chairs to a small bar table. "Are you and Rita still together?"

Kelly shook his head and smiled at Marty. "No, not anymore."

"Sorry, man, she was so cool."

"Yeah, what about you and Gina. You ever see one another anymore?"

"No, I missed out. She's happily married."

"Well, looks like we both lost out then," Kelly said with a smile.

"I guess we'll live," Marty said sadly.

"Say, Marty, can I use your phone for a second?"

"Sure, man, help yourself."

Kelly made a quick call to Cortez and returned to his seat.

"So what are you doing in Great Falls?" Marty asked.

"I came to make you a deal, Marty."

Marty gave him a quizzical look and said, "What's it going to cost me?"

"I want to invest in your studio. Say twenty-five thousand dollars for starters."

Marty sat stunned. "Kelly, please don't be fucking with me. I have serious bank issues right now, and my stupid business partner is off drunk somewhere. You probably heard me begging for my life on the phone when you came in."

"I'll give you five hundred dollars cash right now. Go find your business partner in whatever bar he's in and buy whatever interest he has and get his signature. I have a form for him to sign. It's all filled out for you to use. All it needs is your two signatures, and you're clear of him. I will become your new business partner. I will write you a check for ten thousand dollars right now so you can pay the bank note off, and then you can help me."

Marty's mouth was hanging open. "Damn, how did you find out about all of this anyway?"

Kelly had his corporate sources find out everything about Marty's business and his financial woes. He planned everything out so he wouldn't have to waste a lot of time. He had little time to execute the rest of his plan.

"Marty, I have resources," Kelly said simply. "I will let you run this operation without my interference as long as you help me with the studio, band, and recording work." He paused. "And you don't ask me any questions about my sources or money. Okay?"

"Well, shit, as long as everything is legal. Is that it?"

"One more thing, I will take ten percent of everything you earn. If you get your smash hit, only ten percent for me. Is that fair enough? Anything I earn from this venture I will split with you fifty-fifty."

"Okay." Marty shrugged and smiled. "I'm in, Kelly. When do we start?"

Kelly went out to his truck and got his checkbook.

A week later, Kelly drove to a private Great Falls airport, and with his overnight bag, boarded a private Gulfstream to San Bernardino. During his flight he was going over the plans that he had set in motion with Marty. Kelly had written a song for Rita that he hoped one day he could personally sing to her. It was clear to him that this was never going to happen. He cut two different demos at Marty's studio; one was for KC, the song he had sung at her home, which she seemed to like. He would give it to her when he met her in Las Vegas. The other was a song he'd originally written for Rita; he made five copies. He would, along with Marty's copies, have them delivered and pay for the airtime to play them, and Marty would distribute to country stations. They would be sent to the top stations in the Southern California area. It was expensive but a real lark for Kelly. He was curious to see if anything would come of a song he had written. Pure ego maybe, but he had to know. If this could get Marty on the right track and get him noticed, then it would be worth it. Marty had continued to write, compose, and sing his songs, never gaining any traction. Operating out of Montana was a huge drawback that Marty hadn't taken into consideration. Hopefully, this would get him the exposure he needed. Kelly enlisted Cortez to make all the arrangements. Upon landing at the Bernardino airport, there was a car and driver waiting to drive him to Morongo. Nance and Jenks would be there for a pre-planned business meeting.

Upon arrival at the Villa, Victoria was the first to greet him with a kiss on the cheek and a hug. "Kelly, God I've missed you," she said. "Come on in, let's catch up."

Nance and Jenks followed the two into the house as Victoria linked her arm with Kelly's as they walked into the grand living area. "What a strange turn of events for you," Victoria said, squeezing his arm smiling up at him.

"Jenks, at least two people I have talked to said you have quit your job and have found another. What have you heard?" Kelly kidded.

"Some rumors to that effect," Jenks responded with a grin.

All four sat down on comfortable leather chairs facing each other, and Kelly leaned forward and handed Victoria five new one-hundred-dollar bills.

"What's this?" she asked.

"I told you I'd pay you back," Kelly said.

She turned red and said, "Kelly, you didn't have to do this. It's too much anyway."

Kelly looked at Nance. "Have you told her everything?"

"Only that you had received a *generous* inheritance," Nance said.

"Victoria, I'm apparently now an owner of a large corporation," Kelly started. "My brother, Frank, who was far more business savvy that anyone gave him credit for, created this… I guess the best way to describe it is as an empire. I hired your husband and Jenks full time to help me run it."

She looked over to Nance, who was looking at his hands placed in his lap. "Is this why you've been acting so strange and sneaky lately?" She narrowed her eyes as she looked at her husband.

"I felt I needed Kelly to tell you himself," Nance said quietly with a small smile on his face.

Jenks picked up the conversation. "As of last night, value of all assets is over one hundred seventy…million."

She looked at Jenks and her mouth fell open as she slowly shook her head and flushed red again. "My God!" she exclaimed. "The person who deserves it most in this world finally gets something."

"Victoria, keep the money. There's plenty," Kelly assured her.

Between the three men, they related all that Frank had told them in the brief time they'd had with him. Victoria listened with rapt attention. "Are you still going to live in California?" she asked Kelly.

"We are reactivating the ranch in Montana, and I'm having it completely refurbished. I will probably spend summers there and winters down here. But I will do a lot of travelling, so I will be spending a lot of time in Long Beach and LA, as it is my home too," Kelly answered.

A business meeting with the three men was convened in the den. Victoria was allowed to attend and to hear all that was involved in upcoming business for that week. "God, there's so much going on here. It makes my head hurt," Victoria declared after two non-stop hours.

The four met in the dining room for a late lunch and Jenks led the conversation. "So, Kelly, How's KC doing?"

Kelly nearly choked on his soup, scrambling to compose himself and immediately catching Victoria's attention. Victoria raised her eyebrows and looked directly at him with her piercing, dark eyes. "Well, how *is* KC doing?" Victoria asked with a wry smile.

"Who's KC?" Nance asked, looking at each of the others with a confused look.

Victoria doubled down. "Yes, who is KC, Kelly?" She smiled, tipping her head to the side.

"You might as well tell them," Jenks said. "It has to come out eventually. Call it the price of notoriety."

"There's nothing to it," Kelly said sheepishly.

"That's not what I'm seeing," Victoria said, holding her wine glass by the stem with two fingers, elbow on the table. Nance still looked confused.

Jenks said, "KC is Kaitlin Chapin."

Victoria and Nance looked at one another, and at the same time said, "*The* Kaitlin Chapin?"

By this time, Kelly, thoroughly embarrassed, was looking down with a small grimace, turning red. His first thought was, *What is it with this place? Every time I come here my face turns red.*

"You may as well know the whole story," Jenks announced. "Kelly, do you mind if I tell it?"

"Oh, go right ahead," Kelly said. "I couldn't get you to shut up now if the house were on fire."

Jenks launched into his story, going back to the church when Kelly first met KC, to the house party a couple of years later, the subsequent meeting between Jenks, KC, and friends. Jenks shared the phone calls between himself and her, which were always centralized around Kelly. When he finished up, Kelly was busy fidgeting with his spoon.

"My, Mr. Chase and Mr. Jenkins, you boys have been awfully busy, haven't you?" Victoria said.

"Isn't she the one with the brother?" Nance asked.

"Yes," Victoria confirmed. "An overnight success. They have become quite wealthy, I'm sure. Well, I think it's very romantic."

Kelly thought he had better speak up. "You all may as well know she has offered to fly me to Vegas for her last show there this month."

"You told her yes, didn't you?" Jenks asked.

"Sure, but I still don't know what she's thinking. I mean, is she just feeling guilty, or what—"

"I don't think it's like that," Victoria interrupted. "Would it be so shocking if she had a real interest in you?"

"Exactly," Jenks seconded.

Nance was watching and listening with great interest. "Kelly, you haven't told her anything about…" Nance paused. "Have you?"

"No! Absolutely not. I don't think I'll ever tell her," Kelly said.

"Why not?" Victoria asked.

"Because she doesn't need to know. If she knew, she might act differently."

Victoria held up a palm toward Kelly and said, "Did you ever ask yourself if she thinks the same thing about you? That maybe… you're a gold digger? If she's still talking to you, she may already be putting herself in jeopardy. I mean, for all she knows, you're still this messed-up crazy man hiding out in Montana looking for his big-money break. Now you're in her shoes, wondering about possible motives. It seems to me that you are both taking risks at this point. You're worried she may not like you for you, or that she sees you as victim or some helpless recovery project. But maybe she really does like you, meaning she's taking the chance that you aren't some gold digger and that you like her just for her."

Almost in celebration, Jenks clenched his fist and gave the downward yank. "Yessss! What she said!" he yelled, pointing to Victoria.

The other three started laughing. "Damn, Jenks. Whose side you on?" Kelly asked with an incredulous look. They laughed again.

As Kelly prepared to leave, Victoria led him toward a corner of the dining room as Nance and Jenks went back into the office. "I know you need to talk about Rita," she said. Kelly tried not to react to the mention of her name. "She's still very much on your mind. I'm here to tell you again that she has a good life, and the decision you made three years ago was a good one. Now it's time for you to move on as well."

"I was thinking about letting her know somehow. I just want to see her again, is all," he confessed.

"Why don't we let nature take its course for now. Leave it in God's hands and let it play out. I know it's tough on you, but let's leave well enough alone for now. Okay?" She hugged him and kissed him on the cheek. "We will always love you as our son, and this will all work out someday, you'll see." Victoria always softened him, so he gave in for now.

"Hey, before you go, I want to get a picture of you all together," Weena said, scurrying into the room. She ran into the office and retrieved Jenks and Nance.

Weena, the photographer, brought everyone out to the front portico, where she posed and positioned them. She took four pictures of the group with her Polaroid instant camera, pulling each picture free and waving it back and forth to dry. She laid each on the small side table so all could gather around and admire them.

"I will give you your copy next time you come in," she said to Kelly.

Nance and Victoria walked back into the house, holding hands. Jenks walked Kelly to his car and said, "By the way, I leased a condo for you, Century Plaza in LA near the top floor—twenty-fourth story, I think. It will be ready for you next time you come down, furnished and all. I've made the last payment on your old apartment. You should stop by and collect the remainder of your personal items and clothes. I'll plan to have the rest moved to your new address. And one more thing, take this with you." Jenks handed him a black gadget about the size of a deck of cards. "It's a pager. Keep it on at all times, and when it beeps, you'll know to call me from wherever you are. I don't think it works in Montana, though."

"Damn, that's amazing," Kelly said, turning the device over in his hand. "Anything else, boss?" Kelly smiled.

"Well, there is one more thing." Jenks moved in closer and quietly said, "Kaitlin called me back and said that you were up for a dinner date for the three of us next time she's in LA. Is that true? Did you agree?"

"Why wouldn't I? That's what she wanted."

"Okay, just wanted to be sure."

As Kelly drove away, he recalled a conversation he'd had with Nance and Victoria, how they had to be careful meeting at the house. Victoria had to know where Rita was so there wasn't an unexpected appearance. Staying overnight was sometimes too risky, so they'd agreed that Kelly would rarely stay at the Villa overnight.

On the road, Kelly started planning the week ahead. He would stay at his old apartment for the two days he was in Long Beach. He and Jenks would meet for breakfast, and then together they would go in for his VA physical therapy and psychological sessions, which would take the rest of the day. He was sleeping better, but anxiety still overcame him at times. Since the visit to his father, his scar pain had been significantly reduced. This still mystified him. He was able to manage any remaining pain with breathing exercises, meditation, and medication when needed. They would touch base with Nance in the late afternoon. That evening he would go to an AA meeting and get together with Freddy. The next afternoon he would fly back to Montana. His thoughts went to KC. He wondered what she was doing. Probably getting ready for her performance tonight. Why was he so drawn to her anyway? Did she ever think of him? *Don't be silly*, Kelly thought to himself. Then there was Rita. Could he ever be with another woman after her without feeling unfaithful? As long as she was still out there in the world, he doubted he'd be able to do it.

He arrived at his small apartment, and everything was as he had left it only a month ago. It felt like he had been gone much longer. Kelly did some cleaning and dusting, although the place was spotless. He gathered all his personal belongings together and placed everything close to the door. They would have a van sent around to pick it up for him the next day.

The next morning, he drove to the usual breakfast spot where he and Jenks always met before all this craziness happened. Jenks was always there early, as was his habit. As Kelly rounded the corner to their usual booth, he saw Jenks, and across the table sat Henry Barney. Kelly greeted and hugged Henry, whom he hadn't seen in a long while. He looked fit and healthy. Henry had started an art studio locally. He was sponsoring other artists and teaching night classes at UCLB. They relived old times, laughed, and joked like they used to, but Henry had to leave to open the studio. He gave both Kelly and Jenks a business card and a hug and left.

"Boy, sure is good to see him," Kelly said.

"He's making his mark in the art world," Jenks said.

"Well, you sure got your jollies at my expense yesterday—all that talk about Kaitlin," Kelly said. He gave Jenks a grin to allow him some room to play along.

"Just a news report from the front," Jenks said. "Besides, if something bad happens, you'll have two more who will have your back. Nance needs to know about things like that so he doesn't get surprised. And Victoria, she's a strong emotional support for you, always has been. Believe me, I thought about it before I said anything. I didn't mean to surprise you, but I thought the direct approach was best."

"Well, at least it's out there. Besides you, Freddy is the only one who knows."

"Really, Kelly, I want it to work out. Every time I've talked to her she's struck me as a genuine, well-meaning, good person—maybe a little naïve."

Kelly interlaced his fingers on the table and cautiously watched Jenks. "I have to tell you, though, Jenks, there's something going on with her. I don't know what it is, but it's something," he said, trailing off.

"Hmmm," was all Jenks had to say. "On another note, pun intended, have you listened to the radio lately?"

"No, not really."

Jenks placed his hands on each side of him and leaned forward. "You should. There is this new song being played, 'You're Not Here.' It's a very interesting song that really tells a story—by some guy named J. Jacks." Jenks paused for a moment as Kelly froze. "This J. Jacks sounds really familiar. I know I've heard him somewhere before." Jenks leaned even closer. "You wouldn't happen to know anything about this, would you? What I've heard is the record companies have search parties out looking for this guy, looking to sign him up—"

"Oh, shit!" Kelly said as the color left his face.

In her brightly lit office with dark, formal paneling, Rita's stereo softly played in the background. It helped her think and work better as she prepared her report for the laboratory directors. And then, she heard it for the first time.

"You're Not Here"

I only have you in my memories
I know I try to sing them with no tears
I lie awake at night and rue the fears
I wish I could make it right
I never did get to say I'm sorry for the war we had
For the way that it left you sad

I thought every step I took led me back to you
Now scarred, scared, and broken, I'm all alone

You're not here
And I only have myself to blame
You're not here
And I only have this burning flame
Would you be here if you knew the man I have become?
You're not here
Beside me

You don't know that I am near, but you're not here
Yet I pen for you these words you soon will hear
It's only right that I should have the most to fear
I don't know if I saw you out today, I'm trying to remember
Were you in the crowd? Before the picture fades.

I thought every step I took led me back to you
Now scarred, scared, and broken, I'm all alone

You're not here
And I only have myself to blame
You're not here
And I only have this burning flame

Would you be here if you knew the man I have become?
You're not here
Beside me

Love is said to soothe the slash of a hurt so deep
For me it's not to be. I'm only next to you in my sleep
Friends tell me this, too, the pain will heal too in time
I object, I decline in this universe you never will be mine
You don't know I'm here, but yes, I am here.
But...

You're not here
And I only have myself to blame
You're not here
And I only have this burning flame
Would you be here if you knew the man I have become?
You're not here
Beside me

Rita stopped, sat down in her chair, leaned back, and took in the insistent soft beat of the acoustic guitar. The voice rose in pitch and dropped into a soft, resonant, raspy quality as it unfolded the words that transfixed her. Her emotions stirred. *What if?*

Sometime later, as she walked down the hall to the meeting, she wondered when she would be able to listen to the song again. "J. Jacks? I wonder who that is. Strange name."

• • •

As Jenks drove them to the VA therapy sessions, he feverishly spun the tuning knob through the stations trying to find the song. Kelly looked on with concern as Jenks swerved.

"—and you've all been calling for this one, radio heads!" a host said.

The song started to play as the host yelled, "Who are you J. Jacks? The music world wants to know!"

Volume up, song playing. Kelly listened in fascination as Jenks started laughing. Kelly had to admit it sounded rather good, even on Jenks's old Volvo radio. "Better batten down the hatches, Kelly. Rita's probably going to find out too," Jenks said, eyeing Kelly. "And who the hell is J. Jacks?"

"Just something I made up." Kelly winced.

• • •

When Victoria answered the phone, a distressed Rita was on the other end. When Rita suffered from memories of Kelly, she always called her mother. Apparently, Rita had heard a song on the radio that made her think of him. After Victoria spent time listening to her daughter and offering her calming reassurances, she hung up the phone and ran to the unoccupied den, turned on the stereo system, and started thumbing through the stations. Soon, there it was.

She listened carefully, and when the song finished, she said to herself, "Oh, we've got trouble."

• • •

With pre-performance electricity in the air, Kaitlin warmed up backstage and prepared for her fifth and final show in Las Vegas. She was especially uncomfortable because her stomach was cramping as she did her final voice exercises. That damn song she'd heard today. She knew that voice, and it would not leave her head. *Could it possibly be Kelly Chase? But how? He's somewhere in Montana. It isn't possible.*

She was on…

• • •

In Montana, high in the mountains, the old Indian sat cross-legged with his arms resting on his knees and his hands dangling. His long, gray braids extended into his lap. The fire before him was blazing, causing shadows to dance in the treetops. He was trance-like with his unblinking eyes staring ahead far away into the night, the fire reflecting brightly in them. The stars were a glittering blanket of diamonds set in the blackness beyond. The cold mountain air had begun to settle and call for winter.

Chapter 19

Revelations

Kelly landed at a Great Falls private runway. His baggage was collected and taken to his pickup, which was brought near the Learjet. It was running and already warm inside. The October weather had turned cold again, with low-hanging gray clouds approaching. As he drove to the ranch, he thought about recent events. In his last telephone meeting with Nance and Jenks, REO Chase had redoubled its efforts to limit any exposure, should anyone make any connection, whether intentional or accidental, between Kelly, J. Jacks, and the true ownership of the large private firm. J. Jacks was just another guy who happened to get lucky. The conversation had also included Victoria, as she had expressed concerns about Rita's discovery.

"She has her antenna up," Victoria had said. "She wants to talk things over when she and her family come for Thanksgiving in November. I'm not sure I can keep this subterfuge up much longer."

"We need to let it play out," Kelly had said, repeating what Victoria had told him. "It's a stretch to think she'd figure it out so easily. And I should be the one to tell her if the worst happens. I'm sorry I have everybody on edge over this. It probably wasn't one of my greatest ideas."

Everyone was quiet until Nance had broken the silence. "Then you'll be in Las Vegas next Tuesday to meet with Kaitlin Chapin? I want you to have some fun and not sweat over this."

"Call me and give me a report," Jenks had said with a small chuckle.

• • •

As a result of Marty Ames's demo being distributed to the LA country stations, he had started receiving calls from record labels. They were serious about signing him up. Marty, since he had his own record label, was playing coy and listening to all the offers, having fun with the possibilities—or so this was what he told Kelly.

The hunt was still on for J. Jacks, as the demo had created quite a stir. Kelly did not know anything about the record business. He thought he could talk to KC about it without revealing that he was J. Jacks. Then again, it could be too risky.

He made it to the ranch in the late morning on Saturday. There was minimal activity, but he could see noticeable improvements already. Nance had the company conduct interviews for a ranch manager who would be responsible for day-to-day operations. A selection was made, and Kelly looked forward to meeting him this afternoon. As he came through the front door, he could see that work had been done, as was obvious due to the demolished walls and exposed wiring and plumbing, along with a layer of dust everywhere. He had planned for Shelly and little Danny to live in town during the remodeling. Kelly could see the message light blinking on the answering machine. He pushed the retrieve button and heard KC.

"Mr. Chase," she started, "or J. Jacks, or whoever you are." She let out a small giggle. "Call me." Click.

He called her message number and an answering service picked up. He announced himself, was asked to hold, and waited. "Mr. J. Jacks, how are you today?" KC asked cheerfully.

He realized he'd missed the sound of her voice. "How did you figure it out?" he asked.

"A better question is how did you pull the whole thing off? I mean, you are in the middle of nowhere and you manage to coerce LA radio stations to give airtime to some unknown cowboy. How did you do it, Kelly Chase?" she asked with a genuine curiosity. She continued, "You forget I have an ear for vocals and voices. After you sang at our house, there was no way I could forget your voice."

"Can we talk about this later? Maybe when I'm in Vegas?" he asked.

"Okay, I guess I can give you time to make up some wild story to tell me."

"Thanks, KC. Look forward to seeing you." He paused. "Can I see you before the show?"

"Sure, I'll make the arrangements."

She gave him the details on where to go and what to do when he reached the Riviera complex.

Kelly called for a Jet Ranger chopper to pick him up on Tuesday morning at the ranch. He had constructed a landing pad for helicopters, complete with night markers. It was located over the hilltop to the rear of the ranch house. It was an attempt to limit neighbors seeing chopper traffic. If they did notice air traffic, he could explain it away as oil exploration activity. He was dropped off at a private runway at the Great Falls airport. He was escorted to a nearby Learjet, where the ramp was down and ready for him to climb aboard and make his departure to Las Vegas. He was the sole passenger. Sitting on the jet, the anxiety of seeing Kaitlin again was getting to him. He was looking forward to it, but she was smart and knew how to do business, and maybe was not as naïve as some suspected, so he wasn't sure what to expect. She brought out new sides of him, and despite all the surprises that had come his way lately, her desperate need to see him ranked at the top. He closed his eyes as the jet started to rumble, and all he wanted to hear was the sound of her voice again.

A little over two hours later, the jet landed in Vegas. A waiting limousine whisked him away to the Riviera Hotel and convention complex. He followed Kaitlin's directions and was soon escorted to an upper-floor suite. He noticed that she had spared no expense.

Their show that night was scheduled to start at seven, so they would meet in her dressing room at six. The plan was he would attend the show and then fly out the next morning.

Kelly called Jenks to check in. Jenks had investigated the Chapins' record label, B&M Records. He'd discovered that they were a straight-up operation.

"They were having money problems until they took a chance and signed the Chapins," Jenks explained. "Six months later, the brother-and-sister duo had produced what would become a worldwide hit, 'Next to You.' B&M's money problems quickly disappeared. Their ownership is competent, honest, and secure," was Jenks's final assessment. "When are you going to meet her?"

"At six this evening, just before the show at seven," Kelly answered.

"What do you think you guys are going to talk about?" Jenks asked.

"My guess would be J. Jacks." Kelly shrugged. "She's already figured it out."

"She has? How?"

"She's pretty sharp. Her big question will be how I managed to pull it all together. That'll be a tough one to answer."

"What are you going to tell her?"

"The truth, but not tonight. Later, in LA, I hope."

"Good luck with that. She can push pretty hard," Jenks warned. "Call me if you think I can help with anything. Otherwise, I'll hear from you tomorrow morning before you leave. There are some financial things we need to cover."

At a quarter to six, there was a gentle knock on his door. Kelly opened it to find a large Black man with a cleanly shaved head wearing a tightly fitted, black tailored suit.

"Mr. Chase?" the man said. Kelly nodded. "My name is Crosby, and I can take you down to meet Miss Chapin. Are you ready, sir?" he asked in a British accent.

Kelly nodded again, turned back into the room and slipped on his black cowboy jacket, grabbed the large envelope with the demo tape, checked his tie, his cowboy boots for shine, and said to the big man, "Let's go. Lead the way, Crosby."

Kelly had not made a habit of wearing a cowboy hat in most public places, as he considered it too ostentatious. He had let his dark-blond hair grow, so it reached his collar. He thought that he would fit in better. After a long elevator ride down, they reached a lower level. From there, Crosby led him through a maze of concrete hallways until they reached a plain white door with a simple brass plaque: KC PRIVATE.

Crosby reached for the door handle, smiled, and said, "Miss Chapin is expecting you, sir."

Kelly entered the private room. KC had her back to him as she adjusted the collar at the back of her neck. She quickly turned to face him, and his breath caught in his throat. He remembered she was attractive, but seeing her now, she was simply radiant, dressed in a bright-yellow pantsuit with decorative Native piping strips down both sleeves with similar designs along the buttons of her tunic. She greeted him with a generous smile and moved up to him, holding out both hands to grasp both of his. Her hair was long, straight, dark, and shiny, gently collecting on her shoulders. The light vanilla perfume scent he recognized from years ago filled his nostrils. He felt an odd shot of electricity at her touch—something he hadn't felt since Rita. She backed up a step, still holding his hands and looking up at him with those deep brown eyes. Those eyes that held sadness, that mental sliver again.

"Let me look at you, Kelly Chase," she said as she gave him a quick appraisal. "I see my claw marks are gone. You don't look the worse for wear." She smiled as she teased him.

"You look," he paused, "absolutely stunning, KC. I had no idea..."

She seemed to ignore his clumsy compliment. "Come, sit with me," she said as she led him by one hand to the nearby purple, velvet sofa.

With her free hand, she gracefully invited him to sit down. She sat toward the opposite end of the sofa, with her right arm casually draped over the back. She brought her legs up beneath herself. She gave him another quiet appraisal, which was starting to make him nervous.

"I—who," they both started at once, and then became quiet again.

"Who—I," they both started again.

"You go first," she said quickly.

"No, you first," he insisted.

She laughed. "Okay, J. Jacks. You *are* J. Jacks, aren't you? My brother is convinced, and so am I." Kelly nodded silently. "Is that a song for your girlfriend…er...Rita?"

"Yes, it was supposed to be," he said, stunned at how strange it was to hear KC say Rita's name.

"Well, I will tell you that it is just beautiful. It really touched me, Kelly. I have to say, I am a little envious of her." He looked at her quizzically. She continued, "A man who would give her up to save her, risk not ever seeing her again, that is a love few will ever experience."

Kelly turned away from her, placed his elbows on his knees, and leaned forward. He didn't want her to see him—or the building emotion.

"She will never know," KC said. "I'm sorry, Kelly. I wasn't thinking."

He turned back toward her. "That time in the church, I…" He looked away again. "I think you saved my life. Your voice and your touch. I hadn't felt or heard a woman in years. Your voice…" He gripped his knees. Getting the words out was harder than he'd thought. "I can't explain it, but it was with me before that day, like I'd heard it somewhere. Then, after you sang to me, it stayed with me—always. You reached me when nothing else could. Thank you, KC."

He looked back at her, his eyes starting to burn. She reached out for his hand and squeezed it gently, giving him a small smile as tears filled her eyes. Another shock ran through him.

"I can't tell you how much you touched me that day, Kelly. I have never forgotten you."

They both exchanged looks. He reached inside his jacket and withdrew the large envelope. "This is for you."

She took the package with hesitation. "What's this?" When she lifted the flap and peered inside, her eyes came alive. "A tape, for me?"

"It's the song from your party. I recorded a version for you," Kelly said.

"Thank you so much! Is this for me to fall asleep to?" She grinned.

"It's for you. You can use it any way you want. We—I—have lifted any copyright restriction for you. If you want to record it for yourself to sell, you can. It's a gift."

She reached out and took his hand again. "I can't do that. This could be worth a lot of money—money you could use." She shook her head and pushed the envelope back toward him.

"No, no, I insist. Call it repayment for wrecking your party and causing you any trouble with your family. It's for you, KC, to use however you want."

There was a light tap on the door from someone on the other side. "Ten minutes, Miss Chapin."

"You might not even like it," Kelly said. "But if you do, go ahead. I have plenty of money for what I do."

She shook her head as she stood from the couch, prompting him to get up as well. "Kelly, this is really sweet. Thank you so much. Whatever happens, I will treasure this gift, always, because of the spirit in which it was given. Why don't you join us after the show, about nine-thirty, and we'll grab a bite and talk some more. Okay?"

"Sure," he said. "I'd be happy to."

"Good, I'll send someone for you." She gently placed one hand on each of his shoulders and tiptoed up to kiss his cheek. "Now, off with you. I have to finish up here." She gave him a big smile and a nudge toward the door.

Kelly stepped into the hallway and realized that his legs were shaking. *What the hell?*

"You all right, sir?" Crosby asked.

• • •

Kaitlin closed the door behind him, turned, and leaned her back against it, with her hands still clutching the knob. *What the hell is happening?* she wondered. He had nearly swept her off her feet in a matter of minutes.

She started playing back what she had said to him about his girlfriend. *Oh, God, you just had to say that didn't you?* She pressed the heel of one hand to her forehead and exhaled. The memory of them meeting in the church flooded her mind again. How had he gotten so close to her heart? Dammit! Now she was going to have to put Kelly Chase on her list. How many boxes had he checked off?

"Still, no money, though," she said to herself. Immediately followed by, "Stop being so arrogant, KC."

She made one quick call to Brenda. "I think he might be in."

She hung up the phone and left the room.

• • •

Crosby led Kelly to his seat in the packed Riviera theater, which was center stage within a comfortable distance. He was placed between two teenaged girls who were with different groups of friends. They were chattering excitedly among themselves. The Chapins were soon introduced, and Roland came out first to introduce his sister. Throughout the evening, the band played their catalogue of hit songs. When Kaitlin sang, the audience was reverently quiet. Her pitch was perfect, vibrato expertly controlled, and tone exactly right. While playing one of the livelier tunes, Kaitlin approached the edge of the stage, looked directly at him, and gave him a small wave and a smile.

The girls on both sides of him eyed him simultaneously, with one asking, "Was she waving at you?"

Now others in the same aisle were craning their necks to look at him.

"Damn, Kaitlin," he said to himself as he sunk down into his seat.

Kaitlin finished out the set with a drum solo that was, by any standards, impressive.

"Girl's got talent, for sure," he muttered to himself.

After the show, Crosby appeared at the end of the aisle and escorted Kelly to the tour close-out party. As he entered the banquet room, he saw sixty to seventy people in various styles of dress. Band members, roadies, and other executive-looking types. He found a cooler and retrieved a can of cola. He strolled around, eavesdropping in on conversations as he went. He heard all positive reviews as he went along, but he also heard some roadies complaining about having to pack up and head to the Midwest tour starting in two days.

• • •

As soon as they were off stage, Kaitlin grabbed Roland's arm, "Is the audio van still here?"

"Doesn't leave till later," he said. "Why, what's up?"

"I need to go listen to this," she said, holding up the tape and wiggling it back and forth. "New J. Jacks," she said with a smile.

Roland started walking towards two promotors ready to have a conversation. "As soon as I get done here, I'll be right there."

She charged into the large sound van, located the large tape player, loaded the tape, found headphones, and turned on the machine. It was that same magnificent voice churning out those heart-rending words. The high notes were pure, the lower tones were earthy, raw, and just short of a growl. It was a love song with sole accompaniment provided by a grand piano. The recording was high quality. When the song ended, there were tears in her eyes. This man had to stop doing this to her.

• • •

Roland bounced into the van. “Oh, Roland,” his sister said and fell forward onto the floor

“KC, KC—oh, my God!” Roland shouted.

What happened? I thought she was just listening to music?

He knelt and turned her onto her back, and she was out. He pulled the headphones from her ears and checked her breathing. Her color had gone pale. He leaped to his feet and found a jacket hanging over a chair back and placed it behind her head. He then launched himself out the van door, catching two roadies walking by. “Call an ambulance! Quick, it’s KC. She needs help.”

Both men ran to the building to summon help as Roland returned to Kaitlin’s side.

• • •

Crosby approached Kelly. “Mr. Chase, Roland sends his apologies. Something has come up and Miss Chapin will not be able to meet you tonight. Another time, perhaps,” he offered with a sad look.

Kelly saw a noticeable shift in the room. There was a definite buzz of excitement in the whispered conversations. Kelly asked a nearby group if they’d heard if there was anything wrong with Miss Chapin. They all shrugged and stood silently, shaking their heads, looking at the floor, not responding. Kelly went to the nearest telephone and secured an outside line. He called Jenks's number.

"Jenks, something's happened here at the Riviera. I can't get any information, and no one is talking." He told Jenks that he was afraid that something may have happened to KC. "Check the hospitals in the area. Say you're family, rich—anything to convince them to tell you if she's there. I need to know if she's all right."

"Okay, okay," Jenks said, remaining calm. "I will ding your pager when I have something." He hung up.

Kelly felt a tightness in his throat when he found himself outside the banquet room. Everyone had been escorted out and the doors had been locked. Thirty minutes later, his pager beeped twice as passersby looked at him with puzzled expressions.

"Just an update, Kelly," Jenks said. "We have two sources checking things out at nearby hospitals to see if she has come in for any reason. I will page you when I have more."

One hour later, as Kelly was wandering aimlessly about the hotel lobby, the pager beeped again.

"Kelly, you were right," Jenks said, sounding exhausted. He must have been using every resource. Finding information on a celebrity wasn't easy. "She was admitted under an alias. Our man says he contacted the ER doctor, who told him she appeared to have fainted backstage and did not regain consciousness. She's resting, stable, and may be released tonight or early tomorrow morning. I will page you when I know more. Go to bed, Kel. Get some rest. She'll be fine," Jenks reassured him.

• • •

Kelly woke with a start, immediately hoping there was news about Kaitlin. He rubbed his eyes and realized he had fallen asleep with his clothes on. There it was again, a soft tapping on his door. He roused himself, answered the door, and peeking out into the semi darkness of the hallway. Crosby stood with his undiminished smile.

"Sir, I have a message for you," Crosby said and handed Kelly a small, white envelope. "She's okay," he whispered.

Kelly nodded curtly, and Crosby strode down the hallway.

Kelly closed the door and looked at the clock on the nightstand, just after two in the morning. He turned on the lamp and quickly tore open the envelope and read her neat cursive note:

Sorry, Kelly Chase. Had a little unexpected business to take care of. What a crappy date, huh? I'm okay. Please call me and let me know where you will be tomorrow so we can catch up.

– KC

Though Kelly wanted to know more, the relief of knowing she was all right was enough for him to fall back asleep.

• • •

The next morning, Kelly had just entered one of the casino shops when his pager beeped. Three people looked his way and then around him, searching the source of the sound. Kelly retreated to a house phone.

"She has been released," Jenks said right when he picked up. "There were some tests, but she seems fine. Just some sort of fainting spell. Her brother found her on the floor in a mobile audio van," Jenks explained.

"Okay, Jenks," Kelly said. "I'll call you in about an hour so we can talk business. And thanks again. Sorry to keep you up last night."

"Hey, I was worried too. She's a great person, and I don't want to see her get hurt."

Kelly called KC's number, but it went to the answering service and he was asked to leave a message. "Hey, KC, no harm done. I'm still at the hotel. I will be in my room for about another hour, but then I must get back to Montana to finish some business. Call me if you can. Otherwise, I'll see you in LA…or whenever," he finished awkwardly.

He got a fried-egg sandwich to-go and hurried back to his room. Forty-five minutes later, his phone rang.

"Kelly?" KC said weakly on the other end of the line.

"KC, are you okay?" Kelly didn't want to sound too concerned.

"I'm fine. I will be tied up with some business matters today, and I apologize for last night and not being able to see you again before you leave. It was fun spending time with you, and I enjoyed your company. Thank you for the gift." She sounded further away with each word. "My brother wants to talk to you before you leave. Can you meet him in room three-twenty-five at about ten this morning?"

"Sure, I'll stop there on my way out." He felt the tightness in his throat again as panic seized him. "KC, I'm worried about you. You don't sound well."

"I'm fine," she reiterated. "Now, I'll call you when I," she paused, "get done with my business. Go see Roland, okay?"

Kelly reluctantly said goodbye and hung up. The tightness wasn't leaving, but it was turning into a full-on attack. He ran to his bags, dug furiously for his emergency pill supply, and took a double dose with water. He sat down on the bed to give his symptoms time to subside. He felt clammy, unstable, and short of breath. Half an hour later, he regained some composure, washed his face, grabbed his bags, and went to meet Roland.

He arrived at Roland's room just before ten and tapped on the door. Roland opened the door just enough to look around the hallway and then motioned Kelly into the room.

"Good to see you again, Kelly," Roland said as he warmly shook Kelly's hand with both of his. "Sorry to drag you up here like this, and sorry KC couldn't be here. She has some personal things she needs to take care of."

Kelly laid his bags down. "I'm worried about her, Roland. I just talked to her on the phone, and something is wrong with her. She doesn't sound right."

Roland stopped, looked at Kelly, cleared his throat, and gestured to a chair. Kelly sat down, and Roland said, "I don't know what's up with you two, but you've had some kind of effect on her. I know she likes you."

"Nothing is *up* with us. We're friends—I hope."

Roland took a deep breath and let it out as he walked over to look out the window, considering what he would say next. He turned to look at Kelly. "Look, she doesn't eat right sometimes, and it causes problems. She didn't eat much yesterday, and it caught up with her."

Kelly was quiet. He knew he was getting close to a boundary he should not cross, so it was best to drop it. "I'm sorry for prying, Roland," he said. "Just a little worried."

"That's fine, Kelly. Thanks for your concern." He cleared his throat. "Now, KC told me about your gift. It's quite something. Are you sure you're okay with her—with us—having free reign to rearrange and release it under our label?"

"Yes, it's a gift with no strings. Call it a formal apology for the party disaster I created. She's welcome to do what she wishes. Copyright has been waived."

"Then you know about copyrights?"

Kelly nodded. "Whatever money she makes, she keeps. It's that simple. I want her to have it. I have enough money for the way I live, so I don't need anymore. I'll make it lawyer-official if you want."

Roland collapsed in the chair opposite Kelly and said, "No need. It's just that normal people don't do that sort of thing. You must understand why I'm suspicious."

Kelly was quiet for a moment. "Look, I get that she is in a position for someone to try and take advantage of her," he said, "or try to get close to her in some devious way. Maybe I'm guilty of that. I saw it as a way for her to trust me. God knows we got off on the wrong foot." Kelly shrugged, hoping this would comfort Roland some. "I'm going back to Montana; I have some business to attend to. I will hopefully see her next time you guys are back in LA. She wants to go to dinner with me and my friend. You know Jenks?"

Roland nodded, looked at the floor, and smiled. "You know, that's the second time you've made her cry—that I know of," he said as he continued to look down.

Kelly gave Roland a curious look. "What happened?"

"She had just finished listening to your tape when she collapsed. She'd been crying, and KC is not a crier. You have a strange effect on her, so I'm begging you…don't hurt her. She has had her share of disappointments."

"That's not my intention, Roland—ever!"

Roland reached out to shake Kelly's hand. Kelly took it, forcing Roland to look at him. "I promise," Kelly said, "I won't do anything to hurt your sister."

• • •

Kelly called Jenks after his talk with Roland. "Jenks, I'm worried about her, but I don't know what to do. It's really none of my business. I think I've interfered too much already."

"I can have some friends we know keep tabs on her. You know, in case there's trouble again. They can do some sleuthing and see what they can find out. Some things are bound to come up."

Kelly thought for a minute. "Gee, I don't know." He paused. "I wouldn't feel right about invading her privacy that much. Just keep an eye on her, okay?"

"Man, I think you need to spend some time with Freddy. When are you coming back into town? Do we still have a dinner date with her?" Jenks asked.

"I don't know. I need to wait for her to call me—if she does."

"Oh, she'll call, Kelly. She likes you," Jenks said with a small chuckle.

• • •

The next day, Kelly called Freddy.

"Hello?" came the gruff smoker's voice.

"Freddy, it's me," Kelly said.

"Well, well, how's life in the fast lane? Running with a pretty big pack, aren't you? I hope you don't mind that Jenks has already told me about your newly found financial circumstances."

"No, not at all. I just wasn't sure how to explain it all, so I asked him to help and explain it to you."

"You realize that this will really complicate your continued sobriety. You will need your recovery program more than ever. Your problems are not those of most men. You are now at a substantially higher risk of relapsing. Money can do things to people. Remember our talks about power, property, and prestige? Well, you have all of that now. It is a breeding ground for piss-poor, arrogant behavior." There was a silence between the two men. Kelly heard him strike a match, light a cigarette, and inhale deeply. "I want you to come and see me first thing when you get back to LA. Okay? So, what else is going on?"

Kelly told him about the trip to Las Vegas, leaving nothing out.

"Sounds like you have a bit of a problem, Kelly." Freddy laughed. "In love, huh?"

"What? Um, I wouldn't call it that," Kelly sputtered, totally taken aback.

"Some advice from an old man," Freddy continued, not seeming to notice Kelly's reaction. "Be careful about bullshitting yourself into thinking it's okay to hide a bad motive under a good one. Don't be playing games with anybody on this. Somebody will get hurt, and it might just be you." He cleared his throat. "And don't be spying on people. It's sneaky and underhanded. Don't go there. You're too good for that."

"But what if something else happens to her?" Kelly asked, not bothering to mask his concern.

"If you need to know, someone will tell you. Keep your distance from shit that is none of your business, Kelly. Trust me on this. And remember… Rule sixty-two."

"Rule sixty-two?"

"Yeah, don't take yourself so fucking seriously!" Click.

Upon his return to the ranch, Kelly followed up on the scheduled modifications. His new ranch manager, Del Bonds, was a middle-aged, tall, thin man with a mop of white hair. It hadn't taken the company long to screen the applicants and make a selection. Two company men from Minneapolis had flown in, and in three days, they had hired the manager. Del had only been in place for a little over a week and already had grasped what Kelly had in mind for the place. Del was from Sidney, Montana, and was an original stockman. He knew his way around animals and was intimate with construction. Kelly thought he looked Indian, further emphasized by his speech and mannerisms. Del and his wife, Stella, had set up shop in the newly remodeled bunkhouse and kitchen unit. Kelly asked him if he was sure that the accommodations were suitable.

Del smiled and answered quietly, "Mr. Chase, if I need something, I will let you know. I'm not shy. That okay with you?"

"Yep," Kelly replied.

They understood one another perfectly. Del had the answering service number and could leave a message for Kelly, night or day.

It was the end of October, and Kelly had decided to return to California for the winter. He was anxious to get back to familiar surroundings. There were also several meetings planned with Nance, Jenks, and other high-level managers for the company in the LA offices. Kelly, too, was excited about the new condominium that Jenks had set up. Then there would be the uncomfortable meeting with Freddy.

Kelly hopped on a Jet Ranger to Great Falls with his duffel bag early the next morning. He watched the ranch disappear below until city lights took its place. He arrived in Los Angeles in roughly three hours, landing at a private strip. The Gulfstream smoothly touched down and cruised to a stop. Jenks stood at the end of the stairs as Kelly bounded down to greet him. Jenks helped him put his duffel in the rear of a new Volvo.

"Nice," Kelly said.

"Finally decided I could afford one," Jenks said sheepishly.

"Good," Kelly approved.

After they drove onto the main road and Kelly was comfortable in the passenger seat, he said, "You know, Freddy was pissed about me putting a tail on KC."

Jenks looked puzzled. "What tail?"

"The deal we talked about a couple of weeks ago," Kelly reminded him.

"I don't have the slightest idea what you're talking about," Jenks said, eyeing him seriously as he continued to drive.

There was a silence between the men, so Kelly thought it best to change the subject. "How's that condo shaping up?" Kelly asked.

Chapter 20

Company Business

Kelly and Jenks soon entered a gated complex surrounding a twenty-plus-story building. Kelly had no recollection of this building located somewhere west of Hollywood, so he guessed it was new.

"This is Century City," Jenks said in his best tour-guide voice. "The street we came in on is the 'Avenue of the Stars,' exclusive and private. You may see some people you recognize, so don't be foolish."

They both laughed as they cruised into a tiled portico that led into a magnificent glass, chrome, tiled entryway. On one side of the circular driveway were three white fountains surrounded by lush, green grass with bushes and flowers all along the sidewalks and driveways. A valet tried to assist Kelly with his bag, but he insisted he didn't need any help. Jenks swooped in with a five-dollar bill and a smile. The valet tipped his hat and moved on. Kelly was gawking around like a tourist. They stood in front of a chrome elevator door giving a distorted funhouse view of them. Once inside, Jenks placed a key into a lock, turned it, and pushed the number twenty-four. Kelly was getting that weirded-out feeling again. How had he been transported to this magical land? He shook his head as the elevator whisked them upward, unable to hold back a smile.

"You okay, Kelly?" Jenks asked.

"Yeah, I think so. This is all so unbelievable."

"Talk about rags to riches," Jenks agreed.

Though barely noticeable, the elevator stopped and the doors silently slid open. Kelly's jaw dropped as he dragged his duffel bag into the most beautiful living space he had ever seen. A water feature about ten feet high with water cascading down a granite wall astounded him.

"It's not real rock," Jenks said. "Had me going too."

Kelly was speechless. Beyond the water feature was a bank of south- and west-facing floor-to-ceiling windows surrounded on the ends by light-colored drapes. The area was open and flowed into a dining room and kitchen with professional-grade, stainless-steel appliances. The views of Los Angeles and the Pacific Ocean from the twenty-fourth floor were stunning. The space was completely furnished and included wall hangings, one showing a copper relief of Montana state with a complementary frame. Kelly appreciated the masculine details, though it still had a comforting female touch, which reminded him of his mother. If only she'd had the chance to see this.

Toward one end of the living area was a dark grand piano. Kelly dropped his duffel and hurried over to the instrument. He lovingly stroked the closed lid and the key cover, noting the important Steinway brand. He pulled out the stool, sat down, and felt the piano cover again, and then reverently lifted it and sat back in wonder.

"Damn, Jenks, how did you know?" Kelly asked.

"Oh, just a wild guess," Jenks said with a smile.

That was when Kelly saw the picture of his mother, captured in a five-by-seven color photo encased in a simple dark-brown frame. It sat on a side table next to the piano. Kelly had never seen this picture before.

"Where did you get this?" Kelly asked, his expression one of wonder as he picked it up and gazed at it.

Jenks stood with his arms crossed, watching Kelly. "The day you asked Rita to marry you."

Kelly set the picture atop the piano and started to play "As Time Goes By." Jenks listened quietly as the powerfully clear notes filled the air. It changed the entire mood of the condo and gave it more character, christened it. As he ended the song, Kelly looked up at his friend.

"Thank you, Jenks." Kelly started to tear up. "This is a true gift."

Jenks turned away and cleared his throat. "Well, we had better get moving. We have a meeting downtown in about an hour," he said, walking toward the bedrooms.

Kelly followed along and finished the tour, continuing to be impressed. "We need to leave pretty soon if we're going downtown," Kelly said.

"That's the beauty of it. There's a helipad on the roof, so we'll be taking a chopper and landing on another downtown helipad. Takes about fifteen minutes." Jenks went on to describe the rest of the condo's features. "If you want to take a dip, there's a large pool, a spa area where you can go for a massage—whatever you want. It's all very private. My understanding is nobody pries into your business, and you are expected to do the same. I had all your clothes from the apartment cleaned and put away in the back bedroom. You have time to freshen up and change."

Kelly nodded and retreated to said back bedroom, still coming to terms that this was now *his* bedroom. As he was getting dressed in a suit and tie, he considered that maybe this was all some sort of hallucination that could end at any time, leaving him in a bamboo cage.

Forty minutes later, they were exiting onto the thirty-ninth floor of a forty-story building at 611 West in downtown LA. The long reception counter had a wood and chrome REO Chase logo mounted behind a receptionist who was busily answering phones. The area was large and sumptuous.

"Hello, Mr. Chase and Mr. Jenkins," the receptionist said with a cordial smile. "They are waiting for you in the conference room." She pointed down the wood-covered hallway with her pencil.

They entered through the double doors at the end of the hall. The meeting room was large and had extremely high ceilings. The windows extended from floor-to-ceiling with sunlight filtering through the gauzy window coverings. The walls, Kelly noticed, were dark, shiny wood with panel inserts. Pictures of numerous oil drill rigs noted the locations, depth, and yield of each. Photos of buildings and what appeared to be shopping malls were interspersed. There were twenty or so men and women chatting quietly and standing around the long conference table. When some looked their direction, all talk died down as they started taking their seats, each looking comfortable in the padded leather chairs.

Nance waved Kelly over. "Welcome, Kelly. So glad you could meet our great California upper-management team." Nance introduced each of them as they smiled and nodded. "Would you care to say a few words, Mr. Chase?" Nance said, putting Kelly on the spot.

Kelly hesitated. "I'm not one to do much talking." He nervously shoved his hands into his pockets. "Good to meet you folks. I look forward to getting to know you all better. Thank you."

There was a polite applause from the group as Kelly sat down with Jenks at his side. The meeting lasted well over two hours, and most of it was well beyond Kelly's comprehension.

Nance finally leaned over and whispered to him, "Don't let this intimidate you, son. After what you've been through, this is a walk in the park. You will learn what this all means in no time." He patted him on the back.

Kelly was grateful to have Nance and Jenks. He wasn't sure what he would do without them. The meeting ended and everyone gathered into smaller groups. A young lady opened the double doors and announced that there would be food and beverages up on forty. They made their way into an open courtyard area surrounded by a mezzanine with a wide, curved, carpeted stairway. Kelly had to continuously close his mouth as he continued to stare in amazement. *This is just not something someone sees every day*, he thought.

With the whole of southern California at his feet beyond the glass windows, it was nothing short of spectacular.

“Come on, Kelly, stop gawking like a tourist. Let’s grab some chow,” Jenks said, elbowing him.

Kelly spent the remainder of the week staying by Nance’s side and moving from one meeting to another on both floors of the building. Kelly made time on the second day to meet with Freddy, who did not have any harsh words or criticisms. He only offered continued caution and urged Kelly to re-double his recovery meeting schedule.

“You call me if you feel like the wheels are starting to fall off,” Freddy said. “I will see you at our next meeting.”

On Friday morning, he, Nance, and Jenks were sitting and having coffee in a private office on forty when Kelly asked, “Any word on J. Jacks?”

Both men looked at him, and Nance said, “The furor is apparently dying down, but that only means the efforts have gone underground. Still looking, from what I’m hearing.”

“And Rita?”

“She’s talked with Victoria a couple of times, still stuck on the idea that the voice sounds like yours and that maybe you did make it back and just don’t want to see her again. She wishes it were you but doesn’t want it to be you, either.” Nance shrugged. “I have a funny feeling it is going to come to a head sooner rather than later. But Jenks here tells me that a couple of people have figured who J. Jacks is.”

“Kaitlin Chapin and her brother knew it was me right away,” Kelly admitted. “But they have nothing to gain by exposing me.”

“I understand you two have a dinner date coming up?”

“I think so, if she’s up to it.”

“What do you mean *think*?” Nance laughed and shook his head. “One of the prettiest, most talented girls around and you don’t know?”

Kelly wanted to call her, but he didn’t want to interfere with whatever she had going on. He didn’t want to talk to Jenks about it, because he was afraid. Afraid he might tell him something he didn't want to hear.

"Well, you better call her," Jenks said. "Because I, for one, am looking forward to it."

Kelly had been thinking about her practically every moment since Vegas. He was trying to mind his own business, as Freddy had suggested. But maybe he had better call. Maybe she had made other plans and decided not to see him again. Then there was Rita, and though it hurt his heart to admit, he still loved her. He was so guilt-ridden over her that another relationship was impossible. So why even consider it? He had spent his nights alone in his new residence, trying his hand at cooking, playing the beautiful piano, and writing music. The views at night were beautiful, but he was just as alone as he would have been in his little apartment in Long Beach.

"Can I use the phone?" Kelly asked.

"Sure, please excuse us," Nance said. "Come and find us when you're finished, and let us know if we can help."

Kelly dialed his answering service first, and there was one message for him. It was from KC: "Call me." Kelly nervously dialed her number and was put on hold.

"Kelly Chase, where are you?" KC said right away.

He found his stomach aflutter at the sound of her voice. He thought for a quick moment, recalling Freddy's advice about never lying to her. "I'm in LA moving into a new apartment and going to my monthly VA therapy treatments."

"Are you okay?" she asked.

"Of course, but I should be asking you that," he said.

"I'm okay, just hoping that you would call me. I started thinking that maybe Roland said something to you that—"

"No, no, KC. I didn't want to bother you. I know you're busy."

"I wish you would have," she complained. "Look, we're in Chicago, getting set to leave this afternoon. We have a short break, and I'll be back in LA on Tuesday."

They were both quiet for a moment.

"What are you—" they both started at the same time then stopped.

"Oh no, not again," she said with a laugh, then continued. "Dinner at seven, Montoni's. Don't forget to bring Jenks."

She did sound better. It was good to hear the vibrancy back in her voice.

"Well, you've made my day," Kelly said. "Jenks has been pestering me about this for a week."

"Please tell Mr. Jenkins that I look forward to seeing him—and tell him I've missed him."

"He'll be over the moon. He adores you."

"He does have good taste," she said wryly. "And you, Kelly Chase? How about you?"

Kelly was at a loss. God, she could be so damned direct, which was one of the things he loved about her. Loved? Where did that come from? He threw it back at her. "I think you know."

She was quiet for a moment, and then started, "I can only suspect—"

"Okay, okay. I've been worried about you, and I think about you a lot—"

"I get it," she interrupted. "See you at seven." Click.

Now she was picking up Freddy's bad habits.

Kelly searched for Nance and Jenks, who were standing side by side, leaning on the mezzanine rail, and chatting quietly.

Jenks noticed Kelly first and said, "Did you reach her?"

"Looks like it's on for Tuesday night," Kelly said. He could not suppress his grin.

Jenks was smiling back, while Nance turned with his back against the rail, his arms crossed. "Jenks and I have been discussing your relationship with her," Nance started. "You can't keep this," he raised his arms and looked at all the luxury that surrounded them, "from her if you feel it might be standing in the way of things moving forward. Jenks feels that if things don't work out, she is not the type to expose you. What are your thoughts? Keep in mind you are the boss and can do whatever you want. We just thought we should give you some support if it helps."

Kelly was relieved; he was worried that the whole thing would fall apart and everyone would be mad. She might get mad; he wasn't sure how she would react, and maybe she would feel that he was trying to manipulate her with the song he had given her. There was so much left up to chance, and Kelly was worried that he wasn't doing any of this right. Still, he would go to dinner. He knew backing out wasn't an option—not that his body and heart would even let him.

• • •

Kelly and Jenks were dropped off at Martoni's by a company limousine. Both men were dressed in slacks and sport jackets—Jenks with his ever-present tie with a maroon dress shirt. Kelly wore a pale-blue shirt with one button undone at the collar, accented by his short beard stubble and his dishwater-blond, shaggy hair. Kaitlin had already made reservations. The waiter led them to a cozy, back-corner booth with horseshoe seating. The restaurant's atmosphere was warm and inviting. Many spicy aromas filled the air. Since Martoni's was a celebrity draw, it was known to discourage autograph seekers and encourage privacy among its staff and guests. Both men sat facing each other, fumbling and fidgeting with utensils, water glasses, and coffee cups, nervously waiting.

"We've agreed we're going to do this, right?" Jenks asked.

"I think so," Kelly said. "What happens if this doesn't work out?" Kelly's brow furrowed.

"If it really goes bad, I'll say I need to make a phone call and you need to go to the bathroom, or something, so we meet and figure out what to do next."

"What does that mean: 'really goes bad'?"

"If she flies off the handle and really gets pissed, I guess."

"If she gets mad, I only need to beat you to the door, so she can have you for dinner. I am outta here," Kelly joked.

"Very funny. You're the one with the guilty conscience and truth serum," Jenks shot in a hushed voice.

Kelly caught sight of the waiter coming toward them, closely followed by two of Kaitlin's friends from the party.

"Uh oh, something's wrong already," Kelly whispered.

They both stood to greet Brenda and Ramona. "Good evening, ladies," Jenks said. "What brings you out tonight?"

Both women were in classy black dresses and looked magnificent. "Hi," Ramona said. "I know you weren't expecting us."

"Yeah, KC couldn't make it, so she sent us to keep you guys company," Brenda interjected.

Both men had an identical reaction. Shoulders slumped and heads hung as if the power to them had been turned off, followed by a heavy silence.

"I told you!" Ramona said seriously as she elbowed her sidekick. Both women shared a smile as they looked at one another.

"God, we're so sorry. We were just playing a little joke on you guys," Brenda said.

"I told you it wasn't going to be funny," Ramona complained. "KC *is* here. She only sent us in to make sure the coast was clear and that you guys were here. We're really sorry. Hope you'll forgive us."

"Sure, no problem," Kelly said, instantly relieved.

Ramona held her arm high and twirled her hand. Kelly and Jenks both let out a sigh and regained their composure. Ramona escorted Brenda out by her elbow. "Don't you ever embarrass me like that again, Brenda," she hissed.

People at neighboring tables looked at them briefly, then returned to their conversations. Kaitlin appeared at the end of the aisle, walking toward them and giving a small wave and a shy grin. She was wearing a flawlessly tailored, sharply creased black pantsuit with a white blouse and black, mid-high heels. Her dark hair was finely coiffed, hanging in gently waving tresses around her shoulders. Kelly could swear she was glowing. He thought she was thinner than the last time he'd seen her. *Probably just imagining things*, he thought.

Kaitlin hugged Jenks once she was at their table. "You okay, Jenks?" she asked. "You look a little…odd."

She released Jenks and gave Kelly a tight hug and a kiss on his cheek. She looked back at Jenks, and then again at Kelly. "What's going on?" she asked, looking perplexed by their sudden awkwardness. "All right, what did those two do to you guys?"

"Oh, they were just having a little fun," Kelly dismissed.

"I will find out later. You can bet on it," she said, sending a quick glare toward the end of the aisle.

"KC, you look great. It's really good to see you," Kelly said.

She locked eyes with him, giving that deep, brown-eyed stare. He stood motionless.

"Well, are you going to let me sit down?" she asked with a smile.

"Kelly!" Jenks snapped.

"Oh, yes, of course," Kelly said as the spell broke.

KC eased past Kelly, and her hair slightly brushed his cheek as she moved into the booth. He drew in a deep breath of her perfumed scent and felt himself sway. He sat down more with a plop than anything gentlemanly. Both men eased themselves closer to her as she situated herself at the end of the booth. People at other tables briefly took note of who had entered the room, considered her for a moment, and returned to what they were doing.

As the three settled in, Kaitlin picked up a menu, and without looking up, she said, "Don't pay any attention to what Brenda says, Jenks. She just has a crush on you."

Jenks had just begun to sip his water and immediately spilled it all over his shirt, and he quickly grabbed for his napkin, his face beet-red. Kelly covered his mouth with one hand to suppress a laughing fit.

"Well, it's true. Can't you tell?' Kaitlin asked Jenks with all seriousness.

Jenks was incapable of responding, still too stunned. Kelly laughed out loud now, not able to contain himself any longer. Kelly looked at KC with watery eyes as she sat with the primmest little smile, still looking at her menu. He went into another fit, but soon regained some measure of composure. *Damned if this one isn't special*, thought Kelly.

"Seriously, Jenks, when you met with us three the day after the blow up..." She looked at him and winced. "Sorry, Kelly. It was the most touching and truthful thing anyone had ever done for me. You should know, too, that no one ever talks to me like that. They always try to keep me insulated from the rest of the world and the truth, including my mother and my brother. It's no wonder Brenda is drawn to you."

Jenks turned red again, the candle on the table enhancing the color.

KC reached over and clutched Jenks's hand and squeezed. She then took Kelly's right hand, capturing them both. "And you," she said, stopping to smile at Kelly, bringing color to his face as he looked down. "This feels like the safest place in the world for me right now."

The three ordered dinner and talked back and forth as they dined. Jenks talked about how he loved his new job, and Kelly talked about the ranch in Montana. KC was constantly getting the two to try bites of her dinner to elicit their approval. Kelly took note. Kaitlin was especially interested in how Kelly could produce demo tapes and get them to play at LA radio stations.

"It would be nearly impossible to do this from any LA studio, but from somewhere in Montana... How did you pull this off,

Kelly?" She leaned forward, resting her chin on the heels of both hands, with her elbows on the table. She narrowed her eyes, but her smile was friendly.

"I have a friend in Montana who has a recording studio and connections. He's good at what he does, and he owes me," Kelly explained, hoping that would be enough.

She leaned back in the booth, giving him an appraising tipped-head look, as if deciding whether she should believe him or not. "Jenks, what do you think of Mr. Chase's story," she pressed. "Is it believable?"

"Whoa, don't get me involved in any of this J. Jacks stuff. I don't know a thing about it." Jenks held both hands up in mock surrender.

Kelly met her eyes. "There is more to the story, and I will tell you all of it. I just need to protect someone for a little longer. Are you willing to wait for the rest? I will tell you right now if you want me to, but it might be better if you wait."

She nodded, suddenly looking much smaller. "You know, the plane ride from Chicago was really rough." She went on to explain how she got little sleep.

"Yeah," Kelly said, sneaking a quick glance at Jenks. "I know, my Learjet can get a little rough sometimes too. I think it depends on which one I use." He casually sipped his coffee.

"Very funny, Kelly. Now you're mocking me."

Ignoring her, Kelly continued, "Lately, I've taken to flying the Gulfstreams. They are much smoother and faster too. You should get one."

"Okay, I get this is payback for what those two did, but you can stop now," she said, looking a little shaken. Jenks and Kelly both looked at her without expression, not smiling. "You guys are starting to scare me now. What's this all about?"

"Before my brother, Frank, became ill and died, he created a remarkably successful business," Kelly said. His grip on his coffee cup tightened as nerves crept in.

Kaitlin was giving him her full attention. "Well, that's great news. Maybe someday you can lease a Lear like we do," she suggested seriously.

"KC, Kelly's company is worth about two hundred million dollars," Jenks stated bluntly.

She frowned and became quiet, leaning back in the booth and crossing her arms. It was clear to them that she was starting to shut them out. "Come on, you guys, please don't try to impress me like this. It's beneath you."

Kelly had his elbows on the table with his forehead cupped in his palms, looking down at the table. Jenks had interlaced his fingers and was looking at her intently. Both men were quiet, contemplating their next move.

Kaitlin heaved a sigh of frustration. "Okay, what is the name of this company?"

"Damn, Jenks, we almost had her," Kelly said, looking at Jenks smiling and shaking his head. They broke into nervous laughter.

She instantly leaned forward and gave Kelly a backhanded swat on his arm. "God, you guys are bad," she said with obvious relief on her face. Kelly caught a hint of disappointment in her eyes as well. "Seriously, what is the name of your company?" KC asked.

"It's not important," Kelly said.

"No, please tell me," she insisted. "I want to know."

"REO Chase," Kelly said in a small voice, clearly embarrassed.

"I'm sorry. I didn't mean to offend you. Please forgive me," Kaitlin said softly.

"You are forgiven if you allow us to escort you home," Kelly offered.

Jenks chuckled, his eyes darting between Kelly and KC.

"That can be arranged," she said, smiling. "Let me go to the ladies' room and make a phone call to Ramona and we can go."

Kaitlin paid the bill, slid out of the booth, and made a call at a nearby payphone. Jenks also hurried to a phone to summon a limousine. When she returned to the two men, Kelly thought she looked pale. "Are you okay, KC?"

"Sure, why do you ask?" she said casually.

Kelly shook his head dismissively.

Upon departing the restaurant, a large woman in a colorful muumuu beckoned, "Kaitlin Angela Chapin! I do declare, I haven't seen you in ages. How are you, little darlin'?" She approached Kaitlin and clasped her hands. "You really must come by and see me and John before you leave town again."

"Hi, Catherine," Kaitlin said as they hugged. "Yes, I will. It's just been so busy. You understand?"

"Oh, I do, honey. Touring is a pain." She acknowledged Kelly and Jenks with a nod. "See you soon," she said as she continued into the restaurant.

"Angela, that's your middle name?" Kelly asked.

"Yes, after one of my dad's aunts, or something," Kaitlin explained.

"That's such a beautiful name." He repeated the whole name once again.

KC looked from one man to the other, smiling broadly.

A long black limo cruised to a stop in front of them. A chauffeur promptly exited and held the door open. "Good evening, Mr. Chase, Miss Chapin, Mr. Jenkins." He touched the bill of his small cap.

Kaitlin looked surprised. "Oh, you really didn't have to do this, you guys."

"Nothing but the best for a princess," Kelly said, offering her his hand and helping her enter the limo.

• • •

High up in the mountains of Montana, as early spits of snow swirled about, the old Indian sat in his lodge before the open fire. He stared, trance-like, unblinking, into the distance as the firelight danced in his eyes. A tear rolled down his cheek.

Chapter 21

Odds Are the Goods Are Odd

Kelly, Jenks, and Kaitlin got comfortable as the chauffer closed the door behind them. They eased onto the large, soft leather seats, and Kaitlin moved next to Kelly so they both faced Jenks.

"Impressive, Kelly Chase. Great taste," Kaitlin commented.

"Where to, KC?" Jenks asked, somewhat distracted.

"I'll be staying overnight at my mother's house. She wants to see me in the morning. You know, where Kelly crashed the party." She squeezed Kelly's arm. "Sorry," she offered.

Kelly gave her a rueful smile. Jenks relayed the address he remembered to the driver. Kelly noticed that Jenks had a relieved look on his face as he adjusted himself in his seat.

"Where do you live?" Kelly asked.

She looked at him with a coy smile. "I'll tell you later," she teased. "What about you? Where's your new apartment?"

Kelly noticed Jenks had visibly stiffened. "I'll tell you later." He winked.

"Fair enough. Next time we meet, then?" she asked expectantly.

"What are you going to do with your new song?" Kelly asked.

"I listened to your recorded version, and it was absolutely stunning. I'm afraid to do anything with it," she admitted.

"You should try. It would be perfect for you."

"Roland can't wait to do some experimental arrangements and re-composition, but that's his normal reaction."

"I would love to hear it after you put it together."

"Whoever put the demo together did a quality job. My compliments to the chef."

"I will pass it on."

Kaitlin pursed her lips and looked down, like she was making a decision.

"When will you be leaving on your next road trip? Will you be back for Thanksgiving?" Kelly asked.

"Busy recording, but we will be back the week before Thanksgiving to work over the holiday weekend up near San Francisco. Maybe we could get together at the end of that week? Dinner or something? I'll call you," she offered.

"It's a date, Miss Chapin," Kelly said, smiling down at her.

The car quietly approached a stoplight. Kaitlin looked through the moonroof and saw it. In red, block, illuminated letters at the top of one of the taller downtown buildings was "REO Chase." She sat erect at the same time her eyes fell upon a small, bronze identification plate on the window behind the driver. "REO Chase LA Unit #24." Both men had given up on convincing Kaitlin of Kelly's wealth. The stop at the downtown intersection was not planned, but it had obviously stirred something in Kaitlin. She sunk back into her seat.

"KC, are you okay?" Jenks asked.

"Oh, I'm okay. Just thinking about tomorrow," she said.

Kaitlin moved closer to Kelly and laced her arm through his, and they enjoyed the sweet sounds of the Beach Boys playing through the speakers until she dozed off.

"We're here," Jenks announced.

The driver opened the door and Kelly stepped out and took Kaitlin's hand.

"You're walking me to the door?" she asked, pretending to be amazed.

Kelly was blushing in the low light of the front door, not knowing if she noticed. She turned and looked up to him. He leaned down and they enjoyed a soft, lingering kiss as his arms encircled her waist and hers wrapped around his shoulders. After a moment, Kaitlin pulled away, looking somewhat embarrassed.

She started, "I usually don't—" Kelly placed a finger on her lips and brought her hand up and kissed it. "Kelly, thank you and Jenks for the most fun I've had in ages. You guys are so good to me, and I don't deserve it."

"You deserve to be treated like that every day, and you should never live another moment without being treated like the princess that you are."

"Will you call me tomorrow?" she asked, finally looking up at him again.

"Can't wait," he said.

She turned, unlocked the door, and opened it. She moved quickly and gave him a quick kiss on the cheek, turned, and disappeared into the house. Kelly felt faint as he wobbled toward the car. Before he realized it, he was in the limo sitting across from Jenks.

Jenks eyed him suspiciously. "Are you going to be okay?"

Kelly appeared to be coming out of a stupor. "Man, she does something to me," Kelly said, looking toward the house. "She just pulls me in whenever I'm around her."

"Shit, I guess," Jenks said, almost to himself. He tapped on the window behind his head, and the limo drove off into the night.

• • •

Kaitlin closed the door behind her and leaned back against it. What was it this man did to her? From the very first time they met in the church some years ago, she had this undeniable feeling that she was somehow connected to him. It was a struggle to pull herself away from him that first time, as she was pulled away by her agent. She remembered her last look at him. The tears and pain in his eyes from something that had broken him, something big.

Such a great sadness for one human to carry. She was not an overly emotional person, but on that day, she started crying before she reached the back seat of the car. And it had just happened again. It was all she could do to tear herself away from him. He had treated her so wonderfully gentle, and what he'd said about her being a princess made her feel more special than she ever had. She was now left to contemplate what she had just seen in the car. She had to add up the evidence and find out the truth, no matter what. She did not want to raise the issue of Kelly's business again after she had dismissed them both so stridently. How could she have been so rude and unbelieving of these two men whom she had come to trust? Kelly even appeared willing to overlook her pudgy figure and care for her. She did not want to blow this relationship like she had done with so many others. Her mind raced. Where had she secreted her stash of laxatives? She kept moving them around to keep one step ahead of her mother's prying notions. *Yes*, she recalled, *in my second car in the studio garage.*

• • •

After riding in silence for most of the drive, Kelly said, "What's going on, Jenks? You've been acting strangely since we left the restaurant."

Jenks shook his head. "I was afraid you two would compare notes and find out you lived at the same place," he admitted.

"What?" Kelly said, leaning forward in his seat.

"She lives two floors below your condo. Honestly, I had no idea when we purchased it—just a coincidence. I mean, who would have ever thought to check on something like that?" Jenks explained.

Kelly leaned back in his seat, taking a deep breath and slowly exhaling. He would never doubt his friend for a minute. "I believe you. Despite your best efforts at matchmaking, I believe you," Kelly said, smiling at him. "How did you find out?"

Jenks looked away and said, "You don't want to know."

They cruised to a stop in front of his building, where Kelly was dropped off and Jenks was driven away shortly after Kelly stepped out toward his new home. As Kelly made his way up to his condo, he could not take his mind off KC, how wonderfully charming and funny she was. *Angela*, he thought. *What the hell is wrong with her?* She did look a little thinner, but not by much. *God, maybe it's cancer, or something.* He started to feel the tightness in his throat, and his breathing suddenly accelerated as he entered the elevator and keyed himself into his condo. *No, no, it can't be. I wonder what else Jenks knows.* He slept little that night, worried for the woman he thought he loved.

• • •

Kaitlin was up early the next morning, for she seldom slept any appreciable amount of time. She decided to go to her condo and forgo any visit with her mother. She was in a better mood than she had been in days and did not want to ruin it with a motherly encounter that undoubtedly would turn into a disagreement. The aftereffects of those encounters tended to hang around for days after, souring her mood. It always took a major effort to put them behind her. She was still curious about the previous night's discovery and had to get ahold of Brenda and Ramona once she reached the condo. Grabbing the keys to her second car, she went over her plan and headed for the garage.

Upon arriving home, she called and left messages for both of her friends, and then went through her ritual of weighing herself, followed by a long treadmill run. Exhausted and dizzy, she weighed herself a second time. One hundred four pounds. That couldn't be right. She knew she weighed less than that. She clutched her stomach as it cramped in protest when she stepped into the shower. Afterwards, her friends called and set a date to meet for coffee later that afternoon. Kaitlin needed some caffeine before then, so she made and drank some coffee and ate a small portion of oatmeal. Then she scrubbed her shower, cleaned an already spotless condo, and pressed her clothes and hung them in exact alignment. Her mother called, but Kaitlin let it go to voicemail. She did her hair and makeup, dressed, and left.

As she rode the elevator down to the parking garage, she had a vague sense of uneasiness that something was wrong with her, something like an unseen sliver in a finger, something nagging.

• • •

Bradley Jenkins was in his company office the morning after their dinner with Kaitlin. He nervously dialed the number he had placed in his wallet on that Sunday meeting with KC and her two friends. An answering machine picked up. He, still nervous, left a message for her to call him back at the number and extension he gave her. He rolled his office chair back, rose, and walked to the bank of windows overlooking the southern California landscape. He thought he should go to Nance's office and wait for Kelly to arrive, but then his mind wandered to the dinner with KC last night. It had turned out to be a wonderful evening, and he was shocked to learn of Brenda's interest in him. He knew KC was serious and would not kid about that sort of thing. He decided to leave.

As he placed his hand on the door handle, a voice from his desk speaker came through and said, "Sir, a Miss Brenda on line two."

"Hello, Brenda?" he asked with some trepidation, not sure if she would want to talk to him.

"What took you so long?" she asked without hesitation.

"I just called to see if you would want to go to dinner with me this Friday," he ventured.

Brenda was tall, her long, almost white, blond hair was something that always drew second glances from both men and women. Jenks thought she was out of reach for a mere mortal like himself.

"I thought you'd never ask," Brenda said. "It took you long enough. Did KC say something?"

Whoa, a loaded question if ever there was one. "Well, she may have mentioned you once or twice," he admitted.

"I'll have to talk to her about that," Brenda threatened in mock fashion.

Jenks and Brenda organized their first date as Jenks's heart started to race with excitement.

"Say, Brenda, we had a wonderful time with KC last night," Jenks said. "I—we—were wondering if she was okay. I mean, does she have any physical problems?"

Brenda was quiet, and then said, "Why? Didn't she eat anything?"

"It was kind of hard to tell—"

"Damned girl, we've been trying to get her to eat more," Brenda interrupted. "She's become obsessed about her weight and how she looks. Some press guy once called her chubby, and she took it to heart. Now she doesn't eat anything. I, Ramona, and a few others, including her family, have been begging her to eat more. If you can get her to eat something, you would sure win some new friends. We are all worried." Jenks was shocked to hear the words out loud, but he wasn't entirely surprised. "You know she fainted backstage in Vegas?"

"Really?"

"She just doesn't eat."

"Brenda, I've got to run. I look forward to seeing you Friday, and I'll call you later tonight. Can't wait to see you."

"Same here, Jenks."

As Jenks walked to Nance's office for their morning meeting, he made up his mind to reach out to some people in the medical community to see if he could get some answers. How could somebody just stop eating? How was that even possible?

After several telephone conversations throughout the afternoon, Jenks had been linked up to some high-profile physicians, two of which called themselves "eating disorder specialists." They were both located on the East Coast. Dr. Bender, after some conversation, asked Jenks if this concerned someone in his family.

"No, just a very special friend, a young lady we all love. We are all worried about her," Jenks said, trying to be delicate.

"Ah, of course," the doctor commented. "It's called anorexia nervosa."

"What?"

The doctor repeated himself, carefully spelling it out and pronouncing each syllable. "There is much we don't know. But I can tell you this, it can be fatal when things ultimately reach a breaking point. The best we can do as physicians is feed them intravenously or directly through the nose or mouth, which is extremely uncomfortable."

Jenks, who was standing at his desk, fell into his chair in shock. "Why don't they just eat!" he exclaimed.

"I tell you what, there is only one person I know of who can probably answer that question. She is a professor at a university in Houston, Texas, a psychiatrist specializing in this sort of thing. Dr. Brush, I believe is her name."

Jenks heard the doctor opening and closing drawers, then the rustling of paper as he gave Jenks her contact information. Jenks thanked him profusely and hung up.

"Fatal? Shit!" Jenks exclaimed, still stunned.

Who had ever heard of such a fucking thing?

Jenks walked out of his office to the mezzanine rail, absently gazing to the floor below, watching the busy comings and goings of company employees. As he leaned on the rail, he wondered if he was making too much of this whole thing. Was it really any of his business?

Jenks jumped as Kelly yelled his name after quietly coming up behind him, closely followed by Nance.

"We haven't seen you all day, so we came down to check on you," Nance said.

"Yeah, been kind of tied up," Jenks said with a deep frown creasing his features. "Can we talk in my office?" Jenks extended his hand toward his door.

Once the three were alone, Jenks explained everything that he had learned that afternoon and what his suspicions were. Nance and Kelly were incredulous.

"I think there might be something to it. There is something going on with her," Kelly said. "Did you notice that she barely ate anything last night?"

"Yes, she gave most of it to us a spoonful at a time."

"Pretty slick. It means she's perfected her methods," Kelly pointed out.

"Why would you two even suspect something was wrong?" Nance asked.

Kelly and Jenks looked at each other, and came to a silent, mutual agreement.

"We know she fell unconscious in Vegas after her show and had to be hospitalized," Jenks said.

"She disappeared for a day or so afterward. Her brother admitted she doesn't eat like she is supposed to," Kelly said.

Jenks said, "Then her friend, whom I just talked to this morning, says she never eats and keeps losing weight."

"She looks to be getting thinner each time I see her," Kelly added. "It doesn't seem as though her family and friends have any answers."

Nance slowly shook his head. "My advice is to steer clear of this whole thing. It's really none of your business."

"Jenks, do you remember when you and Freddy came to see me in the hospital after…" Kelly started.

"Yes, I do, but what's that got to do with this?" Jenks asked.

"Can you just humor me and tell Nance what you remember?"

Jenks leaned back in his chair, his hands behind his head, and related the hospital incident where Kelly seemed to have died and then came back to life saying he was told to come back for the angel. Jenks went on to explain how Kelly had changed after that. Jenks, and Kelly's sponsor Freddy, had both heard the same thing, and neither had an explanation. Kelly remembered something about an angel he had to come back for, more of a feeling, really.

Nance listened, with his elbows on each arm of his chair. Kelly continued the explanation. "Then, last night we discovered her middle name was Angela!"

"By God, that's right," Jenks said, bringing himself forward in his chair.

Nance lifted his head and looked at them both. "Do you really think—"

"I don't know," Kelly said. "Now, I've never told anyone what I am about to tell you guys. Nance, do you remember when I went up in the mountains and found my father?"

"Yes, you did tell me you found him, but no more than that."

"That's because you would have thought me an absolute lunatic. My father, Aloysius, is said to be a healer by the Blackfeet people. They say he has powers." Nance and Jenks were both watching him, waiting for his next words. "When I found him, I knew it was him, but he had changed so dramatically. He knew things—said some things. He knew Frank had just died and that I would one day return home. He knew I was alive, and he knew I'd died in that hospital." Kelly stopped to collect himself. "He did a sweat ceremony with me, and it was like I went through my POW years and that death again. I saw myself outside of myself. God, this is not making any sense, is it?"

Both men shrugged, not saying anything but waiting for more.

"I felt as if I'd been burned up from the inside out," Kelly continued. "Then I found peace, a feeling I'd only known after my death.

I was completely free of any nagging pain. I slept for an entire day in his lodge after the sweat. When I awoke, he told me some things that didn't make any sense. But the one thing I do remember is he told me that I had to come back for the angel. And he told me to bring the angel to him. I remember that because of what you and Freddy heard me say. Now, her name: Angela."

The three men said nothing for a time. Finally, Jenks said, "Kelly, we have one more call to make. Nance, do you want to sit in?"

"Given the circumstances and potential company liability, I suppose I should," Nance said.

• • •

Jenks called Brenda later that evening from home. He wanted to make sure their plans were firmed up for Friday night and that nothing had changed. Truth was he only wanted to hear her voice again and take his mind off the phone call with Dr. Brush.

"Hello," Brenda said when she answered.

"It's Jenks," he announced.

"Gosh, first I hear nothing and then I can't shoo you away with a stick."

"I just wanted to ask you where you wanted to go tomorrow night."

Without hesitation, she said, "The Rainbow on Sunset. We can do some stargazing."

"I'll make the date."

"What in the world did your boy Kelly do to KC?" Brenda asked, though she didn't sound too serious.

"Why? Is she okay?" Jenks asked with genuine concern.

"She is crazy for Kelly—I can tell you that. Man, we've never seen her this way. Ramona and I had a late lunch with her, and she is beyond the moon, actually tearing up at one point. KC doesn't cry, so that's weird for her."

"Then that makes two of them," Jenks blurted out before he could stop himself.

"That makes me feel better, Jenks. Ramona and I are worried about her, and I don't think she can take an emotional hit right now. She has a lot going on with TV and interviews coming up in the next two weeks. There is one thing we are still concerned about," Brenda continued. "We know that KC had an item on her list." She hesitated. "I don't want this to seem unkind in any way, more of something to look out for," she said with warning. "She wants that special person to have some substance."

"Substance?"

Brenda let out a heavy sigh. "Money, Jenks, money," she stressed.

"Oh, yes, that." Jenks sighed. "From what I understand, they've worked that out. It did come up last night."

"Really? Then everything is okay?"

"As far as I know," he said. *Except for the fucking fact she might die*, he thought.

• • •

Upon arriving at the Century, Kelly asked the limo driver if there was another entrance he could use. He was directed around the side of the building to a more discreet entrance. His condo key worked in the electric lock provided. He wondered if she was home and was tempted to knock on her door and surprise her, but he remembered he did not have access to her floor. He would have to call her first. She may not even be there. In any event, he needed to go to his condo and think about what to do next. He had been on the edge of an anxiety attack all afternoon since his talk with Jenks and Nance. Then there was the call with Dr. Brush.

The doctor had accepted the conference call with the three men. Company contacts had been able to gain an hour of her time.

Dr. Brush greeted them in her heavy German accent after they had introduced themselves. Jenks managed to lay out their suspicions about Kaitlin's condition. He was sure to point out that the young female in her early twenties was someone well known. The young woman did not know they were calling about her or that they were distraught. Jenks recapped his talk with Dr. Bender and explained how he'd been referred to her. Jenks and Kelly shared what they knew about Kaitlin's history to the best of their ability, doing their best to paint the picture.

She started, "Anorexia nervosa, or AN. There is still much we do not know. However, I have made it my life's work to learn as much as I can about this disease and develop methods to treat it. I have had some success and have observed some recoveries. I have also had to watch some die—those none of us could save. Heartbreaking." She went on to explain how complex AN was. "Possibly stemming from the delusion that they are overweight, not thin enough. This may be complicated by the need for approval from members—or a member—of their immediate family. They are in constant need of approval from this person, but they never receive it. Love is withheld or no recognition is offered by this key person. Those suffering from AN feel out of control and in a state of wanting. The individual's perception of being overweight only worsen the condition. They will sometimes become substance abusers, which again, complicates the disease even more." She paused, sounding like she was taking a drink of water.

Earlier, Jenks had described to Kelly what had happened the night of the party after he had stormed out. How Kaitlin and Roland's parents had come in and her mother exerted control over the two. How she admonished Kaitlin in harsh tones and, as if flipping a switch, exhibited complete compassion toward Roland. Then she had chastised her daughter again as Kaitlin was practically carried upstairs by her two friends. Jenks looked at Kelly, and Kelly gave a small nod.

Jenks explained the incident at the party, which precipitated the mother's involvement, in turn leading to brief details of Kelly's life.

"Alcoholic?" Dr. Brush asked bluntly.

"Yes, ma'am, recovering," Kelly added.

"Very interesting," she observed.

Kelly could feel her reading him over the conference phone speaker. "Then you know that we cannot simply demand that the alcoholic stop drinking and expect that to happen right away. Same goes with someone suffering from AN. We cannot simply demand that they eat!" she stressed. "With the alcoholic, they need to stop doing what they are doing, or it will end fatally. The opposite is true with an AN sufferer; they must start doing what they are not doing, or it will end fatally. As much as we would like to think as doctors and psychiatrists that we can fix alcoholism or AN…we cannot," she admitted. "We can add a component to aid in recovery, but we do not have a sure-fire solution. We do the best we can, and as I said before, sometimes we succeed, sometimes not. It is important that we get help from the person or persons in her family whom she appears to have problems with, and then have them help in the recovery process. For her, it is about control. She turns to the only thing she can control: her own body. Just as there is no known cure for alcoholism, there is none for AN. The best we can hope for is to put it in remission and remain vigilant. As a recovering alcoholic, Mr. Chase, you know this. You also know that a spiritual component or encounter can have a profound impact on putting this malady into remission. The same is true for the anorexia sufferer. I would be happy to help her if she is willing," Dr. Brush offered. "You must know that those with anorexia have a wholly distorted view of themselves. It affects how they see themselves. They look in the mirror and see a heavy person. There is no simple way to dissuade them from this fun-house view of themselves. Oh, how I wish it were so. They, too, have amazing willpower. Think of what agony one must endure to starve oneself to death." She held a long silence before continuing. "This is someone you love, Mr. Chase," she stated flatly. "Please convince her to come see me, for I think I can help. God bless you, Kelly," she said, and then quietly hung up.

Tears rolled down Kelly's face as he tried to sniff his emotions back. Jenks was standing, looking out the large windows, his hands deep in his pockets, head down. Nance sat in his chair, looking down at the floor.

Nance finally spoke up. "I had no idea something like this even existed."

Kelly stood from the desk and moved beside Jenks at the windows. Kelly could see he was crying. Nance approached and stood quietly behind them.

Kelly turned to face Nance. "My god, what do we do?"

Nance pursed his lips and met his eyes. "We do nothing. It's none of our business. We just need to let it play out. I understand how both of you feel about her, but you need to realize that we've already gone too far. Do both of you remember the promise we made to Frank Chase, that we would never intentionally harm anyone?"

Kelly met Jenks's red eyes. They both turned to Nance and nodded their agreement.

• • •

Kelly's thoughts were interrupted as the elevator opened to his home. The message light was blinking on his phone. The answering service clicked over to the message left by KC. "Kelly Chase, can you call me? Love you," she added, and quickly hung up.

Kelly sat on his piano stool, folded the key cover back, and plunked a few notes as he thought about how he would be able to talk to her without losing control. Yet he needed to hear her voice to know she was okay. He dialed her number. The answering service made the connection.

"Hello, Kelly!" Kaitlin said excitedly.

"Hi, princess," he quickly responded. "I'm so sorry I didn't call you today. I was incredibly busy with personal things." He felt the tightness starting as he struggled to keep his emotions in check. He heard her hitched breathing on the other end.

"So was I, no problem. Thank you for dinner and the marvelous time. I realized today that I can't…lose you again. Things would fall apart for me if that were to happen." She held her silence for a moment. Kelly, afraid to say anything, lest his voice break, waited until she continued. "Please tell me that I'm not being foolish, Kelly. Please tell me now before it's too late. Shit, I'm already afraid it already is," she said as she sniffed back her tears.

"KC! I have been in love with you since the first time I met you in that church. The song you sang—" Now it was too late for him; he was losing it. They were both exchanging small intakes of breath, holding back tears. "I love you, KC. I never want to lose you…ever." A new round of emotion seized him. His fear was that he was going to lose her no matter what he did. He could hear her blow her nose softly and clear her throat.

"I need to see you again, but I have recording sessions tonight through Friday. Could we meet at Martoni's again on Friday night, just us two?" she asked.

"Then you will tell me where you live?" he asked.

"Better, I'll show you."

Chapter 22

Powerlessness and Love

Late in the afternoon, Rita Siva and her son, Jacob, drove into the circular driveway at the Villa. She had arrived on the Friday before Thanksgiving week. She eased the late model Mercedes to a stop, drinking in the surroundings and the home she grew up in. She loved this place. Her husband, Ben, would follow her up next week after his work was finished. Rita had still maintained her beauty. Her hair still long, black, and lustrous. Her dark eyes ever intense, highlighting her still flawless complexion. Her high cheekbones only emphasized her overall exotic look. She was dressed casually in blue jeans and a simple off-white, long-sleeved blouse with an open-button collar.

A smiling Victoria came out to meet them, greeting Jacob first with kisses and hugs. Jacob endured with the typical four-year-old resistance. Victoria moved to greet and hug the daughter she had not seen for months. "I'm so happy you could make it to see us this year," Victoria said.

"I had to come see you, Mom. I just need to talk to you. I've been having dreams about Kelly, dreams about him still being alive," Rita admitted somewhat sheepishly, but she thought it was best to get it out straight away. Her mother's face flashed white for a moment, and Rita grew suspicious.

• • •

Victoria's trouble alarm went off. She suspected the time was near when the awful secret about Kelly had to be revealed. Now, there would be hell to pay, and Victoria would be at the center of it. She was always thinking of how to tell Rita. She had yet to come up with a good plan. She could have Kelly come to the house to do the deed. After all, he had offered many times. Victoria, with inward resignation, knew that ultimately it would be her responsibility. She had to do it herself. How she would do it was the question, but she was determined to make Rita's Thanksgiving visit the right time—though she suspected that Rita would not take it well.

• • •

As Rita and her mother walked into the Villa, Rita said, "I need to call Ben and let him know we've arrived safely. Oh, and leave Ben's clubs in the back in case Dad wants to hit the course with me later."

She walked directly to her father's den, noticing Victoria hadn't followed her, stood behind the desk, picked up the phone, and dialed Ben's office number. A receptionist answered and told Rita that Ben was at another attorney's office in San Diego. The receptionist offered to give her the phone number to reach him. Rita opened the center desk drawer to look for a pen and paper to jot down the number. There before her were two photos—photos showing her mother, father, Jenks, and…Kelly! She picked up one of the pictures, bringing it up close to her face, unconsciously hanging up the phone. Yes, and smiling! Kelly standing between her parents, both of their arms around his waist. It was him looking a little older, but it was him! She felt her body numb and slump into her father's chair, and then she screamed for her mother.

As soon as Victoria rushed into the office, Rita held the picture by its corner and thrusted it toward her mother. "Where is he? Where the hell is he?" Rita growled. "You tell me right now! Does he have an address, what town, where?" Rita was screaming at this point. Managing to get out of the chair, she stepped toward her mother. "The address, now, Mother!"

Rita held out her hand with an expectation. Victoria, her face red with frustration and confusion, hurried to the desk, found paper, and wrote down Kelly's Century Plaza address.

"It's not at all what you think, Rita. You have to let me explain," Victoria said, remaining calm.

"How could you be part of something like this?" Rita yelled, tears flowing down her face. She snatched the address from her mother's hand and ran out the front door to her car with Victoria trailing close behind. This was too much, too big of a secret. She had guessed her parents had been hiding something from her for a long time, but she hadn't thought they were capable of this. Kelly was alive. She hadn't dared to believe such a thing until now, not wanting the impossible to creep into her mind just to be taken away again. Her own family had hidden this from her. *Why* didn't matter to her at this point. What did, was finding Kelly. He had to pay for what he had put her through.

Victoria tried to grasp her daughter's arm. "It's not what you think. Please! You'll be sorry if you don't listen. Stop!" Victoria begged.

Rita snatched her arm away from her mother, ran to her black Mercedes, jumped in, and screeched out of the driveway, roaring down to the main road.

• • •

Later in the early evening, Kelly and Jenks quickly made their way out of the Century's main entrance. They walked toward a black limousine parked farther down the circular drive. They were both stopped by the sound of scraping metal, horns honking, and someone yelling. Both turned toward the commotion. A black

Mercedes was pushing another Mercedes into the Century Plaza grounds. Someone was clearly running the gate. Both men stopped to watch. The damaged car careened and roared up the driveway toward them, stopping just short. It was impossible to see who was driving for the broken windshield. The driver's door was suddenly kicked open—and out bolted Rita. She held a golf club and marched directly toward them.

As she approached Kelly, he could see she was out of control with rage. Kelly didn't know what to do as he backed away toward the fountains and grassy area, holding his hands up toward her. "Rita, I can explain. Please let me explain," he pleaded.

Jenks backed away and started yelling, "Rita, you're making a big mistake! Please stop, please!"

Kelly felt the first blow from the club across his cheek, instantly opening a wound. She continued forward as he used his sleeve to wipe his cheek and continued to back away, now in severe pain.

"You son of a bitch!" Rita screamed. "If you didn't want to come back to me, why didn't you just have the guts to tell me. You motherfucker!"

Rita swung again as Kelly partially blocked the club with his forearm, but it still connected hard with his left temple, stunning him and knocking him to the ground. Though Kelly's vision was starting to blur, he could see Kaitlin and Brenda exiting the building into the middle of pandemonium. *Oh, no...*

• • •

Kaitlin and Brenda moved closer to the commotion to get a better look.

"That's Kelly!" Brenda yelled.

Kaitlin moved closer, but a white limousine separated her from the action. Kaitlin's mind was reeling as she tried to make sense of the scene playing out before her. She saw the felling blow to Kelly's head. The person she cared for most in the world was getting beaten and not offering any resistance. Other people were keeping their distance, choosing not to become involved.

Two security men ran toward Rita. Kelly yelled at them and waved them away. "No, leave her be!" The two men stopped, traded concerned glances, unsure what to do.

Kaitlin felt powerless to stop it, yet she knew she must try. Kaitlin bolted around the limousine, trying to reach him. Brenda, close behind, managed to grab Kaitlin's arm to pull her back. She twisted and struggled to break free from her friend's grasp. Brenda finally managed to bear-hug her and lift her off her feet, with Kaitlin kicking in the air.

"Let me go! God damn it!" Kaitlin shouted.

Though Kaitlin didn't know what had led to this, she knew she had to get to Kelly. He was so close, and she had to save him. No one else was even trying, so she had to.

• • •

Jenks ran to Rita, trying to grab for her. In her rage, she shrugged him off and he fell backwards and slipped on the wet grass. Kelly rolled onto his elbows and knees in a feeble attempt to protect himself. He knew he deserved this. All he'd ever wanted was to keep Rita from pain, and here she was. He was the one bleeding, but he could feel that Rita was suffering more than him, and he'd caused this. In all his efforts to shield her from this truth until the time was right, he'd messed it up.

Rita let loose with four or five more blows to Kelly's back, and one more to the back of his head. The crack resonated across the courtyard. Before the world went black, Kelly smiled, for Rita was here. Though she was angry, she was here, and that was enough to smile about. He kept that smile until he lost consciousness.

And then, Kelly was no longer moving.

• • •

"Get up and face me, you fucker!" Rita shouted.

Rita latched onto the first thing she could, which was Kelly's shirt tail. She gave it a violent yank. Buttons gave way with a series of loud pops. She pulled the shirt up around his neck, and then realize that he was limp and motionless. Jenks had finally grabbed her shoulders from behind, struggling to control her. Rita suddenly stopped, staring at the welted, scarred back of her former lover and friend. The back of his head started to ooze blood. The club slipped from her hands.

She brought her hands up to her mouth in shock, her eyes wide. "Oh, my God. Oh, my God."

Rita shook herself free of Jenks's grasp and staggered backward until she bumped up against her still-running Mercedes. Confused, she bolted for the driver's door, jumped in, and squealed around the circular driveway. The metal screeched as she shot through the partially open gate, sparks flying.

What have I done?

• • •

Kaitlin saw Jenks run to Kelly, who had not moved. "Kelly, Kelly!" was all Jenks could say as he gently laid his hand on his friend's scarred back, where new welts rose.

Kaitlin finally reached them, kneeled by Kelly, and lowered her head down to his. "Kelly, it's KC," she said, and his breathing quickened, and he groaned, regaining consciousness. "It will be okay, baby. I'll take care of you." She gently placed a hand on his shoulder, feeling his body shake as he cried.

"No, no, Rita. Please, I'm so sorry," Kelly moaned.

Kaitlin and Jenks helped Kelly to his knees. He was beyond measurable grief. Blood was running down his face and running freely down his back. Kelly tilted his head back, his eyes clinched tightly closed.

"This is not how it was supposed to end. They should have killed me," he said. "I should have died. I shouldn't be here," he cried, slurring and blowing small red bubbles with his lips.

KC was in tears as she embraced him, holding him as tightly as she dared. An ambulance was wailing in the distance, getting closer. Through his pain, Kelly managed to say, "No ambulance, no hospital."

A mixture of blood, snot, saliva, and tears hung from his nose and mouth. Jenks and a security person managed to get Kelly to his feet. Someone brought a towel, and Jenks pressed it to the back of Kelly's head. Residents, some very well-known, had gathered around. They parted as the group passed them, murmuring among themselves in curiosity and shock.

"Take him to my house," Kaitlin said.

Brenda gathered Kelly's bloody shirt, which had fallen from him, and the golf club and followed close behind. Suddenly, two, three, four, bright camera flashes lit up the group. Security men moved quickly to gather up the errant photographers. They rode the elevator in silence to KC's house.

• • •

Victoria was traveling west on Highway 10, carefully watching traffic going east, trying to locate her daughter. She was desperate after she had finally reached Nance and told him the news that they had both dreaded for years. Nance said he would start his search at Century Plaza and contact her later. In the darkness on a highway turnout going east, she saw a black car pulled to the side and a solitary figure illuminated by a lone headlight. Victoria turned around and parked behind the car. It had sustained damage—that was clear. She found her daughter on the passenger side of the car throwing up in the weeds.

Rita staggered toward Victoria as she approached. “Oh, Momma, I’m so sorry! What did I do?” Rita cried.

Victoria held Rita close and stroked the back of her head. “Shh, shh,” she cooed. “It’s okay, baby. You couldn’t have known. Kelly is really tough, so whatever you did, he will be okay.”

“No, Mom, it’s not okay. It will never be okay!” She sobbed, clutching her mother even tighter. Victoria helped her to her own car, turned off her daughter’s car, and took her home.

Later that night, Victoria had finally managed to see her heartbroken daughter to sleep, lying with her until there were no more tears left. Victoria knew there was no way to fix this—only time and…love.

• • •

Kelly was helped into Kaitlin’s home on the twenty-second floor. The men carried him into a large, neat, back bedroom. KC pulled the covers back on the bed and everyone helped lower him down. Jenks removed his boots and trousers. The security man made a quick retreat and left the house. Kelly was in a trancelike state, still unmoving. Kaitlin removed the bloody towel from his head. He was quiet, not talking, only looking straight ahead, his face a mask of sadness. Kaitlin carefully cleaned his wounds with damp towels since the bleeding had stopped. She found a first aid kit and started cleaning and tending his wounds. His rear head wound was small but had temporarily bled profusely. She wrapped a gauze bandage around his head and placed another bandage across his cheek. Jenks moved Kelly as Kaitlin directed him. She brushed his blond-black hair aside, revealing old scars and wounds that took her back to the day they first met. As she worked, her eyes were brimming with tears. *Why has this one been brought such sadness in his life?* she wondered.

She found a sleeping pill and some aspirin, and then tipped Kelly’s head forward so she could give him the pills and a sip of water.

They moved him onto his side so his new back injuries would not be aggravated. Kaitlin sat there with him for a while, but she didn't touch him, in fear she would only hurt him more. He needed to rest, but she wanted to help. She had never felt so helpless.

• • •

Nance received a call from Jenks just as he was on his way out of his office. Jenks described the reunion with Rita, and what he could only describe as "not very pretty."

"I'll be right over," Nance said. "Where are you?" Jenks explained where they were. "How in the world?" Nance exclaimed.

"It's complicated," Jenks said. "I'll explain later. Can you bring a doctor? He's going to need one."

"I'll make arrangements and have him meet us there."

"Nance, is Rita okay?"

"I don't know," Nance admitted. "I can't reach anyone. Victoria is out searching. I'll be there in an hour."

Nance called Victoria but couldn't reach her, so he left a message and told her what had happened. Nance made another call, putting things in motion to restrict any information getting out to the press. He didn't have high hopes for succeeding. He also contacted the management of the Plaza grounds, ensuring that the company would pay for all damages and that money would not be an issue. Here he was again, handling the logistics. He was between family, business, and a man he considered a son. Right when he thought things were looking bright, it had all come crashing down.

• • •

Kaitlin sat on the edge of the bed for a long time, and then gently kissed Kelly on the cheek. "Get some rest, baby," she said softly, stroking his hair.

She rose, turned off the light, and closed the door. Out in the main room, she could see the city lights happily twinkling in the city below. Brenda was standing at the window, looking out with her arms crossed. Kaitlin looked down at herself and discovered there was blood on her white blouse. A tall, dark stranger stood before the fireplace with his back turned. He wore a white dress shirt with the sleeves rolled up and carried a suit jacket draped over his arm. He was staring at a portrait of her and her brother until turning at the sound of her entry.

Smiling, he said, "Pardon me for barging in, Miss Chapin. I am Nance Siva, Mr. Chase's friend, company attorney, and advisor."

Kaitlin approached him, held out her hand, moved forward, and grasped Nance's offered hand in both of hers. "You must be Rita's father," she said. Nance looked down contritely, with his hand still in hers. "I can't tell you how much I hurt for all of you. I know the whole story."

Nance looked up and met her eyes, two deep, brown pools of compassion with an overall sadness that was hard to describe.

Kaitlin turned and raised a hand toward Brenda. "This is our friend Brenda; she was involved as well." Her dress too had smeared blood. Nance gave a smile and nodded to her.

"Miss Chapin, I'm so sorry for all of this," Nance said, eyeing her blood-stained blouse. "A doctor should be here shortly to help with Kelly. Jenks has gone down to escort him up."

The elevator doors slid open, and a tall, thin man with a female aide came in with medical bags. Jenks led them to the back bedroom, and when he returned, Kaitlin backed up a step and turned to him. "What were you and Kelly doing at the Century, anyway? Were you stalking me?" she said with a small smile.

"No, it's actually worse than that," Jenks admitted. "Kelly lives above you on the twenty-fourth floor." He quickly added, "It was all my doing. I was the one who purchased the condo for him, but really, KC, I had no idea you lived here, honestly." He was using arm gestures and shoulder shrugs to make his case.

“Jenks, we’re friends for life, remember? I will always trust you,” she said, “and I know that you’ve been having me followed.”

All the color drained from Jenks’s face. “Kelly doesn’t know I’m doing it. He told me not to, but I did it anyway. It’s my fault,” he confessed. “After Vegas, we—I just wanted to make sure you were going to be okay.”

“Well, Mr. Jenkins, you’ve been a very busy boy, haven’t you? When did Kelly find out I lived here?”

“I told him after our night out last week. He was as shocked as I was when I found out.”

Kaitlin sat on the nearest chair, with her back straight, and placed her interlaced fingers on her lap. “I’m not angry, Jenks. You’re in a long line of protectors I have had. The only difference is, you don’t have a selfish motive, while nearly everyone else around me does, especially my family.”

Kaitlin was also thinking of the coincidences that kept pulling her and Kelly together, like some unseen force pushing and pulling.

Nance stood by taking in the conversation. “Excuse me, Miss Chapin, can I use your phone, please?” he asked.

“Certainly, Mr. Siva, and call me KC.”

“Only if you’ll call me Nance.”

They both nodded, and once in agreement, Nance went to the phone.

Jenks turned to Brenda. “I’m going to stay and make sure Kelly is going to be okay. Maybe we can do this another time?”

“I’m not going anywhere,” she quickly responded as they both walked into the kitchen.

Nance was finishing up on the phone. He returned to Kaitlin and asked, “Can I have a word with you Miss—er—KC?”

She nodded and offered him the seat across from her. Nance sat down and placed his jacket on the sofa next to him. “I have a daughter who is in extreme distress,” he said. Though he spoke calmly, it was clear he was worried. “And I have a young man in the bedroom who is the closest I have to a son. Victoria, my wife, and I love him and think the world of him. What Rita has done is unforgivable, and she is now suffering for it… They both are…and now you…" Nance stopped to collect himself. "My wife and I bear responsibility for this as well, for we were complicit." He hesitated again. "When Kelly was brought back, not telling Rita about him seemed to be the right thing to do at the time. We agreed to it knowing there could one day be a reckoning. To be honest, there was some real doubt by doctors and others that Kelly would survive long term because of his experiences…that he might die. For his sake, we agreed to help him." Nance slowly shook his head as tears started to fall. Kaitlin knelt before him and grasped both of his hands. They shared a silence until he could continue. "While we are both deeply sorry for what has happened, we need to try and put some pieces back together, if we can."

"Is there any way I can help?" Kaitlin asked.

"We know we need to bring Kelly and Rita together and try to work through this. Maybe you can help us do that."

"Anything, Nance, you let me know. Let's see what the doctor has to say, okay?"

The doctor and his aide came out of the back bedroom. "Good job on the wound care," the doctor said to Nance and Kaitlin. "You must have given him a sleeping pill," he said, glancing at Kaitlin. "Sleep is the best thing right now. There are no signs of a concussion, but I've decided to order a private ambulance to take him in for X-rays. I would also like to keep him at least overnight so we can monitor him and clean him up. It's better to be cautious with this. Where in the world did he get those horrendous scars?"

Nance spoke up, "Vietnam, POW."

The doctor shook his head. "The ambulance is downstairs right now." Jenks returned to the room and made his way to the elevator to get the medical crew.

• • •

The four exited the elevator and passed the concierge desk, where three policemen had the attendant cornered and asking him questions. In the portico were two police units sitting with flashing lights. They were assisted into an REO Chase limousine that eased past workers repairing the damaged gate.

"The police will be asking us questions eventually, and there will likely be an investigation," Nance said. "We'll make everything right, and Rita will take responsibility for her part."

Nance and Jenks sat opposite Kaitlin and Brenda. They had changed clothes and had freshened up before the trip to the hospital. Nance watched Kaitlin as she stared absently out the window into the dark streets. He remembered the telephone call with the German doctor who had explained the potentially dreadful outcomes awaiting Kaitlin Chapin. A great sadness washed over him as he weighed the darkness gathering around all the young people in his and Victoria's life. He started to despair. *How will any of this ever be fixed?* Kaitlin suddenly looked at him and gave him the biggest smile. *A ray of sunshine on an impossibly dark night.*

The doctor met the four outside a private room at Cedars-Sinai Medical Center. He was tall and balding, with eyeglasses perched on the end of his nose as he looked down at his clipboard. "X--rays have proved negative for a concussion, but his head wound required about six stitches. He has some welts on his back and other superficial cuts and scrapes. He should be up and around in a couple of days. We will release him tomorrow; we want to keep him tonight, as we have administered some medications that will allow him to sleep and recoup. Is there a responsible party in the group? One that we can stay in contact with?"

"Yes, Doctor, that would be me." Jenks stepped forward and raised his hand.

"Good, check in at the nurses' station and she will take your information. And you should know that there is a police officer in the waiting room, and he wants to talk to someone in your group. Unless there's anything else?" He gave a curt nod, smiled, and left.

"I will go see the police before I leave. Don't any of you worry about it," Nance said.

Jenks and Brenda went to the nurses' station as Kaitlin took Nance aside. "Nance, you say you represent Kelly as his business attorney?"

"Yes, at REO Chase," Nance said.

"Is it a large company?" she asked hesitantly.

"He didn't tell you?"

"Well, they tried, but I wouldn't believe them." She looked at the floor.

"Yes, whatever they told you is true. REO is Real Estate and Oil." Kaitlin grimaced. Nance continued, "It must have been difficult for Kelly. He doesn't like to talk about himself like that, so he gets embarrassed."

"I feel so ashamed for not believing them," she said.

"Look, he wanted you to know so there wouldn't be anything standing between you two. He told me that he could trust you not to tell anyone else, and from what I've seen, he was right."

She bit her lower lip. "Thanks, Nance, I appreciate that. One more thing. Can I take Kelly back to my house in the morning? I promise to take care of him."

Nance smiled at her. "I think Kelly would love that. I'll have Jenks set it up."

Kaitlin, Jenks, and Brenda stayed at the hospital in case anything came up. Nance was anxious to get back home to his family.

• • •

The next morning, Kelly resurfaced into consciousness. He started to sit up until pain shot through his head, and he immediately lay back down.

"Hurts, huh?"

His vision was still blurred, but he would know that voice anywhere. "KC, is that you… Are you okay, princess?" She moved close to him and carefully kissed him upon the cheek while holding his hand. "Where am I?"

Jenks and Brenda stepped into the room. "You're in Cedars, Kelly," Kaitlin said. "The doctor thought it best if you stayed overnight."

He suddenly remembered what had happened. "Rita!" He tried to rise again.

Jenks placed his hands on Kelly's shoulders. "Easy, buddy, you're not ready to fly yet. Nance called this morning. Rita is at home, and her mom and dad are looking after her. She's fine, Kel. Now relax."

"They are going to release you within the hour, and we're going to take you home," Brenda said.

Kelly relaxed and held out his hands. His friends came to him and held them. "Thank you, guys," he said with a smile.

Once Kelly was checked out of the hospital, they drove him to Kaitlin's, where the three finally maneuvered him into KC's back bedroom, administered his pain meds, and made sure he was comfortable and near sleep again. Jenks and Brenda left to get some sleep. Kaitlin curled up on the bedroom chair and drifted off to sleep at the same time as Kelly.

• • •

When Rita finally awoke, she sat up quickly and yelled, "Jake!"

She scurried out of bed and suddenly sat back down, feeling as if she had a bad hangover. Pulling on a robe, she made her way to a small dining nook off the kitchen. It was her parents' favorite breakfast spot. Both sat at the round table, each reading a newspaper. Little Jake sat beside Victoria, playing with his toy cars and making engine sounds as he puttered about.

"Mom!" Jake yelled and jumped from the chair and ran to her.

Rita bent down to scoop him up. Nance and Victoria quickly came to her, enveloping her in a hug.

Nance said, "We're so happy to have you and Jake here. We missed you so much."

Victoria took Jake from Rita and made a motion for her to sit at the table with her father as she took her grandson away to get dressed for the day.

The night before, upon returning to the Villa, Rita was in an emotional stupor. Victoria, with the help of house staff, carefully helped Rita into the guest-wing bedroom, laying her down in bed. She quickly assumed a fetal position, facing away from her mother. Victoria sat next to her and placed a hand on her shoulder.

"Honey, you need to hear this," Victoria said, taking a deep breath. "Kelly was returned to the States in July of 1971 after spending three years as a POW in the jungles of Vietnam. He was kept in a small cage and endured endless torture and misery. He was taken to the San Francisco Veterans Hospital. He called us, looking for you and asking where you were—if you were okay. We put him off until we could see him the next day. It was hard to see him like that…battered, cut, scarred, emaciated. He resembled the Kelly we once knew, but very little. He could barely speak, his voice so hoarse and wispy. He asked about you, but it was clear he already expected the news that you had moved on with your life." Rita turned to face her mother, still curled up, her face red, hair tangled, and staring straight ahead. "We agreed to go along with Kelly and not tell you of his return. Was it wrong? Maybe, but to refuse him at that point was something we just couldn't do. Kelly didn't want his return to interfere with your new life and family. He didn't want you to suffer anymore because of him. It was one of the saddest days of our lives. As time went by, the secret that we kept was getting nearly impossible to contain. It was for Kelly too. We were all three distraught, not sure what to do anymore."

Both remained quiet until Rita finally broke the silence. "Mom, I still love him." Saying it out loud caught them both off guard, so she said it again, "I still love him. But Ben and Jake are my life. What am I going to do? Not only that—I attacked him. I let anger take hold of me, and I hurt him."

"Honey, I think Kelly knows that. I think he understands your anger too. He's known that since his return. He loves you too. Me and your dad know that. It's been killing him. We know he descended into alcoholism and dropped out of sight, and for a couple of years, we didn't hear from him. One day Jenks called us to say Kelly had nearly died but finally seemed to be on the road to recovery. Recently, some good things have happened to him, and we think he has decided to move on with life. This is a very painful thing we are going through. We'll just have to see our way through it."

Rita started to weep softly. Her mother sat stroking her hair until she finally fell asleep.

The next morning, Rita sat down at the table with her father. A breakfast plate with orange juice was placed before her. The helper picked up other plates and withdrew, leaving them alone. Nance reached out and grasped his daughter's hands in his. "We are so sorry for having kept this from you."

"Mom told me everything last night, Daddy. I understand." She looked down. "I just need to pick up the pieces and move on. But now some pieces are missing, and I don't know what the picture looks like. It's so confusing. That stupid war keeps taking and taking long after it's over."

"I'm going to talk to Kelly later and ask him if he would be willing to meet with us when he is feeling better. Maybe later this week. Is that too soon?"

Rita shook her head. "Daddy, I don't know if I can do that." Her face contorted as she squeezed her eyes shut. "Not after what I did to him yesterday."

"Oh, my beautiful girl, you are talking about a man who loves you and has probably already forgiven you."

"Daddy, is he okay? Where is he?"

"He is spending the night at Cedars under observation. His doctor says he will be fine in a couple of days. Don't worry about him. He's as tough as they come."

Chapter 23

Family

Kelly was in the bamboo cage; it was pouring rain. The cover was wrenched open with the creaking of hinges. His chief captor looked down at him with a grin, reached down, and grabbed him by the hair and pulled him up out of the cage. Kelly, with hands bound, could do nothing. He was pulled through the mud face-down until he felt the first stinging slap of the cane on his shoulders, then the next, and the next. The rain was cascading down his face as he clambered to his knees, feeling the blows continuing to rain down. He started to scream, and scream, and scream.

• • •

Kaitlin bolted upright. She saw Kelly kneeling on the bed, with his arms reaching for the ceiling, screaming, his entire body drenched in sweat. She saw his back muscles bunched with the red puffy scars that were more vivid than she remembered. She ran to him and hugged him from behind, pulling him close to her to try to calm him with soothing words. He sagged back onto the bed, not coming fully awake, still twitching. She lay next to him, looking at his back. She softly stroked the scarred landscape of his body, quietly singing one of her love ballads. As she reached for him and pulled his head to rest in her neck, she continued to sing. He stopped moving, and his breathing eased and relaxed.

He mumbled from a dreamy state, "Angel, angel," and then he slept again.

She fell into the deepest sleep she had had in months and

dreamed of an old Indian with long gray braids, sitting cross-legged before a fire. He was singing in a low voice.

Her dream turned the song into words: *Bring the Angel. Angel, the Creator loves you. Come to me.*

The fire was reflected in his eyes brimming with tears. Kaitlin felt warm, safe, with a lightness in the pit of her stomach that glowed, radiating from the core of her body as she awakened. She was clinging to Kelly, who was still asleep. She could see light streaming in from the hallway. How long had they slept? She eased herself from the bed and stepped into the hallway. Looking back at Kelly, she smiled and closed the bedroom door. She felt no need to run, scrub, or purge. It was as if she were floating through her home while getting ready for her trip.

Kaitlin ate a small cup of oatmeal without thinking much of it. She hadn't felt this good in months. She wrote a note for Kelly after she had packed her bags, but she had second thoughts about leaving Kelly alone. What if the doctor had missed something and he took a turn for the worse? She called Jenks's number and left a message. Her call was returned immediately.

"Jenks, can you come back to my house and watch over Kelly?" Kaitlin asked Jenks. "I have to be in Chicago tonight, and he shouldn't be left alone."

"Where are you, Jenks? How soon can you get here?"

"Ah…ah," Jenks stuttered.

"You don't have to explain yourself to me," Kaitlin said. "We're friends, remember? I need to leave within the hour, though. Can you hurry? I will buzz you up."

Kaitlin gathered the rest of her things while she waited for Jenks to arrive, and when he stepped into her house, she hurried to him and grasped both of his hands and gave him a quick hug. "So glad you could make it," she said, relieved. "He's still asleep. I've washed his clothes and set out other things for him to wear. Here is a prescription for him. He can stay here as long as he needs to. I will be back tomorrow afternoon. I'll call your service when I make it in."

Organization was the only thing that would keep her sane while she was away from him.

"KC, I know you don't want to leave. I will take care of Kelly just fine. It's what I do," Jenks assured her.

Kaitlin adjusted her bags and glanced back at him. "How's Brenda this morning?"

"Umm…"

"I'm just messing with you."

"I knew that," he said, sounding unsure.

He helped her down to a waiting car, and she handed him her elevator key. "Don't be throwing any wild parties," she said, winking as she disappeared into the back seat of the limo.

Kelly roused himself around mid-morning. He felt amazing given the punishment from Friday evening. He felt his cheek and head wounds, which were tender but manageable, and he only had a slight headache. Kelly could smell Kaitlin's presence in the bedroom, mainly on the pillow next to him. When he opened the bedroom door and peeked out, he didn't see her. He ventured out a little farther, only in his boxers. He called out for her but no response. Kaitlin's home was larger than his, so neat and clean it made him give a small whistle in wonderment that instantly hurt his face. Moving to the large dining table, he saw a note written in immaculate cursive script.

Kelly,

Hope you are feeling better this morning. You had a rough night with bad dreams. I was lying beside you to calm you down—hope you don't mind. I feel fantastic this morning, and I don't know why. I just do. I think having you here is what I needed. I am in Chicago and will be back Monday afternoon. More importantly, you need to call Nance as soon as you can. It's about Rita. Call me when you can, please.

I love you,

KC

P.S. Stay there as long as you want. KC.

As he finished the note, he heard a toilet flush. Jenks suddenly appeared far down the hallway, still adjusting himself as he came out of a bathroom. "Kelly, how do you feel, man?" he said when he saw Kelly. "Come here and let me get a look at you."

"Hi, Jenks. I don't feel too bad. Damn, she really gave me a going over, huh?" He reached behind his head and winced. "What day is it?" "Sunday and everything is okay. KC is in Chicago and you can call her after her show this afternoon.

"Why don't you get your stuff together so we can get you up to your place so you can clean up."

Kelly went back to the bedroom as he tried to recall recent events. His next thought was how to find out what happened to Rita. Kelly saw his jeans were folded and freshly cleaned, along with a neatly folded black sweatshirt on the small table in the bedroom with a small slip of paper with his name attached. He held the shirt up and admired the Chapin logo prominently displayed, causing a big smile that hurt his face. He carefully eased the shirt on, mindful of the new and painful marks on his back. He cleaned up as best he could and made it back out to his friend and they went up to his house.

Kelly took a hot shower, continually thinking about Rita and remembering only slightly being helped up to KC's house. He looked in the mirror and examined his bruised cheek with a skillfully placed gauze bandage over the wound. He peeled it off and examined the wound—not serious by his standards. He removed the bandage around his head and felt stitches. It wouldn't leave a scar—thank God—he already had enough of those.

After Jenks went down to retrieve some things out of his Volvo, Kelly sat down on the piano stool, picked up the phone, and dialed Freddy's number.

"Hello," came the gruff greeting.

"It's me," Kelly announced.

"How are you doing, Kelly? Good to hear from you."

"I've been better," he admitted.

"Lay it on me, son. I'm all ears," Freddy said in resignation.

Kelly told Freddy everything that had happened since their last talk. All about things with KC, Rita, and Jenks. Freddy could be heard occasionally taking a drag from his ever-present non-filtered Camel cigarette, not interrupting.

"So, why'd you call me?" Freddy asked when Kelly was finished. "Sounds like you got everything under control."

Oh, no, thought Kelly, *it's going to be one of those conversations.*

"If you're just looking for sympathy, find a dictionary. It's between shit and syphilis. Are you still spying on her?"

"I…I'm not—"

"Careful, son, careful," Freddy cautioned. "Remember, there are sins of commission and then sins of omission. Which is this one?"

Kelly hesitated, feeling trapped. "I told Jenks not to do it, but I knew he was going to do it anyway. I just sort of let him," Kelly admitted.

"Not something to harp on as long as you get the lesson attached. You do understand, don't you?"

"Yes," Kelly admitted again sheepishly.

"What are you going to do about Rita?"

"I'll come clean about everything, apologize, make amends, do everything I can to take her pain away. I will ask for nothing."

Freddy was quiet, taking a drag from the Camel. "For what it's worth, you did the wrong thing for all the right reasons. I won't ever try to second guess what you did. It's a tough spot to be in, for all of you, including Jenks. Good luck, and call me and let me know how it turns out. And stop fucking spying on people." Click!

His elevator doors opened, and Jenks stepped in. "How are you, Kel? Have you talked to Nance yet?"

"No, where is he, the office?"

"Home, looking after Rita. "

"By the way, if you are still having KC followed, you'd better stop. Freddy knows, and he's not happy with me."

"How in the hell did he know?"

"You know how he is. He just knows shit."

"It doesn't matter, anyway. She knew all along. I was busted," Jenks said in resignation.

"How the hell did she know?"

"Let's talk about something else," Jenks said.

"Boy Howdy!" Kelly exclaimed.

"Huh?" Jenks said, giving him a curious look.

• • •

The midafternoon sun was streaming through the large bay windows into Kelly's home. Jenks had gone out to fill Kelly's prescription when Kelly received a call back from Nance. Nance asked Kelly how he was doing and apologized for Rita.

Kelly brushed it off. "I expected no less from her and have always been dreading the moment she would find out. I knew it would be hard on all of us. It was just a little more *physical* than I expected," he said, inwardly cringing. "How is she doing?"

"Victoria talked with her last night in the bedroom until she finally went to sleep. She tried to explain everything to her. This morning, her and I had a talk over breakfast. She has agreed to talk to you on Tuesday if KC agrees and you're up to it. I know she's still confused and upset. It's such an emotional thing to process. I often wondered if it was a bad decision we made back then. I—" Kelly could hear him sniff back his tears.

"It's okay, Nance. It was my decision, my choice. You and Victoria didn't do anything wrong."

Nance regained his composure, waited a moment, and then

asked Kelly, "Do you think you can make it this week, Tuesday maybe, to meet with her? I know it's short notice, but we cannot leave it this way."

"Sure, anything to help."

"About one p.m. then. I hope you don't mind, but I met with Miss Chapin Friday night after you were tended to and asked her if she would be willing to accompany you as moral support."

"What did she say?"

"She was more than happy to help. Kelly, she is the sweetest person I have ever met in the music business. My previous experience has been with several pretentious assholes. I was concerned for you, but after talking to her, I can see why you are attracted to her. Wonderful person," Nance added, almost to himself. "We also talked about REO Chase. She understands and agrees that you and Jenks were telling her the truth. She is smart, as she had already figured it out somehow."

So far Kelly's plans to mislead the women in his life when he was trying to protect them wasn't working out. It was time to be upfront and honest.

• • •

The Chapins' private jet had just taken off from LA and had reached cruising altitude when Roland asked, "Are you okay, KC? You seem distracted. We missed you at the house yesterday. We didn't even hear from you."

"Oh, yeah, just hung around the house and decided to stay in and relax," Kaitlin deflected.

Roland nodded, leaned back, and announced, "Chicago, here we come."

Kaitlin couldn't wait to get to Chicago so she could check in on Kelly. She thought back to Friday night's events. She suddenly sat up in her seat as she recalled the flashes—someone had taken photos. It was followed by a flurry of security men scrambling to remove the invaders. This memory had been lost to her in all the excitement. Now she was fearful that the private life she valued was in danger.

• • •

Late that afternoon, Kelly called Kaitlin's service number and left a message. "It's Kelly. KC, thank you for taking care of me last night. I was pretty messed up. I got up this morning feeling surprisingly good in spite of everything, and Jenks is here to help out. Call me. I'm worried about you getting so little sleep. I love you, princess."

Thirty minutes later, his phone rang. "KC," he said excitedly.

"I told you I was going to show you where I lived." She laughed.

Kelly had to chuckle at that one. She had such a great sense of humor. "How are you doing?" he asked.

"I have a couple of minutes before we go on. I can't wait to get home and talk to you. I had the strangest dream when I fell asleep next to you last night. There was this old Indian singing by a fire…" Kelly shot to his feet from the piano stool. "And his words were something about saving an angel, or something," she continued. "I woke up this morning feeling better than I have in months—years. What do you suppose that's all about?"

Kelly was too stunned to respond.

"Kelly, are you okay?"

"Sure, KC, sure. Just not sure what to say," he said.

"Well, it seems to be wearing off now. God, that felt good, whatever it was. Then my mother called just a while ago. She is angry with me, mad at Roland too. She found out about us, who you were. Don't ask me how."

That "knowing thing" had been going around lately.

"Mother said," Kaitlin paused, "you are different from us and that I was to stop seeing you. Besides, she said you didn't have any money. So you are just a poor, broke Indian, and I'm supposed to dump you and move on." Kelly remained silent. "I told her that was not going to happen. She flew into a rage over the phone, demanded to talk to Roland, screamed at him, and then hung up. I don't know what she's going to do, and I don't care. I am coming home to you, and we are going to go see Rita and get things fixed as best we can."

"KC, you don't have—"

"Kelly! Yes, it *is* going to happen, so don't argue with me," she demanded. "I've already talked with Nance, and it's settled. We can take my car and drive over. I know you are too poor to afford one." She giggled.

"I never—"

"Man, I'm kidding. Jesus! Men!" Click!

What is with this Freddy-hang-up stuff, anyway? Kelly wondered.

• • •

After talking to Kelly, Kaitlin hurried to the venue stage and sang for an hour before an excited, appreciative crowd. Something was different that night, and the audience must have felt it too. She was always confident on stage, holding that microphone and watching jaws drop, but tonight, she felt brighter than ever. She would be there for Kelly, no matter what her mother said. For the first time in a long while, Kaitlin felt in control.

After the band finished their set and the cheers subsided, Jerry Mellis, their manager, stepped between Kaitlin and Roland and moved them to a quiet area backstage. Jerry glanced around, making sure no one was close by.

"We might have a problem," Jerry confided. He removed a tabloid magazine from under his arm and showed it to them. "This arrived by courier during the show."

Roland took the paper and unfolded it to read the headline splash: "Bloody Brawl at the Plaza." There were two pictures below the headline. One showed Kaitlin walking toward the camera followed by two men carrying a shirtless and bloody Kelly Chase. The second picture showed Brenda trailing behind carrying a soiled shirt and a blood-stained golf club.

Roland's eyes lit up. "Hey, that's you and Kelly Chase, isn't it?"

Kaitlin said nothing.

"Kaitlin, do you have an explanation for any of this?" Jerry asked.

Kaitlin was still quiet.

"It says here that Kaitlin Chapin had to be physically restrained from becoming involved in an apparent family fight. Something about an attack with a golf club," Jerry said.

Kaitlin ventured forth in a low, confidential voice: "You guys, it's a long story. Jerry, is there any way we can keep a lid on this?"

"Kaitlin, I…"

"I know, I know, we're not supposed to kill anybody. But is there *anything* we can do?"

"With this showing up in Chicago, I can only imagine how big it is in California by now. Let me make some calls to see what I can find out. If it's any consolation, it's pretty exciting, but I'll deny I ever said that." Jerry executed a small nod, smiled, and left.

"KC, what the hell were you doing?" Roland said, crossing his arms. "Damn, when Mom finds out…"

"Roland, I can't get too deep into it right now. Just know that it's a deeply personal thing that Kelly is involved in—a disagreement with an old girlfriend."

"Disagreement? Holy cats, she attacked him with a golf club!"

"Well, she was a little upset."

"No shit, KC. And why were you trying to get involved? You know we can't have things like this going on. It's bad for business."

Kaitlin hung her head. Like with her mom, it was the "business" part that mattered most. She wasn't going to let it trump what was important: Kelly. "Roland," she said just above a whisper. "He's the one."

Roland was suddenly quiet, his eyes softening as he looked at his sister with compassion.

"I love him. And this whole thing is not what you think. Please give me some time, and then I will tell you the whole story."

He reached out and placed his open palm on his sister's cheek. She gave him a hopeful look. It was then when she felt like her brother finally saw her.

• • •

Kelly was roused by his bedside phone. "Hello?" he answered groggily.

"Kelly, how are you feeling? Are you up? Can we talk?"

His head cleared. "Sure, KC. Are you okay?"

"Well, not really. We have a problem."

Kaitlin told him about the photos, the related article, and the band's manager's concerns. Kelly sat up on the edge of the bed, instantly alert. She said she was worried about what trouble this could cause for everyone involved.

"I don't think they know who you are," Kaitlin said, "but there is still a chance they could find out. I just wanted to warn you so you wouldn't be surprised. I'll call Brenda too. Can you tell Jenks? Roland is mostly worried about what our mom and dad will say."

"What paper is it?"

"Some rag, *Star Gazer Daily*. I'm so sorry, Kelly."

"It's not your fault. Let me do some checking and see what I can find out."

"I will call you when I get in. We're just getting on the plane. Love you."

Kelly immediately called Jenks and told him everything. Jenks was still up.

"Damn, don't you ever sleep?" Kelly asked.

"No, just waiting for your call," Jenks said. "Let me check some sources and see where this tabloid originates from and who owns them. Maybe we can still head this off somehow."

Kelly had no choice but to leave this up to Jenks. He wanted to move past the incident and work things out with those involved, so the last thing they all needed was the public eye—or more negative attention from Kaitlin's parents. Unable to fall back asleep, he waited for Jenks to call back, which wasn't until after midnight.

"It's a Chicago-based publication," Jenks said, "owned by a larger media group. It's a hack operation dedicated to sleezy stories and gotcha journalism. I found out who manages the operation and had sources check on the foundation of the photographs. Apparently two of their ace reporters from Chicago were dredging for celebrity photos. They managed to out-fox Century security and slip in. They were probably hiding in the bushes on site when all the excitement took place. They were captured and thrown out but managed to keep their camera—don't ask me why. They hopped on a flight back to Chicago with the scoop of the century, hoping to capitalize. They managed to get some copies out the next afternoon at local outlets in Chicago. That's how the Chapins found out so fast. Want to hear the good news?"

"Don't keep me in suspense."

"You own the major media group that owns them."

"No shit?"

"Nope. I've made arrangements to have the whole thing stopped in its tracks. We have sent people out to collect all remaining local outlet copies, and we managed to get the camera, all photos, copies, and negatives. The operation will run an immediate retraction with an apology to those highlighted in the story. They will explain that editors had been duped by a pair of ne're-do-wells that faked the photos and the story. I assumed that you wouldn't want to be connected to the operation any longer and have asked that the major media group cease the *Star Gazer Daily's* operations next week after the retraction is published and distributed. Hopefully, this never finds its way to California. If it does, we will take care of things there."

Give Jenks a coffee and a few hours and he can work miracles, Kelly thought.

"Does Nance know?" Kelly asked.

"I had to tell him, Kel. He helped me put the thing back in the bottle."

"Good work, Jenks. I think I need to give you a raise."

"Just tell KC she owes me one."

"Boy Howdy."

"Huh?"

"Bye, Jenks."

Kelly was sleeping on his expansive leather sofa with a radio station softly playing in the background when he was jolted awake by the sound of elevator doors opening. He staggered to his feet, clad only in his boxers, as a light came on in the elevator foyer. He became more alert and edged around the large granite fountain, straining to see who was there.

"Kelly?" she whispered.

Kelly let out a breath and relaxed. "KC, what are you doing breaking into my house?" He stepped into the light and saw her smiling and dangling a key on a chain.

"Jenks," she said. "He got me a copy."

She dropped her coat on the floor and jumped into his open arms, hugging and kissing him deeply. He lifted her carefully and carried her to his bedroom, where he helped her undress in the semi darkness of the room, both eager with building desire. Kaitlin was warm and soft, delicate in a way that contrasted Kelly's rugged body. It had taken so long for them to finally be together in this way, and it wasn't until this moment when he realized how desperately he needed it—needed her. They made love for the first time, neither wanting to stop. Two fated souls finally merging and both needing what the other had. Kaitlin clutched his scarred body to hers as she cried at their release. Kelly's heart slowed as she rested her head on his chest and softly stroked and kissed the puckered wounds.

"I love you, princess," he whispered into her ear.

She giggled like the sensation was tickling her. "I'm never going to leave you, Kelly Chase. Never."

She propped herself on his chest and gave him another warm kiss and settled back down.

"How did you know I lived here?" he asked.

"Jenks and Nance. Between them both, they spilled the beans on your secret life. The company you own, the condo, everything. I hold your life in my hands, cowboy."

"Are you going with me tomorrow to see Rita?" Kelly asked.

"Oh, I insist. Wild horses couldn't keep me away. I will be there for you."

Kelly lay quietly thinking how wonderful it felt having her next to him, with no more secrets between them except for one. The one he was powerless to do anything about. He pulled her close and spooned her. "I love you," he whispered in her ear.

Neither said anything more as they drifted off to sleep.

Both dreamed of the old Indian singing his song in ancient words, fire dancing in his eyes, a small smile on his face. "Angel, angel, come to me. Let the Creator love you until you can love yourself," he chanted again and again.

• • •

The next morning, after Kelly and Kaitlin made love, they showered, dried one another, and gently caressed each other with a tenderness each had never offered another before. They both felt a fluttering sensation in their stomachs as they drank coffee in silence, wordlessly communicating their love.

Kaitlin seemed to float down to her house while in the elevator, marveling at the lack of gravity in her body. She did her makeup and hair, and dressed in a pair of denim jeans, a black UC sweatshirt, and white deck shoes. On her way out, she grabbed a heavier fur-lined jacket and went back up to get Kelly.

"Miss me?" she said as she ran into him after letting herself in.

"Breakfast?" he offered.

"No, you go ahead. I had something downstairs," she said.

He scooped the eggs and bacon onto a plate and set it on the nearby small table, and with a flourish, produced a fork. Holding it in front of her face, he said, "I insist. How dare you turn down my first breakfast offering to my princess."

KC reluctantly took the fork, with a small involuntary frown, and sat down while he poured her another coffee. He sat to her left with his plate and started to eat. She took a small bite, and then with another fork full, offered it to Kelly.

"Hey, this is pretty good. Try mine," she offered.

"No, I have mine. Thank you," he said as he smiled at her with his mouth full.

She started to eat again and surprisingly found it somewhat enjoyable. *Why wouldn't I?* she thought. The nagging sliver came back.

• • •

With Kaitlin driving her little Mercedes, they made their way to the Morongo Reservation. "Have you heard anything about the pictures yet?" Kaitlin asked, hiding behind her sunglasses.

"Don't worry about it, princess. We've taken care of it," Kelly assured her.

Kaitlin turned and gave him a deep, unbelieving frown. "Kelly, you better not be putting me on. This is serious."

"I know. Jenks and Nance took care of it."

Kaitlin pulled over to the side of the road. "I've been worried sick about this whole thing, and Roland is beside himself thinking we're finished."

"Turns out we own the company that owns the company that was responsible for the photos," Kelly said simply.

"How in the world?"

Kelly went on to explain the details and how Jenks and Nance had saved the day. Kaitlin removed her sunglasses and was staring wide-eyed at him. "If I didn't know you better, and love you so much, I'd say you were full of shit. But I know by now to never doubt anything you tell me. I have to find a phone and call Roland. He's gonna shit!"

She pounced on the little car as it squealed back out into traffic. Kelly was surprised by her driving skills and reached out to brace his hand on the dashboard.

"Maybe you could just tell him that a concerned party took care of things for you," Kelly said. "I don't think he's ready to hear about my involvement. I still need to stay under the radar."

Kaitlin shrugged her shoulders.

They stopped at a roadside diner for Kaitlin to use the phone booth. Now Kelly understood the large sunglasses, for as she ran over, she did so discretely to avoid unwanted attention. But once she reached Roland, Kelly could see her in the booth making animated gestures while she smiled and explained to her brother that things had been fixed and not to worry any longer.

Two young girls bounced down the metal stairs of the diner. As they walked by the booth, they stared at Kaitlin with curious looks and turned back to each other, stopping momentarily, like they were comparing notes on whom they thought they may have just seen. A second, larger group exited the diner and joined the girls. Roughly ten people met behind the Mercedes, with some pointing at the personal California plate. Kaitlin noticed and finished her call to her brother and hung up. Kelly watched her frown at first, but then she appeared to steel herself, brought up a big smile, and exited the booth. Two girls tentatively approached her as more people started coming out of the diner, curious about the gathering in the parking lot. Kelly sat rooted to his seat, unsure what to do. He decided to get out and be at Kaitlin's side to help however he could. Kaitlin nodded a couple of times and smiled as excitement grew among the group, the volume rising quickly.

Kelly reached her side and attempted to shield her from any harm. Papers, pens, and outstretched arms came from every direction as everyone clamored and called out her name. Kaitlin started signing each offering and greeting each person by name, personalizing her autograph to each paper plate, napkin, hand, wrist, or whatever was offered. She signed each one with precise, neat, and perfectly legible writing. Others wanted pictures with her. Kelly was getting caught up in the photographs as well. Kelly did his best to preserve space around her, extending his arms protectively.

Finally, Kaitlin announced, "That's all the time I have for right now. We must be on our way. Please forgive me for not getting to all of you, and thank you for stopping and visiting with me."

The group responded with a smattering of applause as Kelly managed to make a path for her, open the passenger door, and close it behind her. Kelly, managing a smile, made his way around the car and let himself in. He tried to ignore the fact that several pictures were taken of him as he jumped in beside KC. Kelly looked down at the numerous knobs, dials, and gauges on the Mercedes.

"How do I start this thing?" Kelly asked, feeling panic settle in. The crowd likely thought he was some sort of bodyguard, so he didn't want to drop the act.

Kaitlin reached over and turned the key and moved the shifter into reverse. "Push the gas, Kelly," she said, waving goodbye to those daring to stalk closer to the car.

They shot backward into the parking lot, luckily missing the group of fans. Kelly slammed on the brakes, and Kaitlin shifted into drive. They pulled away from the diner, screeching onto the road in a cloud of dust, briefly swerving into the oncoming lane.

"Geez, Kelly. Am I going to die on Highway Ten?" she teased.

"Sorry, I haven't had much practice lately," he admitted sheepishly. Kelly turned to look back. "Where did all of those people come from? We're out in the damn desert."

"Kind of caught me off guard too," she said with a smile.

Kelly began to realize for the first time what it must be like for her. It wasn't possible for her to go anywhere without having the rush of fans making demands.

"Are you okay, KC?"

"Sure, I really like and appreciate them, but I can only take so much." She sighed and leaned back in her seat. "Be ready, my love. Now they have your picture alongside me. They'll start asking questions, and pictures and rumors will start appearing in some rag before the end of next week, and you won't be able to stop it like last time."

"I don't care, KC. They'll have pictures of me with the person I love most in this world. It's you and me till the wheels fall off."

Kaitlin hunched her shoulders and looked straight ahead. "I love you, Kelly Chase."

She brought his hand to her lips and gave it a gentle kiss.

"At least there won't be as much blood in these photos," Kelly said. "How's Roland?"

"Unbelieving, but hopeful. He's still unconvinced."

Kaitlin found a Beatles tape and shoved it into the tape player. She apologized for doubting him about his newfound wealth, but he dismissed her with a wave.

"It just sounded impossible," she said. "You know what's funny, I realized it was true before you dropped me off that night." She told him of the two almost simultaneous revelations she had experienced in the car.

"Why didn't you say something?" he asked.

"I felt so guilty about not trusting you guys, I couldn't bring myself to say anything. Then I verified it with Nance. I'm still embarrassed about it." She kept glancing his way, gauging his reaction.

He nodded and looked at her. "KC, I would never hold that against you. What's important is that you know."

"What's it like having all that money?" she asked.

"It's probably no different than you, but I don't have to deal with that," he said, hiking his thumb over his shoulder.

"Not yet," she warned.

"I can't allow it to change me. You know I'm already messed up, and now this? I hope it's not too much. How about you, princess?"

She loved it when he called her that. "Me? I've discovered how little freedom I have. We are mining for gold while we can before the fame dries up. There's immense pressure to tour, record, travel, and repeat. I love the people, and I do love what I do, but it just becomes too much sometimes." She looked at him with a rueful smile.

Kelly said, "It must have been quite a surprise for you to see me and Jenks at Century City, especially with Rita. We were waiting at the front door to tell you where I lived when Rita showed up. I'm still not sure how she managed to find me, some coincidence."

"Shocked would be putting it lightly. I couldn't believe what I was seeing, and everybody was just standing there watching!"

They were both quiet for a stretch.

"Kelly?" Kaitlin said, reaching over and placing her hand on his shoulder. "Is this going to work? I mean, with all our money, business, touring, my family…everything. Will it drive us apart and destroy us?"

"KC, I'm yours as long as you'll have me."

She felt wounded. "But I'm so messed up. I can't count the relationships I have ruined and the people I've let down. I'm just a failure."

Kelly immediately pulled to the side of the road and stopped.

"KC, honey, I don't ever, ever want to hear you say that about yourself again. It just isn't true. You are a beautiful, talented, and successful woman. I love you for you. It's not your money or your fame. I have money, and I can have fame if I want it. You just proved to me how well you handle fame back there at the diner. Most people would have run, maybe been rude. Not you. You treated them all with kindness and respect. You gave them your time and attention, and I could see they genuinely loved you for it. No, honey, you're not a failure. You are the most successful kind of human being, one who cares for her fellow man. Back there, I fell in love with you all over again. If you are anything, you are a true 'one off.' There are very few like you. You're stuck with me, Church Girl."

Kaitlin turned in her seat and placed both hands over her mouth as tears slid down her cheeks. She scrambled over into his seat, onto his lap, and squeezed him tightly, letting sobs rack her body and hot tears flow onto his neck.

"Kelly, please don't give up on me," she said. "No matter how messed up I get…promise? I need you in my life no matter what." She drew back, looking at him with red eyes, then kissed him.

"We better get going before we have a big problem," he said.

She smiled at him as their foreheads touched. "Okay, Piano Man. You're the boss."

As he pulled back onto the highway, Kelly thumped the steering wheel. "Shit, I forgot to call Freddy."

"Who's Freddy?"

Kelly described his relationship with Freddy, which included Jenks. By the time he finished, KC had slipped into hysterics and was laughing loudly.

"He really said that about shit and syphilis?"

"Yep, he's a regular comedian."

"I can't wait to meet him."

• • •

Just before one p.m., Kelly and Kaitlin pulled into the circular driveway of the Villa. Jenks's Volvo was already there.

"Kelly, are you ready for this?" Kaitlin asked.

Kelly sat quietly, nodding to himself.

"Just remember that the Church Girl is with you, okay?" she said.

He nodded again, feeling like that was all he was capable of.

As they got out of the car, Kelly noticed it was much cooler than he'd expected. KC donned her jacket. Kelly, grateful that he had taken his jacket as well, slipped it over his "Chapin" sweatshirt. Kelly reached behind him, searching for KC's hand, and her gentle, smooth touch came, which quickly soothed him as she fell in step beside him.

Nance appeared, dressed in his casual attire of a sweater and jeans. Victoria slipped in by his side, grabbing his right hand. She was dressed in her usual elegant attire, a black pantsuit with a white blouse. They both smiled as Kelly introduced Kaitlin to Victoria. Jenks stood nearby with Brenda standing close behind him.

"So nice to meet you, Mrs. Siva," KC said as they both reached out to each other.

"Thank you for coming, Miss Chapin. I'm sorry you were dragged into all this."

"No problem. I'm glad to help."

"Come in," Nance said, extending his hand to the doorway.

Kelly started, "Is she—"

"Yes, she is," Victoria assured him. "She'll be with us in a moment."

"Let me take your coats," Nance offered.

They made their way into the high-ceilinged great room. Kelly caught movement to his right. Rita was approaching him carefully, her hands covering her mouth. He turned to meet her; she was just as beautiful as he remembered, with her long raven-black hair. She moved hesitantly, then quickened her steps as she threw herself into his arms for the first time in nearly six years. She pulled him close, her arms around his neck. He lifted her up to him. She buried her face into his neck, and he could feel her hot tears. He breathed in the long-lost smell of her, his emotions flooded, and his eyes started to burn with his own tears. The world had finally righted itself; his Rita was with him again. Kelly could feel sobs racking her body as she continued to squeeze him tightly. She kissed his cheek, ignoring the gauze covering. *Wait, I must stop. This is not right. Now what do I do?*

"Oh, my god, I am so sorry I didn't wait. Sorry I left you, sorry about hurting you. Please forgive me, Kelly. Please forgive me," she begged, the words tumbling from her.

He could feel her butterfly-like kisses on his cheek and her hot breath in his ear. His words would not come; he was lost in her emotional embrace. She pulled back from him and kissed him on the mouth and on the other cheek.

"I'm sorry I didn't tell you. It was all my fault. I was stupid and selfish. I caused all this and hurt you. I'm so sorry," he admitted.

She stood back and slipped her arms around his waist and laid her head against his chest, her sobs subsiding as they gently rocked side to side. "It's okay, Kel. I forgive you, if you'll forgive me." She stood back from him, deep concern on her face. She reached up and touched the bandage on his face, gently moving his head to one side to examine the wound on the back of his head. "God, look at what I did to you. Are you okay?"

"I'm okay Rita, honest. I've had a lot worse."

She released a small breath and sniffed back her tears. Kelly reached up and placed his hands on her cheeks, using his thumbs to wipe away her tears. "How do we fix this, Kel?"

"I don't know. I'm just so happy to see you."

"We have so much to talk about," she said as she caressed his wounded cheek.

Everyone else froze in place as Kelly and Rita formally reunited for the first time. Nance had his arms draped around Victoria's neck, and both were smiling through tears. Jenks stood by Brenda and held her hand. Kaitlin was holding Brenda's other hand as they looked on with glistening eyes.

"Come on, you two, we'll have plenty of time to work on that. We're just all happy that you two are together again and talking," Victoria said.

Everyone visibly let out a breath in relief. Kelly leaned down and kissed Rita on the cheek, then on the forehead, smiling at her. Kelly stepped back and turned. "And this is my friend Kaitlin." Kaitlin nodded and smiled. "And this is our other friend Brenda."

"We have already met," Brenda said.

Rita eyed Kaitlin with curiosity. "Do I know you? You look really familiar."

"I don't know," Kaitlin said.

"Did you go to Long Beach?"

Kaitlin nodded. "Yes, I did," she said with a coy smile, clearly enjoying herself.

"Here, let me take your coats," Nance said. He helped KC remove hers and then took Kelly's from him. Rita saw the Chapin sweatshirt that Kelly was wearing, and he saw her making the connection as her dark eyes darted about the room looking between himself and KC.

"Kaitlin Chapin?" she said more as a question.

"Ya got me," quipped KC, smiling.

"Oh, I adore you," Rita said.

Kaitlin moved to Rita to spare her the embarrassment and hugged her. KC stood back at arm's length, looking into her eyes. "I am so happy that you are back together again. God bless you."

Rita was stunned to silence. She looked at Kelly, at KC, and back again. "Are…are you two together?" she asked in amazement. KC nodded with a smile. Rita let out a small laugh in relief, rubbing at her tears. "Boy, can my guy land on his feet, or what?"

Everyone laughed in relief, unsure what would happen with the revelation about Kelly's new relationship with KC.

"Are you folks ready for dinner?" Grandma Weena said in a loud voice from the end of the great room.

"Dinner?" Kaitlin asked, looking nervously at Kelly.

Kelly winked at her as he offered one arm to her and the other to Rita. Both clung to him as they walked into the large dining room. It was furnished with a heavy antique carved table, chairs, and dark, wood-trimmed walls. There was a smaller fireplace burning, creating a warm, comfortable, inviting atmosphere. The table was set to seat the group comfortably. Kaitlin and Rita sat on either side of Kelly. Nance, at the head of the table, Victoria to his right, with Jenks beside Brenda. The small staff moved about busily setting dishes and pouring drinks before the guests. Weena stood at the other end of the table, tapped on a glass, and asked for everyone to be quiet as she offered a short prayer to the Creator as all bowed their heads.

"Everyone, dig in," Weena announced. "And no food fights!"

Rita started asking Kelly questions. She said that Jenks and her mom had given her some details of his experiences, but that they would need to wait for Kelly to fill in most of the blanks. Kaitlin leaned in, and Kelly realized she was probably curious and interested as well. Kelly hesitated until he felt KC reach for his hand under the table. He started describing the events of the day of his capture. He was careful not to get too graphic and skimmed over his friends' deaths, his torture, and some of the most physically abusive experiences. He reminded them that he only remembered bits and pieces before his rescue and waking up in the San Francisco VA Medical Center.

"How did you get those scars?" Rita asked.

Kelly squeezed KC's hand, stopped, and put down his fork. "You sure you want to know?" he asked Rita.

"What's going on with the ranch in Montana, Kelly?" Nance interrupted from the end of the table.

Kelly exhaled with relief, inwardly thanking Nance for the

rescue. "We are undergoing a full-scale renovation. It's going to be a great getaway once things are finished," Kelly said proudly.

"Where is it exactly?" Rita asked. Kaitlin perked up too.

Kelly did his best to describe the location and what the countryside looked like, with its rolling hills surrounded by high mountains in the distance.

"It sounds desolate and boring," Kaitlin observed.

"I think that's what we Montanans like most about it, the peace and quiet of it all. The opposite of LA," Kelly noted.

Small talk continued during the remainder of the meal, most of the conversation moving toward Kaitlin as she answered every question asked by her new friends. They were respectful, caring, and compassionate. Kelly was happy to see Kaitlin being welcomed like this, for he suspected her hectic LA lifestyle was much different.

• • •

After dinner, as the group was returning to the large fireplace for after-dinner drinks and coffee, Rita walked alongside Kaitlin.

"Kaitlin, were you there Friday evening?" Rita asked. Kaitlin nodded as she walked. Rita winced. "God, I'm so sorry you had to see that. I made a complete fool of myself—plus the sheriff was after me yesterday."

Kaitlin stopped and looked at her. "You're kidding. What for?"

"Well, I broke about half a dozen laws with some property damage thrown in. Plus, I haven't told my husband about the car yet." Rita hunched her shoulders and cringed.

They stopped briefly, and Kaitlin said, "First, you should call me KC, because I think I am part of your family too. Second, you let me know if you need any help with things, Rita. I know some people who can help with just about anything." Kaitlin gave Rita's arm a reassuring squeeze. "Don't worry, we're family now. Nothing will come between us."

Rita gave her a hug. "Thank you, KC. You are such a beautiful person."

Kaitlin wasn't sure why Rita's acceptance meant so much to her, but she liked being a part of this family unit. She felt like she belonged.

• • •

Kaitlin and Rita took their seats on either side of Kelly on the soft leather furniture surrounding the fireplace, and Kelly sat on the edge of the couch with his fingers interlaced and looking down at the floor. He still wasn't sure he could do what he had come to do, yet he knew he must. Rita deserved to know everything, as did KC and the others.

He started, "They beat me with sharp canes—a lot—broke my fingers with rifle butts and hammers—many times." He told of gruesome experiences he endured during his three-year ordeal, stopping several times to collect himself. At times, an involuntary sob would escape and a tear would fall to the floor.

Each time, KC and Rita would move closer, each hugging one of his arms. Kelly was determined to push forward. The small group continued to listen in breathless silence. He related his hospital experiences and talked about the decision to not tell Rita he was alive because he did not want to upset her new life. He told of his lost years and recovery. He told of his brother's death and his coming into a large fortune.

Rita leaned away from him. "Whoa, Kelly Chase, this is the first time I'm hearing of this. What, like a hundred thousand dollars, or something?"

She looked to her mother and father, but Nance did not look up and simply shrugged.

Jenks came to Kelly's rescue. "Kelly owns a company, REO Chase, which dabbles in mostly real estate and oil. It's worth about a hundred and seventy million, last I checked. You should know, too, that both your father and I work for Kelly."

Avoiding Rita's gaze, Kelly sat on the edge of the couch with his face hidden in his palms.

After a silence, Rita was finally able to muster up a response. "Well, Mr. POW, is there anything else missing from the headlines that you want to tell me?"

Kelly gave her a sidelong glance as he shrugged and came out of hiding. "Not unless you want to know about the J. Jacks thing."

Jenks and KC chuckled, and Nance and Victoria stared at the ceiling. In an even voice, Rita said, "No, I haven't heard that one, so please tell me more."

Kelly took a deep breath and confessed to her how he had produced the recording as J. Jacks.

"It *was* you!" she hissed. "I knew it." She playfully punched his arm and looked at her mother with self-satisfaction, letting out a laugh. KC and Jenks could no longer control themselves and laughed out loud.

Victoria asked, "Aren't the record companies still looking for you?"

"Yes, but the song belongs to KC now. They'll never find me. I don't need the money, so that should be the end of it."

The group stood up to refill their drinks. Kelly went to the bathroom to rinse his face and freshen up. His shirt was damp from the stress of the last hour; he was physically and emotionally spent. Upon his return, the three women were standing and talking.

"How did you and KC meet?" Rita asked.

KC glanced at him, as if gaining approval. She then told the story, starting with their first meeting in the church and how their paths continually seemed to cross, and how Jenks played an important role in their coming together. Rita was enthralled, tearfully admitting that it was the most beautiful love story she had ever heard. Rita thanked KC and hugged her tightly.

Weena joined the group and struck up a conversation with Jenks. Kaitlin found a phone and was talking to someone. Rita and Kelly took the opportunity to go off by themselves next to the piano.

"Rita, are you going to be okay?" Kelly asked.

"I think so," she said. "Other than the fact that Ben, my husband, is going to kill me. That was his car I destroyed." She sighed. "I could never imagine that Kaitlin Chapin could be such a wonderful person. She makes you whole—that much is clear. For a man I love, I could never ask for more." She gently kissed him and said, "Kelly, I still love you dearly, but my husband, Ben, and Jacob are my life. I would never walk away from that. We are still family. Mom and Dad love you like a son, and that will never change. I hope you understand."

Kelly looked at her, smiled, and kissed her cheek. "We are family, and that's what's most important for me *and* Kaitlin."

"You two must come for Thanksgiving. You can meet Ben and my son, Jacob. Jacob did come down with me, but we have him staying with Gina's parents today. We thought this might be something he wouldn't understand." She paused before saying, "I love you, Kelly Chase." She moved away slowly, giving him one last backward glance before joining her parents.

As he watched her leave, Kelly remembered the conversation he had had with Freddy about having both women in his life, two people who would always love him. He had found the idea unbelievable at the time, yet here it was unfolding before him. KC came to him and put her arm through his.

"That was my father. He wanted to warn me that Mother is up to something. He doesn't know what, but she has been complaining about you and professed to get you run out of town, or something like that."

Kelly's eyebrows arched. "Don't worry about me, princess. I always land on my feet."

Chapter 24

Awakenings

Kelly and Jenks were in the offices early the morning after the get-together at the Villa. They were brainstorming any ideas that could blunt any plans Marie Chapin might have. They would give it some thought and meet each morning to discuss. Kelly and Kaitlin had seen each other at least once a day since they had been to the Villa. Not once had he seen her eat anything of substance. He had watched her during dinner at the Villa as she expertly moved her food around and took a few small bites. Kelly feigned disinterest as she glanced at him occasionally. Did she suspect that he knew something? She seemed to be losing weight again, and he was at a loss for what to do. It was always a topic of discussion each day. Kelly became more concerned when taking out the trash one afternoon and one of the garbage sacks split and the contents spilled on the floor. Numerous capsule containers scattered across the floor. They were so numerous he had no idea where they had come from. He eventually found a label that identified them as a well-known over-the-counter laxative. But there were so many. Where had they all come from? He suspected that Kaitlin had been using them. But, for whatever reason, he could not understand. He decided to call Dr. Brush and ask her some questions. She explained to him that it was one of the best tactics that those suffering from anorexia employed in an attempt to limit weight gain. The overdosing of these products could reach unbelievable amounts. This behavior would be used in conjunction with induced vomiting to expel recently consumed food. Kelly was speechless. He began to watch Kaitlin more closely when she was with him. She was spending a lot of time taking bathroom breaks. He caught her coming out of the bathroom once looking as if she were ready to faint. She was pale and glistening with sweat. He was now certain that she was in the grip of something evil.

Kaitlin's band had been spending a lot of time in recording sessions, so she seemed preoccupied whenever they were together. As he stepped into his house a few days later, his phone was ringing.

"Hello?" Kelly answered.

"Mr. Chase?" Kelly recognized Roland's voice. "It's Roland. Sorry for calling you so late, but I just wanted to chat with you a bit."

"Sure, Roland, and call me Kelly, please."

"Kelly, it's about my sister. A couple of weeks ago, you two had apparently spent a day together out of town." Kelly didn't say anything. "The next day at the studio, she was the happiest I had seen her in months. I wanted to thank you for being a positive influence on her. Other men have tried, and it never seemed to work out. You appear to be what she needs, and I just wanted you to know that."

"Thank you, Roland," Kelly said, happy to get some sort of approval from Kaitlin's family. "I think we have something special and princ—KC—has brought me real happiness too."

"Kelly, I need to tell you that our mother is on a tear because of you. After the photos and articles in the weeklies about you and KC, she has accelerated her campaign. She has been haranguing KC every day, sometimes twice a day. She's been working on me too. Any happiness KC found a couple of weeks ago has been drained by our mother. I'm afraid she's not eating again, and she's being driven to the edge by this daily harassment from our mother."

"What has she been telling her?" Kelly asked.

Roland stayed quiet for a moment, and then started, "I… don't—"

"It's okay, Roland. You can tell me. I can take it."

"She tells her that you are just a lazy Indian and will never amount to anything," Roland blurted out. "She tells us that she will get you run out of California if it's the last thing she does."

"Do you believe any of that?"

"No, not at all. I think you're a very determined, talented individual, and that you will be a great success at some point." Roland continued, "What's more important to me is my sister's happiness, which means more than anything. I want that happy girl who showed up two weeks ago back. I think Mother is having you followed, trying to catch you doing something. She's gathering evidence to try and convince KC that you're a bad person."

"Your mother told you this?"

"No, I overheard a couple of phone conversations with her friends."

"Roland, you are eventually going to find out that I am the opposite of what your mother is suggesting. You might even be amazed by some of the things you learn. Right now, I need to convince your mother to help KC instead of hurting her. I have a plan, and I promise I will not harm your mother." Though it hurt that Kaitlin's mother was more interested in who he was on paper, and how much was in his wallet, he needed to do whatever he could to get her off his back—and Kaitlin's. "I want you to know that I'm trying to help KC get on track and enjoy the Chapins' success again."

Kelly could hear Roland heave a sigh of relief. "Kelly, if you could do that, I would be eternally grateful. By the way, I don't know how you were able to get us all out of the golf-club thing, but we are certainly thankful. Good thing Mother didn't see it. Hopefully you have patched up your differences with your ex-girlfriend."

"Thanks for asking, and yes we have."

After hanging up, Kelly reflected on the articles he had read. "Who is the hunk travelling with Kaitlin Chapin?" and "Happiest she's ever been!" and "Who is the mystery man?" All these articles were positive, but they weren't enough for Kaitlin's mother. Kelly had to stay one step ahead.

Company security picked up Kelly's followers the next Monday. And the followers now had followers. It was determined that they were reporting back to Marie Chapin. It was time for Kelly and Jenks to put their plan into action. They drove in Jenks's Volvo to their frequent breakfast hangout, making sure they were followed. While at the restaurant, Jenks called for the largest limousine the company had available. A short time later, it swooped in to pick them up. Both men walked slowly and talked before entering the vehicle, making certain they were seen and possibly photographed. They went directly to the closest private airfield, drove through a secured gate, and were taken to a new Grumman Gulfstream II that could easily be seen from those outside the security fence. Company security verified that the followers had seen Kelly and Jenks board the plane. The jet took off, having filed a flight plan to Great Falls, Montana.

The men waited until one of the employee flight-line personnel had exited the gate. As expected, one follower approached the employee and asked if he would be willing to share a little information, holding out a fifty-dollar bill. The employee, who was prepped by Kelly, relayed the information as he was told. They were flying to Montana to check out a new oil well. Kelly had told him to say, "That's what I heard them talking about. They said they would be back this afternoon about two o'clock. That's all I know."

Kelly and Jenks returned at two, making certain they still had followers. They entered the waiting limo and were taken to the Rolls-Royce dealership in Beverly Hills. They were dropped off and the limo disappeared into traffic. Kelly had the company plan for a two-day test drive of a fully loaded Silver Shadow. As Jenks drove from the dealership, Kelly sat in the back seat with the window down long enough to expose himself clearly to any photographer. From the dealership, they made their way into one of the wealthier areas of Beverly Hills, constantly checking to see that their followers were still there. They soon arrived at a large, gated estate, where the gate automatically opened in anticipation of their arrival. The gate closed behind the Rolls, leaving the followers wondering what to do next. While in conference, a groundskeeper in a pickup triggered the gate from the other side and drove through. A follower approached the groundskeeper with a fifty-dollar bill in hand, just as he had done earlier that day. As Kelly expected, the groundskeeper, an actor hired by Kelly, looked confused, then concerned, playing his part to a tee. He sheepishly took the bill, looking around surreptitiously. Kelly imagined the conversation went something like:

"Who owns this property? Is it the Joneses' estate?" the man asked.

"No, Señor. Señor Chase owns the property and estate. He's a nice man," the groundskeeper said.

"Very rich?"

"Sí, Señor, he's very rich." Kelly hoped he'd add a vigorous nod for flare.

"How long has he been here?"

"I think maybe six months."

"Is he an actor?"

"I think oil, maybe property."

"You mean real estate?"

"Sí, Señor. Yes! That's it!"

"And oil wells?"

"Sí."

Once the scene had played out and the follower left, the actor found the first phone booth and called Kelly. "I think they bought it," he proclaimed in perfect English.

Kelly thanked him and hung up. "I'm glad we are only renting these things for a couple of days, Jenks," Kelly said. "I would not want to drive a Rolls or live in a place like this," Kelly said as he turned from the phone.

• • •

Upon hearing the report, Marie Chapin sat down on her sofa, absently hanging up the phone. She looked at the pictures sent by special messenger as she spoke with the follower on the phone. Could they have tailed the wrong man? How could this be the same slovenly, roughly dressed Indian from before? He also appeared to be the same man who had appeared in the weekly entertainment magazines with her daughter. Now here he was being chauffeured in a limousine, riding in a new Rolls-Royce, and living on a large estate. Marie was feeling the earth shift below her as she contemplated her next move. She lifted the phone and dialed her financial advisor, Michael Holmes.

• • •

Jenks, using his contacts in the financial investing markets, two days earlier had placed a call to Michael Holmes. Jenks discussed a certain unnamed someone who would call him asking specifically about Kelly Chase.

"Here is what I need you to tell this person when they contact you." Jenks told Michael Holmes the information he wanted him to deliver. "It's all the truth, so you don't need to be concerned about ethics, and no public companies are involved. I know you would not ordinarily give out this information, but in this case, you have a limited exception to tell this one person."

The agreement was made.

• • •

"Hello, Mrs. Chapin," Michael said when he answered Marie's call, remembering that decorum was important to her. Marie made her request.

“I need you to tell me what you know of a certain Mr. Kelly Chase,” Marie demanded, getting straight to the point. “I think he’s originally from Montana. What can you tell me?”

“Mrs. Chapin, it would not be—”

“Michael! How long have the Chapins been trusting you with our investments?”

Michael held his silence for effect, finding some pleasure in Marie’s frustration with his hesitation.

“Mrs. Chapin, what I’ve heard is that the two Chase brothers originally struck oil on their land in Montana about five or six years ago. Since that time, their holdings have expanded exponentially from oil and gas production to major real estate investment holdings. Their company, REO Chase, has a recently audited book value of over two hundred million dollars or so—that’s on paper,” he added dryly. “One of the brothers recently died, and total holdings and leadership of the private company has been passed on to the older brother, Kelly.”

Michael paused for effect again after he heard an audible gasp from Marie Chapin.

“Keep this under you hat, Mrs. Chapin,” Michael lowered his voice conspiratorially, “but I’m hearing rumors that REO Chase is looking to acquire the Stonewood mall complex here locally.”

This was too much. Michael could hear a clatter as the phone apparently fell to the floor.

• • •

The Chapins were performing their last night of a five-night engagement at a venue just outside of San Francisco, and Kelly and Jenks had decided to go see them. Their show was flawless. As Kelly watched, his eyes were always on Kaitlin, noting every move and voice intonation. He had become more concerned about her the last week before this short tour run, as her mood had become sullen despite his attempts to cheer her up. Hopefully, after he and Jenks had gotten Marie Chapin's attention, things would change for the better. He was still having re-occurring dreams each night for the past week about his father, the old Indian. He continued to urge Kelly, "I can help you save her. Bring her to me."

In the dreams, there were visions of Kaitlin falling onto the floor; there was blood, and her eyes were wide open, lifeless. She was surrounded by medical personnel, with a continuous beeping sound piercing the room as masked doctors shook their heads in unison. Kelly would awaken with a start, drenched in sweat and feeling a loss so deep he knew he would not survive it. On one night, Kaitlin was with him, so she soothed and calmed him until his panic subsided and he drifted back to sleep. The dreams and visions would occur whenever he closed his eyes for any length of time. The dreams were pushing him to take an action he knew was logically beyond reason. Ultimately, Kelly became convinced his father held the key to healing Kaitlin. He recalled having awakened from a heavy sleep in his father's lodge, how serene, rested, pain-free, and secure he felt. That same feeling would still wash over him whenever he thought about it.

On stage, Kaitlin was putting on a masterful vocal performance. When watching and listening to her, one would not suspect the inner turmoil brewing, especially when she played her drum set on two numbers; she was the picture of pure joy. Midway through her last song, her voice faltered noticeably, something that never happened. She took a step back, then forward, swayed side to side, and fell backwards into the rear staging deck. The lights immediately went down, then off. The crowd was quiet, and then gradually grew louder expressing alarm, many rising from their seats. Kelly was immediately on his feet and moving, his aim to get on stage. There were low house lights coming on as he found his way around and up on stage, one security man grabbing for his arm after Kelly had maneuvered around him. Kelly arrived to see her surrounded by band members and others trying to help. Someone held a flashlight overhead, so he could see blood pooling around Kaitlin's head, mixing into her matted hair. Two large security men grabbed Kelly under each arm and dragged him off the stage. They formed a solid human fence with other security that he was unable to penetrate.

Kelly finally found Jenks at a lobby phone bank trying to talk to someone on the phone amid the chaos. Jenks turned to Kelly. "We're just going to have to wait," Jenks said before Kelly could get a word out. "We have people working on finding out which hospital they took her to."

Kelly was starting to panic. "I need to go outside," he said, moving toward the doors.

Jenks waited by the phone for a return call.

An hour later, Jenks came running out with notes in hand. "They have a car waiting for us up front. Let's go," Jenks said, leading Kelly toward the car.

Upon entering the hospital, they found a man in a blue casual suit. "Hi, I'm Anthony Dale," he said calmly. "I have some information for you." Anthony related the ICU location, floor, and the attending physician. "She is stable but unconscious. I understand that they are trying to get permission from her family to feed her intravenously. She's anemic and is underweight. Doctors feel that was the cause of her collapse. Her head injury has complicated treatment, so nothing more can be done until x-rays have proven conclusive. Probably a concussion with a good-sized wound. They are trying to keep her stable right now so they can develop a treatment plan. That's it for now."

"Is it possible for us to get close to her, to see her?" Kelly asked.

"I can get you to a nearby waiting room, but you should know that her family is there, and it might be uncomfortable," Anthony warned.

"We'll take the chance," Kelly said.

They eventually stepped from an obscure freight elevator and found their way to the main ICU corridor. Halfway down, there was a wide opening with soft light glowing into the dim hallway. The men made their way down the hallway, passing ICU rooms filled with trauma equipment. Anthony led the way and gingerly peeked around into the waiting room, ducked his head back, and gave Kelly a nod. Anthony and Jenks retreated down the hallway. Kelly entered the room. Seated along one wall was Roland staring ahead blankly. Jack Chapin was asleep lying on a small sofa at the end of the small room with a light blanket covering him. Sitting opposite of Roland was Marie Chapin. It was quiet on the floor. The only sounds were the beeping of monitors and the hushed murmurings of nurses. Kelly closed the glass door behind him as Marie Chapin looked up and met his eyes directly. *She knows as much about me as I want her to*, Kelly thought.

Roland leaped to his feet in total surprise; Jack continued to sleep.

"Mrs. Chapin, I'm Kelly—"

"I know who you are," Marie snapped.

"Forgive me for barging in, but can you please tell me how Kaitlin—er—Miss Chapin is doing?"

Marie considered him for a long moment. Kelly's azure eyes grew more intense as she broke away and glanced at Roland, then back to Kelly. "She'll be fine. Clumsy girl stumbled, fell, and hit her head," Marie said without emotion.

"Mother?" Roland questioned.

Marie dismissed Roland with a backward hand wave, staring back at Kelly again. He could sense she was making a decision. "Sit down," she said, indicating the empty chair across from her. Kelly sat next to Roland, who sunk into his chair. "Apparently you and my daughter have some sort of relationship." More of a statement than a question. "I'm only allowing you in here because I know you aren't after her money."

Jack Chapin suddenly emitted a loud snort, rolled over on the couch, and continued to sleep.

Marie clucked her tongue, glanced at her husband, and rolled her eyes. "Other than checking on her welfare, is there something else you wanted?" she probed.

"Marie, it's not just a bump on the head. Otherwise, she wouldn't be in the ICU. Your daughter hasn't been eating. That's the real reason she collapsed," Kelly said bluntly.

Kelly could see Marie's eyes blink in surprise.

"Your daughter has a condition called anorexia nervosa, AN for short. It's a disease. She's in the beginning stages, and if left untreated, it will be fatal," Kelly continued. "Force-feeding her, as they are planning to do, is only a temporary fix. It will not cure it."

Marie frowned, keeping her eyes from him. Roland had turned to look at him, his mouth open.

"And you know this how?" Marie finally managed to say.

"I'm in love with Kaitlin, and because I've been around her quite a lot, I've seen her aversion to food. My first thought was 'just eat.' Telling her to do so only encourages her to dig in her heels and increase her laxative use and self-induced vomiting, especially when she is forced to eat and can't wiggle her way out of it."

Marie could not stifle her involuntary gasp. Roland remained quiet, slumping back into his chair.

After a moment, Kelly continued, "I've found the only expert on this little-known condition. She's a professor at a university in Houston. Although she's on sabbatical in Montana right now, she's willing to help Kaitlin, but she says that she needs your help, Marie, to treat the condition." Kelly was tempted to tell Marie that her controlling nature contributed to Kaitlin's condition, but he had to be careful.

Marie was still quiet. As Kelly looked at her, she looked at the floor, slouching and letting her hands fall into her lap.

"How can you know all this?" Roland asked.

"He has more money than God, Roland," Marie hissed. "He can find out anything he wants." Roland again turned to Kelly in disbelief. "What does Kaitlin know about you?" Marie asked.

"Everything. Because I love her, I do not hide anything from her," he stressed. "Apparently, she has told neither of you anything, showing that my trust in her is not misplaced. Marie, if you are willing, the doctor will take your call at any hour. I have made all the arrangements. She knows who Kaitlin is and the sensitive nature of the case. You only need to give the word and we can go to a nearby private phone and you can talk to her."

Marie wiped the tears from her cheeks with the heel of her hand, her expression still serious, and nodded her head twice, fixing her mouth in the same frown that Kaitlin would often display.

Two hours later, Marie came out of the small private office, visibly shaken. She held a balled-up tissue in her hand. Kelly suspected Doctor Brush's assessment and information had been sobering, blunt, and emotional. He hoped she had come to terms with knowing that she may hold her daughter's life in her hands. Kelly needed her help, and he watched her closely as she walked numbly down the hallway toward them in the waiting room.

"Have they said any more about her? Is she okay?" Marie asked with genuine concern.

Kelly and Roland rose from their seats. "Mother, they said she's resting comfortably and out of danger," Roland explained. "They're going to move her to a private room tomorrow morning. They want to start feeding her with a tube—"

"Absolutely not! Not yet," came Marie's immediate response.

During Marie's absence, Kelly had shared all he needed to with Roland. He answered his questions about AN and his relationship with Kaitlin. He told of his financial independence, to a point, choosing not to reveal more than what Roland needed to know.

"Kelly, you warned me, but this is the last thing I expected," Roland had said. "I'm happy that my sister has finally found the one. She was in near complete despair having to choose a career over a relationship."

"She's not out of the woods yet. There is work to do," Kelly had cautioned.

After Marie received Kaitlin's update from Roland, she looked for Jack. "Where is your Dad?" she asked.

"I sent him to the hotel, Mom. He was starting to snore."

Kelly approached Marie. "I apologize for handling this the way I did, but I saw no other way. I'm terribly sorry, Mrs. Chapin. I know I was blunt and rude. Please forgive me."

She looked up at Kelly, her eyes glittering. "Please call me Marie, Kelly. You've earned it." Finally, she smiled. She turned to Roland and embraced him, giving him a kiss on the cheek. "Now off with you. I will attend to your sister."

Roland seemed dumbstruck by his mother's odd change in mood, but he didn't ask any questions.

"Marie, may I wait with you?" Kelly asked as he held out his arm to escort her to a chair, and then sitting down beside her.

A woman he had thought to be made of stone had softened. Kelly knew Kaitlin's wellbeing meant the most to her, and so they could share this moment together.

• • •

Kaitlin drifted into consciousness. Her vision gradually cleared as she became aware of her surroundings. A hospital. *Not again*, she thought.

She became aware of two figures by her bedside as her vision cleared a little more. She blinked her eyes twice, three times. A dull pain in her temples ached, and then she saw her mother on one side and Kelly on the other, each holding one of her hands.

"Welcome back, Kaitlin," her mother said in a soft voice she couldn't recall hearing in years.

"How are you doing, sweetheart?" Kelly asked as he gently lifted her hand and kissed it.

Kaitlin smiled at him. "Kelly," she said and weakly squeezed his hand. She looked at her mother and weakly greeted her. "Hi, Mom," she said in a whisper.

Surely she must have been dreaming. Her mother and Kelly in the same room, both with her. How could this be? Confusion washed over her face as both of her visitors seemed to be enjoying her puzzled expression.

"What happened? How?" she whispered.

"You fainted on stage, my girl. You fell and hit your head," her mother explained in an unfamiliar compassionate voice.

Kaitlin worried about how Kelly saw her now, seeing his Church Girl looking weak, sick, and her head wrapped in a gauze bandage. His eyes filled with tears, and he looked away, struggling to control himself.

Marie came closer to Kaitlin, grasping her hand with both of hers and starting, "Kelly and I have come to an agreement. We are taking you to see someone who can help you as soon as you are released to travel."

"With what?" Kaitlin asked with a serious look.

"You have an eating problem, honey—"

"No, Mom, I'm okay. Really, I'm fine," Kaitlin said, almost begging, her voice starting to return. "There's nothing wrong with me. I'm just a little too overweight. That's all, really."

Kaitlin knew she'd chosen the wrong words, for as Marie stood erect and looked at Kelly, there was no doubt that she could not convince her mother she didn't have a problem.

"Kelly," Marie said, giving Kelly a single nod.

Kelly bent down and gave Kaitlin a tender kiss on her cheek, like he was trying not to break her. "Get some rest, princess. This is me not giving up on you," he whispered.

Kaitlin did not respond. She was angrier than she'd ever been.

• • •

Kelly and Jenks planned for a private medical flight out of a nearby private airstrip. It was a self-contained aircraft able to handle any emergency medical transports. Kelly also paid for Doctor Brush to meet him, Kaitlin, and Marie at a leased office suite in Great Falls not far from the airport. Kelly had paid for all of Dr. Brushes expenses with a lucrative fee for her specialized treatment for Kaitlin. The doctor was truly dedicated, and while she admitted that the money was a plus, she was extremely interested in Kaitlin's case and was looking forward to the challenge and wanted to help. Dr. Brush wanted to meet with Kaitlin alone on two consecutive days so she could get familiar with her and give them a chance to establish a treatment relationship and a plan to move forward. Kaitlin's family would then become part of the treatment plan. Marie had agreed to be involved. Kelly was going to commit a sin of omission. He had delayed the initial meeting between Kaitlin and Dr. Brush by three days. He needed some time to spirit Kaitlin away to meet with the old Indian. They needed to do this, for now it had become an undeniable force he could no longer resist. The nightly manifestations had become more and more demanding.

Kelly had Jenks set everything up from the first landing at a small former military airfield in Cut Bank. They would then take a short medical chopper flight to East Glacier Village, the small town where the brothers had dropped their father off years earlier when he had left them. A specially equipped four-wheel-drive Jeep would meet them there to continue the journey to "Lower Two Medicine Lake." Sheriff Potter would provide escort services, as the road was officially closed. Ranch Manager Del Bonds would bring in a truck, trailer, and two horses, complete with tack and gear. At nearly mile-high elevation, the small road to Lower Two Medicine could be difficult to navigate in the winter. All this planning had been complicated by the winter storm that had struck the night before, leaving one to two feet of snow in places. The temperature had dropped to ten degrees and had only warmed slightly. Sheriff Potter had thoughtfully made arrangements for a snowplow escort to the lower lake.

It was almost six o'clock in the morning, still dark, when the vehicles all converged at East Glacier to continue the trip to the lower lake, with the snowplow leading the way. Once they arrived at the lower lake, Del and Sheriff Potter busily set about getting the two horses and gear prepared for the assent by Kelly and Kaitlin. Their destination would be the same as Kelly's earlier trip to see his dad. Somewhere near Upper Two Medicine Lake, about six miles up through cold, snowy, rough terrain, the snowplow had managed to turn around and head back to the garage. Kaitlin was bundled in blankets, and only her face and dark-ringed eyes were visible.

She had started out on the journey from San Francisco in a bad mood, which finally began to brighten at the experience of a helicopter flight. She was cleared medically to make the trip to Montana, but she was weak and tired. Kelly knew he was taking a big chance bringing her up on the mountainside, but he was convinced this would help her. Jenks was not in the best of sorts either, as he continued to badger and complain that Kelly was unnecessarily putting Kaitlin's life at risk. Kelly kept reassuring Jenks that it would be okay, but Jenks wasn't buying it. He had gone silent during the last two miles of the Jeep ride.

The two horses were standing by the trailer with all the gear loaded, saddled, and ready to go. Kelly and Jenks gently encouraged Kaitlin to perch upon Mush. She was secured into the saddle and stirrups, with her hands holding the saddle horn. She was dressed in a snowsuit with knee-high, fur-lined boots and mittens, a ski mask, and hood to protect her from the wind.

"How do you feel, baby?" Kelly asked her.

"Where are we going?" she asked, looking confused. "Kelly, do you still love me?" she asked suddenly in a weak voice.

"Honey, you're my one and only," he reassured her. "I need you to hold on tight to Mush and yell at me if you need me to stop. Okay?"

She managed to nod several times. It was as if she was going in and out of a trance. She had eaten little in the last few days, and she was getting weaker. Kelly prayed he wasn't going to add to her misery with this trek up the mountain. The second horse, named Sniff, was packing food, shelter, extra blankets, water, and other necessary items. Kelly slung his rifle over his shoulder. With Mush tied to Sniff, he would lead.

Sheriff Potter handed Kelly a communications radio. "When you get halfway down, we should be able to pick you up again. Or call us if you get in trouble. The frequency is set. Call us when you're ready, and we will be waiting for you."

Kelly had hoped to reach his father by early afternoon, weather cooperating, and if he could follow the map with the snow blotting out many landmarks. Jenks was standing nearby, lost in his large, blue parka with a fur-lined hood.

"Why can't he come down to see us?" Jenks asked.

Del Bonds said, "He's camped on land that is said to be sacred ground by the Blackfeet. It holds great power, according to the ancient ones. Those who hold great medicine have been known to inhabit this place. The line of medicine holders was broken many years ago, and no one has been present. Now we are hearing of a holder who resides again on the mountain. He's called 'the chaser of bad sprits,' who some have said has great power to heal."

Kelly was stunned to hear this from Del. Del looked up to the mountain, nodded, turned, and walked back down to the truck. Jenks went to Kaitlin and placed his hand on her knee.

"Please come back to us, KC. We love you," Jenks said in a quivering voice.

She looked down at him and gave a small smile, still trance-like. "I love you too, Jenks," she softly responded.

Jenks smiled at her, then turned and glared at Kelly.

"Don't cry, Jenks. Your tears will freeze," Kelly warned.

Jenks looked away in disgust and stomped back to the Jeep.

"Good luck, son," Sheriff Potter said to Kelly.

• • •

Jenks stood by the Jeep and watched the two people he cared for most in the world disappear into a swirling foggy haze as early daylight struggled to overcome the low overcast sky.

Sheriff Potter told Del and Jenks to go back into town and grab something to eat and warm up. He would stay and monitor Kelly and Kaitlin as they made their way.

Del was driving the Jeep as Jenks sat quietly. "You know that's his father up there, don't you?" Del said.

Jenks looked surprised. "What? You mean the medicine man?"

"Yep."

Jenks was quiet again, he remembered something about Kelly's experience with his father and how he worked some unbelievable magic on Kelly's pain. "Do you believe all this nonsense, Del?"

"Mr. Jenkins, I have seen many unusual things in my life, and I've become convinced. Yes, I do. You should try to keep an open mind and reserve judgment."

Jenks looked ahead, watching wind gusts blow the snow across the road in swirls. He said a prayer to the only God he ever knew.

• • •

Kelly and Kaitlin struggled up the steep, wide, rocky ridge, where the wind had blown away the snow to expose the ground beneath. The great trees swayed as clumps of snow occasionally landed around them. Kelly stopped to check on Kaitlin. Her head was down as she tried to avoid the sudden bursts of wind and stinging snow.

"Are you okay, princess?" Kelly yelled through the elements.

Kaitlin raised her head, and Kelly heard her weakly respond, "Yes."

"Are you getting cold? Are your feet or hands numb?" he asked again.

She shook her head. Mush turned his head like he was inspecting the rider. Kelly took out a small, insulated canteen and drank a few gulps and offered her a drink, which she refused.

"You yell at me if you get thirsty—or if anything gets numb or you need to stop," Kelly shouted.

Kaitlin nodded gamely at him, the dark circles around her eyes standing out clearly against her pale skin visible through the ski mask's eye holes. Kelly checked on her every five minutes as they made it through another two hours of slowly gaining ground, hesitating each time Mush missed a step or slipped on an icy patch. After another check on Kaitlin, she was complaining that her fingers were numb. He loosened her hands and massaged them through her mittens for a minute, then secured them again.

"Do you want to get down and stretch, try to move around?" he asked. She nodded, so Kelly reached up, lifted her, and placed her next to Mush. "Here, just lean against him while I help you."

She leaned against the horse and grasped his mane with one mittened hand. Kelly took off his gloves and laid them across the saddle. He rubbed and massaged both of her legs, working his hands up her body to improve circulation. He briefly warmed his hands inside his parka under his armpits, and then he removed her mask, checked her skin, and then rubbed and massaged her face. Her eyes came into focus as she looked at him.

"I love you, Piano Man," she said.

He instantly felt a hard lump in his throat. "I love you too, Church Girl." He hugged her and kissed her cheek. "How are your feet?"

"Okay," she said, but she didn't sound too confident.

"Do you need to go to the bathroom?" he asked. She shook her head. Kelly reached into the saddle bag and pulled out a small slab of beef jerky. "Want some?"

Again, she shook her head. He separated a piece and popped it into his mouth, savoring the sweet, flavorful juice. He reached into another small bag and pulled out an egg and offered that to her as well. She turned up her nose with that familiar frown. Kelly debated stopping to create a warming camp. They would lose momentum and might not be able to continue if they had to spend a night in the open. He decided to go a little farther. He, too, was suffering from exhaustion and was wearing down quickly. He gave the two horses some water, put her mask back on, and lifted her back onto Mush.

"Just hold tight, baby," he said. "Yell at me if you need to stop."

They continued up the mountain but made two more stops during the next four hours. Kelly had lost track of time and had gotten into a plodding rhythm, following the ridgeline, stumbling occasionally when he heard it—the far-off cadence of a drum, then a gentle voice singing in Blackfoot. Kelly turned to check on Kaitlin, who had fallen forward with her head resting on her hands and the saddle horn. He panicked. Had he lost that much time? The sound of the voice grew louder.

Kelly hunched his shoulders. "Come on, Mush and Sniff, we're almost there."

Kelly looked up when the voice suddenly stopped. Standing before him was his father, Aloysius Chase, "The Chaser of Bad Spirits," who stood wrapped in a buffalo fur, his gray hair catching the light snowflakes as the wind suddenly died down.

"You have brought the one of great value, the angel," his deep, resonant voice announced.

Kelly didn't remember his father's voice ever having such great presence. He seemed to have grown in size. Was that possible? The old Indian stepped forward, passing his son. He effortlessly lifted

Kaitlin from the saddle and cradled her in his arms. Kelly followed with the horses, stumbling to keep up, and then he realized that his feet and hands had gone numb. His nostrils were frozen nearly shut, and his face was without feeling. The scars on his body were aching and on fire. He could barely see his father disappear into the lodge, with Kaitlin hanging limply. He found his way to the horse shelter and shook the remaining water out of his canteens for each horse, as most of it had turned to blocks of ice. After tending and clearing the loads from the horses and covering them with the skins provided, he made his way to the lodge.

Kelly entered his father's warm lodge to see him pulling the heavy, cold outer coverings from Kaitlin. He had uncovered her head, exposing the bandage wrapped around it. The old Indian stretched her alongside the small fire and started massaging her bare hands and feet, gently pushing warmth back into them. He covered her in a large buffalo fur and turned to his son, beckoning to him silently. His father delicately unclothed his son and rubbed his hands, face, and body to bring back sensation. Aloysius covered Kelly with another fur and helped him lie by the fire, with Kaitlin's head just inches from his.

"Rest, my son. I will bring you some food and drink," Aloysius said.

The scars on Kelly's back were soon in flames. His hands felt weak and tingly. His feet turned hot and painful as his blood began to warm his body. His father brought him warm roasted fish with roots, sweet berries, and water. He struggled to pick up the food with his fingers, as cold numbness refused to release its grip. He ate what he could.

"There is more if you want it," Aloysius offered as he sat cross-legged by Kaitlin, continuing to massage her body. Kelly reached out and stroked the sweet face that he loved. "We will begin with her tonight. She's okay now, just needs to rest and warm up."

Kelly soon felt it impossible to keep his eyes open. He vaguely recalled seeing his father removing Kaitlin's head bandage as she slept. He stroked her hair with a damp cloth as he cradled her in his lap. The old Indian again sang softly, chanting in the old way. Her eyes had lost most of their darkness, as there looked to be a small smile on her face. Kelly could hear the wind buffeting against the lodge as he drifted away.

• • •

Kaitlin felt unbearable heat as she surfaced from a deep sleep, realizing she was in a small tent or shelter of some kind. It was so hot she felt as if she were going to burn up at any moment. She tried to get up but found she could not move or speak. An old Indian with long, gray braids was leaning over her. He was slowly waving a large feather over a small clay dish beside her head, with smoke slowly rising and directed toward her with the feather. The aroma was sweet and immediately put her at ease as she breathed in the soft smoke, her nostrils burning from the hot air contained in the sweat lodge. The old Indian was singing a song, but she could not understand the words. It suddenly came to her that this was the man she'd heard singing the strange song in her dreams. Those dreams always made her feel so good when she awakened. It was strange that she only had those dreams when she was sleeping next to Kelly.

Kaitlin started slipping back into a dreamlike state. She found herself looking down at her body as she hovered above. She was in the sound trailer in Vegas with headphones on. She could see herself collapsing onto the floor as her brother entered. She called out for him as she fell: "Oh, Roland." He was on his knees yelling her name and checking her pulse and her breathing. He ran out the door and screamed for help. She watched herself be put into an ambulance and delivered to a hospital. She saw doctors surrounding her, expressing great concern, and talking about testing for anemia—and how she appeared underweight. The scene switched to her on stage, again in San Francisco. She saw herself stumbling, swaying back and forth, dropping the mic, and collapsing backward, landing hard and hitting her head on the backstage platform. She could see blood pooling around her head as chaos ensued. She saw Kelly trying to climb over security to get to her, his attempts futile—his face full of fear. The scene quickly showed a scale displaying eighty-five pounds. She saw herself having a screaming confrontation with her mother, until her mother wept as Kaitlin stormed out the door. Then, in a closet, she slowly slipped to the floor. She was not moving or breathing as emergency workers tried to revive her.

Why was she seeing all this? This had never happened.

The scene flashed to a hospital setting, where doctors worked furiously on her while other emergency nurses and aides leaned against the walls and slid onto the floor weeping, crying, and reaching for one another. All were crying out her name. The doctors stopped, and their heads hung in defeat. The scene went dark, and she could only hear her mother, father, and brother crying out her name in pain. In the background, she could hear the oscilloscope signaling a flatline. And that's when she saw true devastation: her lifeless body on a gurney.

"No, this is not happening," she moaned in her sleep. "Please, please make it stop," she begged.

The old Indian sang and chanted again. The tension left her body as the gentle voice resonated through her. She felt the heat growing again, then a sensation building in the core of her body—a warm glow building within. It was a light, giddy feeling that continued to spread, working to consume her entire body. The tips of her fingers and toes glowed. Then everything was taken over by the eerie inner glow as it grew within her entire body, becoming a white hotness until it felt like she would burst into flames.

Kaitlin was plunged into a cold that shocked every fiber of her.

Her first reaction to scream was stifled by the intense cold. It froze her throat, and no sound could escape. She involuntarily took in a deep breath, the cold burning her lungs and freezing her nostrils. Then she felt like she was being lifted.

Fully awake, she was looking up into a gray sky. Water dripped from her body and from her light leather garment. She had been lifted out of a glacial stream that had not yet frozen over. She saw the face of the old man looking down at her with a gentle smile.

"It's going to be okay now, little angel," he said, taking her into the large lodge and humming a song as he set her down by the fire and helped her remove the wet leather covering from her shivering body, blotting her dry with a large chamois. He helped ease her between two soft buffalo furs and tucked her securely away, leaving only her face exposed to the warming fire. Kaitlin saw Kelly sleeping soundly on the other side of the fire. Starting to warm, she snuggled within the soft fur coverings. The mysterious glow returned to her body as she sailed off into a deep sleep.

• • •

Kelly was prodded awake by Aloysius. He sat up, cleared his head, and looked for Kaitlin.

His father laid a hand on his shoulder. "Come."

Aloysius helped Kelly to his feet and wrapped him in a buffalo robe. Kelly looked at his princess, but he could only see what showed through the folds of the fur coverings. He noticed the darkness around her eyes was gone. Although it was hard to discern by the light of the small fire, he was certain he saw a smile.

Kelly followed his father to the sweat lodge. The sky had started to darken, and it was getting colder. He had lost complete sense of time. Kelly dropped the robe just before entering.

"How is she?" Kelly asked once he had settled across from his father.

The old man poured water over the newly stoked stones. Steam filled the small lodge as the rocks popped and sizzled in response. Sweat instantly beaded on his body.

"The angel will be okay," Aloysius said. "She still has work to do, but she'll be different in some ways—in good ways," he added.

Kelly sat motionless as the strange inner glow quickly came back to him. It overpowered his entire body and sharpened all his senses. He experienced that same weightless state he had felt on his first visit. The large scars on his body quickly grew hot, hotter, ever hotter. It felt like they were about to explode. He screamed, but no sound came. A fog rolled in. He saw a vision of his brother, Frank. A much younger Frank. He was happier than he ever remembered him being. Then Kelly realized that his mother was standing behind Frank with her arms around him, holding him tightly with a face filled with joy only a proud mother could feel. Kelly felt his own tears as he reached for them both. The scene changed to a vision of Jonesy and Clemons being executed, then Kelly lying in the cage with rain cascading down, him shivering and cold curled in a ball. Another scene with him struggling through thick jungle, staggering under the weight of ammunition boxes. Another switch, seeing himself with the old mama-san as she dug bullets from his chest, him writhing in pain. The last cane-beating came into view, the rifle butt coming down on his head. Rita coming after him with the golf club, him surrendering to her, accepting the punishment she demanded for the trouble he had caused. He felt as if his body had swollen to twice its size, completely filled with pain, ready to explode. The pinpoint of heat deep in his stomach was now growing larger and larger as it consumed every bit of his body. All the air was sucked from his lungs as his body was consumed with a hot fire—he could not breathe. He felt himself struggling to take a breath and realized that he had collapsed into nearly nothing. Suddenly, an explosion of cold. Cold air rushed into his lungs, filling him completely, the feeling utterly glorious. The cold so complete he felt death eminent. Then silence. The sensation of weightlessness again. He was being carried. His body was being dried and then placed between two warm buffalo furs. Sleep again took him.

The next morning, Kelly struggled to come awake, his eyes feeling stuck shut. He reached up and rubbed them, feeling the eye crumbs on the backs of his fingers. His vision cleared. His mouth and throat were so dry each breath he took burned his throat. He exhaled with a slow moan.

Kelly sat up instantly, jarred fully awake with panic as he searched for Kaitlin. She sat on the opposite side of the fire, sitting cross-legged and fully dressed.

"Come on, sleepy head. Grab some breakfast," she said with a smile—perfectly radiant.

The old man sat behind her, carefully brushing her long hair with a relaxed smile across his face. She held a bowl of something and was taking bites with a small spoon.

"You know, you didn't even bother to introduce me to your father," she said. "You should be ashamed." She wagged her spoon at him. Kelly could hear her scraping the bottom of the bowl. "Can I have a little more, please? It's so good. What is it, anyway? Can I get the recipe?"

The old Indian looked at her as if expecting another question before he dared answer. "Little angel, best you don't know what it is. It's good for you, and you'll be able to keep it down. I will send some with you to eat on the way down."

Still stunned, Kelly thought he might be dreaming. In a hoarse voice, he said, "KC, meet my father, Aloysius Chase." Posed as more of a question, he added, " The Chaser of Bad Spirits."

Kelly was lying on his side, propped on his elbow. The old Indian looked down at Kaitlin, nodded once, and got up to take the empty bowl for a refill. His father returned with a large gourd of water. Kelly eagerly drank with large, unrestrained gulps. He downed the entire gourd, finishing with a long sigh.

"Well, get dressed and eat. We have to get going," Kaitlin said, an eagerness filling her voice.

Aloysius took the empty gourd and quickly returned with another bowl and a water gourd for Kaitlin. She noisily slurped the water as she looked over the top of the gourd at Kelly with her big brown eyes. It was clear there was a light in them that was not there before.

"Thank you, na-ahks," she said, and then she continued speaking to the old man in Blackfoot in the old way.

Grandfather, thank you for your home, food, and healing, Kelly managed to translate to himself.

With warm eyes and a smile, she looked up at the old man, who, as he placed his hand on her head, responded in Blackfoot, "Little angels are always welcome here."

"Come on, Kelly Chase!" Kaitlin shouted. "Get going! We have business to attend to." She wagged her spoon at him again.

Kelly pulled a fur over his shoulders, stood, and made his way around the fire to her. He folded her into his arms tightly, kissing the top of her head as he closed his eyes, drinking in the smell of her and the feeling of her closeness.

She rested her head on his chest and closed her eyes, tears working at the corners. "I love you, Kelly Chase."

"I love you too, princess. How do you feel?"

He stood back, holding her shoulders and appraising her. There was an unmistakable brightness in her eyes, something deep, a twinkling. She looked back at him, and he hoped his love for her was clearer than ever before.

"Now get dressed and grab a bite. We need to get going," she said as he turned.

She playfully pinched him on the butt and giggled. The old man stood with his back to them, giving a small laugh.

• • •

As Kaitlin helped Kelly dress, he realized that all of his physical pain was gone. The nagging pain in his fingers and back was completely gone, replaced by the lighter-than-air giddiness in his stomach. His father had been busy preparing a plate of food for him. Warm venison, potatoes, local vegetables, and sweet berries.

"There's more if you need it."

"How long have we been here, Dad?" Kelly asked.

"About two days."

Where has the time gone? Kelly wondered in amazement. Had he been sleeping all that time? What had happened to KC? "That long?"

His father nodded with a smile as he chewed a piece of pemmican. After Kelly had finished his meal and KC had tidied up the lodge, Aloysius said, "Let's smoke."

His father prepared the pipe, sat down, stoked the fire, and lit the pipe. He gestured for both of his guests to join him, pointing with his chin. The three gathered around the fire. The pipe was passed to KC. She took the long pipe and looked unsure.

"But, Grandfather, I don't smoke," she said in the perfect old tongue.

"Go ahead, Angel. We won't tell anyone," Aloysius said with a sly smile.

She took her first puff and didn't wince, looking like she found it pleasant, and the smell of tobacco and raspberries filled the air. They shared a quiet moment, smoking in silence, which gave the two visitors time to reflect and collect themselves.

The temperature had warmed considerably, and clouds had parted to show blue skies above. The horses were loaded, and everything was set for the journey down. It was still morning, and they would make good time on the return. Kelly's dad had mysteriously come up with clothes for Kaitlin. Blue jeans, denim shirt, cowboy boots, and a brown, fringed leather coat, which all fit her perfectly.

“Now you won’t stick out so much in Montana,” Aloysius said, helping her put on the coat and brushing her shoulders and back, working out any wrinkles.

She turned to him and hugged him. “Hamma tenshai kum-cha—na-ahks.” *I love you, my grandfather.*

She kissed him on the cheek and hugged him again.

“Come see me again, little angel,” Aloysius answered in Indian.

Kaitlin nodded at him, her eyes turning misty. Kelly helped her climb atop Mush as she stroked his mane. Kelly handed her the reins. “He will be gentle with you, and he’ll follow me and Sniff,” Kelly said as he motioned to the other horse with his hat.

Aloysius disappeared briefly and returned with a dark Stetson hat. “One last thing, little angel,” he said as he handed her the hat.

Kaitlin took it with a big smile and placed it on her head, her long hair trailing behind her in a leather wrap. *Damned if she didn’t look like a top hand*, admired Kelly. Kelly embraced his father as Aloysius leaned forward and gave him a small kiss on the cheek.

Aloysius turned away. “Make sure she sees the German woman,” he said, not turning as he disappeared into the woods.

Kelly stopped, lifted his hat, scratched his head, shrugged his shoulders, and climbed aboard Sniff.

They made their way down the mountainside, zig-zagging to accommodate the rough terrain. KC talking almost non-stop. She said maybe she had died during the experience with his father. She told of seeing herself dead and how terrifying it was. She tried to put into words the glowing lighter-than-air sensation in her stomach and body that had come to her and how it was still with her. How safe, loved, and secure she felt. She had finally awakened from her sleep and felt hunger, and it was only natural that she ate to satisfy it. She spoke with awe about the things that she had experienced, how everything was new and more colorful.

They stopped occasionally to rest and water the horses. On the last stop, they admired the view of the valley vista below through the parted clouds. The sun streamed through the opening and lit up the valley floor below, creating a breathtaking visual splendor—reflecting the snow-covered ground made it ever more beautiful. One could see for miles to the next range of mountains to the west.

"This must be the most beautiful place on earth," Kaitlin marveled.

Kelly didn't answer, only nodded in agreement. It was as if he were seeing it for the first time as well. Having lived here most of his life, he realized just then what he had been taking for granted. He moved next to KC, put his arms around her from behind, and brought her close to him. He breathed in the scent of her and kissed her check tenderly.

"It's a long way from LA and Hollywood, huh?"

"It's so quiet," she said, still expressing awe. She turned to him, took both of his hands, and held him with her intense, deep, brown-eyed gaze. She kissed him tenderly. "I probably will never understand what happened with Grandfather. But I feel so light, free…and I'm starving." She ate the last of the special dish that the old Indian had prepared for her. "I wish I knew what this is. It's so good."

"Trust me, if the old man made it, you really don't want to know," Kelly quipped.

During the last leg of the descent, each of them sang a song as they rode. When KC raised her usually soft voice in this place, it rang out powerful and clear. Kelly thought it sounded like a choir in a cathedral. He looked over at her, and she was emotionally lost in the song—her eyes closed. *She could never be more beautiful*, he thought.

• • •

Using Sheriff Potter's radio, Kelly had arranged to be met at the pick-up point, where Jenks waited anxiously. The sheriff, Del

Bonds, and Jenks stood by the two trucks, craning to see the two riders that had come into view.

Upon arriving at the trucks, Jenks ran up to Kaitlin and placed his hand on her knee. "KC, are you okay?" Jenks suddenly froze as he looked up at her. Her brown eyes met his, as did her smile. *Is this the same person?* he wondered.

He helped her dismount from Mush as Del held the reins. "What happened?" Jenks asked in amazement.

Kaitlin started talking to Jenks in Indian, "na-ahks," and then she suddenly stopped and said, "Er, an old Indian did something, just not sure what."

Jenks gave a puzzled look.

"Her grandfather," Del said, interpreting as he walked by, stopping briefly to tip his hat to KC.

"Yes, Grandfather," she echoed.

Kelly remained aboard Sniff, taking it all in.

Jenks saw that she was all right but that something had changed. Kaitlin had a presence that she hadn't had before. She radiated, almost glowed, her eyes holding a light. Her smile was genuine and warm, hiding nothing. Her attire, too, set her off even more. Where had she gone shopping on a mountain?

Jenks was speechless. Kaitlin went to Jenks and gave him a long hug and kissed him on the cheek. He responded with a crimson flush. Kaitlin stepped to the front of Mush and stroked his soft muzzle and hugged him. Mush let out a small whinny of appreciation.

"I love this horse," she announced.

Kelly, still sitting with his wrists resting on his saddle horn, said, "Good. He's yours, but you have to feed him and take care of him."

The sheriff and Del both laughed as Kelly dismounted Sniff and went to Kaitlin to hug and kiss her. Jenks looked at his old friend and saw the same light in his eyes. One that was not there before.

• • •

Kelly and KC rode with Del back to the Chase ranch. They followed Sheriff Potter and Jenks. The temperature had warmed up even more, and the late-afternoon sun came out to clear the road and melt the snow.

"I didn't know you were Indian," Kelly said to Del.

"My Dad is Blackfeet," Del said. "He knows your father and many of the old ways."

They got off on the typical conversation of who was related to whom. Something Indians always did—it was customary. Sitting in the middle of the two men, Kaitlin's head turned from one to the other as they shared some unusual names of relatives near and far.

She giggled at one of the more obscure names. "Oh, sorry," she said with a sheepish grin.

When they finally entered the ranch gate, Kelly could see drastic improvements. Kelly and KC entered the house, where according to Kelly, a majestic transformation had taken place.

"Well, how do you like it?" Shelly called out.

Jenks followed them in and joined the group in staring in amazement. A fire was burning in the large stone fireplace, the wood occasionally popping. Leather furniture and scattered Indian features were prevalent.

"This place feels so warm. I just love it," Kaitlin gushed.

Skylights were a predominate feature built into the new cathedral-like construction, and there wasn't a dark corner in the fully transformed home. Kaitlin toured the new kitchen. It was warm and had all the latest innovations. She let her fingers linger on the countertop as she walked along.

"Soup's on," Shelly announced.

Kaitlin managed to eat a light, soft meal that Shelly had specially prepared for her. Kelly had warned Kaitlin that their trip up the mountain was not an authorized adventure, so any phone calls were not a good idea.

"Dang it. I can't call my bookie?" she asked with mock concern.

Jenks went to Kaitlin. "I don't know what happened up there, but you both look amazing." She tried to explain what happened, but he stopped her. "If I believe in miracles, then I will just accept this and move on." He hugged her as she kissed him again on the cheek.

"You are so precious to me, Jenks."

Kelly and Kaitlin spent their first night together at Chase Ranch. They lay afterward and talked of their experiences. KC was full of questions about her new grandfather. Questions about his mother, his brother…everything. Kelly explained the plan to see Dr. Brush and the story of how she became involved. Kelly apologized for involving himself in her personal business. He was worried she would still be angry with him and reject the help he was offering.

"I know you would never do anything to harm me—or my family—I believe you. You still haven't given up on me."

The next morning, they explored the reconstructed suite with all the latest conveniences. KC was in love with what Kelly had created.

"This is a place where I've always wanted to live. It's my dream palace," she said.

After breakfast the next morning, Jenks flew out in a Jet Ranger headed for Great Falls, then on to New York. Kelly and Kaitlin drove in Kelly's truck to Great Falls to meet with Doctor Brush. They stopped along the way and did some shopping and sightseeing. Kelly bought her some more Montana clothes so she would fit in. She was dressed in denim jeans, a faded red snap-button shirt, and, of course, her boots and leather jacket. She had on a colorful headband that was tied and hung to her shoulders. Kaitlin sat next to Kelly as they travelled. They found a country radio station and started singing.

• • •

Kelly and Kaitlin entered Doctor Brush's expansive, richly appointed, remote office that REO Chase company had created for her. Plush red carpet, floor-to-ceiling windows looked down from the third floor. It was expensively furnished with one wall of bookcases and only a few books occupying the shelves. Two dark, leather settees faced opposite, separated by a low, large table. To one side was a round worktable with four chairs. There were open books, a writing pad, and other paperwork on the table, evidence that the doctor used this as her main work area. Dr. Brush was a small woman in her mid-sixties. She had graying hair pulled up in a tight bun. She had intense, ice-blue, laser eyes that were offset by an ever-present soft smile. She had on a deep-blue dress with a white collar and wore small, dark-rimmed, round glasses that further softened her look. She approached Kaitlin first and extended her hand, their eyes meeting. She stopped in the middle of her greeting and tipped her head to one side.

"Hmm? Interesting," she said. "I'm sorry. I'm Doctor Brush, and it's a pleasure to meet you, Kaitlin," Dr. Brush greeted in her heavy German accent as she politely took her hand.

"Thank you, ma'am," Kaitlin responded, nodding politely.

Dr. Brush's stare dwelled upon her for another moment before she addressed Kelly. Looking into his eyes, she narrowed her gaze briefly then nodded to herself. "So nice to finally meet you, Mr. Chase," she said, finishing her introduction.

She offered each of them a seat on the nearby leather couch as she eased herself down opposite them. Dr. Brush saw a light in Kaitlin that she had never seen in any of her previous patients. They, by contrast, were dark, drawn, pre-occupied, and depressed. She saw the same light in both her guests.

Dr. Brush started, "Kaitlin, can you tell me where you've been in the last couple of days?"

“I was with na-ahks,” Kaitlin said, but before Dr. Brush could ask what that was, Kaitlin restarted in English. “I was with Grandfather on the mountain, and something special happened.”

The doctor turned to Kelly. “And you?” Kelly nodded without speaking. “Kelly, will you give us some time to get to know each other? Come back in about an hour. We should be done by then.”

Kaitlin answered the doctor’s questions as fully as she could, going into every detail she could recall from her experience with the old Indian. Doctor Brush was making copious notes as they went along. At the conclusion, Dr. Brush put together a continuing treatment plan for Kaitlin as they agreed on dates, times, and ground rules. Dr. Brush opened the door to the outer reception office to see Kelly approach them with a smile, seemingly anxious to greet Kaitlin and give her a hug.

“Are you okay?” he asked.

“Never better, Cowboy,” Kaitlin said. “Ready for lunch?” She turned and winked at Dr. Brush. The doctor smiled at her.

“Mr. Chase, a word please? And, Kaitlin, no phone calls, please.” Dr. Brush turned to Kelly after closing the door. “It’s clear something profound has taken place here. I don’t doubt it for one minute, and I’m not going to question it. It has created an opening by which we can proceed with treatment for Kaitlin. It has enhanced her chances for recovery immensely. You have both been blessed.”

• • •

Arrangements had been made for Dr. Brush to meet with Kaitlin’s family the next morning. Kaitlin and Kelly arrived at nine a.m., as instructed, and waited for fifteen minutes before the door to the doctor’s office finally opened and Dr. Brush stepped out to usher them into the room. Kaitlin’s father, mother, and brother stood in front of the doctor’s desk facing her. Kaitlin greeted them with a smile as she stood alongside the doctor, with her hands clasped in front of her. The eyes of all three family members widened when they saw her. Kaitlin hoped it was because they sensed something had changed, the light dancing in her eyes telling the story. Her genuine smile and relaxed look enhanced her being as she stood before them. She felt nineteen again, having gained some weight.

"My God, KC, you're back!" Roland exclaimed, and he ran to his sister, wrapped her in his embrace, and kissed her on each of her cheeks.

Kaitlin could feel his tears on her cheeks as her own eyes began to brim. Her dad joined them and hugged and kissed her, lifting her gently to her tiptoes. He held her at arm's length and assessed her.

"So now you're a cowboy?" he chided.

"I love you, Dad," she said.

Marie waited until Jack and Roland parted for her. Marie was never one to show emotion, but Kaitlin saw love in her mother's eyes, knowing how much she had put her through. Though a hard woman at times, Kaitlin knew Marie cared for her, and after this journey, they'd both had their share of breakdowns. Kaitlin suspected it happened to Marie more often than she'd admit, opting to hide instead of show everyone. In the end, they didn't want to lose each other.

Tears had already started down Marie's cheeks as she slowly approached her daughter. Mother and daughter embraced deeply in a way that had not happened for years. Kelly kept his distance and stood at the open door, fingers in his pockets as he watched a family brought together after years apart.

"I have never told you this, but I love you," Marie said. "You are the most beautiful, talented daughter a mother could ever wish for. I am so happy that you are mine."

Dr. Brush removed her glasses to dab at her eyes with a small lace handkerchief. Her family surrounded her, embracing her as Kelly stepped away to give them privacy.

Chapter 25

Gratitude

Jack Chapin escorted his beautiful daughter down the aisle through the Villa courtyard as organ music played. It was the proudest moment in his life, for only months earlier, he had finally gotten his daughter back. The brightness he saw within her as a teen had returned. She had been, from all outward appearances, happy, but Jack knew there was something deeply troubling his girl. Her weight loss was a red flag that could not be ignored. Jack had seen a remarkable change in Kaitlin since her relationship had blossomed with Kelly, and the little German woman had entered their lives.

"I do, Kelly Chase, I do!" Kaitlin said loudly so all could hear.

Kaitlin and Kelly kissed for the first time as man and wife. The entire house broke into cheers as organ music started again.

• • •

Kaitlin clung to Kelly as they joined the crowd, unable to contain her joy after having just married the man of her dreams. What had started with the old Indian had closed one door and opened another. The overwhelming force that had gripped her so tightly before was gone, replaced by an ever-present peace and serenity. Her treatment sessions with Dr. Brush were productive and reinforced her new behaviors. Her mother was present during her first few therapy sessions. It was extremely difficult for Kaitlin to watch her be opened painful piece by painful piece. Sessions with her brother and her father were much less stressful. By finally dealing with the demons that had lingered deep inside her, improvements were dramatic.

The private wedding was held the Friday before Easter weekend. The Villa was crowded with friends, relatives, and many well-known music artists and record executives. The reception eventually gave way to the Chapins performing one of their well-known tunes, with Kelly adding to the harmony. After their performance, many guests complimented Kaitlin and Kelly on how gorgeous she looked. Kelly moved in beside his new bride and kissed her on the cheek.

"Mrs. KC, have I ever told you how beautiful you are and that I love you?"

"Not in the last hour, Mr. KC, or is it Mr. Jacks?" she teased, smiling up at him.

She wrapped her arms around his neck, tiptoeing up and kissing him deeply. This was cause for the guests to hoot and whistle again, many holding their glasses high in salute to the newlyweds.

Kaitlin loved this man. Not in her craziest dreams did she ever think she would end up with the street-begging piano player from the church. He had completely captivated and broken her heart all at once. She had thought of him so many times after that first meeting, always wondering what had become of him. Now here she was, married to him. This beautiful man who had saved her life and brought joy into her world. And his father, her grandfather, was another beautiful human who had taken her to the edge of existence itself—then brought her back and breathed new life into her. And her precious friend Jenks, whom she suspected devised numerous matchmaking schemes to get them together.

"Well, it worked," Kaitlin said to herself as she held Kelly's arm tightly.

She had somehow been led to these wonderful men who loved her unconditionally. And how her mother had changed, wrapping her in a love that she had withheld for so long. And Nance and Victoria, who had stood by Kelly as he walked a tortured existence on his way to reach her. And her new friend Rita. They shared a love for the same man in different ways, yet the same. They would forever be bound in a most unexpected way. And her brother, Roland, who had spent many anguished days and nights over the dilemma his sister had presented to him. She became aware of the wonderful floaty feeling again in the core of her being.

• • •

As the reception started to pick up and people were laughing and telling stories, Marie approached Kelly. "Can I have a word with Kelly, honey?" she asked her daughter.

"Sure, Mom. I wanted to go talk to Dad, anyway," Kaitlin said, and she gave Kelly's hand a squeeze and left to find her father.

"Kelly, I never really had a chance to thank you…formally," Marie said. "Thank you for bringing me to my senses. I was lost when it came to Kaitlin. I knew there was something wrong, but I didn't know what to do. I distanced myself from her, wishing it would just go away. So…thank you." She kissed him on the cheek and hugged him. Kelly nodded and smiled at her. She continued, "I've also heard your story with—you know—Rita. And your time," she paused, "away, and how you and Kaitlin first met. What incredible odds you and Kaitlin have had to overcome. We love you and welcome you into the family. She stepped up and kissed him on the cheek again.

"Thank you, Marie. I wish my mother were here to meet you," Kelly said. "She would have loved your grit and determination."

Marie smiled and stepped away as Roland stepped up. "Kelly, you were right," Roland said. "I still can't believe some of the things I'm still hearing about you. I want to welcome you home." He stepped back and gave Kelly a snappy salute—a rather good one.

"Thank you, Roland. I appreciate you." Kelly hugged his new brother-in-law tightly.

"Mother," Roland said, offering his arm to Marie and escorting her away.

Nodding to Kelly with a smile, after Marie and Roland passed her, Rita said, "Hi, darling. As I've said before, you've managed to land on your feet, and we wanted to congratulate you."

Rita's husband, Ben, came alongside her and held out his hand "J. Jacks, I presume?"

Kelly laughed. "Hey, that's supposed to be a secret."

Ben gave the cross-my-heart motion and finished with a boy-scout salute. Kelly laughed again; he already loved this guy. His Rita was in good hands.

Little Jacob muscled his way through the grown-up crowd and ran to Kelly. "Uncle Kelly," he said as he hugged Kelly's leg. Kelly reached down and picked him up.

"And I have a little cousin for you to meet later. His name is Danny."

Rita and Ben were both radiant as they took their small son and joined in a dance tune that was playing.

Kelly walked over to Nance and Victoria and hugged them both. Victoria kissed him lightly on the cheek.

"Thank you for doing this," Kelly said.

"Nonsense, you are our son. We would do anything for you," Victoria said, reaching up and touching his cheek.

Nance stood by smiling and nodding. He moved in for a hug when KC came up to the group. "We love you kids and are so happy to have you in our family," Nance said.

"What'd I miss?" came a raspy voice behind Kelly and KC. They turned to see Freddy. Kelly broke into a big smile and hugged Freddy tightly. "Easy, sonny. I'm an old man," he grouched, winking at Nance and Victoria.

Kelly introduced Freddy to KC, Victoria, and Nance, telling them that he was a special friend. "You ever see a guy that could get himself in so much god-damned trouble and still come out smelling like a fucking rose?" Freddy asked in his smoker-heavy voice.

"Oh, my," Victoria said, moving a hand to her mouth.

Nance emitted an abrupt laugh. KC erupted into a constrained laugh, hugging her sides.

"I guess I can't say you didn't warn me, Kelly," KC said to her new husband.

"Thanks, Freddy… I think," Kelly said, giving Freddy a sideways glance.

Jenks moved into the group. "Hi, guys. Can I steal this guy for a minute?" he asked.

As Kelly and Jenks stepped away, Henry Barney stepped up. "Henry!" Kelly exclaimed. "God, I'm so glad you could make it." Kelly hugged him as Henry licked his cheek. "Damn." Kelly wiped his cheek with his sleeve and threw a fake punch at his friend.

"It looks like your snaggin' days are over," Henry said as he winked at Kelly. "Let's get together down at the gallery next week. I have something for you."

"Thanks, Henry. I'll call you."

"Where are you two going for your honeymoon?" Jenks asked.

"KC wants to go to Montana, the ranch probably. It's quiet and private there."

"Good," Jenks said, looking anxious as he shuffled from one foot to the other.

"Okay, Jenks, spit it out. What's up?"

"Er…ah… Would you be my best man?"

Kelly smiled. "Brenda?" Jenks nodded. "Congratulations, Jenks. You bet! Count me in." Jenks lit up with a smile. "Jenks?"

"Yeah?"

"Come here." Kelly grabbed his friend and hugged him tightly. "Thanks for being my best man and my best friend. Thank you for putting KC in my life. I owe it all to you. I'm sorry if I ever made you uncomfortable or hurt you. I owe you my life." He stepped back from his friend, both near tears.

"Boy Howdy," Jenks said as he turned to go, Kelly assumed, to find Brenda.

Joe and Marty had managed to slip into the reception, suddenly appearing before Kelly. "Hey, Kel, we both received your invitation but weren't sure what to make of it," Joe said. "We both said the same thing when we read it: *the* Kaitlin Chapin? How in the world did you work all this magic?"

The three came together in a hug. "Damn, just lucky, I guess."

"Ya think?" Marty said, marveling at the celebration taking place.

"I sure am happy you fellas could make it. Marty, I understand you have a couple of hit records."

"Yes, and we would like to thank you for that, brother," Joe said.

"When can you introduce us to the bride?" Marty asked excitedly.

"Tell you what, fellas, I will gather her up when she is free and we will come find you, okay?"

"You bet," said Marty.

Kelly moved out to the courtyard. A well-known band was making an impromptu stage appearance and had the crowd rocking. Kelly joined his bride in the center of the happy celebration. Both danced and enjoyed their friends and family till early in the morning.

• • •

One month later, the Chapins had booked a small tour in the Southern California area. No one had seen them make any public appearances since November of the previous year when Kaitlin had collapsed. On the first evening performance, Kaitlin took the stage as Roland introduced her. She quickly walked to center stage and waved and smiled to the crowd. She wore a black knee-length dress that hugged her new figure and exposed her shoulders. She had filled out in all the right places. A closely monitored workout regimen had toned her body and brought slight definition to her arms and legs. Spending some time in the sun had brought her color back. Her dark hair was long and lustrous. The crowd was on their feet applauding before she could say anything. Roland handed her a mic and kissed her on the cheek. The applause continued as hoots, hollers, and a few wolf whistles came from the crowd.

Kaitlin executed a deep bow. "Thank you all so much." Then she started to sing.

• • •

Three years later, Kelly and Kaitlin were leaning against the big tree near the pond on the ranch. By Kaitlin's order, all the unsightly oil pumpjacks had been removed from the property. It was a beautiful Montana late-spring day. A gentle breeze softly moved the leaves above. They had their heads together, leaning close, enjoying the Montana quiet—only to be interrupted by a loud braying in the distance.

"Burrass again. Noise blackmail from a jackass until he gets fed," Kaitlin said with a giggle. Kelly chuckled in response.

"Mommy, Mommy!"

They both looked up as a small girl with a pastel-pink dress ran toward them with a handful of wild daisies. She pushed herself into her mother's softness. She looked up at her mom, showing big brown eyes and a light scattering of freckles across her nose.

"I brought you some flowers, Mommy."

"Oh, thank you, baby! I love you, Karen Anne."

-THE END-

The following chapters are the alternate ending to *Saving KC,* intended to be read after chapter 24.

• • •

Author's Note to the Reader

I know you're wondering why there are two endings to *Saving KC.* The truth is, when I wrote the ending to the original manuscript, I had to make a decision. Would I write the ending my readers expected, or would I write the ending I wanted? As all authors do, I fell in love with my characters, so harming them more than I had already would be emotionally rough for me. So, I did what any self-respecting chicken-shit would do: I folded.

In the weeks following the book's release, I continued to feel this nagging guilt that I had not done my best and had failed in some way. So, I mustered up the courage, and my publisher and I hatched the plan to re-publish to include both endings. Now, the ball is in your court, reader. You can decide which ending best suits you. I am eager to know your response when you write your review.

GD

Chapter 25

Gratitude

Jack Chapin escorted his beautiful daughter down the aisle through the Villa courtyard as organ music played. It was the proudest moment in his life, for only months earlier, he had finally gotten his daughter back. The brightness he saw within her as a teen had returned. She had been, from all outward appearances, happy, but Jack knew there was something deeply troubling his girl. Her weight loss was a red flag that could not be ignored. Jack had seen a remarkable change in Kaitlin since her relationship had blossomed with Kelly, and the little German woman had entered their lives.

"I do, Kelly Chase, I do!" Kaitlin said loudly so all could hear.

Kaitlin and Kelly kissed for the first time as man and wife. The entire house broke into cheers as organ music started again.

• • •

Kaitlin clung to Kelly as they joined the crowd, unable to contain her joy after having just married the man of her dreams. What had started with the old Indian had closed one door and opened another. The overwhelming force that had gripped her so tightly before was gone, replaced by an ever-present peace and serenity. Her treatment sessions with Dr. Brush were productive and reinforced her new behaviors. Her mother was present during her first few therapy sessions. It was extremely difficult for Kaitlin to watch her be opened painful piece by painful piece. Sessions with her brother and her father were much less stressful. By finally dealing with the demons that had lingered deep inside her, improvements were dramatic.

The private wedding was held the Friday before Easter weekend. The Villa was crowded with friends, relatives, and many well-known music artists and record executives. The reception eventually gave way to the Chapins performing one of their well-known tunes, with Kelly adding to the harmony. After their performance, many guests complimented Kaitlin and Kelly on how gorgeous she looked. Kelly moved in beside his new bride and kissed her on the cheek.

"Mrs. KC, have I ever told you how beautiful you are and that I love you?"

"Not in the last hour, Mr. KC, or is it Mr. Jacks?" she teased, smiling up at him.

She wrapped her arms around his neck, tiptoeing up and kissing him deeply. This was cause for the guests to hoot and whistle again, many holding their glasses high in salute to the newlyweds.

Kaitlin loved this man. Not in her craziest dreams did she ever think she would end up with the street-begging piano player from the church. He had completely captivated and broken her heart all at once. She had thought of him so many times after that first meeting, always wondering what had become of him. Now here she was, married to him. This beautiful man who had saved her life and brought joy into her world. And his father, her grandfather, was another beautiful human who had taken her to the edge of existence itself—then brought her back and breathed new life into her. And her precious friend Jenks, whom she suspected devised numerous matchmaking schemes to get them together.

"Well, it worked," Kaitlin said to herself as she held Kelly's arm tightly.

She had somehow been led to these wonderful men who loved her unconditionally. And how her mother had changed, wrapping her in a love that she had withheld for so long. And Nance and Victoria, who had stood by Kelly as he walked a tortured existence on his way to reach her. And her new friend Rita. They shared a love for the same man in different ways, yet the same. They would forever be bound in a most unexpected way. And her brother, Roland, who had spent many anguished days and nights over the dilemma his sister had presented to him. She became aware of the wonderful floaty feeling again in the core of her being.

• • •

As the reception started to pick up and people were laughing and telling stories, Marie approached Kelly. "Can I have a word with Kelly, honey?" she asked her daughter.

"Sure, Mom. I wanted to go talk to Dad, anyway," Kaitlin said, and she gave Kelly's hand a squeeze and left to find her father.

"Kelly, I never really had a chance to thank you…formally," Marie said. "Thank you for bringing me to my senses. I was lost when it came to Kaitlin. I knew there was something wrong, but I didn't know what to do. I distanced myself from her, wishing it would just go away. So…thank you." She kissed him on the cheek and hugged him. Kelly nodded and smiled at her. She continued, "I've also heard your story with—you know—Rita. And your time," she paused, "away, and how you and Kaitlin first met. What incredible odds you and Kaitlin have had to overcome. We love you and welcome you into the family. She stepped up and kissed him on the cheek again.

"Thank you, Marie. I wish my mother were here to meet you," Kelly said. "She would have loved your grit and determination."

Marie smiled and stepped away as Roland stepped up. "Kelly, you were right," Roland said. "I still can't believe some of the things I'm still hearing about you. I want to welcome you home." He stepped back and gave Kelly a snappy salute—a rather good one.

"Thank you, Roland. I appreciate you." Kelly hugged his new brother-in-law tightly.

"Mother," Roland said, offering his arm to Marie and escorting her away.

Nodding to Kelly with a smile, after Marie and Roland passed her, Rita said, "Hi, darling. As I've said before, you've managed to land on your feet, and we wanted to congratulate you."

Rita's husband, Ben, came alongside her and held out his hand "J. Jacks, I presume?"

Kelly laughed. "Hey, that's supposed to be a secret."

Ben gave the cross-my-heart motion and finished with a boy-scout salute. Kelly laughed again; he already loved this guy. His Rita was in good hands.

Little Jacob muscled his way through the grown-up crowd and ran to Kelly. "Uncle Kelly," he said as he hugged Kelly's leg. Kelly reached down and picked him up.

"And I have a little cousin for you to meet later. His name is Danny."

Rita and Ben were both radiant as they took their small son and joined in a dance tune that was playing.

Kelly walked over to Nance and Victoria and hugged them both. Victoria kissed him lightly on the cheek.

"Thank you for doing this," Kelly said.

"Nonsense, you are our son. We would do anything for you," Victoria said, reaching up and touching his cheek.

Nance stood by smiling and nodding. He moved in for a hug when KC came up to the group. "We love you kids and are so happy to have you in our family," Nance said.

"What'd I miss?" came a raspy voice behind Kelly and KC. They turned to see Freddy. Kelly broke into a big smile and hugged Freddy tightly. "Easy, sonny. I'm an old man," he grouched, winking at Nance and Victoria.

Kelly introduced Freddy to KC, Victoria, and Nance, telling them that he was a special friend. "You ever see a guy that could get himself in so much god-damned trouble and still come out smelling like a fucking rose?" Freddy asked in his smoker-heavy voice.

"Oh, my," Victoria said, moving a hand to her mouth.

Nance emitted an abrupt laugh. KC erupted into a constrained laugh, hugging her sides.

"I guess I can't say you didn't warn me, Kelly," KC said to her new husband.

"Thanks, Freddy… I think," Kelly said, giving Freddy a sideways glance.

Jenks moved into the group. "Hi, guys. Can I steal this guy for a minute?" he asked.

As Kelly and Jenks stepped away, Henry Barney stepped up. "Henry!" Kelly exclaimed. "God, I'm so glad you could make it." Kelly hugged him as Henry licked his cheek. "Damn." Kelly wiped his cheek with his sleeve and threw a fake punch at his friend.

"It looks like your snaggin' days are over," Henry said as he winked at Kelly. "Let's get together down at the gallery next week. I have something for you."

"Thanks, Henry. I'll call you."

"Where are you two going for your honeymoon?" Jenks asked.

"KC wants to go to Montana, the ranch probably. It's quiet and private there."

"Good," Jenks said, looking anxious as he shuffled from one foot to the other.

"Okay, Jenks, spit it out. What's up?"

"Er…ah… Would you be my best man?"

Kelly smiled. "Brenda?" Jenks nodded. "Congratulations, Jenks. You bet! Count me in." Jenks lit up with a smile. "Jenks?"

"Yeah?"

"Come here." Kelly grabbed his friend and hugged him tightly. "Thanks for being my best man and my best friend. Thank you for putting KC in my life. I owe it all to you. I'm sorry if I ever made you uncomfortable or hurt you. I owe you my life." He stepped back from his friend, both near tears.

"Boy Howdy," Jenks said as he turned to go, Kelly assumed, to find Brenda.

Joe and Marty had managed to slip into the reception, suddenly appearing before Kelly. "Hey, Kel, we both received your invitation but weren't sure what to make of it," Joe said. "We both said the same thing when we read it: *the* Kaitlin Chapin? How in the world did you work all this magic?"

The three came together in a hug. "Damn, just lucky, I guess."

"Ya think?" Marty said, marveling at the celebration taking place.

"I sure am happy you fellas could make it. Marty, I understand you have a couple of hit records."

"Yes, and we would like to thank you for that, brother," Joe said.

"When can you introduce us to the bride?" Marty asked excitedly.

"Tell you what, fellas, I will gather her up when she is free and we will come find you, okay?"

"You bet," said Marty.

Kelly moved out to the courtyard. A well-known band was making an impromptu stage appearance and had the crowd rocking. Kelly joined his bride in the center of the happy celebration. Both danced and enjoyed their friends and family till early in the morning.

• • •

One month later, the Chapins had booked a small tour in the Southern California area. No one had seen them make any public appearances since November of the previous year when Kaitlin had collapsed. On the first evening performance, Kaitlin took the stage as Roland introduced her. She quickly walked to center stage and waved and smiled to the crowd. She wore a black knee-length dress that hugged her new figure and exposed her shoulders. She had filled out in all the right places. A closely monitored workout regimen had toned her body and brought slight definition to her arms and legs. Spending some time in the sun had brought her color back. Her dark hair was long and lustrous. The crowd was on their feet applauding before she could say anything. Roland handed her a mic and kissed her on the cheek. The applause continued as hoots, hollers, and a few wolf whistles came from the crowd.

Kaitlin executed a deep bow. "Thank you all so much." Then she started to sing.

Chapter 26

Give and Take

After an engaging, well-received performance, Kaitlin and Roland left the stage for a boisterous backstage welcome. They were surrounded by family and team members offering congratulatory hugs and well wishes. Kaitlin could feel the warmth radiating from everyone. The moment was exciting and brought a measure of redemption from her unexpected lengthy absence. For the first time, she could finally claim the fame she had denied herself for so long. There again was that delicious glow inside her that emanated outward from the pit of her stomach. She was urgently searching the crowd for Kelly. She knew he would attend their performance after his arrival, coming off a two-week trip to the Montana ranch. She reasoned he must be running behind, as she did not see Jenks either, although he had been in attendance earlier.

There must have been some problem, she thought as she moved toward Roland. "Have you seen Kelly anywhere?"

"No, I haven't seen him at all. Do you think there's a problem?" Roland asked.

"I don't know, but I need to find Jenks. I'll let you know," she said.

"By the way, KC, congratulations on your performance. It was perfect."

"Thank you, brother, love you."

She moved toward the rear exit, finally spotting Brenda, who had just arrived. Brenda came up short, surprised at meeting Kaitlin so abruptly. "Have you seen Jenks or Kelly?" Kaitlin asked.

Brenda wore a concerned look. “Kaitlin, we need to talk,” she said as she lightly grasped Kaitlin’s elbow and guided her toward a small equipment room. “Kelly did arrive here just before the show, but Jenks took one look at him and took him to the hospital. I am unsure what the problem is, but something is wrong for Jenks to be that concerned.”

Kaitlin thought back to her talk with Kelly the night before, and he seemed a little off and distracted. She had chalked it up to possible business issues.

Brenda gave her a number to call, which she did right away. “Nurse station two,” someone answered. Kaitlin asked for Mr. Jenkins and was put on hold.

“KC?” It was Jenks.

Her questions unfolded in rapid fire. “Jenks, is he okay? What’s wrong? Where is he?”

“KC, please calm down—take a breath,” he advised. “They have admitted him and are running tests. There are some concerns that it may be a serious bout with reoccurring malaria. They won’t know anything until later tonight. I’ve sent you a car and an escort.” He gave directions on where to go when they arrived.

Kaitlin could feel a wave of nausea as her panic level rose. God, if something were to happen to her Kelly, she would just die; she knew it.

Once Kaitlin and Brenda arrived at the hospital, they quickly found Jenks and Nance in a small, private waiting room. She hugged them both. “Any news?” she asked. “Where is he, and can I see him?” She was beginning to panic.

“He is in intensive care right now with no visitors. We were told a doctor was coming down to see us right now. We are also getting our own medical team involved to see if they can help,” Jenks explained.

“How did this happen, Jenks? When did he get sick?” she asked.

“He said he felt a little odd when he left for Montana, but he thought he would shake it off. I hadn't heard from him in the last couple of days until I saw him when he arrived at the performance venue. He looked horrible; his color was off, and he was running a fever. I took him straight here, and they didn't mess around; they admitted him right away."

Kaitlin could feel her legs shake as she shuffled backward onto a nearby chair.

"I'm sorry, KC. I should have been more on top of this. I should know by now that he thinks he's Superman and doesn't complain or bellyache."

"I know, Jenks. It's not your fault."

Nance said, "I have contacted Victoria, and she is getting the word out to the family. They will be here later tonight or in the morning."

The door opened, and a man in a neatly trimmed gray suit entered and closed it. His expression was unreadable as Kaitlin watched him closely.

"Good afternoon, Mrs. Chase. I am Doctor Morgan, ICU chief here at Valley Hospital." As he moved to take Kaitlin's hand, everyone moved toward the doctor. "Kelly is having a serious malaria episode—something he picked up while in Vietnam. Depending upon which form, the disease can reoccur throughout a person's life. It can be dire if not treated immediately and effectively. In this case, Kelly was delayed in seeking treatment, which has complicated things. The strain Kelly has can sometimes lie dormant for years. It is a parasite that usually finds its way to the liver and camps there, sometimes dormant for a person's entire life, or as in Kelly's case, can come out again to wreak havoc. This case has been particularly aggressive and has compromised Kelly's vital organs, such as his liver and kidneys, which, all to say, is very serious. We have placed Kelly in a medically induced coma for now while we try our best to get ahead of things. We will know more tomorrow as we continue to perform further testing."

"But he's going to be okay, right?" Kaitlin asked with imploring eyes.

Doctor Morgan looked around the room. "He has had many physical challenges in recent years, which has not been helpful." He hesitated and looked at the floor.

Kaitlin felt her legs start to fold. Nance and Jenks moved to her side to support her. "He's going to be okay, right, Doctor?" she repeated in a forced voice.

The doctor continued, "Given Kelly's fast-moving, aggressive symptoms…" The doctor stopped and looked directly at Kaitlin, meeting her eyes. "Mrs. Chase, you should prepare yourself."

The floor fell from beneath her. Jenks held her, and she clung to him. "Please, Jenks, do something. Please, fix it—you can fix anything—please," she begged unreservedly. She felt Jenks start to break as he held her close and began to cry. "I can't go on without him. I won't make it, Jenks. I need him—I need him."

Jenks did not respond, as his grief had overwhelmed him. Nance moved in and enveloped them both in his arms, softly comforting them while trying his best to stay strong. Brenda added herself to the group, weeping softly as she hugged them.

• • •

The next day, other family members arrived: Kaitlin's mom and dad, Victoria and Rita, Henry Barney, and Freddy. All were gathered in the ICU waiting room and sat quietly, just waiting, as there were no more words or prayers to say, just waiting.

Kaitlin had been taken to Kelly's room to spend time with him. He had been brought out of his coma and was being made as comfortable as possible. KC moved in beside him, and his appearance had changed so dramatically. He appeared weak, barely able to open his eyes. His off-color appearance was difficult to behold. Her handsome knight was reduced to this indignity. She prayed it would end soon. He reached out a hand. That hand that she had come to know, with bent and misshaped fingers, a hand she loved. She took the hand in both of hers and kissed it deeply, tasting her salty tears. She held the hand to her cheek and closed her eyes, remembering when she had first met him, aching for that time again. Her tears again returned, blurring her vision; she could feel herself slipping but was determined to stay strong.

"I'm here, Piano Man—I'm right here," she managed.

"Church girl," he said in a wispy, airy voice. "What a crappy date, huh?"

"No, honey, not at all," she said, stroking his cheek and kissing him softly.

"Do you know when I first knew I was in love with you?" She shook her head, smiling down at him. He continued in his small voice.

"It was that time in Vegas, in your dressing room." He paused and swallowed. "It was the first time I had seen you since I blew up at you. He took a deep breath. "You had your back to me, then you turned and looked at me, and I was a goner. We sat and talked, and you treated me with such kindness I thought my heart would melt and I would have to run out of the room." He gave her a weak smile as a tear peeked from the corner of his eye and ran down the side of his face. Kaitlin caught it with her finger and brought it to her lips, tasting the sweetness.

She said, "Do you remember the ride home from Montoni's? I knew when you walked me to the door that I wouldn't live my life without you." She softly stroked his hair as they stared deep into each other's eyes.

"KC, please don't let me feel any more pain; please let me go when it's time. Promise?" She gave small, jerky nods, trying to control her tears with the heel of her hand. He gave her a small, weak smile. "Please, princess, I've had enough." He drifted off before she could say anything else.

She found herself in the corridor, sliding along the wall, not knowing what to do next, lost in grief where she could not see the end.

"KC, KC?" a voice came to her. Rita found her and grabbed her in a supportive hug, taking her into a small waiting room. Rita held KC until there were no more tears between them.

Early the next morning, Kaitlin held Kelly in her arms as she sang him a gentle song that he loved. She held him close until she could feel his spirit leave, and he slowly went limp. "I love you, Kelly Chase, forever."

It was a beautiful Montana spring day. Everyone was gathered at the small cemetery where Kelly's mother and brother had been laid to rest. Kaitlin was surrounded by all her closest friends and family and those who considered themselves part of her family. Jake and Brenda were now married: Ramona, Nance, and Victoria; her mother, father, and brother; Henry Barney, along with the Ames brothers, Freddy; various band members and record executives. Kaitlin was especially comforted by her forever friend and sister, Rita. They were rarely seen apart during Kelly's last days and had become one in their grief. Many residents had come to know Kelly and Kaitlin and wished to celebrate Kelly's life.

Toward the end of the service, Kaitlin noticed a lone figure on a nearby hill mounted on a paint horse. She looked closer and saw the long gray braids of Kelly's father, her grandfather. He was clad in knee-high buckskin fringed moccasins, wearing a loin covering, and was bare-chested. She could see that both he and the horse were painted in various colors to signify mourning, she guessed. He carried a long lance, which he held high; he then pierced the sky with a long, keening wail, shaking the lance at the sky. He spurred the horse into action, riding the pony back and forth across the hilltop while issuing his heartbroken message to the creator. Everyone watched silently, tears welling in their eyes until the rider disappeared and was silent.

• • •

Kaitlin was sitting under the big tree at the pond three years later. By her order, all the unsightly pump jacks had been removed. It was a beautiful summer day; a breeze softly moved the leaves above. She could always feel Kelly's spirit here; this had become the center of her world. She was thinking about her last talk with her grandfather, Aloysius Chase. He had come down to see her about two months after the funeral. He held her in his arms for a long time.

"You know he had died once already?"

"No," she responded with a frown.

"Yes, but he was sent back." After a long pause, he continued, "He was sent back to find and save you." She tipped her head and looked at him with suspicion. "He honored his end of the agreement and was called home. Your separation from him is only temporary. You will meet again; your love will be forever."

As she fondly remembered their conversation, she again felt the joy that had set her free.

"Mommy, mommy!"

She saw her little girl running up to her with a small handful of wild daisies. She pushed herself into her mother's softness, looking up at her with large azure eyes and a light smattering of freckles across her nose. "I brought you some flowers."

"Oh, thank you, baby. I love you, Karen Anne."

-THE END-